Tlasht Bade, Supreme Commander of Invasion Forces, scowled at the message from Atmospheric Flyer Command. It read: "Warning! Tornado sighted approaching main base!"

Runckel leaned over to read the message. "What's this?" he said angrily. " 'Tornado' is just a myth of the humans. Everybody knows that."

Bade snapped on the microphone to Aerial Reconnaissance. "What's this 'tornado' warning?" he demanded. "What's a 'tornado'?"

"Sir," came the answer, "a tornado is a whirling severe breeze of destructive character, conjoined with a dark cloud in the shape of a funnel, with the smaller end down."

Bade squinted. "This thing is dangerous?"

"Yes, sir. The natives dig holes in the ground, and jump in when one comes along. A tornado will smash houses and ground-cars to bits, sir."

"Listen," snarled Runckel, "it's just *air*, isn't it? Holy fang-jaw! Air can't hurt us. What's bad about a breeze, anyway?"

Bade took Runckel by the arm. "Look there!"

On the nearest wall screen, a wide black cloud warped across the sky, and stretched down a long arc to the ground. The whole thing grew steadily larger until the screen fell dark. There was a thundering crash, the ship trembled, tilted, heeled, and slowly, painfully settled back upright as Bade hung onto the desk and Runckel dove for cover.

The sky began to lighten. After a moment, the first estimates of the damage came in. One of the thousand-foot-long ships had been tipped off its base. In falling, it struck another ship, which also fell, striking a third. The third ship struck a fourth, which fell and split up the side like a bean pod.

The humans chose this moment to land their heaviest missile strike in weeks.

—from "The Gentle Earth"

Baen Books
by Christopher Anvil

THE TROUBLE
WITH HUMANS

by
Christopher Anvil

Edited by
Eric Flint

BAEN

THE TROUBLE WITH HUMANS

Copyright © 2007 by Christopher Anvil

"We From Arcturus" was first published in *Worlds of Tomorrow* in August, 1964.
"The Underhandler" was first published in *Analog* in November, 1990.
"Duel to the Death" was first published in *Analog* in June, 1965.
"Shotgun Wedding" was first published in *Astounding* in March, 1960.
"The Law Breakers" was first published in *Astounding* in October, 1959.
"Compensation" was first published in *Astounding* in October, 1957.
"Merry Christmas From Outer Space" was first published in *Fantastic* in December, 1964.
"The Plateau" was first published in *Amazing* in March, 1965.
"Captive Leaven" was first published in *Astounding* in September, 1959.
"Sinful City" was first published in *Future SF* #32 in 1957.
"Behind the Sandrat Hoax" was first published in *Galaxy* in October, 1968.
"Nerves" was first published in *Fantastic Universe* in November, 1958.
"The Gentle Earth" was first published in *Astounding* in November, 1957.

A Baen Books Original

Baen Publishing Enterprises
P.O. Box 1403
Riverdale, NY 10471
www.baen.com

ISBN 13: 978-1-4391-3330-9

Cover art by Bob Eggleton

First Baen paperback printing, January 2010

Distributed by Simon & Schuster
1230 Avenue of the Americas
New York, NY 10020

Library of Congress Cataloging-in-Publication Data:
2007018797

Printed in the United States of America

10 9 8 7 6 5 4 3 2 1

TABLE OF CONTENTS

WE FROM ARCTURUS

Boglis Kamm stood at the edge of the woods and squinted at the factories, the whizzing cars and the shiny aircraft slanting down toward the rich valley spread out before him. Unconsciously, he licked his lips.

"There are so many loose ends and unprotected flanks," he said, "You hardly know where to start to eat them up."

Slint, Kamm's companion in Test Infiltration #6, sank the hooks of the Sirian camouflage cloth into the sod around the little Arcturan-made personal-spacer.

"It looks easy," said Slint. "But what happened to Test Infiltrations 1, 2, 3, 4 and 5? They came down around here, too, you know. All in the last ninety days. And not a peep from any of them."

1

Kamm scowled, and cast around through various telepathic communications channels. "Nothing but static," he said. "And we've seen their transport and building techniques. All physical."

Slint picked up a crude shovel—made by his own race: with a ragged edge, no bend for leverage where the blade joined the handle, the blade braced by a pair of crisscrossed mending plates and the handle wrapped in a yard of tape at a weak point. Slint looked at the shovel with distaste, then shoved it under the camouflage cloth and straightened up.

"Let's hope this planet has a few mechanized hand tools. Every time we hit a rock too big to teleport, we end up working on it with a crowbar and that miserable shovel."

Kamm nodded. "The thing takes up altogether too much room. It's bad enough, having to convert to Arcturan form to use the spacer. But to have to ooze around that shovel and the damned crowbar every time you want to move is just too much."

A low rumble interrupted their conversation. Kamm glanced apprehensively at the big gray clouds gliding overhead.

Slint said, "How do I look? Okay for a native?"

Kamm critically studied Slint's regular human features, the hang of his arms and set of his head on his neck, the action of arms and legs as he walked, his quiet gray suit, white shirt and blue tie. He checked to be sure Slint had four fingers and one thumb on each hand.

"Look satisfactory."

"Okay. I'll check you."

Kamm strode briskly across the clearing and back again, till he was again looking down the hill.

Slint nodded. "Good. Matches the 'color TV' and what we've been able to pick up telepathically."

"Fine. A few more details and we can go."

Kamm reached into a side pocket, pulled out his Aldeberanian protoplasm-coagulator, checked it carefully and slid it back in his pocket.

Slint glanced at the sky, and hesitated. "Should we just go now, while there's time? Or do we have to—"

"Hmm," Kamm squinted at a formidable black cloud sliding across the sky in their direction. "But what if we get back and they question us on procedure?"

Slint groaned. "I'll get it out, and we can go through it out here. When it lets fly full-blast in that little constricted cabin—"

There was a heavy rumble of thunder.

Kamm nodded. "Okay. Nobody's around to overhear it, and they couldn't understand it anyway. Maybe the thunder will even drown it out for us."

"No such luck," growled Slint. He vanished as he teleported himself into the personal spacer, then reappeared a moment later holding a small recorder of Centauran make, which he hung on a dead lower branch of a sizeable pine tree about twenty feet back from the edge of the clearing. He threw a switch.

"*Citizens*!" roared a voice from the recorder box, speaking their native tongue.

The Sirian camouflage cloth over the Arcturan spacer had now adapted itself to its surroundings, and looked like a gentle mossy swell of ground.

"*Soldiers*!" shouted the recorder.

There was a rumble of thunder.

Slint growled. "I hope it gets it over with quick."

"It never does," said Kamm.

"*Conquerors!*" screamed the box.

"Ho-hum," said Kamm.

"You go forth," bellowed the recorder, "to glory and to triumph! To rend another glowing jewel from the violet orb of space! To place it in the diadem of the Only True Race! Victory and glory are yours! Yours the triumph! Yours the splendor! Of the greatest race of conquerors ever to span the stars!"

"If," murmured Slint, "your gravitor doesn't conk out."

"Or your heat-control," said Kamm.

A heavy crash of thunder providentially drowned out the next part. When they could hear again, the recorder had finished off its opening generalities and got down to details.

"That," it intoned, "which distinguishes Us from all other known life-forms is Our adaptability.

"Anyone can strut and glory in mere physical force.

"Hundreds of races take pride in puny intellect.

"Scores boast the power of telepathic and clairvoyant communications, the telekinetic ability to exert force at a distance.

"Only we, of all known races, can also take the form, and reproduce the structure, of all the rest, and thus conquer silently, efficiently, destroying even the telepathic by our temporary assumption of identity with them!

"Such supernal capacity is not bought without a price.

"Magnificent protoplasm-condition must be rigidly maintained. Clean living is essential. Healthful conditions must be upheld or our unparalleled protoplasmic control is impaired. This is the only requirement. This is all. There is nothing more. But it is essential.

"You, as you go forth upon your mission, can, must and *will* maintain yourselves uncontaminated, for the glory of conquest!

"For the triumph of the race!

"For the—"

There was a blinding flash of light, and a crack of thunder that made the earth shake. Rain poured down, drenching them in an instant.

Slint ran to get the recorder, now blaring martial music through the downpour. Kamm and Slint teleported themselves into the little spacer, where they fit as uncomfortably as two sardines in a pea-pod. From overhead, the rain drummed on the camouflage cloth and gurgled as it ran down under the cloth and filled up the spaces between the spacer and the dirt it sat in. The recorder, after an instant of impressive silence, let go with a final crashing crescendo that left them all but deaf.

When they had the recorder jammed into its cubicle, Slint said angrily, "Now what do we do? Reconvert to Arcturan form so we can stand it in this shoebox?"

Kamm twisted to get one of the spiny control-handles the Arcturans were so fond of out of his ribs. "Well, we can't see through that downpour. And I don't care to wind up inside a steam boiler, or halfway through a wall. So teleportation's out."

"Personnel Control and their fool idea that no one can go on a Test Infiltration if he's got good clairvoyance!"

Kamm experimentally tried to see mentally and got his usual fuzzy, vague, near-sighted image.

"Well," he said, "I'm certainly not going to trust myself to *that*."

"I suppose," growled Slint, "that they're afraid we'll only look from a distance, instead of really test-infiltrating, and some slick psi race might fool us."

"Lower creatures are sometimes superior in lower skills," said Kamm, trying to console himself for his miserable clairvoyance. "But," he added, changing the subject, "we're still stuck here."

"Tell you what," said Slint. "You remember those six-legged, web-footed mud-divers on Grinnel II? *They* wouldn't have any trouble with this weather."

"Good idea," said Kamm. "And we can make up a couple of waterproof suitcases to carry the clothes in. I saw a late-night TV movie where you can get into a 'hotel' easier with a suitcase."

* * *

Two hours later, a pair of monsters eased out from under the camouflage cloth and, walking on five legs with another leg apiece clutching a suitcase, ambled out of the forest and down the hill.

Part way down the hill was a highway, and here a problem manifested itself.

"Look at that," growled Kamm, "there are *still* a lot of cars on that road, despite the rain."

"And heaven help us if they see us."

Kamm considered various details of information picked up from late shows on TV. This planet, being subjected to regular eruptions of giant apes, huge ants and spiders, enormous sea monsters and invaders from other planets of the local solar system, was no doubt all set up to squash a pair of web-footed mud-divers in nothing flat.

"On the other hand," he said, exasperated, "even though we can now *see* across this road, we can't teleport across it."

"Burn out the nervous system," agreed Slint.

"Hmm." Kamm looked around. "Well, we certainly can't risk being seen. Maybe we can detour *around* this road. The forest seems to run along the hill for quite a ways, to give us cover."

"Worth a try."

∗∗∗

Fifteen or twenty minutes of this disclosed another problem.

While the mud-diver's body was not at all disturbed by the downpour, the creature's feet were unaccustomed to the comparatively hard soil and its muscles and bones were designed for a planet with lighter gravity.

"Phew," said Kamm, shifting the suitcase from one limb to another. "I'm going to have to strengthen the creature's muscles."

"That will mean larger attachments at the bones, and a better blood-supply."

"Which will mean a larger heart—"

"And better lungs—"

"And we've already turned ourselves inside out, just fitting the creatures to speak simple words."

Slint groaned. "Let's sit down a minute."

"How? Where do you put all the legs, and these webbed claws?"

"I forgot. The things don't sit down to rest. They go out into deep water and float."

Kamm strained the mud-diver's vocabulary with some well-chosen comments.

The upshot was that half an hour later he and Slint came out from under a large, big-leaved tree, walking erect, looking human and carrying the suitcases in their left hands.

"Possibly," snarled Kamm, "the other five infiltration teams drowned to death."

"It might be," said Slint. "It certainly is a sorry thing that with all our superior abilities we can't even keep from getting wet."

"That's a thought." Kamm tried teleporting the rain drops as they fell, but they poured down so thick and fast that he was worn-out and frazzled in no time.

A particularly heavy crash was followed by a downpour like a waterfall.

They squished down the hill toward the road. The rain momentarily faded to a steady shower.

"Why," said Slint, "didn't we run off some of these 'umbrellas' on the fabricator? You know. Like what we saw on the TV. What they carry around in the London fog to hide under when they stop people on the late-night movies."

"We didn't run off any umbrellas because we were too busy following *your* idea of making the trip as mud-divers."

They trudged in a strained silence to the highway.

⁂

At the highway, the first five cars gave them a wide berth, the sixth ran through a nearby puddle and soaked them again to the skin, the next three in quick succession accelerated past as if afraid they might be attacked, and then a car braked to a stop and backed up. The door opened, disclosing a beat-up interior, the rubber floor mat in bits and pieces, and the stuffing showing through worn spots in the seat cushions.

"Hop in, boys," said the driver jovially. "You're wet, but that won't hurt this jalopy."

"Thanks," said Kamm, climbing in.

"Thanks a lot," said Slint.

The driver reached over and slammed the door. "I've walked many a mile, rain and shine, and I know what it's like. Have a smoke?"

He took some whitish tubes in a little paper box and held it out to them. Having seen this on TV, they knew what was expected, and each took one of the little cylindrically shaped things and stuck it in his mouth.

Kamm murmured telepathically, *I think our luck has changed for the better. This native is friendly. We should be able to get some information.*

Yes, but more immediately, we have to "light" these what-do-you-call-thems. How do we do that?

You notice the driver just pushed a little plug in the car's control board. When that pops out, we just hold it to the "cigarette" and smoke will come out. I saw it in a late movie.

"Yes *sir*," said the driver amiably, "there's nothing like a car—so long as it runs. Yours is broke down, I suppose."

"Yes. Yes, that's the trouble."

They sat draining on the seat in a friendly silence.

Slint's thought came to Kamm. *I fail to see why the other five teams failed to report. Look how friendly and unsuspecting this specimen is.*

They certainly seem like natural victims, thought Kamm.

The amiable driver cleared his throat. "Don't happen to know what's wrong with your car?"

Slint spoke up, his voice faintly mimicking that of a stranded farmer they'd both seen on a TV show.

"Rod jumped out through the side of the block."

The driver grunted. "Too bad."

Slint thought, *Whatever that may be.*

I wondered myself, thought Kamm.

They certainly are unsuspicious. I'll see what I can find out. Aloud, Slint said, "Is that serious?"

The driver boggled, and the car almost ran off the road. *"Is it serious?"*

"Just thought I'd ask," murmured Slint, to pass the subject off. He tried to look nonchalant.

The driver took a fresh grip on the wheel and cast a sidewise glance at Slint and Kamm.

The little plug popped partway out, and Slint took it out and held the handle of the plug to the tip of his cigarette. He waited patiently for some smoke.

Kamm, thrown off-balance by the powerful aura of suspicion suddenly emanating from the driver, forgot himself and spoke out loud. "No, no. The other end."

Slint took the cigarette out of his mouth, turned it around, and tried the other end. "What's the difference?"

The driver reached under the seat, and came up with a short length of one-inch pipe, which he slipped out of sight under his coat, hoping he hadn't been seen.

No, no, Kamm was saying telepathically. *The plug. The other end of the plug. Turn it around. Careful!*

Slint worked the plug and cigarette clumsily, got smoke coming out of the cigarette, and then for some reason immediately went into a coughing fit.

The driver's thought came over fuzzily, obviously impelled by some powerful emotion:

Couple of nuts escaped from the State Hospital. Have to unload them first chance I get.

Kamm had the bare words of the thought, but couldn't make out the background ideas and shadings. Seeking to calm the driver, he put the plug back in its hole, pushed it in knowledgeably, and remarked in a friendly tone, "If you can get us to a—er—" A desperate search through remembered television shows failed to turn up the exact word he was looking for, so he borrowed a couple of words, that he was sure meant the same thing, from a commercial. "Automotive specialist," he concluded.

"Sure," said the driver, his left hand under his coat.

The plug popped out, and Kamm, striving to act like a natural Earthman, casually pulled the plug out, stuck it against the cigarette, sucked, blew, sucked, blew, sucked—

Glowing spots swam before his eyes. His stomach rolled over, throat constricted, and tears ran down his cheeks. Hot volcanic gases seemed to circulate through his insides. The fumes traveled around his lungs, and he had a sensation like a sledgehammer smashing him between the eyes.

The car swerved to the side.

The driver leaned across and opened the door. His voice, filled with false cheer, boomed out. "Here we are, boys. Service station. They'll take care of your car here."

Kamm and Slint reeled out of the car. A door slammed, brakes screeched momentarily, then the whine of the engine dwindled and faded into the distance.

Kamm looked through a soaking drizzle at a large rough bench, a trash can, and a sign, "Parking Area."

There was a crash of thunder, a blast of cold wind, and the rain picked up again.

Slint groaned. "This is no service station."

"There's got to be one along the road somewhere."

"I just want to lie down and—"

"Walk," said Kamm dizzily. "If we lay down in this rain, these human-type bodies will get a 'chill,' there'll be 'congestion'—" he remembered a TV ad—"Maybe even 'sinus!' "

"All right," said Slint wearily. "I'll walk."

They staggered out onto the road, and the cars passed by monotonously.

Thirty-five minutes later, they trudged into a service station. The big door of the shop was slid up, and they went in.

An attendant appeared from somewhere, cigarette dangling from lower lip, and stared at them. He disappeared into a kind of office. There was a sound of gurgling liquid, and he returned carrying two paper cups.

"Cold medicine." He grinned. "The best. You guys look like you need it. Car broke down?"

"Thanks," said Kamm, taking the cup of brownish liquid.

Slint also murmured his thanks, and added, "Yeah, our car's broke down." He added warily, "We don't know what's wrong with it."

They gulped the cold medicine, aware from the TV ads that a human body with a cold wasn't pleasant.

The cold medicine slid down their throats, and momentarily coiled in their stomachs.

There was the clang of a bell.

"Customer," said the attendant. "Be right back." He ran out.

The cold medicine seemed to flash into hot vaporous fumes surrounding them.

The top of Kamm's head felt as if it rose up about three inches, to let steam blow out his ears.

"Strange sensation," came Slint's voice, from somewhere.

***

The garage was traveling in slow circles around them as the attendant came back in.

"You're in luck. My partner was out to eat, but he just got back. Tell you what. Go in that washroom, if you want, and wring your clothes out. Only take a few minutes. Then go out there to that truck and show him where your car is, and he can tow it back. I'll wait till he gets back, then take you up to the Roadside Inn with me, and you can dry off in there. It's warm, and if you want you can hire a cabin and rest up while we get your car fixed. Okay? You're not wrecked, are you?"

Kamm felt pretty well wrecked, but Slint got the meaning better.

"No, the car just—It doesn't work."

Kamm and Slint wrung their clothes out, dried off with a convenient endless roll of paper towel and put the clothes back on, after which they felt colder and wetter than before. Then they staggered out to the truck, where "Sam" called out cheerfully, "Climb in, boys. She ain't comfort, but she's sure transportation."

The battered door clanged shut, the gears ground, the engine roared and Sam rolled up his window and turned the heater on high. "Almost forgot. Don't want you boys to catch cold." He relit the end of a short thick black cigar and puffed convulsively. Clouds of greasy gray smoke began to circulate around the inside of the cab. The gears ground again, the truck rolled faster, and Sam shouted over the engine noise, "South, ain't she? Down that way?"

Kamm nodded, his eyes smarting as Sam puffed.

"Hokay," said Sam cheerfully, "here we go."

The gears ground again, the engine speeded up, the heater threw a blast of recirculated hot air, Sam puffed busily, and shouted over the roar of the engine, "How far?"

"Oh—" said Kamm dizzily. "About—"

"Mile? Mile and a half?"

Slint spoke up, his voice growing louder and fainter. "Down at that—at the—"

Kamm caught on as Slint signaled telepathically for help.

"The Parking Area," said Kamm.

"Oh. To the left of the road?"

Kamm didn't know for certain what "left" was, but he caught the mental picture. "Yeah."

The truck ground noisily along, bouncing two inches at every one-inch bump in the road. The heater labored heroically at the captive air. Sam lit a fresh thick black cigar, and stuck the smouldering stub of his old one in an open ash receptacle on the panel just in front of Kamm. Slint, next to the door, had his nose against a crack between door and cab, but Kamm got fresh and stale smoke both.

Ahead of them, a big truck labored under a pall of black smoke coming out a pipe thrust up in the air, and blowing straight back at them.

"Diesel," grunted Sam, around the end of his cigar. "Ain't they stinkers, though?"

Slint recoiled from his crack.

A new odor blended with the fresh cigar, wet clothes, stale cigar, cold-cure fumes, hot grease and faint leak of exhaust gas from a hidden crack somewhere. Dutifully the heater blended and recirculated them all, at a slightly higher temperature.

A desperate question jumped from Kamm's mind to Slint and back again.

Simultaneously, they teleported back to the clearing. Leaning against a tree trunk, they gasped for air.

***

"Great space," groaned Kamm.

"We're whipped," said Slint, choking in big gasps of air. "If this planet is like this all over, we're done for. We'll have to go back and admit it's hopeless."

"It *can't* be that bad," said Kamm. "We've just had bad luck, that's all. Look, it's stopped raining. We can teleport right into the city."

Slint looked up. There was a cold wind blowing, and ragged dark clouds rushing by, but that was all. A flicker of hope passed over his dispirited featured. "It *has* stopped raining, hasn't it? Of course, with these soggy clothes—"

"Nothing simpler. We'll run them through the fabricator, and they'll come out minus the water."

As with one mind, they teleported into the spacer, where they were immediately jabbed by all manner of jutting levers and handles, most of them fitted with the jagged projections that the Arcturans were so fond of, because they helped them get a firm grip.

"Uh," grunted Slint. "Can't get them off in here. But there's that icy wind outside—"

Kamm was draped around trying to get at his shoe, but the jagged end of the Number Four gravitor-control bar was in the way.

"Phew," he said, "nothing to do but reconvert to Arcturan form. If we start thrashing around in here and hit the wrong thing, we'll be in a mess. You can't control the miserable ship unless you're jellyfished out like an egg on a pan, gripping half-a-dozen levers in opposite ends of the cabin, and working them all at the same time.

Let us knock just one of these out of position, and we'll get flipped end-for-end, and wrecked."

"Yeah, nothing else to do," groaned Slint. "We'll have to reconvert."

Kamm relaxed and made an effort. Slint muttered something under his breath.

Kamm grunted with effort.

Slint spat out a curse.

Sweat ran down Kamm's face.

Nothing happened.

Slint said, "I can't do it!"

Dizzily, Kamm tried again.

Again, nothing happened.

Slint burst out furiously, *"Now I see it!"*

"Watch out!" yelled Kamm. "Don't move! You'll wreck us!"

"Let's get out of here."

"All right. But no sudden moves."

They teleported to the outside.

"The trouble," said Slint savagely, "is that we're protoplasmically poisoned. That's the very thing that imbecilic recorder warned us to look out for before we started."

"You're right," said Kamm. "But what was it? The cigarette, the cold cure, the cigar smoke, or that truck?"

"I don't know *what* it was, but we've had it."

"Phew!" said Kamm. "Then we're stranded. No one but an Arcturan can run that ship. And if we can't convert to Arcturan form—"

"We'll just have to purify ourselves," said Slint. "We'll have to stick right with the ship, eat from the fabricator, breathe fumeless air—"

Kamm squinted at the city in the distance, noticing the smoke blown away from the tall smokestacks.

"How do we work that?" he demanded. "Look there. And exactly how do we eat from the fabricator if we can't reconvert? Those controls are *recessed*, remember? Like the communicator controls."

Slint groaned. "How do we let anyone know the spot we're in?"

"I don't think I'd want to. They'd assume we went native."

"Well, we can't just stay here and *starve*. We've got to do some*thing*."

"Let's head for that city. Maybe it's not so bad as it seems."

***

They teleported into the city in two fast jumps, landing on a sidewalk near a busy street corner.

The traffic light changed, and cars streamed past two abreast on both sides of the street. The air filled with a faint blue smoke. Gasoline fumes surrounded them.

"No good," snarled Kamm.

They teleported back to the clearing.

Slint stared exasperated at the city.

"That stuff will infiltrate everywhere. There are *thousands* of those vehicles. *Tens* of thousands. *Hundreds*—"

"That's out," said Kamm.

"Well, what do we do? How about the country? A nice quiet farm? We could work as laborers, herd the animals, eat pure natural food—"

"Good idea!" said Kamm. "Let's go."

By a series of teleport jumps, they got out at open country, located a farm—

—Where a tractor *put-putted* across several hundred acres of open fields, dragging behind it a contraption that sprinkled greenish-white dust over the rows of little plants. By the farmhouse, a woman guided a machine with an attachment that squirted a cloud of bug spray at the side of the house. A lanky youth in blue jeans came out of the house with cigarette trailing out of the corner of his mouth, threw it on the grass, stepped on it and leaned into the open engine compartment of a car. With one hand, he reached in the car window and pushed on something as he worked the flat of his hand up and down on some kind of cylindrical opening.

Gray smoke rolled out the tailpipe. The boy worked furiously, jumped inside the car, got the smoke pouring out, emerged jubilantly, stuck a cigarette in the corner of his mouth, lit up—

"Uh-uh," said Kamm. "Chemical dust on the plants, spray on the house, gas fumes, cigarette smoke—Maybe a—what do they call it?—'Home on the range'—you know, where they ride along slowly—"

"That's no good either," said Slint. "I saw a—I think it's a 'documentary?' Well, anyway, now they don't use horses. They use something called 'eeps.' They run on gas."

"There must be some place on this planet. Something primitive, but yet where we can fit in easy, so we won't starve or get irreversibly poisoned, or have to fight savages with blowguns, like in that late-night movie where the two men and the girl—"

Slint snapped his fingers.

"I've got it. All we have to do is round up maybe a hundred fake documents, and with *our* talents, that should be easy!"

"What is it?" demanded Kamm, hardly daring to hope.

"I'll tell you. On the TV the other night, there was this item, remember?" He threw it to Kamm telepathically, and Kamm's head spun with the beauty of the idea.

"Come on. Let's not waste time!"

* * *

The recruiter was beaming as he shook hands with them. Not everyone eagerly volunteered for the most primitive possible territories. The special feather in his cap was that this was the sixth pair of husky, upstanding, highly-recommended young idealists to volunteer through *his* office in just the last ninety days.

"Men," he said, "you may find it rough and tough, the pay low and the conditions miserable. But the important fact is the comradeship and the service to all humanity. That, of course, is what you volunteered for. To serve humanity."

He blew out a cloud of cigarette smoke as their eyes filled with some unnamed emotion.

"Men," he said, "I'm proud of you."

And thinking of the near-miraculous reports that had filtered back about the other five pairs of volunteers from his district, he beamed emotionally upon them, ground out the cigarette and gripped them by the arms.

"Welcome to the Peace Corps!"

THE UNDERHANDLER

James Hardesty, officially known as "Expeditor—Allied Governmental Liaison/Control," familiarly called "Chief" in a variety of tongues, stood far below Earth's ravaged surface in the Communications Center, HQ WestEurope. Overhead, the morning sun cast its wintry glow on missile craters, wrecked buildings, and smashed green-and-violet war machines. Down here, Hardesty coolly studied the projected image of a maze of struts, beams, braces, tubes, and cables that crisscrossed and looped around a number of weird forms watching him out of a big three-dimensional grid.

Hardesty, waiting for the tone that would tell him the technicians were reasonably sure the conference would not be interrupted, briefly looked over the occupants of the grid, noting those of types he had met before, usually

21

on the other end of some murderous technological device. Then he devoted his attention to the one directly in front of him, the most nearly human-looking of the lot.

***

Gar Kranf, overlord commanding sector XVI of the Coequality, did his best to put the fatigue of the trip behind him. He leaned forward in the command ship's conference grid to study the three-dimensional image in the clear space before the grid, that resolved itself into an incredible entity that defied its home planet's gravity to balance erect on half its sparse allotment of limbs.

Kranf watched alertly as the creature inspected the conference grid, turning its head to examine the nearer occupants.

Kranf, waiting impatiently for the technicians to finish their checks, held down the silence stud to make sure what he said was not transmitted. Bad as it was to be hastily called in on a disaster only after it got to this stage, it would be worse yet to let the opposition find out just how hasty the call had been.

Kranf cleared his throat. "Acclimatization."

A small voice said, "Sir?"

"This creature before us, in solid image. This is its natural form?"

"Yes, sir."

"That's all there is of it?"

"Yes, sir."

"It hasn't, perhaps, lost part of its structure due to wounds?"

"No, sir, that's all there is to it. Actually, they manage to compensate pretty well. They make their equipment with their own limitations in mind."

"This one is typical of what we've been up against here?"

"Yes, sir. They don't have much variation. More or less all of them look like that naturally."

"And do they normally loom straight up off the surface like that?"

"Yes, sir."

"Can they move around?"

"Oh—they can move fast."

"The one we're looking at hasn't taken root there?"

"Oh, no, sir."

"Well—does it have spikes on its feet? If not, how does it do it?"

"No, sir. These creatures seem to have some kind of body-centering mechanism that enables them to equalize the pull of gravity by minute muscular movements. It can be proved that if you've got all the different structures of the body set off one against another around a common center, and the support is located under that center, a sufficiently strong structure will not get pulled over by gravity."

Kranf took another look at the weirdly balanced alien. "How does it calculate all that?"

"H'm . . . Well, sir, quite a few of them were cut open before the Ecology Center got vaporized, but no one was quite able to figure it out. There should be something corresponding to our pressure-regulation plexus with nerves running to receptors in the soles of the feet. But no one could actually find it."

"They can keep this up?"

"They tire finally, but it takes a long time."

Kranf exasperatedly asked himself just what, if anything, the significance of this might be, and why no one had bothered to mention it before this face-to-face confrontation. All he had heard was complaints about the locals' ferocity, their rocket production, bacterial agents, and innumerable guns of every size and description. Then he noticed that the weird entity in front of him was again looking directly at him, and he, Kranf, in turn studied it.

***

Hardesty, conscious that he was at the focus of attention of the monster in front of him, asked himself how he knew it. It could only be by the focusing of the creature's eyes. He gave the prearranged hand gesture to be sure what he said wasn't broadcast. "Miller?"

"Sir?"

"Am I right in thinking this is a new one—this quasi-human in front of me?"

"Looks like it, sir. We can't find any record to match that one. There are one or two others there that we've seen before."

Hardesty glanced from left to right, to see, partly hidden by what looked like separate elaborate control consoles; first, a creature with an upper body like a wolf; second, this new individual suggestive of a human with an extra set of arms and hands; and third, a creature like some variety of octopus, but with a larger number of long flexible limbs. Further back and off to the sides were others, unpleasant enough to look at or contend with, and evidently less exalted in rank.

What the lower extremities of some of these entities might be was hidden from this angle, though experience told him that they were all generously provided with limbs of one kind or another. A flicker of motion higher up caught Hardesty's attention.

Directly above the relatively manlike creature in front of him, Hardesty caught a glimpse of a thing like an oversize spider that faded out of sight in the general vagueness around the edge of the image.

Hardesty uttered a low murmur, but his mouth scarcely moved, and his expression remained blank and uninformative as he focused his gaze on the creature directly in front of him, and waited.

***

Gar Kranf, sector overlord, heard the tone signaling that all elements of the connection had been checked. He growled, "I can now speak to the creature?"

"Yes, sir. Just let up the silence stud, the automatic translators will take over, and you will be speaking directly to their local overlord."

***

Hardesty heard the tone, but something in the manner of the entity in front of him suggested feelings of superiority that Hardesty intended to dent, one way or another. He ignored the tone, signaled that the transmission be delayed, and said, "Anything new on the title of this latest quasi-human here, the one right in front of me in this maze?"

"Still not clear, sir. We think it means 'Higher Commander,' not 'Supreme Commander,' but we can't be sure."

"But it is clear this one outranks the previous one?"

"Yes, sir. Our best guess is this one's a level up, came here to find out just what was going on, and superseded the local commander because he didn't like what he saw."

"H'm . . . And am I right in thinking that catwolf nearby is someone we've run into before?"

"Yes, sir. A general by the name of Yraang. We think it's the ranking combat officer in their local command structure."

Hardesty took a brief glance at the creature, seeing in his mind the tigerlike lower body concealed by the console, then looked at the octopuslike entity on the other side of the plainly impatient Higher Commander directly in front of him.

"Do we have anything on that squid?"

There was a brief silence. "No, sir. This is the first time we've seen anything like that. It's not just that it's a new individual. We've never even seen that type. It apparently came in with the new commander."

"OK. The conference can start anytime, as far as I'm concerned."

"Yes, sir . . . well . . . Now *they've* signaled for a delay."

***

Kranf, who disliked the idea of a sector overlord of the Coequality awaiting the pleasure of an alien monstrosity, however ferocious, held down the stud. "There's a little problem with the automatic translators that sometimes shows up on occasions like this."

"Ah—yes, sir."

"Any slip in translation, when the automatic translators are providing the illusion of easy and free interchange can be ruinous."

"Yes, sir. But—"

"You realize that?"

"Yes, sir. We do. But—"

"One misunderstood word, and millions of unnecessary casualties can result."

"We do our best, sir. But perfection is outside our reach. Even where two entities are nestmates, with no translation machine involved, there are language errors. We can't eliminate the risk."

"I understand. But if there seems to be the possibility of some error, don't hesitate to point it out, because you will be held responsible."

"Yes, sir."

"All right. I will now speak to it." Kranf looked around at the weirdly balanced creature, moved his head slightly to try to get a view of the rest of its body, which of course was not there—that was all there was to it, just two arms and two legs. Then Kranf smoothed out his face muscles, and methodically relaxed both sets of arms and the rest of his limbs lest some trace of tension, which might suggest uncertainty, should show in his voice as he said, putting overtones of Command Power into the words:

"You have received our offer of a Truce?"

Hardesty's eyes glinted.

"We got it."

Kranf considered the peculiar overtones as the automatic translators rendered the reply. Was that due to the device, or was it in the original? He spoke again, his voice rising as he bore down hard with Command Power:

"You explicitly acknowledge and agree to all terms?"

Looking on nervously from different locations in the grid, Kranf's experts winced and braced themselves.

The local overlord said flatly, "We agree to none of your terms."

Kranf felt as if he had been hit in the face. Evidently the translating machine had got the right tone to begin with.

Kranf tried again, easing off on the Command Power, and letting curiosity show in his voice. "Then what do you propose?

."We will discuss terms of a suspension of hostilities while you withdraw your remaining pests, attack animals, and war-machines, and get them out of our Solar System. Once we agree on that, we will consider terms of peace—provided you make up for the damage you've done here. This is all we're willing to talk about."

Kranf kept his face blank, pressed down the silence stud, and glanced to his right, toward the creature that had reminded Hardesty of a large wolf.

"Yraang," said Kranf.

There was a noise like shells crushed under heavy rocks, and a moment later the translator gave audible words in a deep brisk voice:

"At your command, War Chief."

"You heard this entity?"

"I heard it."

"What are the chances of success if we put the sector reserves into this fight?"

"Including the war hordes of Thrang and Guyul?"

"Yes."

"They will have to come a long way, and will get here late, which complicates the calculations."

"Your best opinion?"

"My personal estimate is that we would be able to maintain control of possibly two-thirds of the southern hemisphere of the planet, and our base on the planet's moon. Our lodgements elsewhere would be eradicated. The final outcome is uncertain."

"H'm." Kranf kept the silence stud pressed down. "Threletok?"

From overhead came a high piping tone, transformed after a moment into a somewhat heavy pedantic voice: "My estimate is equally speculative. But I would point out that under pressure of sustained attack, their weapons production and tactics have developed, not retrogressed. The prospects are not promising. There is no likelihood of surprising them. Our supplies and reinforcements come from a distance. Their resistance is solid. And their last counterattack shattered any illusion of our inevitably winning. We are in their net, not they in ours."

"What if we use the full resources of the sector?"

"How do we do that? And when? Our resources are at a distance. The problem is that we are losing on the ground, and in the immediate vicinity of the planet. The enemy is fully aware and working at full power to finish us. We may either withdraw to regroup, or fight it out where we are, trusting to prompt reinforcement. If we withdraw, we spare our troops, but the enemy will turn this planet into a fortress, make its moon an advance base to move out in force into the Solar System, and when we renew the attack, they will be much tougher than they are now."

"Suppose we don't withdraw? Suppose we hold our moon base and the bulk of our lodgements on the planet?"

"Then we will have to throw in reinforcements as they get here, in order to hang on. There will be no point when we can bring our superiority to bear all at once. The reinforcements will get ground up piecemeal. And while we put our reserves into this problem, difficulties may arise at—heh—trouble spots elsewhere."

"M'm." Kranf maintained his pressure on the silence stud. "Let's have a brief summary from the local planetary assimilator. And I mean brief."

A weary miserable voice said, "To summarize my request to be relieved of command:

"On approach, we found a single-dominant-species planet varying in technological development from region to region. Electromagnetic surveillance revealed enormous differences in local languages and customs. It was obvious we couldn't have a binding agreement with such a collection of fragments. However, these differences seemed to offer excellent chances to defeat the locals one by one. And they were dependent on fossil oil to run their technology. Our analysis showed that a large part of this fossil oil came from a comparatively undeveloped region locally known as the Middleast. If we attacked this region, we might do several things:

"First, win a quick local victory.

"Second, overawe the rest of the factions.

"Third, paralyze these other factions at will, by withholding from them our portion of the fossil oil.

"Fourth, adroitly play off one faction against the other, using the fossil oil as a bargaining counter.

"After all, they would be unprepared, and how could they possibly guess what would happen to them once we got control of the fossil oil?"

The voice came to a stop, and Kranf, frowning, said, "Then what?"

"Well—the relatively undeveloped region, for some reason, turned out to be overloaded with weapons. There was a little delay while they got over their surprise, then we got hit with everything—bullets, bombs, rockets, gas—it was like stealing meat out of the claws of a dozing thrakosnarr. Then the outside factions that we planned to finesse later on, came piling in. They had warplanes, long-range rocket-bombs, monster sea-borne floating fortresses, and every description of armored ground attack machine you can conceive of.

"Well, what could we do? We'd planned a neat surgical strike with minimum losses. Instead, the locals went berserk. There was no way we could hope to militarily fight it out on their terms—they had the whole resources of the planet at hand, and we only had what was with us. The obvious thing was to use our scientific superiority to hamstring them."

"Specifically?"

"We set up bioduplication bases, got out our stock of tailored pests, found out which ones seemed to fit, dropped around twenty thousand flights of sixteen-legged jangerls, stingbats, and burrowing trap-adders to poison and terrorize the natives, and give them a little warning that they'd better cooperate."

"How did that work?"

"Well, till we used the pests, there was tough resistance. After that, it got vicious. These split-up groups formed an alliance, got this native here, in front of us, to run things overall, and he got them actively working together. Before long, their measures and their counterblows were on a level we hadn't even imagined was possible. They even adopted a simplified common language to be able to hit us harder. Everything got worse after we started using pests. But what else could we do?"

"Be specific. What incident led you to call for help?"

"Well, we'd just landed two or three million forty-legged flatstings genetically engineered to kill natives, and the natives had come out with a dust that killed flatstings, and then they fired a swarm of missiles that came up off the planet and shot out into space. Only a few came anywhere near us, so we figured their control was breaking down. That was when I sent that report that we were getting the edge on them. Well, these missiles kept coming up, but we were happy to see them waste their firepower, figured we'd won, and called on them to surrender. About then, a missile streaked in from nowhere and hit us from behind. The next thing you knew, they were coming in from all directions, and we realized all these seemingly wasted missiles had been set to come back at us. There was no possible way we could defend against this.

"These things blew up the Moon Command Base, the bio-teams, the germ-synthesis labs, Tactical Combat Center, and Fleet Refit Base, and all that survived were our forces actually on the planet, and our ships in transit.

"That's when I called for help, sir. I've done my best, and every move I've made has been computer checked for maximum damage to them and maximum gain to us; but nothing worked. I'm out of my depth. Maybe somebody else can solve it."

"H'm," said Kranf, and looked back at Hardesty.

Hardesty eyed him coldly.

Kranf glanced uneasily to his left, where Selouel, the sector underhandler, lay back comfortably, half-a-dozen limbs twined amongst the beams, pipes, and cables, a few crossed thoughtfully in front of him, another half-dozen or so trailing over the edge of his big saucer-like couch. As usual, the sight of the underhandler did nothing to improve Kranf's mood. One glance at the creature, and Kranf felt as if his teeth were coated over with chalk. He tried to swallow, and the saliva wouldn't go down.

"M'm," said Kranf, looking away. "Has anyone any suggestion? This native entity here has refused a truce. It demands that we get off the planet. It further insists that we pay for the damage done . . . Any ideas?"

There was a silence, then a gruff comment from Yra-ang, to Kranf's right. "Get out. And pay them."

A piping voice came from overhead. "Agreed. The prize is not worth the risk."

The haggard voice of the former planetary assimilator spoke up: "I fought them. And look what happened."

Kranf glanced sidewise and to his left, where Selouel had judiciously intertwined several more unoccupied limbs, and now thoughtfully opened his large eye. His voice, before translation, had a condescending tone that set Kranf's teeth on edge, and despite the automatic translators, a certain amount of this got through:

"One might, perhaps, with a bit of thought, bring about a moderately satisfactory conclusion."

Kranf felt as if he had been slapped in the face with a length of wet rope.

To Kranf's right, Yraang gave a low grunt and growl.

Overhead, Threletok hissed.

Selouel disengaged a tentacle that was wrapped around a brace, and trailed it lightly through the air.

"A certain degree of subtlety is called for. This isn't the usual sort of flounder-and-bungle job you military and bureaucratic types can luck through by routine. A bit of intelligent finesse is required."

Kranf exhaled very slowly, then drew in a fresh breath, and spoke with care. After all, the worst of dealing with Selouel's kind was not their infuriating air of superiority. The truly unbearable part was what was almost certain to come next, unless Kranf was able to get through it just exactly so.

Carefully, Kranf did not try to sound jovial; he did not strain for a flattering comment; he did not even lean over backward to try to get all the rage out of his system before he spoke. He merely let the intense curiosity sound in his voice:

"How?"

Selouel's large eye fixed him in a bright benevolent gaze.

"Dear fellow, 'how?' 'How' indeed! Think!"

Kranf let his breath out raggedly. No, he hadn't succeeded. Now there was this to go through. The price of failure was humiliation, and Selouel's kind did not stint in dealing it out.

"Now then," said Selouel, "try to think for a moment. You know this native, 'Hardesty,' is their leader. You have heard that he has been successful in welding together a diverse lot of these incongruous two-legged two-armed monstrosities, and making a cohesive force out of them. Now, then, how will these locals regard their leader?"

Kranf groped mentally. He had to have Selouel's suggestion. Not only did the miserable creatures—who were almost totally worthless for any ordinary useful routine—not only did they somehow hit on the right answer in a good proportion of desperate cases—but once they did offer a suggestion, the responsibility was off the commander who followed out the suggestion. The underhandler was then stuck with the responsibility. But first Kranf had to somehow get the suggestion out of Selouel.

Now, how will the natives regard their leader?

"Aaahh," said Kranf, groping mentally. "They will be obedient to him."

Selouel's benevolent gaze cooled. His numerous limbs froze briefly, then gave a faint convulsive twitch.

"Come, come," said Selouel, irritation creeping into his voice. "You can do better than that."

"Respect," gritted Kranf. "They will regard him obediently, and with respect and veneration."

Selouel's gaze brightened.

"Exactly. Veneration. Now, let us make no mistake." Selouel settled back, and gazed off abstractedly into the distance. "No, we cannot count on having it all our own way here. But we can neutralize them for now, and perhaps incidentally draw their fangs for the future, who knows? We can certainly give it a try. Here's what we will do, if you are agreeable. And I suggest that we proceed quickly. I will tell you just what to say to them."

***

Hardesty, observing the consultation, consulted with his own experts and subordinates, who watched intently, and were recording all this though they could hear nothing.

"What does anyone make of this?"

An ironic voice, belonging to his Deputy WestEurope, replied, "It's a question, sir, whether they should drop twenty million sixteen-legged rats with teeth on both ends, and infected with a cross between rabies and the black plague, or whether they should try a dose of some new stuff that promises to turn all the vegetation on the planet back into carbon dioxide and water vapor."

"Would fit, wouldn't it? Any other—"

Abruptly, Kranf began to speak: "Very well. After due consultation, we have decided to accept your terms."

Hardesty froze, momentarily unable to grasp what he was hearing.

Kranf went on: "Our initial attack was wrong, compounded by the fear of the local commander to admit his blunder when he finally realized it. Your race is of such capabilities that an able leader would have requested your cooperation in joining the Coequality. An error in sampling provided our local commander with a false picture of your nature, and led him to use unacceptable methods. We are sincerely sorry.

"If you agree, we will withdraw our forces at once, and we will attempt to pay in full—insofar as payment for such an offense can be made. We will do everything we can to make this up to you."

Hardesty, stunned, struggled to recover his mental balance.

Kranf said, "Because of the severity of the attack, and the distance our supplies must be transported, we feel that a long time must necessarily elapse before we can make good the damage, and ease the ill will it has created. But we believe you can understand that. Our offer is as follows:

"First, we will withdraw at once, retaining, with your permission, only a few supply distribution centers on Earth, and a base on your moon, for the importation of goods and supplies.

"Second, as we feel that some among you might naturally seek revenge, we ask that you refrain from constructing any numerous or sizable warships for interstellar use until we have completed our repayment.

"Third, because of the possibility of outside interference, we will provide defense of your Solar System, and will protect your interests against any outsider until such time as you choose whether or not to join us.

"Fourth, to assure us of your good will as we make repayment, we ask for a hostage. We ask to take your leader, Expeditor Hardesty, on a long journey at extreme near-light speed. Due to the contraction of time at that speed, he will experience a comparatively short period of absence. But during this absence, we will have time to repay you for the damage we have done you.

"Fifth, by the time Expeditor Hardesty has been returned to you, we will attempt to have repaid you, to your and his satisfaction. You may then choose whether to continue with us, or to go your own way alone.

"We regard this as a fair offer, and it is the best offer we know how to make. Please bear in mind that we will do everything we can to provide full repayment, freely and willingly, to undo this injustice as far as we are able.

"Since we do not know what your answer may be, we want to mention the alternative. If you should refuse this offer, we will consider it a sign of your implacable enmity. We will then bring our main forces to the scene for a war of extermination.

"Whatever you decide, we offer you our sincere apology for a wrongful attack made by us in error.

"We await your decision."

***

Hardesty, at HQ WestEurope, waited before speaking, and chose his words with care: "We accept your apology. We will now give your offer very careful consideration."

***

Gar Kranf spoke the customary formula that came to him by habit: "May wisdom and forethought guide your deliberations."

The two-legged two-armed creature before him, still weirdly balanced upright, somehow conveyed an impression of benevolent good will, then vanished as the contact was broken.

"H'm," said Kranf, turning to Selouel, "this may work, at that. Now, what's the trick?"

∘ ∘ ∘

Some hours later, Hardesty sat frowning as the recorded images of the conference, projected on the screen, faded out and the room lights came back on. He glanced at the typescript of the peace offer. He looked around as the various delegates and experts sat up, scowling. Hardesty cleared his throat, turned to the projectionist, and glanced around the room.

"If there is no objection, I wonder if we could see that again."

There was a murmur of agreement.

The lights faded out.

Once again the screen lit with a view of the conference amongst Kranf, Yraang, Selouel, and their less clearly visible compatriots. There was no sound, but there was plenty to look at.

This time, when the lights came back on, for just a moment Hardesty didn't see the room around him. He was still seeing the crafty glint in a large eye, and a number of sinuously waving limbs.

"H'm," said Hardesty, glancing at the copy of the peace offer.

Around him, this time, there were not only murmurs, but curses.

Hardesty balanced the peace offer in his hand. He glanced around the room, and cleared his throat.

"Would anyone object to watching that again? It's true that they're all aliens, and there's no sound, but it seems to me there's something that comes across plainly enough from that conference of theirs."

There being no objection, once again the room darkened.

***

Gar Kranf, sector overlord, stared at his underhandler.

"Are you serious? There's no trap in this? It's a straight offer of friendship?"

Yraang, to Kranf's right, turned to stare balefully at Selouel.

The underhandler's large eye beamed benevolently as several of his tentacles turned gracefully upward.

"Would we want," said Selouel, "to give fresh cause for offense? If the estimate of the potential trouble from this planet is correct, such a course would be ill-advised, to express it mildly."

Kranf felt the uneasy sensations of one sledding across a frozen bog on a hot spring day. "Yes. No doubt that's true. But still—"

"Though," said Selouel, "if it should just happen to turn out to our advantage and their expense, that would be merely a just reward for our sincere generosity."

Yraang's fur rose up in a ridge along his back. He clamped his jaws shut, and looked away.

Overhead, Threletok hissed.

Kranf suppressed a curse, and waited before speaking. "Look, if I have it straight, we are planning to freely and openly repay these people for the damage done them. And that damage was terrific. Are you telling me that is all there is to it?"

Selouel delicately turned a tentacle in the air, admiring its graceful form, and the delicate purple flush that flowed along it as the color cells were activated. A glowing pink followed the delicate purple, to be followed by a soft turquoise, which gave way in turn to a sort of quietly gleaming ivory, and then a lavender blush—

Yraang's tiger body came half out of his seat, his white daggerlike teeth gleaming. Kranf hastily got hold of the rough fur with three of his hands, his voice low but earnest: "Never mind. Let's not let it bother us. Except for a few final details, the whole mess is now his responsibility. Let's just hope the locals accept the offer, whatever's behind it."

❋ ❋ ❋

James Hardesty, Expeditor—Allied Governmental Liaison/Control, cleared his throat and eyed the assorted monstrosities in their grid.

"In the name of the Allied Governments," said Hardesty, "and speaking in the exact spirit in which the offer was made, I accept your offer of peace and repayment, and I agree to serve as hostage in the meantime."

❋ ❋ ❋

Gar Kranf, sector overlord, finished what he hoped was the final report on this all-time indescribable shambles, and looked it over without enthusiasm. This last report, amongst other things, gave the details of the removal from the planet of some five million cocoons of winged green firestings, each and every one of which had had to be located by visual search, and then cut down with meticulous care, in order not to jar the touchy short-tempered inhabitant of the cocoon.

The locals were now more or less mollified, but Kranf had not missed the fact that the first crates of supplies had gone straight into roboticized bomb-proof examination centers especially fitted out, if Kranf's information was correct, with sectioning and sampling equipment, electron microscopes, electronic sniffers, specially trained dogs, and chemical, physical, and biological laboratories devoted to finding anything whatever that might be peculiar about the supplies provided. This did not strike Kranf as a promising sign. But he was prepared to let Selouel take the responsibility for whatever happened. The main thing was, Kranf's part in this unmitigated disaster was about over.

Kranf's assistant, looking sober, came in carrying a headset.

"Sir, the master overlord."

Kranf winced. A catastrophe of these proportions within his sector was bound to involve explanations, at the very least. He took a deep breath, reached out, and, as he slid on the headset, was rewarded by a view of one of his own kind seated on the far side of a desk, with a huge transparent all-sectors globe behind him.

Kranf said courteously, "Greetings, sir."

The master overlord looked him in the eye. "Greetings. I've just finished your report. Kranf—what in—that is to say, what exactly is behind this solution you've arrived at?"

Kranf struggled to keep any oily tone out of his voice. He said straightforwardly, "Sir, according to regulations, I turned the problem over to the sector underhandler, at his suggestion."

The master overlord looked at Kranf, frowning.

Kranf looked back frankly, squarely.

The silence stretched out.

The master overlord leaned forward.

"Kranf."

"Sir?"

"What is the solution?"

"The underhandler, sir, didn't explain it in detail."

"You mean you don't know?"

"According to regulations, sir," said Kranf frankly and openly, "I turned the matter over to him, and followed his instructions strictly to the letter. Regulations are not clear that the underhandler must explain the matter to the sector overlord."

The master overlord sat back, then leaned forward, all four hands gripping the sides of his desk.

"Are you telling me that if I want to know the plan, I will have to go to your underhandler and get it out of him myself?"

"No, sir. But—"

"Tell me what you do know about it."

"Sir, the idea is that we are to claim the attack was all a mistake; that if we had realized the capabilities of the locals, we'd have invited them to join us; that we'll do all we can to undo the damage; though, because of the distances and amounts involved, it will take us a long time, unavoidably; that we will invite them to join us, after we've made up for the misunderstanding and the damage as best we can; and that, meanwhile, their leader is to go on a long near-light-speed trip on a courier ship, as our guest, to guarantee their cooperation."

"That's it?"

"Yes, sir. Along with various details, and incidental odds and ends."

"Then this report isn't missing anything? All right. What's the point?"

"I—ah—"

The master overlord leaned forward. "Listen, Kranf, did you ever yet know an underhandler to come out with a simple straightforward plan?"

"I—well—no, sir . . . now that you mention it."

"Where's the catch?"

"I don't know."

"All right. Now listen to me. The usual underhandler plan is designed to trap its victim, by using some failure or weakness—of the victim's. That's not their only stunt. But that's where the teeth are, generally. Now, I have examined this very carefully, and I have yet to find the hook."

"Sir, I couldn't figure it out, either. But Selouel is the sector underhandler, and he did straighten out that mess with that race of hardshells we ran into a couple of centuries back. The trouble is I just—dealing with them is so—well, it just seemed to me that if he chose not to volunteer the information, still, he knew himself what he was doing in his own specialty, and it was strictly his responsibility—just as long as it works, that's all."

"The trouble is, I have to know what this plan is. It may not be your responsibility any more, but it is still my responsibility. And I am going to find out that plan."

Kranf drew a deep ragged breath, and said nothing.

The master overlord leaned forward with an imitation friendly conspiratorial smile.

"Wouldn't you like to know, yourself, what the plan is? Be frank, now."

Kranf's instinct for self-preservation overpowered his natural response.

"Yes, sir. I'll go ask him."

***

Selouel was in his study, a few limbs trailing in a gigantic open bath tank full of steaming water, several other limbs leisurely clasping a musical instrument equipped with a hundred or so strings, with a quadruple row of pearl-colored push-buttons along the base, a sizable leather bag attached to one end, with a kind of lever and pump on the side. Horns, drums, and dangling steel strips, rings, and disks protruded from the frame of the instrument, while little mallets with brass, steel, or leather heads hung from it on slender gold and silver chains.

As Kranf entered the study, there was a rhythmical clank-clank-clank in the background, as Selouel worked the pump lever with one limb, meanwhile idly caressing the strings with the tip of a second tentacle, along which waves of bumps and twists traveled to sound other strings in passing. The tip of another tentacle was tapping first this and then that pearl-colored button, as one horn after another emitted its blast, squeak, whistle, grunt, or squeal. Various other limbs hovered in the air, to suddenly snatch this or that hammer, to create a throb, tinkle, clunk, rattle, or clang.

The whole performance, so far, was no worse than being stuck in heavy traffic in a polyglot city with drivers of many kinds of engine-driven and animal-drawn vehicles all jammed together slowly winding their way through a busy factory district, so that the sounds of the metalworking shops, the horns, the bells, and the cries of the animals, and calls and curses of the drivers were all mingled together in one deafening chaos of clashing noise.

So far, it was endurable.

The trouble was, Selouel was only idling along. His kind could go a lot faster and louder than this, and think nothing of it. On top of that, at any moment, Selouel might begin to sing. In ordinary conversation, the under-handler's voice, with its undertones, overtones, and untranslatable intonations, was hard enough to bear. Raised in song, it was indescribable. Just at a glance, Kranf could see that Selouel was producing the present cacophony while working at a very casual pace. He had his voice and a lot of limbs still in reserve.

"Ah—" said Kranf tentatively.

Selouel's large eye came partly open. Half-a-dozen free tentacles made urgent downward shushing motions.

Kranf shut his mouth, and waited miserably. After all, he had got in touch first and asked if it was all right to come over. Selouel had said certainly, he would be free "in a moment."

Now, damn it, the "moment" should be here soon, shouldn't it?

But Selouel appeared to be moving to a slowly increasing beat. Another tentacle was now joining those already at the instrument.

Kranf glanced around nervously, then froze.

Softly, Selouel had begun to croon.

***

Hardesty, his compartment on the aliens' spaceship set to mimic a twenty-four hour day, noted the gradual darkening of the simulated landscape "outside" the imitation window of his compartment. Hardesty was aware, by now, of the various spy-devices watching him. But he saw no cause to object to the arrangements. Again, he thought over his deductions as to this peace proposal. So far, the conclusions still seemed reasonable.

***

Kranf, jumpy, trembling, nerves on edge, shoved the door of his office shut behind him, sank into his seat, drew a shaky breath, and picked up the communications headset. He was suddenly looking at the master overlord, who was snarling at someone on an angled screen by his desk. A moment later, he turned. "Ah, Kranf. You look done in. You have the plan?"

Kranf winced under the blows of little hammers still pounding inside his head. "Finally, sir."

"Let's have it."

"Just the plan, sir, or the background to explain it?"

The master overlord winced. "He gave that too, eh? All right. The whole works."

"Yes, sir. Selouel says there are two sets of data—those which can be treated logically and quantitatively, and those that cannot. He calls the first 'mathematical factors,' and the second, 'unmathematical factors.'"

"Let's see, now . . . All right. I've got that. Go on."

"We, he says, rely on the mathematical factors, and do moderately well at it, but are disastrously weak where the unmathematical factors are concerned."

"Mmf."

"He was very condescending, sir."

"I can imagine. Well—go on."

"The locals, he said, are also strong on the mathematical factors. Stronger, perhaps, than we. Therefore, to beat them—that is, to have a chance to beat them—we need to use the unmathematical factors."

"Well, granting that what he says is true, and I suppose it could be, that's reasonable. But his plan doesn't guarantee victory?"

"No, sir. He thinks it gives very good chances of a favorable outcome, and the possibility of outright victory. But only the possibility. He doesn't know for sure how it will work out."

"H'm . . . well, considering the alternatives—good enough. Now, let's have the plan. And, just incidentally, has it been computer checked?"

"Ah—since it's unmathematical—"

"Oh. I see. It can't be put into form to check it with a computer?"

"Let me just explain it, sir, and you'll see. According to Selouel, there are three basic positive drives which motivate most living creatures: self-preservation, species preservation, and expansion of territorial control. He claims that these three take various forms, and boil down in essence to just one, and he had a long complicated explanation of relationships, derivations, modes of expression, and—" Kranf noted the glazed expression taking form on the master overlord's face. "If we can just skip all that, sir, it will save time."

The master overlord nodded in relief.

"The practical use," said Kranf, "is to apply these drives of our opponent to tie him in knots."

The master overlord leaned forward eagerly.

"Good. Now, how do we do that?"

"The idea is to pour the necessities and luxuries to them, and be in no way threatening, ourselves. We just provide all their needs, while sincerely asking their forgiveness."

"Generous of us. Where's the payoff?"

"Selouel says we already have the first part, in that the fighting has stopped."

"Well, that's good for a start. But it would be better to beat them. Where's the teeth in this plan?"

"According to Selouel, at any one time, each individual or organization has just so much energy, and the energy diverted from one positive drive normally goes to another. But in this case, the territorial expansion drive is in a state of suspension, while we make payment. And, since we are defending them, the self-preservation and species-preservation drives are also inactive. If so, then no positive drive is in action.

"Selouel thinks the most likely result of this inactivity is that they will degenerate and finally end up as more or less pure pleasure-lovers. This will, incidentally, be reasonably satisfactory to the species-preservation drive, which, according to Selouel, is very persistent and adaptable, and will probably lead them into a mating binge. In short, since it will take us a long time to pay them back, they will have a decades-long bout of dissipation and deterioration, at the end of which they will be over-populated, weak, utterly worthless as warriors, and no danger to us at all. That is, if it works."

The master overlord looked impressed. "It's crooked, after all."

"Yes, sir."

"And there's no way for the locals to detect it. It fits perfectly with our official explanation."

"Yes, sir. But Selouel doesn't guarantee it will work. On the other hand, if it doesn't work, at least we shouldn't have a war with them."

"H'm. It's unfortunate we couldn't have gotten our reinforcements there faster. Then we could have avoided all this expensive subtlety, and just battered them into submission."

"Yes, sir. But if too many of our troops were here, then every sorehead and malcontent on every other planet—"

"Yes, I know. I see the problem."

"So, you see, sir, the underhandler's solution is, if you can't break them, rot them; if they won't break or rot, then be fair to them, because anything else would be too dangerous."

The master overlord sat back. "This experience shows a need for better training and coordination. We will have to hold more Fleet training exercises, and set up new bases closer to Earth. After all, by the treaty, we have an obligation to protect this planet. So, we will need to shift our strength toward Earth. After all, Kranf, if these locals do degenerate sufficiently, they won't be able to look after themselves. We have to remember, they are under our—ah—protection." He smiled.

Kranf, for just a moment, didn't follow the master overlord's meaning. Then he nodded obediently.

⁂

Hardesty glanced at the chart showing elapsed ship-time and elapsed Earth-time. Incredibly, fifteen years would now have passed on Earth. And the time there, from his viewpoint, would now be flowing past even faster than before, as the ship picked up more and still more speed.

⁂

Selouel, relaxed in his big dishlike lounge, reached out his number fourteen tentacle, picked up a few dozen of the tasty salted groundnuts grown locally, and shot them into his open mouth. As he crunched contentedly, his number three tentacle flexed and folded, switching holds with its grippers on the massive third-decade report that described the continuing deterioration of the Earth locals. Selouel, who was somewhat far-sighted, held the report out at a considerable distance as he read it.

The lids slid closer over Selouel's large eye as he worked his way through the report, reading sections on "Death Rate of Former Combat Officers," "Local Avocations," "Usage of Illicit Intoxicants," "Flowering of Useless Leisure-Time Occupations . . . "

The sleep-inducing qualities of the report were such that Selouel almost lost it into the slowly filling bath tank.

Irritated, he switched grips on the report, and considered a section headed, "Mating Patterns of the Indigenous Locals." This section included four page-length tables, each containing long columns of figures, plus two charts, a foldout, and sixteen pages of closely printed text. Doggedly, Selouel read on:

" . . . averaging 5.7 offspring per mating unit (see Chart 22–1). Cross-correlation by factorial analysis against prior data universes (Grumpff and Schnittl, cited above; also see Graggdrith, B.: Annals Investig. Soc./ Popltn. Scien. 156V990 661c-9) downflows to Model 16–1 (Kindly fold out three-dimensional surface). Referencing the Z-plane, note that the current-time data intersection band is concave upward . . ."

The report almost got away from Selouel a second time, and he dumped it onto a nearby bath stool. This was mating they were talking about! And they had achieved such a degree of detached mathematical objectivity that it came across like a maintenance routine for space stations.

Selouel's large eye narrowed. The trouble was, he thought, that the people who made these observations truly believed that everything should and could be reduced to figures and dealt with by purely mathematical methods. But how was the scent of a flower, and its effect, to be accurately described mathematically? How was an emotion to be truly understood and appreciated mathematically? Didn't they sense the risk of overlooking the essence of reality and being left with an empty cloak of external description?

Selouel could feel the approach of an idea, hazy at first, and then—

The jarring buzz of the urgent-communications alarm sounded overhead. Startled, he reached up, and flipped the "Receive" switch. An anxious voice spoke, and Selouel recognized Sector Overlord Kranf: "Underhandler Selouel?"

"If your receiver is functional," said Selouel, groping futilely for some trace of the vanished idea, "who else could you be talking to?"

"With all the steam, I can't see a thing."

Selouel shut off the hot water. "Now what? Are you in difficulties again?"

There was a little silence, then a sigh.

"We have," said Kranf, "a revolt on Triform. The local overlord is in desperate straits. Are you busy?"

"Not seriously. I was looking over the latest ten-yearly report on Earth, which came in along with a sack of the local groundnuts. The groundnuts are excellent. What's your problem?"

Kranf's voice was worried. "Triform has three dominant species, and when we got here, the one that's warlike was so outnumbered that we beat them after a short struggle. Then, just out of normal prudence, the overlord in charge exterminated the survivors of the warlike species. The whole thing was computer-checked. Since the other species were unusually submissive, our people seem to have gotten a little careless. Now, out of nowhere, the extinct warlike species, which was totally wiped out, has suddenly reappeared. Our men barely got out of the last scrape with a whole skin, and the casualties have been terrific."

Selouel half-closed his large eye.

"The information was, of course, fed into the master computer that these species were completely separate?"

"Of course."

"Naturally. Well, after I have a good soak, I'll look into it. I'm sure a heavy weight of data sheets will be on the way."

"The situation is desperate!"

"What's the local technology like?"

"Backward, except in weaponry. There, they are precocious."

"With the blockhead you have running that planet, we can take trouble for granted. Ransack your officer corps for someone with half to two-thirds of a brain; if you can find anyone, put him in charge. Meanwhile, I will check the information coming in, and let you know. So far, it sounds solvable to me."

***

On the near-light-speed courier, Hardesty finished his morning's exercises, and stepped into the shower. His routine on the ship was the same as usual, but time outside was passing now at an incredible rate as the ship curved back on the lap of its trip that would again take it toward Earth. Soon, he should be back home, and he clenched his jaws at the thought. When he returned, his veterans would be gone. It would all be up to a new generation then.

***

Sector Overlord Kranf, on the planet Triform, surveyed the horde of Type Two adults gorging on the latest load of crushed roots and cane sludge. Guns and helmets lay strewn around and forgotten over what had been a battlefield.

"Well," said Kranf, staring at the sight, "it's damned ridiculous. And it's expensive. But it worked."

Selouel said seriously, "The life-form, of whatever type, ordinarily seeks self-preservation, species-preservation, and increased control. Energy for one purpose may, by proper measures, be diverted to another purpose. The entity will usually give up increased control for self-preservation, and self-preservation for species-preservation. There is a point of equilibrium, which varies among individuals and races, as to where the effort will be concentrated, in the absence of immediate stress. If the species is driven back from this equilibrium, a later relaxation of need or circumstances tends to cause a sharp recoil toward and often for a time well beyond the equilibrium point."

Kranf, not given to abstract discussions, took a deep breath and considered how to get Selouel back on the track.

Selouel was going on, " . . . so that, provided the creature genuinely perceives fighting capacity to be unnecessary, then where the forms are convertible, the fighting form usually will revert to one of the other forms. So, the problem is to remove the perception of a need to fight. Now—"

Kranf growled, "Anyway, it worked."

Threletok spoke up: "The time will soon be here to check up on Earth. Everything appears to be proceeding in good order, with the locals spending more and more time on pleasure. Their native overlord will be returned to the planet before long. Should we make arrangements to watch the landing?"

❖❖❖

Selouel, as the date for Hardesty's return drew closer, paid more attention to the mind-numbing reports that flooded in. Uneasily, he set a formidable object headed, "Final Report Planet 'Earth' " on his specially braced holder, and eyed the report as a wrestler eyes a particularly nasty opponent.

Bunching himself up onto a large stool, Selouel got himself situated fairly near the report, then reached out and dipped a tentacle-tip into a sizable washtub with chunks of ice floating around in it. He braced himself, plunged a long flexible limb into the tub, and got a jarring chill that snapped him wide-awake in a flash. Good enough. He began to read the report.

The next few hours crept past to the sounds of crackling paper, low mutterings, sighs, yawns, and sudden splashes of water. Nervous subordinates on the far side of Selouel's door gave it a wide berth.

Then came a prolonged silence. After sitting immobile for some time, Selouel, his large eye narrowed, took a good grip on the report's front and back covers with one tentacle, and slid another in between two diagrams in the middle of the report.

There was a ripping sound as Selouel extracted the first diagram, and got it out where he could lay it beside the columns of figures. There was another tearing sound, and he had the second diagram loose. He stretched out a long sinuous limb, and rummaged through a kind of footlocker in a far corner of the room, to pull out a magnifying glass the size of a garbage-can lid. There was silence as he held the first diagram beside the pages of data, and looked through the glass.

"H'mm ... " He brought over the other chart, switched places with the first, flipped rapidly back and forth through the report, and grew rigidly intent. An hour crept past as he subjected one page, then another, to intense scrutiny. An unoccupied limb stretched out and groped around in a drawer behind him, fished out a large thick pencil and several scraps of paper, which it brought over and placed on the edge of the report. For a while, Selouel scribbled intently. Then another limb groped out, felt its way up the communicator to one side, flipped it on, and Selouel, still huddled over the report, growled over his shoulder, "Get me Sector Overlord Kranf."

There was a pause, then a haughty voice replied, "The sector overlord is busy and cannot be disturbed."

Selouel, his voice abstracted, and his large eye still fixed on the report, said, "This is Sector Underhandler Selouel, and I will either discuss this matter with Sector Overlord Kranf, or I will inform the master overlord himself. What Sector Overlord Kranf will then do to you is a matter of total irrelevance to me." After a brief silence, he added, "Alternatively, I may come in and break your neck myself."

There was a ringing silence, and then a brisk voice: "Kranf here."

Selouel let his breath out with a hiss, and settled back a little from the report.

"Kranf, this final report on Earth is cooked."

"What? Who? Selouel? I can't see you. What's that?"

Selouel gave a complex writhing motion that ended up with him facing the communicator. "I've been looking over this so-called final report, that shows drug use up so much, recreation up so much, such-and-such an increase in DQ—"

"Yes, I read it. The general idea is, everything looks pretty good. 'DQ'? Let's see . . . what's DQ? What do you mean it's 'cooked'?"

" 'DQ' is 'Degeneration Quotient.' By 'cooked,' I mean the report is fake. Rip out those two center charts, and try to match them with the figures they're supposed to be based on."

Kranf stared at him, then turned from the screen. There was a sound as of someone fishing through a large pile of waste paper, then a heavy thump, then a ripping sound. Kranf reappeared on the communicator screen, the charts in one pair of hands, the body of the report gripped in the other, looking back and forth from one to another, his lips moving in perplexity. There was a lengthy quiet, then Kranf looked up.

"H'm . . . You seem to be right. Unless, possibly, these footnotes—" He rummaged around through the back of the report, resting the bulky document on the edge of his desk, looked up with an affronted expression, went back to the body of the report, then shoved it back, frowning. "You're right. But that doesn't prove the information itself is no good. What we have there may be some kind of complicated clerical error."

Selouel nodded. "You don't see it all until you go into it more closely. Then it's overpowering. Take a look at that section on drug use. Whoever set that collection of figures down is more subject to some brand of intoxication than the natives."

Kranf riffled through the pages, settled back, and read aloud, his voice a monotonous drone: " 'Monthly Total Native Hallucinogenic Drug Usage by Weight, per Day, Standard Format Estimate, in Quadrillions of Tons.' Let's see, what in the . . . oh, that's a superscript . . . well . . . Ah, here we are . . . First day of the month, 21.6, next day, 21.85, then 22.08, then 22.10, 22.4, 23.78, 22.5, 23.9, 23.4, 23.85, 23.99, 24.02, 24.4, 24.6, 24.8, 24.75, 24.6, 24.70 . . . Mmf, lost the place . . . 24.79, 24.85, 24.9, 25.1, 25.05, 24.88, 25.3 . . . Well, it looks good. What's wrong with it?" Kranf looked up.

Selouel said, "Think it over and you'll see what's wrong with it."

"The trend of the figures seems to fit in. Daily drug use has been rising steeply for years. This is on trend. So are the other elements of this so-called DQ. This is all satisfactory. What's wrong?"

"Kranf, my boy, for one thing, how many of these natives are there?"

"Billions of them. The reproductive rate is terrific."

"All right. Now tell me—What is 25.3 quadrillion tons of dope per day divided by the numbers of billions of natives we have down there? How much is that for each individual?"

There was a silence, then Kranf gave a grunt, as if he had been hit in the midsection. "That's impossible."

Selouel said, "There is no way the locals can use up that much drug per individual, but setting down those figures keeps the increase in usage 'on trend,' all right. You go through that report an inch at a time, and you will find inconsistencies no one can explain away. But if you just glance it over for a general picture, everything looks fine."

Kranf said doggedly, "There's no way I can go over these mind-benders an inch at a time. Not if I'm going to have any time left to run the sector."

"Exactly. And since no one can read all this junk and stay conscious, much less absorb it, we read the summary and look at the charts, then sling the report in a corner and get back to work. So there's no great problem in faking the whole thing to keep us happy. Incidentally, if you're right that these figures fit with what went before, then they're all fake, except maybe the first few."

"But what does it mean?"

"It probably means the locals have our survey teams—which openly check our own performance, and secretly report local conditions to us—enmeshed in every kind of stupefiant known to the planet."

Kranf exhaled noisily. "A wonderful time to find it out. Their local overlord is about to get back. What do we do now?"

"You get ready to move fast, just in case. This mess is my special responsibility, and I just hope they function the way I think they do."

"We—ah—we've still got this overlord. That is, the hostage. We could—"

"The best thing we can do is hand him back in one piece as promised. They may be able to strike at us. If so, we can strike back. But let's provide them no motive to go berserk again."

"Yes. I agree. Well, who do we notify about this?"

"I will notify the master overlord. As for the rest, why start a panic? Just give the notice that their local overlord is being returned as agreed, and everyone should be alert, in case the locals should, for any reason, try anything."

"If they do try anything, it should start with a heavy blow, and a good time would be when their overlord gets back. Do we attend the ceremony when this Hardesty is returned?"

Selouel said dryly, "By remote transceiver, if possible."

"The locals might get the idea we're afraid to go in person."

"We can say we feel the reunion is a private Earth matter, and we don't wish to intrude."

"And suppose they invite us?"

"Then we go. I've got a suit of ceremonial armor around somewhere."

* * *

To Selouel's discomfort, the locals duly sent out invitations. Selouel, Kranf, and Yraang, along with lesser dignitaries, found themselves in a large forest clearing, looking around at an assortment of rocks, shrubs, moss, ferns, bramble bushes, and worn paths that wound through the landing site, and were visible between hordes of robed enthusiasts carrying large signs and the longbows, target rifles, packs, and other implements of their chosen sport or recreation.

Yraang, looking around, gave a low rumbling growl, and the automatic translators rendered this unpromising noise into intelligible speech:

"A large crowd."

Kranf, uneasily watching Selouel out of the corner of his eye, nodded agreement.

Selouel was busy with a stuck section at the shoulder end of one of his long flexible limbs, where the ceremonial armor, which he hadn't worn for the better part of a century, had proved a trifle small, so he had had extra rings added. Not only had these rings turned out off-color, but they were too thick, their joints with neighboring rings were stiff, and no amount of grease would fix it. One particular ring had got stuck at an extreme up-angle, so Selouel now had one limb painfully groping for the sky.

Kranf looked over the locals. The sight of them, weirdly balanced upright, made him uneasy. Here and there the effect was compounded by large signs giving a message or identifying a group:

"WELCOME HOME, CHIEF!"

"Weekend Parafun Jump Club"

"AAA+1 Marching Society"

"Friendly Order of Berets"

"Queensberry Legal Fellows"

"Recreational Marksmen Club"

"Royal Marine Bathing Society"

"Sweet Pea Karate Fellowship"

"Judo Aikido Chum Club"

"Now," growled Kranf, "are they, or are they not, degenerate?"

Threletok noted the translations of the signs on a convenient screen nearby, and observed thoughtfully, "The organizations seem to be harmless recreational clubs and societies."

Yraang growled, "You see the native in that purple robe—by the welcoming ramp? Watch it keep the crowd back . . . Look at the arms on that monster! True, it's only got two of them. But that's not my idea of degeneration."

Kranf growled, "Is that translation right? How degenerate is a bunch that makes parachute jumps for fun?"

Selouel, struggling with the armor, now had half-a-dozen limbs shoving against the stuck joint, and was aware that his writhings were attracting unwelcome attention from the Earth crowd, where people were now nudging each other, and turning to stare. Threading one limb through several others near their base, and pressing down hard, Selouel managed to build up a kind of compound pressure against the joint in the armor, and—

Claang!

The joint came free.

Selouel wasted a few seconds trying to remember the names of the artificers who had done this work, then he practiced moving around. The joint moved stiffly, like all the rest of the new ones, but it moved. Good enough. Now there was Kranf's question about this crowd. Selouel glanced around.

He took in the crowd's loose colorful garments, the signs, the long hair worn either loose or tied by strings or wisps of colored cloth. His gaze settled on a group under the sign, "Ye Wooozie Smoking Felloweshippe." He grappled briefly with the name, then looked over the individuals. Seated on the hood and blocky front fenders of a vehicle painted camouflage green and brown, they wore outer garments of loosely floating net, had flowers stuck in their hair, and were passing around a mouthpiece on a long flexible tube trailing out from a central pot on a smoldering brazier. As the mouthpiece passed from hand to hand, wisps of smoke drifted out. The smokers clutched at the mouthpiece for another puff.

Well, that looked promising, but there was still something—

"H'm," said Selouel, thinking of the faked data, and the survey teams that had been quietly picked up, and found in a rare state of stupefaction.

"Well?" said Kranf.

Selouel studied the scene with foreboding.

"On top of everything else, there is something—h'm—yes, if I am not mistaken, there is a noticeably low proportion of Earth females here." Selouel's limbs tensed as he looked searchingly around. "Aside from the 'Sisterhood of Nurses' and the 'Ladies Auxiliary of the Hunt Club,' this crowd would appear to be almost entirely male."

"What's the significance?"

"The species-preservation drive prompts the males to protect their women in times of danger. This is not a promising sign."

"Well, here comes the landing boat. Maybe we can tell more from their greeting."

The crowd looked up and moved aside as a glittering rounded cone dropped slowly down.

Selouel noted several Earth individuals casting furtive glances at their guests from the Coequality.

A sickly nasal voice began to moan the words of what must be a popular song:

"Oh, I cry why, Lover—Please tell me why, Lover
. . ."

A tense voice spoke into Selouel's ear-membrane:

"Does their local overlord have the unfortunate seizure now, sir? We can get at him in the landing boat. He may be out of range a few minutes from now."

Selouel had forgotten that provision, imposed on the plan by the master overlord, but with the final decision left to Selouel.

"No," said Selouel into the unobtrusive mouthpiece. "Don't do it—Repeat, do not."

The crowd was reaching into its voluminous robes, pulling out flasks, bottles, jugs, hypodermic needles, long pipes, weird glass cylinders, and sacks of white powder, as the song wailed over the assemblage: "Lover, telll me why-y, should I ever have to die-ie? Life with you's so sweet, so sweeet, so very very sweeEEEeet. So-o, Lover, tell me why-y-y, should I ever, ever have to die-e . . ."

Selouel, who would have been glad to answer the question, was staring at the multiplying paraphernalia for every intoxicant known in this end of the universe. His gaze was caught by a thing that combined glass bulbs, tubes, coils, mouthpieces, syringes, and flasks, and his mind spun as he tried to picture the thing in use.

Threletok, who as yet knew nothing of the faked reports, piped, "It worked! They have degenerated! This is total victory! We have wo—"

The former expeditor appeared in the landing boat's hatchway.

The crowd turned as one person. Bottles, cylinders, hypodermics, weirdly shaped pipes—all streaked toward Kranf and his party, hit the ground some forty feet away, and burst in blinding white flashes.

Ground and sky, trees, grass, vehicles, the crowd, the landing boat—vanished from Selouel's view in a huge puff of smoke.

Kranf jerked back. Threletok screamed. Yraang bared his fangs, and Selouel, conscious that the whole thing was out of his grip now, stayed still as the cheers, shouts, and roars of engines echoed around the clearing. The voice spoke close to his ear membrane:

"The locals are breaking into formed units— Surrounding the expeditor—He is being hustled into a ground vehicle—Euh!—The ground vehicle sprang into the air! All these vehicles parked around the edge of this clearing are taking off!"

With the smoke blowing away, Selouel could not only hear them but see them streaking off overhead.

Now, with his plans in ruins, with the communications chief shouting that a message was coming in for him from the Earth overlord, suddenly Selouel got the idea he'd been about to get when Kranf had called for help from Triform. Now, when it was too late, the whole thing was clear.

"Proceed," he said dryly to the communications technicians, and a few moments later he had the headset on, and was looking at the neat, smiling Hardesty.

"Well," said Hardesty, "I see you kept your promise. It was you, of course, behind the original peace offer?"

"Yes," said Selouel, "and now we offer you the chance to voluntarily join our Coequality."

"At least for now," said Hardesty, "we want independence."

"We honor your decision," said Selouel carefully, "and we would value your friendship. Our guard squadrons will be removed at once. You, of course, will take over their duties?"

"Yes," said Hardesty. "And we expect soon to put somewhat larger ships in space."

"May good fortune attend you," said Selouel, "and wisdom be your guide."

"Thank you. We will remember you kept your promise."

The communications link was broken.

Selouel exhaled carefully, removed the headset, gave it to the waiting technicians, and looked at his companions.

Kranf said dully, "Well, they fooled us. Now what?"

"Now," said Selouel, "we order our fleet back from this bomb of a planet. Then I am going to take a hot bath. After that, if anyone cares to join me, I am going to soothe myself with music. Following that, for all I know, the master overlord may have me pulled to pieces for stupidity. Everything in its due and proper course."

∗∗∗

The master overlord had been dealing with underhandlers for a long time, but this was the first time he had seen one suffering from dissatisfaction with his own performance. The master overlord, who had often hoped to reduce an underhandler to this crestfallen state, perversely found himself feeling sympathetic.

"After all," he heard himself say, "nothing has happened that you didn't warn against. These lack-limb short life monstrosities have followed one of the two possible courses you predicted. The result is certainly unusual, but it's better than the mess we were in when you took over."

"I should have known the reports weren't valid."

"How? Twenty-five specialists who have spent their lives in a field a thumb's width wide and a universe deep get together and write a three hundred page document based on the life-work of ten generations of their own kind, using their special vocabulary. You and I are supposed to pick this thing up, when we have a day's work to do, and understand it? And three years later new observations may show their conclusions were false, anyway. And that's just one report."

"The report isn't all," said Selouel moodily, "though it's bad enough. It was right in front of me, and I missed it."

The master overlord, seeing Selouel droop in every limb, and observing the number of Selouel's limbs, said consolingly, "Well, perhaps we can use it another time. What else do you blame yourself for?"

"How many times have I sneered when I heard someone say, 'Has it been computer-checked?' And yet, where the mathematical factors are concerned, that makes sense."

"Yes," said the master overlord, gratified to hear this admission.

"And," said Selouel, "it would equally make sense to carry out a check where unmathematical—particularly emotional—factors are concerned."

"If we could do it. But you can't accurately represent emotions on a computer. We've tried it, and it doesn't work. No, it's better to rely on calculation, and mangle these unmathematical factors when they turn up. If that doesn't work," said the master overlord benevolently, "well, we have our underhandlers to turn to."

Selouel did not look consoled

"And I missed it," he said.

The master overlord stared at him. "Missed what?"

"There is what amounts to an emotional computer, and we use it all the time. Why not here?"

"This is news to me."

"None of us can function without predicting the actions of others, and interpreting their emotional response. We do it by using what is, in effect, an analog rather than a digital device, namely, our own emotional nature. It isn't perfect, but we have no choice. Well, what does it matter if the others are aliens? We have to allow for variations, but we all have the same basic drives. How could I overlook—"

The master overlord decided that underhandlers were as hard to take humbled as overbearing. Possibly worse.

"Listen," he snarled, "specifically what did you miss?"

"First," said Selouel, "that the viewer was left on as usual when we conferred after their local overlord rejected our first truce offer."

"Well, the idea is to signify that the communication isn't ended. The other side sees its point is being considered, even if it can't hear the details. What's the harm?"

"They got to see our consultation, that was the harm."

The master overlord sat back, and pictured it.

"But—with no sound—"

"A vital point was to present ourselves as perfectly sincere."

The master overlord got a brief mental picture of Selouel looking shrewd, with four or five arms writhing in the air, with Kranf suspiciously looking on, and Yraang leaning forward with bared teeth.

"H'm . . . yes . . . I see what you mean."

"And then," Selouel went on, "as if that wasn't bad enough, I actually imagined that these locals might deteriorate if this hero of theirs should be sent on a long trip!"

The master overlord sat back, his upper right hand clasping his chin, and his other hands clasping various elbows. He said thoughtfully, "We know now that it didn't work. But how could we know at the beginning? It all fit together."

"We should have run it through our emotional computer."

"Should have imagined it done to us, and thought how we would react? All right. Show me."

"Just what would we do if, say, we knew that, after a few centuries, Kakolian or Mardugast would return to us, in the prime of life?"

The master overlord gripped the arms of his chair.

Mardugast! The Master War Chief of the Ages! With an effort, he controlled his emotions. His voice became dry.

"We would not," he said, "spend our time, while we awaited his return, smoking kasheef."

"It would," said Selouel, "call forth our greatest efforts. We would train our descendants, and deceive the opposition, so that all would be ready at his return."

"I see. Yes. With the right comparison, it is clear what happened."

"Clear, but too late."

"Too late for this time," said the master overlord pragmatically. "But we see what happened, and we can be ready the next time. And all this trouble follows, one way or another, from the nature of the locals. You didn't make them. Your problem was to find a way to get along with them. And, at least, they do seem pacified."

Selouel sighed. "That seems true, at least."

The master overlord noted that the underhandler, having unburdened himself of his sins, was looking like himself again. Yet there was a subtle difference, and the overlord, pinning it down at last, asked himself if this horrible planet might not have some good in it, after all:

That lordly superiority that made underhandlers so hard to endure had, after grappling with this world, vanished without a trace.

DUEL TO THE DEATH

The fight began on the 3rd of March, 2363, Terran Standard Time, at 0822 hours by the chronometer in the cabin of the scout ship *Torch*.

It was at this moment that the tiny bell just behind the left ear of Stellar Scout Anthony Conger began to ring, and it was at this moment that the miniature transmitter atop the helmet of Conger's exploration suit transmitted the ringing of the bell. Before Conger himself was fully aware what was happening, the ship's Log had recorded the sound of the bell, and the exact time of its alarm. The ship's transmitter had relayed the information to a signal satellite overhead. The signal satellite had bounced the warning toward a central collector station waiting to slam this message or any other like it through subspace for immediate relay to HQ on Terra.

69

Before this process had time to more than begin, Conger felt a brief piercing sensation at the inside of his left knee, just above the top of one of the high sturdy boots that fit closely over the exploration suit's impenetrable skin.

Conger had time for a feeling of surprise, for a recognition that the bell signaled the passage of something through the supposedly impassable wall of the suit, and for the realization that the bell and the brief pain were connected. He was bending to find the cause, the indescribably sharp thorn or seed-pellet that must have pierced the suit, when the sense of fatigue hit him. He continued to bend, and when he hit the ground he hit it like a sack of mash that tilts and falls from the back of a colonist's truck.

Where Conger lay on the ground, some forty yards from his scout ship, he was among a low spreading moss-like growth that looked like a miniature forest, and he, with his suit, had by contrast the appearance of a gigantic mechanism that had abruptly been turned off, and now lay motionless. If there had been small creatures in the forest, they might have explored Conger, marveling at the size and complexity of his huge alien mechanism. They might have explored Conger, that is, if they could have penetrated the carefully-designed suit.

Inside the suit, Conger lay motionless. But the suit was wide awake. The suit noted, and transmitted data on, the extreme shallowness of Conger's breathing, the drop in his body temperature, the slowing of his pulse, the varying pattern of his brain waves, the alteration in his skin-resistance. The ringing of the alarm bell cut off as four little dots, parts of a pattern of dots that covered the inner surface of one of the thin layers of the suit,

heated and flowed in a molasses-like stream that spread
a layer of sticky fibers over the tiny hole at the back of the
left knee of the suit. A tiny, microminiaturized receptor
traveled spiderlike down the inside of the suit's left leg,
paused at the knee, and swept its electronic gaze across
the smooth tight inner suit Conger wore, and that at one
point held a little droplet of clear blood. The tiny receptor sent back a very slightly fuzzy three-dimensional
image of this blood droplet. After that, the suit maintained its even temperature, held the concentration of
oxygen, carbon dioxide, and nitrogen at the proper levels,
and reported continuously the respiration, pulse, blood
pressure, and other indicators of Conger's condition. And
the suit held itself in readiness to report and seal any
new penetration of its tough layers. But beyond that,
there was nothing more it could do, so it waited.

Outside, the messages sped toward the collector station, reached it, and were hurled in a tight beam through
subspace to the relay that would send them on to HQ.
At the relay, a phenomenon known as "fringe radiation"
sent a faint bubble of garbled transmission expanding
through space from the relay at the speed of light. If
anyone there had been interested, he might have unrav-
eled this garbled transmission, and guessed at the sudden
rise in human activity caused by a minute droplet of
blood many light-years away.

All this took place outside the rough barrier of the suit
designed to seal Conger from all physical contact with
the planet he was exploring. Inside the tough but imper-
fect barrier of the exploration suit, and with due allowance for scale, equally great activity was taking place.
The suit recorded what it could of this activity by the
crude monitors of blood pressure, pulse, temperature,

rate of respiration. But the suit lacked the means to detect the migration of white blood cells toward a point several inches above the droplet of blood that was the only visible evidence of what on a larger scale would have been called an invasion. The suit could not see this. It could not detect the rapid increase in the death rate of the polymorphonuclear cells and the monocytes that now congregated several inches below the left hip-joint. The suit lacked the means to infer, from the form of the brain waves, the minute changes that took place in the controlling centers of the unconscious man's brain. There were only the gross manifestations to suggest the changes in nerve currents, the shifts in electric potential, the violent activity at lymph nodes, the alterations in blood sugar and oxygen levels; the presence of foreign substances that entered the blood stream, were swept to the heart, the lungs, back to the heart and on to reach the brain.

The suit could detect none of this. But it could detect the sudden start as Conger became conscious, as the ancient mechanism that defended the body called, in its need, for help from the conscious entity that occupied the body, and made the need unmistakably clear.

The suit recorded the abrupt alteration in brain waves, galvanic skin response, pulse, respiration, and blood pressure. It could sense, for a brief moment, that Stellar Scout Anthony Conger was wide awake, apparently aware of his mission, aware of the alarm that had rung in his left ear, conscious of the need to correctly perform his duty. Then the gross indicators by which the suit judged altered wildly, and the suit had no way to know Conger, suddenly aware of his body's need, had thrown off all thought of the duties and ideologies imposed on

him from without. The suit could only detect the
moment of abrupt stillness, the indrawn breath, the sudden rush to an upright sitting position. The suit recorded
the scream, dutifully obeyed the commands of Conger's
muscles, multiplied the power of his sudden spring from
the yielding forest of moss on which he lay, countermanded the attempt of his right hand to rip away the
confining suit at his throat, countermanded his attempts
to tear off the helmet, obediently multiplied the power
of each wild movement that involved no injury to the
man or the suit, recorded the desperate plea that burst
from his lips, transmitted the one word, "God," to the
ship that rested some forty yards away, detected but
could not interpret the sudden steadiness that followed
the frenzy, recorded the look of determination that
passed over Conger's face, recorded the shift in all outward indicators, and the sudden faltering of the pulse.

The single word, "God," was transmitted to the signal
satellite, and flashed through space to the collector, as
Conger lay motionless. Meanwhile, the suit detected
anomalies, but did not know how to interpret them. Conger lay unmoving. Within his body, the war was over,
but the battle continued, just as isolated combat units
will fight on, unaware that on a higher level the cause has
been lost. A last message traveled out over the complex
network leading from the control centers of the brain.
The message traveled along many chains of nerve-cells,
from axon to synapse to dendrite, and should eventually
have reached all over the body. But at different points
along the chains of neurons, the message was blocked
between axon and dendrite, and there it ended. The
heart continued to pump feebly, stopped, and then
under the influence of chemical stimulation began to

pump again. The violent resistance of neutrophils and monocytes continued in the abdomen, then in the region of the chest, reinforced by local cells that spat strange molecules at the alien host, that interlocked and clung to it, and then the fight continued along a lymph channel, entered a new and vicious interlude at a lymph node, continued more slowly, moving now along the throat of the motionless body, to pass under the angle of the jaw, the change in skin coloration noted by a watching receptor in the suit, and duly recorded, transmitted, and relayed on a tight beam toward Terra.

And then, after a further interval of quiet, the body moved.

The suit duly recorded the fact.

The eyes opened, and shut.

The hands clenched and flexed.

The lungs drew in a sudden deep breath.

Pulse and respiration returned to normal.

The body stretched.

The eyes opened once more, and came to a focus.

They regarded a tiny receptor poised just above the chin, clinging to the inside of the suit.

An arm of the body hesitantly pulled free of the encumbering arm of the suit, and reached across the chest toward the receptor. The receptor entered a small niche at the edge of the transparent faceplate. The hand tested the strength of the niche, then returned to the arm of the suit.

The eyes closed.

The word "God" arrived at the end of tight-beam transmission through subspace, reached the relay, and was transmitted toward HQ, simultaneously with the faint globular echo that sent it expanding at the speed of light through the universe.

And at that moment, there were two nearly simultaneous transmissions, as viewed from a point halfway along the transmission-line linking Conger's body and human HQ on the home planet.

From the human end of the line came the single order, "Jettison."

***

From the other end, from Conger's motionless body, came a transmission the suit could not detect or record, and that was outwardly signaled only by a light reflexive narrowing of the eyes that the suit duly picked up. But the subject of the message passed, it could not detect.

This message, in the form of impulses on a totally different wave length from that usually used for direct human communication, brought a prompt answer, and transmission and reply flowed rapidly, imbued with a sense of urgency:

"I have the control centers. Not much damage to the host. But this organism isn't fully centralized. There is still resistance."

"You will overcome it. What caused the delay?"

"The organism has a separate exoskeleton. Passing it was exquisitely painful, and even then, the controlling organism was completely separate, covered by another exoskeleton."

"But you are now in control?"

"Yes. But there is resistance."

"What else is it that troubles you? You haven't told us everything. There is something else wrong. What is it?"

"The exoskeleton is occupied by other small organisms. What I have may not be the ultimate control after all."

"You have the information banks?"

"Yes."

"Suspend the vegetative functions and scan."

The suit now recorded, and transmitted, the fall in rate of respiration, the slowing of heartbeat, and other gross indications. Again, later it failed to detect the resumption of a different form of transmission.

"Yes. We have it. Resume the vegetative functions."

"What is it? What does all that mean?"

"As nearly as we can tell, it means you have a find equal to the greatest ever made in our whole history. We also judge that you are in serious danger. The ultimate control mechanism is located outside the exoskeleton, completely out of our reach on another planet. The exoskeleton is partially subject to external control."

"It hasn't resisted in any way since initial entry."

"There is a time-lag, similar to that of impulses passed over a nerve. Your only hope of safety is to leave the exoskeleton."

"In scanning, I saw that this may be fatal to the organism."

"There is no time to explain. Merge your consciousness with ours and let us control the organism."

The suit now recorded a rapid increase in oxygen-consumption, not accounted for by any violent physical activity, and followed by the withdrawal of both arms into the suit. A moment later, both arms struck violently at the large clear headplate, distorting the tough plastic, but not breaking it. Another violent thrust produced a similar bulge, but the plate did not break. A third attempt failed to cause more than a minor distortion.

The one-word order from human HQ, "Jettison," now reached the end of subspace transmission, left the collector, and flashed toward the communication satellite.

The suit, recording a further increase in oxygen consumption, missed the messages that passed back and forth in mounting desperation:

"Can't get out that way. You will have to return the organism to its vehicle, and follow the customary procedure."

"But you said yourselves . . . What if the destruction order is already on its way?"

"There's no help for it. We'll just have to move fast. Get out of the way, and give us control."

"No. This is the only way. I sense it."

"*Give us control!* There's no time to argue!"

"These limbs aren't even strained. That was no maximum effort. There are safety devices . . . "

"*Give us control!*"

The suit recorded a sudden cessation of breath.

The single word "Jettison" reached the communications satellite, flashed to the scout ship, triggered a special circuit—

Simultaneously, the suit's receptors signaled the sudden bursting of the headplate, the unseating of gaskets that sealed the oversize helmet to the body of the suit, and the violent thrust that brought the suit's occupant almost out through the wide neck of the suit.

The special circuit in the ship some forty yards away flashed a message to the suit, and following that, a different message to another part of the ship.

There was a bright flash at the midsection of the suit, and a blast of flame from the mouth of the suit.

The ship quivered, a puff of smoke escaped at the edges of the closed hatch, and a flash of flame showed at a small window, to be followed by a dull roiling visible within, and many spreading cracks in the window itself.

The ship transmitted a last scene of the shattered burned remnant that had been Stellar Scout Anthony Conger.

***

That message, followed by electromagnetic silence, trailed out of the communications satellite, reached the accumulator, streaked through subspace to the relay, ballooned out faint and shadowlike in all directions as an expanding sphere, and simultaneously hurtled into the communications network that quickly cast it in clear visual three-dimensional form on a screen at Luna I HQ.

A tall, strongly-built man, with three comets at his lapel, watched the screen closely, then turned to a shorter man with one comet at his lapel, who in response made brisk rubbing motions with his hands and said, "That ends *that*."

The taller man glanced around the little group of pale, grinning, slightly sick technicians and lesser officers, and when he spoke, his voice grated.

"Play that over."

"Sir?"

"Play that over. I want to see it again."

As the technicians turned to obey, the shorter of the two men, with one comet at his lapel, gave a slight nudge and said to the other, "General Matthews has a cast-iron stomach. That's how the high command is selected." He glanced at Matthews, and there was no response. The superior of the two generals was studying the chaos on the screen. When it was over, he said:

"Play it again."

One of the technicians bolted from the room.

The others bent numbly to their jobs, avoiding the sight.

When it was over, for the third time, Matthews said, "Take the end of that, the last few seconds, and make it up into blown-up stills. And I'll want representative stills of the rest of the incident. From beginning to end."

As the technicians and lesser officers of the headquarters communications center obediently bent to their tasks, the shorter man with one comet at his lapel turned to study Matthews with a look of puzzlement.

"Hell's bells, the thing's dead."

Matthews turned away and said as he walked off, "Come into my office for a minute."

As if drawn despite himself, the other man followed.

Matthews sat down at a large desk, and slid across a box of cigars.

"Help yourself, Cutter," he said, with no particular inflection in his voice.

"Thanks," said Cutter. He glanced at Matthews uneasily. "Say, Brad, I'm sorry if I spoke out of turn out there. I know you've got the rank, and all you've got to do is snap your fingers and I'll spend the rest of my service life okaying requisitions for brass polish."

Matthews' face strained in the effort to produce a smile, failed completely, and the resulting distortion chilled Cutter as no reprimand could have done.

"Sir," said Cutter. "I'm very sorry. Please accept my apologies for the . . . the undue familiarity."

"Yes," said Matthews, puzzled by this sudden shift of attitude.

"We get . . . well . . . pretty free and easy and informal out there on the frontier, sir."

"Perfectly all right," said Matthews. "I understand." He made another attempt at a smile, as his awareness of the situation told him that only a smile would relieve it.

Matthews did not really feel like smiling, but he was accustomed to supply lack of feeling with conscious effort, and he supplied it now, lifting the corners of his mouth consciously in imitation of a warm friendly smile.

Cutter wilted in his chair, all the easy assurance and camaraderie of frontier life burned away in a realization of just how fatally he had angered his superior officer. Matthews' grimace told him plainly what volumes of words could never have expressed.

Matthews, seeing Cutter sink back visibly, took this as a sign of relaxation, and settled back himself, pleased that he had been able to establish a proper atmosphere for what he had to say.

He cleared his throat. "You know, Cutter, this is a serious business. We have taken a great many precautions to protect our colonies from infiltration by unknown life forms. We did this, first, purely on a theoretical basis. But three times recently, on three separate worlds, we have run into this very phenomenon you've had a chance to see first-hand today. You appreciate that it's a serious business if our opponent, whatever it is, succeeds?"

"Yes, sir," said Cutter dully.

"You see," said Matthews, "The first time this happened, it was the cause for a mild alertness on the part of the watch team. The breaching of the exploration suit merely meant that our man on the planet might find himself in trouble from poison or some exotic disease germs. So we didn't stop it quite as fast as we did today."

Cutter, despite himself, said, "What happened, sir?"

"The scout," said Matthews, "gradually changed form. I don't know how to get this across without sounding melodramatic. Before our eyes, we had a demonstration of physiological control. Bodily proportions changed, as if whatever it was that had gained control was putting its new captive through its paces. Testing the flexibility of the protoplasm. Then it reverted to the original form."

"What did it do then?"

"It started to get out of the exploration suit. We destroyed it."

Cutter hesitated. "Sir, what of the next time it happened?"

"The next time was just about the way it was today. We observed signs of a physiological struggle that just about matched what we had recorded from the first instance. We destroyed the suit, and the scout, and the scout ship."

"The three planets where this happened are close together?"

"Relatively speaking. The first two happened to be planets of stars in the outstretched upper limb of the constellation, Felis Major. The third star is roughly in line with the first two. They are all, roughly, in the same region of space. All three planets are Class A, with breathable atmosphere, perfectly suitable for colonization. Except for this."

The two men sat silent a moment. Cutter said, "Haven't I read . . . Isn't there some literature about this very thing?"

Matthews nodded. "The records aren't complete, but there's enough to give a good idea. The old magazines of technological speculation have reference to just such a situation. And we have most of a complete volume on this exact problem."

There was a thud and the soft tone of a gong, and Matthews lifted the cover of a low cabinet built into the wall to the right of his desk. He took out a stack of glossy ten by twelve photographs, in full and grisly color, riffled through them slowly, and tossed one across to Cutter.

"There's our problem."

Cutter looked at the photo, turned it around, and looked up in puzzlement.

Matthews said, "The head, shoulders, and upper body are all in one piece. The head isn't even seriously burned. I doubt that the heart and lungs have been put out of action."

Cutter started to speak, paused, then nodded slowly. He moistened his lips. "It's hard to appreciate that damage like this might not be fatal."

"But that's what we're up against," said Matthews.

* * *

The creature was no longer in pain, having blocked the synapses of all but a few of the nerves leading in from the badly damaged surface of the body. Now, for the first time, it could spare the attention to answer the call that was repeating over and over again, an urgent demand for information.

"It's all right. Nothing serious was damaged. But this body has a capacity for pain unlike anything I've experienced before."

"We thought you had been destroyed."

"The upper region of the body has only superficial damage. The lower region is in bad shape. There isn't much I can salvage. I'll have to discard most of it to avoid poisoning by the decomposition products."

"Can you handle it alone?"

"Not very well. I'm still under attack by the roving nucleated cells that infest this body. I'm hoping that the tissue damage will draw them to the surface so I can have freedom of movement in the interior."

"Stay at the control centers. We'll send help."

***

Cutter handed the photograph back to Matthews.

"What can we do to make sure it's dead?"

"Destroy the planet."

Cutter shook his head. "Sir," he said earnestly, "a whole planet? I don't want to seem chicken-livered, but couldn't we merely find the remains of the scout ship and blast everything within a hundred-mile radius of it?"

Matthews snapped a desk switch and studied a three-dimensional stellar chart to one side of his desk. Scattered sparsely among the stars were pale blue spheres. Matthews shone a pointer of light that touched one of the spheres.

"This is our nearest base." He moved the pointer further out. "About here we will have our roving patrols. From here on out to the trouble spot will take at least twenty days, and that's assuming we're fortunate."

"Sir, how far could a man in that condition go in twenty days?"

Matthews, frowning, studied the chart. He looked back at the photographs.

Cutter said earnestly, "Sir, some day we'll learn how to kill these creatures just as we kill ordinary germs. But will we ever learn to put a planet back together? I've been out on the frontier, and, sir, I know how badly we need every Class A planet we can get."

Matthews, his eyes narrowed, studied the photograph, looked up, and cleared his throat.

***

The creature was more comfortable now, free of the strain of single-handed effort it had felt before.

"Better?" said the voice.

"Much better. I think we have everything under control now. It's much easier with a team."

"As soon as you can, we want you to strengthen the musculature of the host's chest and forelimbs. We are going to move you, and you will have to help."

"No, not yet. The resources of this body are stretched almost to the limit. Before we can accomplish anything else, we have to regenerate the lower portions of the assimilative tract. And there are a number of organs we have to regenerate as soon as possible. For lack of their internal secretions there is an overall loss of tone and an accumulating imbalance that is going to make a great deal of trouble later on."

"There won't be any later on unless we act promptly now. The data we've received from the host's information banks shows that great precautions have been taken by this race's ultimate controlling mechanism to prevent loss of control of even a single *one* of its units. Everything that has happened thus far is known to this controlling mechanism. The control mechanism must know that the initial attempt to destroy this unit failed. Its reactions in that first attempt were fast and decisive. Can we expect anything less now?"

There was a moment's hesitation, then the reluctant reply.

"You're right. I'll take care of it at once."

***

Matthews turned the photograph over, and shook his head.

"In twenty days, we don't know what will happen out there. The only way to destroy the creature, and *know* that we've destroyed it, is to destroy the whole planet."

"Sir, a man in that condition won't go anywhere in a hurry. Even assuming the most fantastically rapid healing, there are bound to be natural obstacles to travel. We *can't* destroy the whole planet merely for the purpose of getting certainty to the last decimal place."

Matthews' eyes glinted. "What would you do?"

"Blast the site and everything for a hundred miles around, *after* getting complete pictures of the whole region from overhead. If the ship, and the remains of the suit and body were still there, I'd call it a day. If the body was gone, I'd roast everything within a fifteen-hundred mile radius. I'd make sure that the ship and the suit were completely destroyed. Pulverized. Burned to dust and the dust scattered. Then I'd ring the planet with satellite planet-busters, and if anything came up off it, *then* I'd destroy the planet, and with it the thing that was on its way up. And, sir, I'd think I had assurance triply sure, compounded, and cubed. *And* we'd still have the planet for use later on."

Matthews stroked his chin.

Cutter said, "Sir, we *need* planets."

Matthews nodded. "All right. There's a fleet being formed off Sental II for the purpose of dealing with all of these planets. I would have said, 'Destroy the lot of them.' Perhaps your way is better. There seems to be very little risk."

"Sir, so far as I can see, there's *no* risk."

"There is, because we're dealing with the unknown. You don't lay down rules to govern the unknown. You only try to confine it within certain borders. You do this by controlling certain elements the unknown has in common with familiar things."

Cutter nodded. "Yes, sir. In this case, the unknown being material, and thus subject to the law of gravitation, this whatever-it-is can't get off the planet without some means of transportation. And can't move body, suit, or ship without showing it."

"Yes," said Matthews. "So it seems. But I am going to modify your plan to be on the safe side. If, on any of these planets, you find the body or its remnants are not there, you will destroy the entire planet."

Cutter drew a deep breath. "Yes, sir."

"Sental II," said Matthews, "is on a short direct sub-space route from here. You can be there by the time the fleet is formed and ready. From there out, it's all problematical. You shouldn't hit any impassable radiation barrier in that direction, but all we know about the region comes from the reports of scouts. Who approached it from a different direction."

"I'm sure we can make it with no trouble, sir. We only hit serious radiation barriers when we try to go outward, toward the rim of the galaxy, or if we go too far laterally. The barriers ease out, like the walls of a funnel, as we move in toward the center. This region is almost directly inward."

Matthews nodded. "I'll wish you good luck, in any case. Your orders will be ready shortly. If, while you're here, there's any message you want to send down to anyone on Earth—"

Cutter grinned. "There is. I'd like a solido hookup."

"Easy to arrange." Matthews picked up one of the several phones. A few moments later Cutter shook hands, saluted, and left the room.

Matthews put the grim stack of ten by twelve color photos back in the wall cabinet by his desk, hit a button marked "microfilm," and another marked "file," and sat down again at his desk.

There was a thud and a click from the cabinet, then the office was quiet. Matthews put his hands to his temples, frowning.

He had a headache, and a faint, sick, queasy feeling.

He looked around the room depressed at the regulation gray he had seen hundreds of times before, with no reaction.

Something was wrong, he told himself.

But what?

* * *

The thing was sick.

Clinging to the centers of control, holding itself in phase against the growing fatigue, it slammed the nerve impulses down the long tracts, conscious of their inevitable decay and automatic amplification by the built-in mechanisms of the captured body. But the resistance was rising steadily. It grew progressively harder to create the necessary tension to initiate the electrochemical process that ended in holding the burned hands clenched and the large muscles of the arms tightened. The chemical stocks of the body were badly depleted, and poisons were accumulating. Strong talons clamped the sides of the body from outside in a viselike grip that interfered with respiration, and yet was not enough in itself to give full support, or allow a moment's rest. From some uncaptured stronghold in the labyrinth of interconnected neurons that was the creature's brain came the faint but insistent hypnotically regular command ordering the dissolution of the body's cells, and this command must be blocked while the need to override the fatigue of the efferent nerve channels rose to a level that required every bit of conscious attention merely to maintain the grip of weakening muscles. And now, somehow, one of the large nucleated free-moving cells found its way into this hidden place, and with a detectable sensation like a growl of content forthwith set about its grisly work of dismemberment.

There was nothing to do now but scream for help, and with every impulse hurled along fast-clogging nerve-channels, the scream went out. Each time it was a little weaker.

"It's all right," came the answer. "You're almost there. Just a little longer. Hang on. We'll have help to you in a moment."

※ ※ ※

Brigadier General Cutter had never felt better. He had his memory of Dione's arms around his neck, and when he thought about it he could feel her lips tight against his, and her tantalizing perfume rising to his nostrils and almost drowning him in its mere memory. He had, in addition, a fully independent command, and a mission that could not have been at the same time more simple or more ominously important. Perform it successfully, as no one with all his wits could fail to do, and he would have commendation, promotion, and a certain ineradicable increase in professional stature. Let the news leak out that he had blocked an order to *destroy* three Class A planets, and he would have political backing all along the frontier. To add to this perfection, he had the ultimate in good fortune, a fleet navigator who had struck a lucky subspace route that knocked six days off the original estimate, making it so much the more likely that he could let this first planet off with a minimal dose. That would look better yet to every frontier colonist who learned of it. And all this, in turn, compounded his original source of ecstasy. Could Dione, already weakening to the pleas of a mere brigadier general, withstand the demands of a major general with the luster of glory on his name and with the whole body of border senators in his pocket? No, the prospective major-general told himself, she could not. His ambition, growing cramped in the constricted bottleneck below the ultimate top levels of command, revived with a rush. The star-flecked dreams of youth returned, and he saw himself with hand upraised, in solitary splendor. The words of the oath of the highest office open to any human in the known universe echoed in his ears, and through his veins there flowed like wine the intoxication of power.

***

The creature was conscious of misery, despair, and a situation inside the captured body that bordered on chaos. He was out of phase with the final elements of the body's control centers, but he had still a vague remembered awareness of up-and-down motion, and of the voice soothing him:

" . . . almost made it. Close enough. All that has to be done now is to draw the body through a short stretch of water and up onto the land. We can do this without your help. Once on land, you'll be all right, and we've arranged for you to get a good deal more help. All we should lose in the process is the transporter. That's going irreversible already, but we should be able to get everyone out . . . There . . . You're on land. Safe."

And that was all he was conscious of for a long long time.

When at last he felt the first flicker of awakening consciousness, the situation was far different. At first, he found that he was unable to reorient himself, and he experienced a moment of panic before he discovered that the control centers of the captured host organism had slightly changed phase. A first cautious contact gave him an entirely different body-sense than what he had expected. Cautiously, he tried again.

This time he realized what had happened. The sensations of pain that he was trying to damp down were no longer coming through. In their place was an awareness of physical good order. He opened the visual receptors of the organism.

Abruptly he realized that he was sitting on a beach, looking at long flat waves rushing up the sand. He had a sense of well-being, aliveness, and awareness, that brought him to his feet in a rush. Unthinking, he sprinted down the beach, whirled, paused, and closed his eyes.

With an effort, he shifted himself slightly out of phase, put the organism in a sitting position, and considered what had just happened.

The voice reached him, amused: "What do you think?"

"This is the best yet. It responds beautifully." There was a moment of astonishment. "The lower limbs have been regenerated!"

"The entire organism has been gone over. We've done a lot of work, believe me. There are parts of the organism that apparently never were properly developed. There were organs partially clogged with poisons, evidences of mistreatment and malnutrition, energy directed along the wrong nerve tracts, habitual enforcement of incorrect or distorted functions. You have to remember that this organism was just a cell in a much larger group organism, and when the functions of that larger organism demanded it, this comparatively small cell was grossly distorted to fit the larger functions. Without that pressure, we've been able to put it into better condition than it's ever been in before."

"It must have taken a great many of us to do this."

"Yes, at first. But most of the work was self-maintaining once we had it properly started. You should have no trouble managing it all yourself, except for one thing."

"What's that?"

"The roving nucleated cells. We've had a great deal of irritating interference from them."

"Could we wipe them out?"

"Probably. But they serve a useful function in keeping down other troublesome organisms. They're not really dangerous to us unless we're in weak condition, or have to stay still in some exposed location. We'll have to try to exist with them, until we can find some better way."

"In that case, I don't want to run this organism alone."

"You won't have to, for now. You'll only have to do that if you should have to give up your companions in taking over other organisms."

That was the last the voice had to say for the moment, and he found himself speculating on it. Everything habitable on the planet was already occupied by his kind. What other organisms were there to take over?

* * *

Brigadier General Cutter studied the staff summaries, looking for the words he wanted to find. The scout ship was "definitely located." That was good. The suit was "apparently located." That was understandable, considering the violent explosion that had partially ripped the suit apart. Good enough, anyway. But the body of the stellar scout was "uncertainly located, possibly owing to complex biological degenerative changes."

What the devil did *that* mean?

Cutter picked up a phone. "Rodner?"

"Sir?"

"What's this on the body? Is it found, or isn't it?"

"We're not certain about that, sir."

"Why?"

"Well, sir, there's been a good deal of violence down there. And, of course, exposure. It's an alien planet. We don't know just what the decay bacteria on the planet can do."

Cutter scowled at the phone.

"I gathered that much from your report."

"Yes, sir."

"Well?"

"Sir?"

"So what?" said Cutter angrily. "What about the exposure and decay? What about the bacteria?"

"That's precisely it, sir. We don't know."

"Don't know *what*?"

"Their effects, sir."

"So?"

The voice was cool. "Well, of course, therefore we just can't say."

Cutter held the phone out and looked at it. He put it back to his head and said, "Are you working on anything right now that can't wait?"

"N-No, sir."

"Then come to my office and we'll talk this thing over."

Cutter jammed the phone back in its cradle, and growled under his breath.

The door opened and a tall, slender, rather sensitive-looking staff officer stepped in. Cutter pinned him with his gaze.

"Now, then, what's this about the bacteria and all the rest of it?"

"Sir? Just what I told you."

"Tell it again."

The officer said patiently, "Owing to the time-lag prior to examination and to the uncertain effects of bacterial action on the planet, we find it impossible to state definitely whether or not the remains we have located are truly the remains of the stellar scout, Anthony Conger."

Cutter smiled and nodded his head. "Very good. Now, Rodner, let's just look over that statement. And before we do that, let's consider, if you don't mind, a few other aspects of this. Shall we? First of all, you have, if I remember correctly, a splendid record in your specialty, and it was this that gained you a temporary commission as major when you were inducted. This is correct, is it not, Rodner?"

The staff officer, watching him with an incredulous look, stammered, "Yes. Yes, that's true, I believe."

"Well, well," Cutter stood up, beaming paternally. "*Major* Rodner. It sounds nice, doesn't it? Much better than, say Pvt. Rodner, or PFC Rodner, or, maybe, T/3 Rodner. Doesn't it?"

The hapless staff officer opened his mouth, shut it, and swallowed. As if despite himself, his mouth opened up again. "Yes, sir."

"Good," said Cutter. The paternal look vanished. "The trouble with temporary rank is, you can lose it anytime. You need to make your superiors happy if you want to keep it. I will now ask you a question: *What do you know about the condition of the stellar scout's body down on that planet?*"

"Sir," said the staff officer desperately, "we have located several sizable masses of proto . . . that is, body tissue—"

"I know what protoplasm is," the general grated.

"We've found several sizable masses of protoplasm, and have definitely identified badly burned human body tissue in some of these masses. These tissue samples are apparently from the lower parts of the body. The remains of the upper part of the body is more thoroughly decomposed—"

"That's natural, isn't it? Wouldn't the charring of the lower parts of the body slow down decay?"

"Yes, sir."

"And the upper part of the body, being exposed to the elements, and there being nothing whatever to slow down decay—that *would* be more likely to be affected by the local decay bacteria, wouldn't it?"

"Yes, sir."

"And that would account for unusual chemical substances in the body, wouldn't it?"

"Yes, sir. To a degree."

"Then what's the problem? And you'd better give me a straight answer."

"There are decay products that couldn't have been derived from normal body chemicals. There is hair that appears to be materially unaffected by exposure, and yet its chemical structure does not correspond to that of human hair. Photographs of the body show, from the purely physical standpoint of appearance, a perfectly normal picture, considering the circumstances. Chemical analysis shows some things normal, and some things abnormal. We're handicapped in working out a definite answer because we can't work on the body at close range.

We have to use servo-dissectors and analyzers, and a variety of remote-control techniques that become awkward when the situation is so far from routine."

Cutter scowled. "And the net result is that the outward appearance of the body is all right, but the chemical structure is wrong?"

"Well, not entirely wrong. But—"

"Ninety per cent wrong?"

"Oh, no, sir."

"Fifty per cent?"

"If you mean, are fifty per cent of the compounds of the body, and of the decay products, wrong. No, sir. Not that many."

"How many?"

"I would say . . . oh . . . two per cent, roughly."

"Well, then . . . two per cent. That isn't much. After all, we're dealing with a strange planet."

"Yes, sir." The staff officer's face showed signs of a struggle for words. "But this two per cent happens to be next to impossible for us to explain on any rational basis."

"Obviously. You don't know everything about the planet."

"We can allow for wide differences in some directions, but not others. For instance, we recognize a human face as human despite variations in height of brow, prominence of cheekbones, width of skull, spacing of eyes, size of nostrils, skin, eyes, and hair color, freckling, beard growth—there can be wide variations in these things, and they aren't critical. We know we're dealing with genuine human characteristics, and there's no special effect of dealing with anything alien."

Cutter nodded. "Well, then—What's the difficulty?"

"Well—Suppose someone walks in with everything perfectly normal except he has a growth of beard across the forehead, and his nose on upside down? Then what?"

Cutter's heart seemed to skip a beat. "You didn't mention—"

The staff officer looked as if he felt sorry for Cutter. "Sir, that's just a comparison. The anomaly is on the chemical level. But, believe me, it's just that bad."

Cutter nodded. "All right. You've given me a straight explanation. That's what I want. Now get out."

The major hesitated, then saluted hurriedly, and went out.

Cutter blew out his breath. Matthews' words echoed in his ears: "If, on any of these planets, you find the body or its remnants are not there, you will destroy the entire planet."

That was an order. It was recorded on tape in Matthews' files, and a copy of the tape had been forwarded to Cutter for his own files, and clipped to the packet containing his written orders.

Whether or not he, Cutter, should destroy this planet depended on how literally he interpreted his orders, and on a purely technical guess as to whether the body was or was not there. And he was not personally qualified to make the guess.

Cutter's gaze fell on his desk solido of Dione. As he watched, she seemed to smile up at him, arms stretched out.

With an effort, Cutter picked up the staff summary, glanced from it to the solido, and wavered.

❖❖❖

The powers of the captured body, once relieved of accumulations of poisons and self-defeating nerve-currents, were intriguing. He slowed the body, stopped, whirled, and glanced back at the ground he'd covered in a brief spurt. Not bad. He glanced up, crouched, sprang, caught the limb of a low weathered tree, and hauled himself up into the knobby branches.

The voice spoke in his head. "A remarkably versatile organism. But hadn't you better go slow at first?"

"No need. The control-information for every single move I've made is coded and stored away in one section or another of the creature's brain. All I do is just let it take over. Watch."

He glanced around.

The tree grew at the edge of a deep rocky inlet. Briefly, he studied the clear water, then arced out from the tree, split the water cleanly, and popped to the surface, aware of a grin that expressed his sense of well-being perfectly.

The voice was reproving. "If you'd gone just a little bit to one side, you'd have split the creature's skull."

"The point is, I didn't go that little bit to one side. The control mechanisms are extremely accurate, once freed of the cumulative poisons and allowed to function properly. I think basically this is a much more finely-controlled organism than any of our others. The beauty of it is, most of the control is automatic. I don't always know just what the mechanism will do, but I have a sense of *readiness*. For instance, when I looked out of the tree at the water, if I looked beyond the rock, I had a feeling of unease and danger. Thus I knew the body could not clear the rock. When I looked at the water in front of the rock, again I had the feeling—this time more a sense of cramping. A little analysis showed that the body would either strike the bottom, because of too steep a dive, or strike the rock, because of too shallow a dive. There was no way to avoid one of these difficulties without running into the other. When I looked to the side, however, there was a feeling of perfect ease and readiness. There was really no need to calculate anything. It was all done by a process of comparison with stored data."

"Then you are ready to test the body against our others?"

"I'm ready, of course. But I don't think there'll be much I need to do except to keep the internal processes and the functioning mechanism of the body in proper condition, and perhaps occasionally make a selection between alternatives. Its operation seems to be largely automatic."

"In that case, we might as well start. We hope to have more specimens before too long, for comparison."

"How so?"

"Several remote-controlled vehicles have come down to examine the remains of the exoskeleton and the host's body. Of course, we've heavily infiltrated the vehicles, in the samples of decomposing body tissue. Thanks to the information we have from previously scanning your host's brain, we've been able to locate the circuits which control the vehicles. They really aren't so much different from nerve circuits, basically."

"What are you going to do?"

"Corrode and wear away a section of a separate circuit designed to trigger an explosion to destroy the vehicles. This is nearly done. Then, when they can't strike back at us by destroying the vehicles, we'll take over the vehicles. They are driven by mechanisms controlled by small motors, and these are controlled in turn by plungers actuated by"—there was a minute pause—"solenoids. Movement of the six sets of plungers determines the eventual movement of the vehicles. The solenoids are small, and the plungers light. All we need do is cut the normal control circuit, and actuate the plungers mechanically."

"That will warn them."

"Of course. We will do this only if they send the signal to destroy the remote-control vehicles. But they have vacillated for some time. The vehicles were ridiculously easy to infiltrate. The sham body we constructed was so closely accurate we doubt they can detect the difference. If they do attempt to destroy the vehicles, we will simply send them up at the larger vehicles off-planet and try to manage just one collision. All we need is to get just one of us inside any one of those ships. And now, if you are ready for the test—"

"I'm ready."

* * *

Brigadier General Cutter strode back across the room, and slammed the staff summary onto the floor in the corner. No matter how he approached the problem, it changed form before his eyes, and the solution he had just arrived at seemed wrong.

The simple, obvious solution was to say, "Destroy the planet." For justification, he could point to his orders, and to the indecisive staff report. But that was just the trouble. The staff report *was* indecisive. Angrily, Cutter turned to the photographs of the body. Certainly, that hideous shambles *looked* authentic. He glanced at the detailed dissection and analysis report. The dissection reports disclosed everything normal, considering the circumstances. Only the chemical structure seemed anomalous, and these anomalies were few and small. It took a specific type of biochemical training to begin to appreciate them.

Cutter shook his head. On the strength of these few submicroscopic differences, he was supposed to destroy the planet. And if he *did* destroy the planet, it would, inevitably, raise an outcry along the whole frontier. Inevitably, there would be an investigation. And this was the evidence he would have to present to justify his case for destroying the planet. He could see himself in the packed Senate chamber, a microphone shoved up to his mouth, a tri-di camera staring him in the face, the question put to him gently, but inescapably:

"And you say, general, your orders were to destroy the planet, if the scout's body was not there?"

"Yes, sir."

"Now, general, I ask you to look at this photograph. Have you seen this photograph before?"

"Yes, sir. Of course, I have."

"May I ask you, what is this a photograph *of*?"

And there he was. Hung up. What could he say? He could answer the question in different ways:

"Senator, that is the body of the stellar scout."

"Now, general, this photograph was taken on the planet you destroyed, was it not? It was taken just before you issued your famous command to destroy the whole planet, was it not?"

"Yes, sir."

"And your orders were to destroy the planet *if the body of the stellar scout was not there*?"

"Yes, sir."

"And yet you just said, *this is a photograph of the body*? Then the body was *there*, was it not? You don't argue, do you, that you took a photograph of something that wasn't there?"

And he was condemned out of his own mouth. On the other hand, he could answer differently. He could say:

"Senator, that is an *imitation* body, constructed by an alien organism."

"It is—what? What was that again?"

"That is not the body of the stellar scout. That is an imitation body constructed to mislead us."

"It is? Why, general, it's a badly decomposed body, but it looks human to me. Here, show me anything here that's nonhuman. Does it have six or seven fingers? I don't see anything. Show me."

"It isn't a question of appearance, senator. Obviously, a sham would be ineffective if the appearance were inaccurate. It is a question of the chemical structure of the body."

"General, when I look at you to see if you're human, I don't have to cut you up and run samples of you through a test tube, do I?"

Laughter in the chambers.

"No, senator, but if you found my body, ran it through a test tube, and discovered it was made of green cheese, you'd be a little suspicious, wouldn't you?"

"Well—That's a point, I have to admit, general. But I have here this sheaf of papers showing the results of anatomical and chemical examination. The anatomical examination showed perfect normality."

"The body was in a state of considerable decomposition."

"Yes, but if this had been simply a matter of scraping together a mass of material and stamping it into an outward human semblance—I'm thinking of that green cheese, general, that you're made of—then the anatomical examination would certainly have shown it, would it not?"

"Yes, sir. But what we're up against works more subtly that that."

"All right. I'm open-minded. But we find nothing abnormal about the appearance of the body. Nothing an ordinary human would notice. And we cut it up and find nothing abnormal about the structure of it. If any doctor had been called to carry out a post-mortem, it would have seemed like a perfectly human body to him. Any anatomist would think it was a human body. *You* say it was the chemical structure. I see here in this report a long complicated series of analyses. It looks to me as if there are only a few substances out of line. Here, point out to me a few of these abnormalities."

"Well, here, senator, in the hair, and here, in the nails—"

"I see. Yes, and I also know that this body was decomposing, on a strange planet, that there are natural variations both in structure and in chemical balance among perfectly ordinary human individuals, and that your orders were to destroy the planet *if the body of the scout wasn't there*. Did your orders say, "Destroy the planet if the scout's fingernails aren't up to specifications?"

"No, sir. But—"

"*But that's what you did, isn't it*? You *did* destroy the planet, didn't you? Because these few chemical compounds didn't happen to be just the way you wanted? *Answer the question!*"

"Yes, sir. Because the implications of those few chemical compounds—"

" 'Implications of the chemical compounds,' " mimicked the senator. "Let's think of the implications of your actions, for a change. Do you know that planet would ultimately have supported *three billion human beings*?

Do you know you blasted out of existence the homes and futures of three billion people—for a set of fingernails? Where will these people go? Their world is destroyed! *You* destroyed it! And if you destroy the future, the possibility of existence, of a human being, how is that different from destroying the human being himself? I indict you, general, for the destruction, the murder of three billion colonists and their descendents, down through the mists of time, they and their children and their children's children, in uncountable multitudes, that can never exist, that have been blotted out of existence, because *you* didn't like a man's fingernails!"

Cutter, drenched in perspiration, looked at the phone resting on his desk, that he could pick up very easily to cause the destruction of the planet and the ending of all doubt. He saw the phone through a mental haze of imaginary shouting jeering people, senators and spectators, their accusing fingers pointed at him, the bright lights dazzling him, his perspiring features reproduced in a billion homes.

"No," he said. "I can't do it. It isn't right. Nobody can ask me to do that."

Driven by the nightmare generated by his own brain, he picked up the phone.

"Sir?" came the waiting voice.

"I want everything within a hundred-mile radius of that scout ship smashed to powder. That's all."

"Yes, sir. About the servo-dissectors, sir—"

"Destroy them," said Cutter shortly.

"Yes, sir."

Cutter hung up. He glanced at the solido of Dione. He looked at it for a long time.

On the other end of the wire, the orders were going out. In one detail, they were different from what Cutter intended. The simple, obvious way to destroy the remote-control devices near the scout ship was simply to leave them where they were. At the center of a hundred-mile radius of destruction, they would be smashed to dust.

But Cutter had only said, "Destroy them." He hadn't specified how. Now the order went out. "Activate the suicide circuits."

Cutter, unaware of this, and seeing an end to his dilemma, began to breathe easily again.

* * *

At Luna I HQ, Lieutenant General Bradley Matthews frowned and leaned back in his chair. He hadn't had again an attack of sickness such as he'd had after Cutter left to make his call to Earth, but he'd had plenty of indigestion. He was having an attack right now, and he asked himself, Why? He frowned. It all dated from that talk with Cutter. He leaned back, scowling, and after a long while, slowly sat up.

He was remembering Cutter's hearty frontier manner, quickly dropped when a little heat was applied. He remembered Cutter's arguments in favor of easy measures to preserve planets for future colonists, and his own reluctant agreement on easy measures, so long as the body of the scout was there.

But there was the cause of his trouble.

Cutter was the wrong man to carry out such orders ruthlessly.

Matthews' indigestion vanished in a sudden burst of anger. His hand shot out and gripped a bright green phone on his desk. He jerked it viciously off its cradle. A voice replied, "Max. Priority." Matthews said, "All traffic outward of Sental III is quarantined, with immediate effect. The direct Sental-Earth subspace route is closed, with immediate effect. Move reserve groups IV, VI, and X forward along the axis Sental-Felis. Halt all traffic moving inward toward Sental, or laterally across the axis Sental-Felis, or breaking from subspace anywhere within range in the region outward of Sental. Attack and destroy without question any traffic which disobeys the halt order. There are no exceptions to the halt and destroy orders for any circumstances whatever. There is to be no physical contact with any of the halted ships for any reason whatever."

"Yes, sir. At once, sir."

Matthews slammed the phone in its cradle, got up, paced the floor, and abruptly snapped on the three-dimensional stellar chart.

❋

The voice spoke inside its head, almost simultaneously with its own shock:

"WHAT WAS THAT?"

Directly across from it was the grapple, a low armored creature with retractile eyes, four very long snaky limbs that spread out and disappeared in the marsh grass and a large and a small set of powerful pincers at one end. The grapple had two of its snaky limbs bunched and pulled back, three of its eyes were extended on wiry stalks, and the large and the small pincers were poised, open, above the bunched limbs. The pincers snapped shut with a loud *click*. Abruptly the eyes swiveled outward, and the limbs violently unbunched, snaking out in the long marsh grass. The pincers dove out of sight in the grass. Two of the eyes retracted almost out of sight, and the third straightened, to wave stiffly and gently among the stalks of tufted grass. The armored body was motionless, like a low lichened rock among the mossy hummocks.

Suddenly the voice said, "It *had* you!"

"I was careless. This body could have escaped. But I forgot that it had no experience with grapples. No stored recognition patterns or get-away reflexes. It was my fault. I should have used direct control."

"The point is, it *had* you. And yet, you *did* escape!"

There was a brief pause, and this fact sank in, to be followed by blank astonishment. "It must have let go. All I felt was the shock of capture. Then I was free."

"We were in contact with both of you. It didn't let go."

"But—that's impossible."

A faint gliding movement caught his attention. Abruptly he was aware that the low "rock" which was the grapple's body was no longer on the far side of the large mossy mound, but had imperceptibly eased alongside of it. Then the grass rippled in a long wave.

He hit the water with a flat slap. The hard grip at his ankles yanked him feet first through muck and grass. A second limb snaked tight around his chest and waist, pinning his arms to his body. Eyes on wiry stalks arched overhead. A large set of pincers loomed above him.

In a flash he saw in clear detail a section of swamp he'd been looking at a moment before. Something happened so fast he was aware only of a brief vague sensation of gripping something beside and around him to thrust his body in relation to it.

He was standing forty feet from the gray "rock" that was the grapple's armored body. This time he did not remain standing there. With little urging on his part, the body sprang carefully and accurately from hummock to hummock, eyes alert for any gray, rocklike thing anywhere ahead or to the side.

The voice spoke in his head:

"WHAT DID YOU DO?"

***

Brigadier General Cutter looked at the phone, scowled, and said, "What's that?"

"Sir, the servosurgeon and servoanalytic rockets aren't destroyed. The suicide circuits won't work."

"Why bother with—Oh I see." He frowned.

"Instead, sir, the probes mounting these devices are headed back toward the ship."

"We can't have that," said Cutter. "Put them back down near the scout ship, and blow them up with it."

"Sir, they won't go back down. They don't respond to signal."

Cutter glanced at the solido of Dione. He hesitated possibly a fifth of a second. "Open up with fusion guns. Burn them up."

"Yes, sir."

Cutter held the phone and pressed down the short plastic bar in the phone's cradle. He glanced at the solido of Dione. He let up on the bar, and said, "Missile Electronics."

There was a brief delay.

"Sir?"

"What are the odds that the suicide circuits on the servo-equipped probes we set down on that planet would refuse to obey the trigger signal?"

"Sir? Just about zero."

"And what chance is there that the probes would then head up on their own and start for the ships?"

"Impossible, sir. Unless someone down there got into the circuits and altered them. Or, possibly, if they had a very small sensitive remote-control tool, and got it into the C-box."

"What's in there?"

"Sir, I'm forbidden by regulations to discuss it. But if a very sensitive complex tool, capable of exerting a small pressure in the right directions, was somehow gotten in there, the probe could be remote-flown from outside."

"Would this be hard?"

"It would be fantastically complicated. The tool would have to be collapsible, capable of being worked in through a narrow channel, and remote-controlled somehow to exert pressure in the right directions. But that's how it could be done."

Cutter nodded. "Thank you."

He put the phone in its cradle, and sat staring at the staff reports.

It stopped the swift running of the body across the marsh, and looked back toward the grapple. Only a bit of the gray body was visible, blending with the low hummocks of moss and clumps of marsh grass.

This time, the shock of capture and escape was more violent. He could still feel the grip of the tight contractile arms at waist and ankles. He could still see the eyes on stalks against the sky, and poised just above him, the powerful pincers. His own reflexive fear of the pain the grapple could inflict on his host, and through the nerves of his host, on him, was compounded by the host body's own reaction—a violent pumping of blood and rapid respiration that built up the sensation of fear. Angrily, he thrust these feelings aside, and concentrated instead on the memory of his escape.

Something had happened. But what? Carefully he scanned the body's central nervous system, seeking the faint traces that would reveal patterns of nerve connections set up briefly, used for a bare instant, then lost again. This failing, he groped to recover the memory of what had happened. Holding the other activities of the brain to a bare quiet minimum, gradually he recovered the memory. Working from the memory, he strove to gain a conscious knowledge of whatever it was that had enabled him to get away from the grapple.

Bit by bit, it became clearer, and as he remembered, he carefully traced the nerve paths, trying to locate the exact form and sequence of nerve currents that had set the process in action.

After a long silence, the voice said, "You have it. That's what happened."

"But will it work if I initiate the process consciously?"

There was a moment's hesitation. "Try it and see."

He hesitated.

"I'm not quite sure of the right sequence. It seems to me there is some sort of master impulse that comes first, and cuts out interference. But right after that—I don't know."

"Try anyway."

"Yes. But what if—"

"*Try*." The voice had an urgency that communicated itself to him, and told him that there was more than curiosity behind the demand.

Carefully, trying to follow the remembered pattern, he sent out the nerve impulses.

Cutter held the phone to his ear. "*Completely* destroyed?" he insisted.

"Yes, sir. Flashed to vapor. We got the lot of them in quick succession."

"They were still headed for the ships?"

"Yes, sir."

"We have complete records of the incident?"

"Yes, sir. Beginning to end."

"All right. Carry out your orders to destroy the scout ship and its environs."

"Yes, sir."

Cutter put the phone in its cradle and got up. He had a hard problem to work out.

After what had happened so far, he was going to have to destroy the planet. There was no way out of that. He would *have* to destroy the planet. After his superiors saw the record of what had happened here, they would crush him if he left without destroying the planet.

But he had to destroy it in such a way that it would look good to the colonists.

He began to pace the floor.

* * *

The initial nerve impulse had gone out correctly, but now instead of finding himself in the plot of tufted grass he had visualized, he was instead swamped with flashes of color, and a sea of unfamiliar verbalizations that washed into his consciousness, drowning him in a flood too great to endure.

Desperately, he choked off the nerve impulses, and the process, whatever it was, faded out entirely, leaving him with a few strings of words that his host's brain belatedly responded to, giving him the thought behind the words:

"I've got to smash this planet. But how to do it and not antagonize the whole frontier?"

And from a deeper level, the thought came through:

" . . . I ought to destroy it now. I ought to destroy it now. I ought to destroy it now . . . "

And from a still deeper level:

"Dione . . . Dione . . ."

Puzzled, very carefully, he permitted the nerve currents to flow again.

And he picked up the welter of verbalizations. But this time he found he was able, like a beast of prey following a trail, to sift very carefully through the confusion for the familiar scent he was tracking.

***

Cutter was standing still, scowling. For a moment, he had completely lost track of his own thoughts. He saw Dione's solido, and was conscious of a sudden, almost embarrassing rush of emotion. An instant later, he was aware of the desperate importance of destroying this planet before it was too late. He reached for the phone, and paused, remembering all the irksome complications that would follow the destruction of the planet.

He wavered, seeing the angry colonists petitioning their representatives, and their representatives calling him and grilling him on his thoughts, purposes, intents, and rational justifications. And it would all take place in a fantastic publicity display that could turn in any direction at all, and leave him suddenly a has-been as a result of one wrong answer in a situation where the basic structure of right and wrong was hidden like a reef till he either hit it and was wrecked, or accidentally came through the unseen channel and suddenly realized with surprise that the ordeal was over.

But if he didn't do it, if he *didn't* destroy the planet—

Suddenly exasperated beyond enduring, by all the pros, cons, and imponderables, Cutter suddenly threw the whole mass of complications out of his mind.

The solido of Dione caught his eye, lush, seductive, demanding.

Demanding?

Cutter blinked, studying the construction of the woman's jaw.

His gaze traveled the curving length of the lush body, came back to the jaw, flicked up to study the shrewd eyes and empty face.

He spat an ugly curse, knocked the solido off the desk, cast a brief glance at the staff report, and picked up a phone.

"Sir?"

"Check out four subnuclear triggers—"

"Sir, we've got half-a-dozen checked out and ready to go. It's SOP on this category mission."

"You've also got suitable target areas selected, to destroy the planet?"

"Yes, sir."

"Destroy the planet."

"Yes, sir."

***

The host's brain interpreted the order, but there was a lapse of time before the full meaning came through. Even then he wasn't certain that this was what it actually meant.

The voice was not so hesitant:

"You're picking up the thought of the commander of a space fleet with the power to destroy this planet. You've got to stop him!"

"But I can't! How could I—"

"We've had time to analyze the process you've followed. You are using nerve paths that the host creatures rarely ever use, and are hardly aware exist. Ordinarily, a great deal of training would be necessary, just to develop the nerve tracks, and special organs involved. But in rebuilding this body, we repaired damage resulting from neglect and disuse as well as injury. We didn't know where to stop, so we evidently developed certain organs that are still normally in process of evolutionary development. You've used these twice to escape destruction. *Now you've got to do it again.*"

"I don't know what to do!"

"The escape mechanism seems to operate when you visualize clearly the place to which you desire to go."

"But if the *whole planet* is to be destroyed—"

"Before you received the auditory sensations a moment ago, there were *visual* sensations. If you could filter out all the distracting sensations, and concentrate on *one clear visual picture*—"

"Yes," he said suddenly. "I see."

"Can you do it?"

"I'll try."

Once again, he let the nerve currents flow, and this time he struggled to recover the flashes of bright color he had ignored before. At first, there was no visual sensation at all. But as he carefully varied the current, there was a brief glimpse of gray, and he concentrated on it intently.

* * *

Brigadier General Cutter was pacing the floor, cursing the vacillation that had led him to waver and debate with himself when the only thing to do was obvious.

The basic cause of his trouble looked appealingly up at him from the floor, arms outstretched. Cutter booted the solido across the room, and felt a vicious satisfaction as it smashed into the bulkhead.

He felt a brief wave of dizziness. His vision nearly blanked out. He caught the desk for support, and then the phone was ringing.

By habit, he groped for it, and held it to his ear.

"Sir, the subnuclear triggers have impacted and fired."

"The planet is destroyed?"

There was an instant's hesitation at this question, then the dutiful answer, "Yes, sir. Certainly."

"Good."

Cutter hung up.

He told himself that he should have felt relief at that comment. But he didn't.

The spell of dizziness had passed away.

Cutter looked up.

⁂

With the effort to control the nerve currents, and to focus precisely on the gray visual image, had come a desperate sense of urgency. He had lost consciousness of everything else in the effort to define that fuzzy image. And when he had defined it, when he saw it clearly, there was a brief moment of unbearable intensity, and then—a sense of relief.

He was standing in a gray-walled room, looking at a man—a host organism just like his own—replace a black plastic "phone" in its black plastic "cradle."

The man looked up—and stared.

⁂

Cutter saw the naked figure, its appearance godlike in the definition of massive muscles and the healthy glow of smooth skin. For an instant, Cutter was unable to move.

The figure stepped forward and clasped him by both wrists.

There was a sharp, piercing pain in Cutter's forearms.

Suddenly Cutter jerked back from the desk, and tried to wrench his hands loose.

The figure on the other side of the desk smiled, leaned forward, and rested its weight heavily on the pinned wrists.

Cutter tried to knock the phones from the desk. He tried to butt the massive figure that gripped him. The silent struggle went on.

Abruptly, Cutter recovered from his shock.

He sucked in a deep breath, to shout at the top of his lungs.

Sight and sound began to fade. He felt a brief dizziness.

The godlike figure stood over the slumped general, looked around the room thoughtfully—and then vanished.

***

He was lonely.

The voice, a manifestation of a whole planet taken over and controlled by his kind, was gone. Wiped out. But it would speak again, in time, if he could spread his kind throughout the ships of this fleet. To do that, he had, he found, to carefully scan the thoughts that came to him, find some that he could identify as coming from one of the nearby ships, focus intensely on the visual sensations accompanying the thought, and find a host organism that was alone. Then he need only restrict his attention to the visual sensations, and when there was that undefinable moment of discontinuity, he found himself physically close to the new host organism, which he seized by arm or throat long enough to pass one or two of his kind, and then he pinned the host organism till the original consciousness of the host lost the struggle for control.

Then he moved on.

Soon he had a host organism on each ship of the fleet.

Unfortunately, not all of the hosts were in controlling positions on their individual ships. To get at these particular hosts required a delay while the reproductive process created new master organisms. But the delay was not important. His kind had gained control of the chief host organism, and that was what *was* important.

***

The body of Brigadier General Cutter moved at the desk, straightened, and looked around. Two of the phones were ringing. Cutter's hand picked up one of them. There was a moment of listening.

"Yes," said Cutter's voice. "We will check both of those planets. There's no reason whatever for a change of plan. And then, when we're through—

"Then we'll head back to Earth."

Lieutenant General Bradley Matthews, the three comets of his rank glinting at his lapel, looked at the incomplete transmission that had just come in:

"LANDING ON FELIS IV TIME"

Matthews looked up at the communications officer.

"This is all that came in?"

"There was a lot of gibberish preceding it, sir. The message ended abruptly at the word 'time.' "

"Let's see the gibberish."

"Sir?"

"The meaningless part of the message. Where is it?"

The communications officer stared at him, then saluted and left the room in a rush.

Matthews looked back at the message.
"LANDING ON FELIS IV TIME"

***

The voice was back.

Not quite the same voice.

Not, perhaps the voice of a brother, but the voice at least of a cousin. Still, it was the voice. The voice that told him he was not alone in a hostile universe, but immersed in the affairs of his own kind. The voice that told him he was no longer one of a little band of lonely explorers, but had the resources of a civilization at his back.

To the eye and mind of the host organism, the planet was commonplace. To him, conscious of the ruling species that controlled all the diverse life forms, the planet was home.

When he left, he intended to take home with him.

***

"There it is, sir," said the communications officer. "That's an exact copy of the original."

Matthews studied the sheet of paper:

AZAZRGHORABNLOKDLDMSARTEEDQHMFA
EQNLARNLDAJHMCANEACHRDZRDANQA

Matthews glanced down the paper. The jumble of letters went on for better than two dozen lines, and it all looked about the same.

"Just gibberish, sir," said the communications officer, frowning uneasily at the paper.

Matthews' attention was caught by the first four letters, "AZAZ." The first and last letters of the alphabet. Idly, he wrote out the alphabet, and below it, the alphabet reversed. The A and Z were now opposite each other at the beginning and end, so that when he glanced over the paired alphabets counterclockwise, the letters at the two ends read "AZAZ."

"Sir," said the communications officer, "if anyone had wanted to send us a message, he could have used the standard code."

"Yes, but what if hadn't wanted the people around him to know what he was saying? Suppose he just wanted them to think he was ' sending . . . say . . . a test transmission?"

"Well—"

Matthews felt more and more certain he was right. Ignoring the communications officer, he substituted the letters of his paired alphabets, and wrote:

ITSJIWYMOJPWOW

The communications officer cleared his throat.

Matthews frowned at the paper. "IT" was encouraging. "IT'S" was all right. But what to do with "JIWYMOJPWOW"

Matthews became conscious of the amount of time that could go down the hole while he wrestled with this.

He glanced up at the communications officer, saw the I-told-you-so look on his face, and suddenly remembered that rank *has* its privileges.

"Get to work on this," said Matthews briskly, "and decipher it. I'm inclined to think it's a substitution cipher of some kind. And demand an explanation of that 'Landing on Felis IV' message that came with it."

The communications officer glanced at the sheet of gibberish, looked blank, said "Yes, sir," saluted, and went out, leaving the copy on Matthews' desk.

Matthews shoved it to one side, and tried to consider other matters. A landing on Felis IV would mean—what?

That the planet was clearly safe? That Cutter's expedition had somehow already been taken over?. That some unforeseeable emergency had forced the landing?

Frowning, Matthews pulled the sheet of paper over and looked at it:

AZAZRGHORABNLOK . . .

***

The voice was still there.

As the fleet moved, the voice moved with it, evidence that the fleet and every creature on it served as transports for an invasion force of the master organism. All that was needed now was a supply of new hosts. To that end, their suspicions must be stifled before they could arise.

A long message went out from the fleet to human headquarters. The main part of the message read:

. . . INFECTED PLANET DESTROYED BY SUB-NUCLEAR ATTACK STP OTHER TWO PLANETS HARMLESS STP . . . COMMUNICATOR MAL-FUNCTION GARBLED MESSAGE WHICH FOLLOWS . . . REMOTE TESTING DEVICES LANDING ON FELIS IV STP PLANET SEEMS OKAY SO FAR BUT TIME WILL TELL STP END OF PRIOR TRANSMISSION STP . . . MISSION COMPLETED STP RETURNING EARTH BY WAY OF SENTAL II IMMEDIATELY STP . . .

***

There was a rap at the door, and Matthews looked up. "Come in."

The communications officer, a sick look on his face, came in and saluted. Wordlessly, he handed Matthews a sheet of paper that read:

SHIPS COMPLEMENT SUFFERING FROM
SOME KIND OF DISEASE OR SPIRIT POSSES-
SION STP THERE ARE LONG PERIODS OF
SILENCE WHEN THEY SEEM TO MERELY INAC-
TIVATE THEIR BODIES STP THEY ACT
TOGETHER AS IF GUIDED BY TELEPATHY STP
I AM SYSTEMS REPAIR TECHNICIAN IRA BENT-
LEY STP TWICE THEY HAVE GRABBED ME BY
THE WRISTS AND HELD ME TILL DIZZINESS
HIT ME STP I THINK I AM IMMUNE STP DO NOT
LET THEM RETURN TO EARTH STP

The communications officer cleared his throat. "Simplest form of substitution cipher, sir, with 'A' inserted
between the ciphered words."

Matthews picked up the green phone by his desk.

"Max. Priority," said a respectful voice.

"The ships of General Cutter's expedition," said Matthews carefully, "wherever they are found, are to be
attacked and destroyed without warning. They are to be
attacked the instant they are recognized."

"Yes, sir."

Matthews put the phone down and glanced at the
communications officer, who saluted and went out.

Matthews briefly studied the star chart, and learned
nothing new from it.

There was little to do now but wait.

***

"We have carefully developed the special organs and
nerve paths of each of these host-organisms in order to
take advantage of undeveloped capabilities of the host.
At this distance, and without more practice, we can't be
certain, but the reports we have been able to get are not
very reassuring. You've had more practice than the rest,

so before we finish the approach to Sental II, perhaps you'd better tell us if you agree with the other observations."

***

Matthews slid the coil back into his fission gun, gave a quarter turn to lock it, thumbed down the safety, and put the gun back in the open drawer, within easy reach. He returned his attention to the report on his desk, turned the page, and read:

" . . . But telepathy is only one of these hypothetical powers. Also mentioned frequently are: precognition —the ability to at least partially foresee coming events; clairvoyance—the ability to see, without use of the visual organs of vision, and unrestricted by physical obstructions; clairaudience—the same type of thing, as applied to hearing; teleportation—the ability to transfer objects, including the body, from one place to another, without visible physical means. There are many others, and also variations of the ones already mentioned.

"Thorough scientific investigation of a variety of persons offering to demonstrate such powers has revealed many instances of fakery, carefully detailed at the end of this report, and also a number of instances in which no fakery was found, so that the investigators were evidently duped.

"Save for a few examples drawn from ancient texts, which have gone through many translations, there appear to have been no instances of commercial or military application of these powers. Indeed, such application is forbidden by various injunctions. This is apparently with the purpose of forestalling in advance any challenge for a demonstration, since such commercial and military utilization could obviously be highly profitable.

"Some few public demonstrations are reported to have taken place, but these can either be duplicated by physical means, in which case their method of operation is clear, or they plainly must be instances of mass hypnosis, hysteria, and confused memory on the part of the participants.

"Thus, impartial evaluation of the records reveals . . ."

Matthews circled the word "teleportation," and read again: "the ability to transfer objects, including the body, from one place to another, without the use of visible physical means."

He was thinking of Cutter's argument that a planet would be safe if ringed by subnuclear missiles, since—how could anything leave the surface of the planet without the use of physical means?

Matthews glanced at the deciphered message: THEY ACT TOGETHER AS IF GUIDED BY TELEPATHY.

Assuming that some minute creature were able to invade the human body, and having invaded it, could take control of it, vary its form at will, and eventually utilize powers that the human himself scarcely knew existed, how could anyone possibly hope to withstand the creature? All that was needed was to blunder onto a planet occupied by it, and the fight was all over. If such a creature existed anywhere in the universe, what chance was there for humanity? First contact meant automatic defeat. How *could* there be a defense against such creatures? All they had to do was to seize control of one human, and all the rest was just a matter of going through motions.

He picked up the green phone and spoke into it, choosing his words carefully.

❖❖❖

The voice was hopeful. "Were we wrong, then?"

"No," he said uneasily. "Far from it. The instant our ships appear off Sental II, they'll be destroyed."

"Unfortunately, we can't approach Earth without either making a long circuit, or else pioneering some new subspace approach—which might bring us out inside some physical object and destroy us—or else coming in on the known subspace route to near Sental II."

"The other two approaches give our opponents time to prepare. Couldn't we do as you did when you seized control of Cutter and his ships?"

"Not this time. They're in pairs. They're well-armed. No doubt, after a terrific struggle, we would eventually get control of the ships of that fleet—assuming we could move fast enough when we broke out of subspace—but what then? What if *those* ships were destroyed? The controlling entity obviously is in a mood to do just that."

"Then we will have to try to bypass all this. We will have to try something else that these organisms seem to be potentially capable of. We will have to try to boost the power of these nonphysical effects. Possibly we can form a linkage, act together at long range, and strike at the nerve center of the ultimate control organism. But we will have to act quickly. The longer we wait, the more likelihood of some disastrous action that will destroy great numbers of the host, to no purpose."

Lieutenant General Matthews heard the soft step, and looked up. Naked, eyes blazing with tension, the godlike figure moved forward in a blur.

Matthews fired, whirled aside, and fired again, as a second figure appeared at the other side of his desk.

Powerful hands gripped his throat from behind.

His right heel smashed down by reflex action, to snap the small bones of an unprotected foot, at the same instant that the raised muzzle of his gun found the head of the figure behind him.

There was a sudden warmth at his left shoulder, but he was free, firing again and again, as the room around him turned into a slaughterhouse, and then suddenly there was no more opposition.

He felt a wave of dizziness, and aimed the gun at his own head.

The dizziness faded.

There was an intense pain at his chest. A gray curtain seemed to fall before him to cut off his vision.

He struggled in vain to raise the gun and squeeze the trigger.

But a delicate thermal switch cemented to the roof of his mouth took note of the typical fall in body temperature, and faithfully sent out its signal.

In a dazzling flash, the room dissolved.

⁂

"Close," said the voice. "Our losses are nearly forty per cent. But the stubbornness of the opposition makes no ultimate difference, since we won. As we had to win. There really was no way they *could* have won. Now it's just a matter of cleaning up."

The messages began to come in now, calling for help from scattered parts of human-controlled space. These messages told of a spreading nightmarish life form, capable of using humanity as humanity uses beasts of burden. The messages called for help from Earth. The replies were always soothing, and the help quickly forthcoming. Once the help arrived, there were rarely any further complaints. The diminishing flow of messages that came in told the story of an interstellar human civilization sixty per cent, eighty per cent, ninety per cent overcome in a fight carried out without quarter by an overwhelmingly superior opponent.

And then, at last, the messages calling for help came in no longer.

The fight appeared over.

It was then, at the moment of final victory, that the radiation barriers began to vary in strength.

The voice was concerned:

"This oscillation of the radiation barriers has never happened before?"

"No. I find no mention of it in any of the records available to the electronic computers the humans used. No record at all."

"And there is no memory of it. We have lost a comparatively small percentage of them, and the memories of those we have all agree. This has never happened before. We know that we have completely conquered the human race, that we have occupied Earth, its home planet, and that we now control the race and all its resources. We know in addition that there is one more radiation barrier, inward, toward the center of the galaxy, that they had not yet reached on their own. Thus, they occupied a very large box of space. We now control them, and through them the suns and planets within the large volume of space. But we actually know nothing of the nature of these radiation barriers, except that they are fatal. So, how will we—"

The frequency of the oscillations varied, all around the enclosed volume of space, as if seeking a value at which space itself would respond.

There was the sudden flare of innumerable points of light.

The stars seemed to multiply.

Space lit in a dazzling haze as interstellar dust burned white.

Spaceships flared and burst.

The atmospheres of planets lit in dazzling auroral displays.

The oscillations came to another fine adjustment.

The stars seemed to dull, as their planets blazed in a fiery glow.

The Voice cried out, then died away.

The radiation barrier farthest out, toward the rim of the galaxy, began to move in, toward the center.

* * *

Lieutenant General Bradley Matthews became aware of consciousness. An instant later, he remembered his last physical actions. He felt a grim satisfaction that he had been able to take a few of them with him, and that he had blocked their attempt to capture him. But then, why could he still think? Where was he now?

"Steady," said a quiet feminine voice, very close to him.

Matthews tried to speak, but was unable. He thought, putting the thought in words, "Where am I?"

"In cubicle 68654 tier AA layer AB of the transit ship *Arcturus*."

Matthews thought this over for a long time.

"I don't understand. How did I come to be here?"

"You volunteered on New Mars, made the necessary qualifications trip through a colonization center, discovered the type of planet for which you were best suited, reported for the first trip, and—here you are."

"I volunteered on New Mars, you say?"

"That's right. I have your file at my elbow."

"I seem to have . . . well, lost my memory. Possibly you could tell me a little more."

"Your age is twenty-four. Your field of specialization is densitization, with particular emphasis on cooling control. You received your B.S. at Max Mann University on New Mars, took your M.S. and Ph.D. (elementary) at the same school. You transferred to Interstel on New Earth and took your Ph.D. intermediate and Ph.D. (advanced) at Interstel. While you were preparing to take the qualifying exams for your electorate, there was an incident in which another student molested a girl you were interested in, was severely beaten, and died from the effects. You were accused of manslaughter. Because of lack of conclusive evidence, an indeterminate verdict was returned against you. You were expelled from Interstel, and for lack of proper educational qualifications, could obtain only menial employment on New Earth. You returned to New Mars, received your Dns.El., *cum laude*, but because the scandal followed you from New Earth, you decided to leave on the next colonization expedition. Word came that an elimination was going to have to be carried out in Nineteen Prime, with an advance of the Border in that region. This meant a great deal of planet-recovery work, with high tax-free pay. You volunteered. Does any of that ring a bell?"

"I'm a little hazy on this idea of 'elimination.' What's that?"

"Well—" the feminine voice hesitated. "Of course, your stat sheet shows you aren't qualified to understand military specs."

"Oh, of course not," replied Matthews. "But it seems to me I should have *some* kind of rough idea."

"You have to take specs outside your own field for granted. When there's an 'elimination,' that means there's planet-forming work afterward. That's absolutely all you need to know."

Matthews' thought came out with what, if he had spoken, would have been a harsh rasping note:

"If you don't know what it means, look it up."

There was a short tense silence, then the click of switches.

A stiff feminine voice said, "Here you are, then. Quote: Owing to the danger of infiltration by quasi-human life forms, mental parasites, telepathic life forms, squoits, class-A complex wave-forms, and others summarized in Table 61 below, external compartmentalization is a necessity. Thus, as the race moves inward, quasi-Earths are seeded well in advance of the actual border regions. Using deep hypnotic techniques and refined methods of planet-forming, the initial generations on these quasi-Earths are led to believe that they have a very long, though somewhat confused, history, usually interrupted by one or more natural catastrophes that have apparently disarranged the 'evidence.' Believing firmly that they are the original and only humans, they proceed to colonize the surrounding region of space.

" 'If successful, they are in due time made aware of their actual line of descent, and are allowed to join forces with the "elder race." If, however, they are invaded by any of the aforementioned life forms, or others not yet discovered, we learn of the danger through taps on their communications system, observation by molecularized detectors, and other means which need not·be detailed here. In such a case, the entire affected compartment of space is subjected to a complex process based on substrate energetics. The result of this process is the elimination of all organized life within the affected compartment.

" 'Following this "elimination," the nearer energy wall of the compartment is advanced roughly two-thirds of the distance to the farther wall, the necessarily slow and expensive planet-forming work is carried out, a new pseudo-earth is seeded in the farther third of the compartment, the outer energy wall is withdrawn, and the inhabitants of the new pseudo-earth, earnestly believing that they are the original and only humans, proceed to carry forward the work of colonization.

" 'This roundabout procedure is a necessity, to prevent infiltration into the actual main body of the human race. This process assures us that the infiltration gains access only to a limited portion of the space under human control, and acquires only the comparatively limited knowledge available to the pseudo-earth race. Before the infiltrating conqueror has time to realize that the preconceptions of the humans it has conquered are false, it is wiped out.

" 'External compartmentalization limits the unavoidable disasters, and enables us, the true, original, Earth race, to continue human colonization of space.'

"End quote," said the prim feminine voice. "And I hope it helps you orientate yourself, though frankly, I *don't* think you can understand it without proper qualification."

Matthews gave a kind of mental grunt, as he slowly absorbed the fact that his whole region of space, with its billions of inhabitants, had been blotted out of existence. At least, he thought grimly, *they* hadn't gotten it.

"What's that?" said the feminine voice, strongly tinged with curiosity.

"I still don't have any clear memory. Are you sure there isn't something you've left out?"

The feminine voice hesitated, then said, "You were depressed when you came on board. You said you had a premonition you would never survive the trip. And you said that after what you'd seen of the way things work out, you didn't much care. I know, because I'm a Med.El., and you talked to me about it. I was assigned to handle your group of the planet-forming crew. Don't you really remember *anything*?"

Matthews told himself that from what little he'd experienced of this only, true, original Earth race, he could see how anyone who'd spent twenty-four years in it could be a little disheartened. But why fold up and quit? Why let a race case-hardened into an academic caste-system get off that easily? A few cracks on the right joints and nerve-centers ought to loosen them up a little.

"You say I'm a Dns.El.?"

"Yes."

"How does that compare with a Med.El.?"

"Well—" she hesitated. "*Some* people say a Dns.El. makes you a professional. I . . . I don't know." Her voice brightened. "*I* don't have any prejudices myself."

Matthews made a hard effort, and ranks of abstruse formulas, and masses of specialized knowledge rose before his conscious attention, and seemed to pass in review before him. Someone, he could see, had labored hard and long to acquire all this knowledge, and what was he at the end? A mere Dns.El., not truly a professional.

Struggling to form some kind of overall mental picture, and to acquire an insight into the inner meaning of all this knowledge, Matthews made the startling discovery that no understandable unifying viewpoint was to be found. None had ever been offered. All this maze of technicalities lay on the mind like a dead weight, crammed at top speed and largely undigested. But naturally, it would have to be, if one wished to acquire his Dns.El. and start making a living sometime in the first half of his life.

Matthews threw it all out of his consciousness. He'd seen enough to know that he could familiarize himself with it rapidly when he decided to. That was all he needed to know about it now. There were other matters to be looked into.

"And I'm twenty-four, is that right?"

"Yes," said the girl, her voice tense.

Twenty-four. That gave plenty of time to get something accomplished, assuming he wasn't cut off right at the beginning. What was the tenseness in her voice for? Spurred by an instinct that seldom, if ever, failed him, he delved earnestly into the memory that opened up to him like the pages of a book.

"You're Sylvia?" he thought.

"Yes," she said, eagerly.

"It's coming back to me. I remember that long talk we had, and the moonlight shining in the big window in the lounge."

"Oh, I'm so glad. I was afraid—Look, you *do* remember now?"

"Yes, I remember. Perhaps at first I didn't really *want* to remember."

"Amnesia is often an escape mechanism," she said knowledgeably. Matthews could see, from memory, that the girl was fairly pretty. Her figure wasn't bad either. But there was something about her habit of thought that grated on him, and he told himself, being careful not to verbalize it, that possibly he could find an ill-educated Ph.D. (advanced) a little less frozen into the rut.

"Excuse me," she added contritely. "Of course, you can't understand that. It's just the way we Med.El's talk."

"Oh, of course. What were you worried about?"

"Well, sometimes someone comes out of depth with a—Well, some of them argue and insist they're really someone else. The psychologists say it's a 'traumatic transference psychosis.' It's out of my field, and I really don't know much about it—"

And neither do they, he thought, being careful not to verbalize, but they've got a name for it, so, of course, it's all right.

" . . . But the psychologists say it's a very serious condition. I was afraid when the amnesia lasted so long—But it's all right, because you remember. Of course, the trouble is, you were motivated badly."

"My motivation is all right now."

"Of course. There's often a heterochronic effect in the alleviation of motivational deterioration." She made a little sound of distress. "But of course, you can't understand." As if sensing that possibly she had trodden heavily on his sensibilities, she said hastily, "In just a little while, when you go to work on the planets, *I'll* be the one who doesn't understand. I think it's always so nice when there's an elimination, don't you? It makes so many opportunities. Here, I'll bring you out."

Matthews considered the fact that the "elimination" she was so happy about had resulted in the death of billions of his own people. But, of course, she didn't know. It was out of her province.

There was a strange sensation as the warm liquid drained away from him, and light burst on his eyelids. There was an instant when a voice seemed to say to him, "You see how they are, and the way they think. These so-called 'only true humans' in this particular space-time compartment are caught in a trap of the mind. They will finally end up in very much the state of insects, on a grand scale, if we can't break them loose somehow. You happen to be the forty-seventh instrument we've chosen to initiate the attempt. Can you at least understand the point? Will you at least *try* to do your best?"

"Don't worry," Matthews thought grimly. "You can count on me."

SHOTGUN WEDDING

Stil Bek, Sector Controller of the Planetary Occupation Service, could tell a real mess when he saw one. With the impressions of jangling confusion still fresh in his mind, he clasped hands in the inner office with Kife, the Initial Penetration Commander. Stil noted Kife's feverish grip and glittering eye as Kife turned to point to a blond wood cabinet with a twenty-eight inch screen.

"With that," said Kife, "I will throw them into total chaos. When I get through, there won't be a sound mind or a stable government left on the planet. Watch."

Kife twisted a knob on the side of the cabinet. On the screen, floors and lighted rooms slid past, as if they looked into a building with one outside wall removed. Amidst a multitude of innocent scenes, Kife paused to show violent arguments, wild drinking parties, a group of people trading malicious gossip, and various couples who looked suspiciously as if they did not belong together.

Kife grinned, "Lies, backbiting, adultery, betrayal. Once a viewer sees these things on the screen, he'll watch them instead of anything else. And it's all *real*. The poison this device will spread will ruin the planet."

Stil felt his back hair prickle. "This is a scientifically advanced planet, Kife. Isn't this a dangerous device to release here? There isn't a world in the Galactic Combine where we'd dare to do this."

Kife didn't seem to hear him. "I've got the distribution problem whipped, too." He spread out a big map that showed the planet's western hemisphere surrounded by ocean, and ringed by selected parts of other continents. Large gray areas dotted in red and green were scattered over the map.

"The gray areas," said Kife, "are population centers. The green dots represent legitimate merchants. If the local governments block those, I've got black-market contacts set up—those are the red dots."

Stil felt the edge of the map with a finger to see if by any chance it wasn't all unfolded. "What about the rest of the planet?"

"I'll hit that later. First, I'll throw this western half into chaos and create a power vacuum. When the other bloc on the planet moves in to take over, there'll be confusion. Then I'll slip large numbers of the device into their territory. Since they work even more by secrecy and deceit, it will wreck them, too." He snapped his fingers. "Oh, yes, there's something else I wanted to show you."

He punched a button on his desk. The door flew open, and a quivering subordinate popped in. Kife scribbled on a pad, ripped off the top sheet, and thrust it out to the subordinate, who scurried out and was back shortly with a folded bundle of paper covered with printing.

"This," said Kife, "is what the locals call a 'newspaper.'" He snapped it open to a big ad headed:

ALL DOORS ARE OPEN
—WHEN YOU OWN AN RTV!

Beneath this was a picture of a family gathered reverently about an oversized screen that showed a circle of men and women in formal clothes.

Stil, who had learned the language in a hurry as his ship hurtled him through space to this planet, understood only snatches of the main body of the ad. But he could read enough to get the idea:

". . . What will ordinary TV *do* for you? . . . Just the same old shows, endlessly repeated . . . But suppose you could touch the magic knob and go anywhere . . . view real life anywhere in the world, in all its surging passion and variety . . . Uncensored! . . . Now, by a miracle of modern science . . . the dream of the ages comes true . . . And better yet, once you own an RTV, it shields you so no outsider can snoop into *your* home . . . Free from prying . . . exercise you healthy urge for reality, unafraid . . . Low, low down payment . . . See us soon."

Stil took a deep breath. "How soon are you planning to distribute the device?"

A look of proud achievement appeared on Kife's face. When he spoke, the words rang in Stil's ears like a sentence of doom.

"I've done it," said Kife.

Stil got some more details from Kife, then left the room in a kind of stupor. A nervous orderly guided Stil to a windowless private room and bath. Stil locked the door and glanced around. He was realizing, as he had in tight spots before, what a fortunate thing it was that the Galactic Combine had means of fast and secret communication. It might be too late for him to do anything, but he could warn others, so the situation might yet be gotten under control. Stil snapped off the room light, and lay down on the bed. He relaxed, and gradually quieted his thoughts. As his mind became calm, the faint hiss of the implanted transceiver grew louder, till it was like the whistle of steam from a tea kettle in a quiet room. Within the whistle, he could hear faint variations, which gradually became more distinct, and then formed words:

"Hello? Stil? . . . Come in, please . . . "

Stil formed a reply in his mind, and heard the words as clearly as if he spoke. "Right here, Dinal."

"Thank heaven. Have you reached 26JB3?—'Earth', as its inhabitants call it?"

"I'm there right now."

"Is it as bad as we thought?"

"Worse. Kife has actually put the sets on the market. Better than eight hundred were sold before I got here, with heavy advance publicity. There are hundreds of thousands more in stores and warehouses scattered over half the planet. We can't squash this now."

There was a silence, then Dinal said, "We notified the Chief."

"What happened?"

"The worst. He didn't explode. He just sent out for the whole file. Meanwhile, he's had no lunch, and no dinner. He's just working through his files. About six hours from now, he'll have the whole picture. He'll also be in a foul mood. Then the heads will really fly."

Stil grunted.

Dinal said, "What are you planning to do?"

"I'm still worn out from that conference on Tikra IV. I got here by ultrafast spacer, under maximum boost, and my control ship hasn't caught up yet. Until it does, I'm going to catch up on sleep."

"You must have iron nerves. Well, good luck."

"Thanks. Good luck to you."

The words faded into an unvarying whistle that died away to silence as Stil lay back, thinking.

In his mind's eye, he could see for a moment the great sweep of the Galactic Combine, holding its thousands of wide-flung planets in unified control. Stil saw his own sector as part of a huge pattern that constantly expanded as scout ships spotted new planets, and penetration teams moved in to study the local life forms, spot their weak points, and subtly introduce a new factor that would set the native populace at each other's throats and make the way easy for later exploitation and integration into the Combine.

Each planet, Stil thought, offered its own challenge. But planets of the type of this "Earth" were particularly tricky. Already split into hostile, scientifically alert factions, they were accustomed to stress, strain, and upheaval, as regular conditions of life. This meant that the disrupting factor had to be selected with care, and subtly introduced at just the right place and time. Otherwise, the planet might erupt into an outburst that would all but blow it to bits, thus losing it for the Combine. Or, the suspicion of outside interference might actually unify the warring factions overnight. All sorts of pitfalls lay in the path of the penetration teams on this type of planet. The strain on the penetration commander was particularly intense. Occasionally, a commander broke, lost contact with reality, slanted his reports according to his private delusions, and was not found out till the catastrophe happened. Then there was real trouble. Just as there was right now.

Stil decided there was no use thinking of it. He got up, washed, lay down again, and soon fell into an exhausted sleep.

Stil woke very early the next morning, the whistle loud in his head. As he held his attention on it, the voice grew clear, and he realized it was not Dinal this time, but Jad, his emergency controller. Jad's characteristic sourness came through clearly.

"Come in," said Jad. "Come in, Stil . . . "

"Right here. Where are you?"

"We've got the ship as close off planet as we can without being spotted. You want the first summaries now, or shall I wait till you come up?"

"Go ahead now." Stil blanked his mind.

Jad's voice said, "The history of the place seems about as we expected. Here's a reconstruction based on the data so far."

On the globe, light lines snaked over mountains and plains, to show the boundaries of nations and racial groups. As each boundary was completed, a voice spoke briefly, saying "Greece, Carthage, Rome, India." With each name Stil saw in a flash the characteristic national traits and habits, the more outstanding attitudes being symbolized by special shades of color, which gradually shifted over the globe as the armies marched and races migrated.

Brief flashes of light marked the inventions of new methods and devices, and Stil saw the effects of these in long-term processes that gradually gathered momentum.

The outward shifts of power now became more rapid, and accelerated into a series of violent upheavals that exploded and regathered till they locked into two huge power groups where the flow of colors brightened and intensified, and vast potential changes seemed to quiver on the verge of reality.

Stil held his breath, waiting. Then Jad's voice said, "At this point, Kife appeared on the scene. He found that one nation, the United States, had many immigrated minority groups still speaking the languages of their mother countries. Kife decided to carry out the initial language training in the United States, where living conditions were good, and where he'd have his men fairly well together. This worked, as far as language-teaching was concerned. Unfortunately, Kife's men also picked up the philosophy and attitudes of the place where they were living. Then Kife sent teams of them to places like the Soviet Union and China."

On the big globe, there flared into life here and there, a shade of color that contrasted glaringly with the color around it. Most of this new color was instantly snuffed out. But scattered fragments survived stubbornly. In the region called China, one began to enlarge like the vortex of a hurricane. It drew in and overpowered the color around it. It grew larger and larger. In the neighboring Soviet Union, the prevailing color wavered, then intensified. Bright lines arced out toward China. In a series of violent nuclear explosions, the transplanted color flared, broke into fragments, and finally died away. This same shade intensified sharply around the globe in the United States.

"That," said Jad, "was what they call 'the twenty-eight days' in China. The result has been to create terrific new tensions within each power bloc. At the same time both are shaken by the ferocity of what happened. This business seems to be what ruined Kife. A number of Kife's men, incidentally, were captured and brutally tortured. In the process, their implanted transceivers were found. The eastern bloc now thinks this means a fantastic scientific breakthrough by the western bloc. The eastern scientists are working on it day and night. At the same time, agents of the western bloc are reporting this to their superiors, who *know* the stuff wasn't theirs."

Stil drew in a deep breath. "Any reports on those sets Kife has distributed?"

"Not many. We've been concentrating on the background material I just showed you. But I think I can give you a few typical reactions."

The blue-and-green globe vanished. In quick succession, Stil saw a series of scenes: 1) A knot of wide-eyed men clutched beer cans as they huddled around a screen where a shapely woman slid a sweater over her head. 2) A group of tough but cheerful-looking men took copious notes as they watched bank officials methodically lock the vault for the day. 3) A poorly dressed man and woman shook their heads and grinned at each other as they watched an expensively dressed man and woman go through a savage quarrel on a big screen. 4) A man in a blue uniform with a microphone close by watched other men in blue fan out and approach the rear of a store adjoining a bank building. 5) A big cabinet sat with a blank screen by a bench, the works from inside the cabinet spread out on top of the bench with two men squinting at them, one of whom turned to the other and said, "Like hell we made it, Fred. And the Russkies didn't either."

The scenes faded out. Jad said, "We'll have a lot more for you later on. This seems to be typical for right now. The only other items of note are that several of these sets are on their way by fast plane to other nations, and the United States has slapped a ban on further sale of the sets in their own country. Whether the ban will last, I don't know."

Stil lay silent a moment, thinking. "How does it strike you this will develop from now on?"

"Like lightning."

"That's what I think. We may need force here, and plenty of it."

"There's a single shock group coming on the run. It's all we can expect till that business on Aret VI is stamped out."

Stil nodded. "Well, get in touch with me as soon as you have a good sampling of later reactions to the device. I'm going to stay till morning and get a first-hand impression of the atmosphere here. I'll be up shortly afterward."

Stil thought over what he'd learned, then went back to sleep. He was awakened shortly after sunrise by the tingling of his alarm watch. He washed, dressed quickly, and went out into the corridor.

He went into Kife's outer office, and found half the office staff trying to look busy, while the other half huddled in little groups over the reports, and quarreled about how to present them to Kife. The door to Kife's office was tightly shut. Stil took a look around, then left word that he was going back to his ship.

He entered one of the booths under the building, held his tab to the scanning slot in its wall, and waited. He had time for his usual twinge of dread at the thought of his body transmuted to electromagnetic waves, bounced from transmitter to relay to relay to receiver, and reassembled again far way. Then the walls of the booth seemed to jump slightly. Stil opened the door and stepped out in the sector control ship, *Co-ordinator*.

Stil walked down the corridor, glanced briefly into busy offices, nodded to hurrying aides, and turned in at a doorway marked "Emergency Control." Several minor officials sprang to attention, and ushered him through a huge room filled with screens, big three-dimensional charts, rows of uniformed men and women at desks and files, and a long curving bank of communications booths with people entering and leaving. In the center of this maze sat a long-limbed man in a swivel chair within a wide, ring-shaped desk. He wore a light headset and a pained look as he stabbed buttons of coded shapes and colors set in sloping banks atop the desk. He glanced up as Stil crossed the floor, and waved a hand in greeting. A section of the desk slid back, and Stil stepped through.

"How is it?" said Stil.

"Terrible," said Jad. "Here, take a look." He handed Stil another headset. As Stil slid it on, he found himself looking at several men in a small room with a couple of flags standing against the wall. Two of the men were standing tensely beside chairs, one was at the edge of the desk, and the other was standing with his head tilted slightly forward, his left hand at his chin. This man looked up, and nodded.

"All right. Go ahead. There's a certain risk involved, but we'll have to take it." The room emptied in a rush.

Stil took off the headset. "What was that?"

Jad looked up. "The President of the United States deciding to lift the ban on RTV sets. Did that look like chaos or panic to you?"

Stil shook his head gloomily. "Any other developments?"

"Well, if there's a technical nation on this planet that hasn't got several of the sets apart by now, I don't know where it is."

"Any disorders?"

"A number of fist fights, so far. A few minor shooting incidents. Nothing big. The trouble is, the local police departments got the sets, too, so they're in a position to break up most of the big trouble before it has a chance to get started."

Stil nodded. "The way it's turning out, I can't see anything to do but wait and hope. We might get the kind of chaos we can use. But I don't expect it."

"Me either. This is going to be a job for the troops."

A few moments later, Stil went to his own office, had breakfast sent in, and got started on the accumulated problems of Sector government. Shortly before lunch, he caught the faint varying inward whistle that told him someone was trying to reach him.

"Hello, Stil?"

"Right here, Dinal."

"Where are you?"

"Back on the ship."

"Anything new?"

"The situation's getting more out of hand, as we expected. But it's too soon to be sure what will happen next."

"What are you planning to do?"

"We're going to wait. It's all we can do. Kife's distribution of the sets seems to be going smoothly. There's still a remote chance things will work out as he predicts. If we were to pull him out now, there would be a lapse in authority down there that might ruin what little chance remains. If worst comes to worst . . . well, we've got troops coming."

Dinal was silent a moment. Then he said, "I hope it works out. This business, right on the heels of that mess on Aret VI, over in Noral's sector, has the Chief in quite a state."

Stil shook his head. They gloomily wished each other luck, then Stil sent out for lunch, and turned to a report from Jad: "Here's the latest, such as it is: Abortive riot in New York, First Privacy League being formed in Boston. Stupefaction in Moscow over design of the set. Peiping warns it has established a no-viewing boundary thirty miles offshore. By actual count, incidentally, there are at this moment seven hundred eighty-two sets focused on China, and several of these sets are in Moscow. This latest survey still shows no tendency that might develop into anything useful to us."

This feeling lasted from one day to the next as the situation on the planet wavered, but refused to collapse into chaos. He immersed himself in routine work punctuated by brief reports from Jad. Among the many reports, some stood out:

"So far, eighty-six murders, one hundred seventeen holdups, eight suicides, and nine hundred sixty-five arrests traceable to RTV sets."

"Uproar in the United Nations over American display of sets focused on Hungary, Tibet, a prison in Moscow, and assorted horrors inside China. Soviet Union Purchasing Commission is now shipping sets home in wholesale lots.

"American display of sets in Moscow showing typical United States workers' homes. Rival Russian display of massed sets across the street focused on assortment of United States slums, ghost towns, and economically-depressed areas—also labeled 'typical United States workers' homes.'

"Scattered acts of assault due to overexcitement on part of viewers. Various ineffectual bills in national legislatures to restrict use of sets."

Stil now received word of a new outbreak on Aret VI. The shock group racing toward Earth was turned around and sent rushing back in the opposite direction. Stil fired off angry messages to no avail, then called Jad.

"I know," said Jad. "By the time they get back to Aret, the trouble will be over. After all that time under full boost, the shock group will be right back where it started from. Next, new orders will come down for them to rush here under all possible boost. The troops will get here one hundred per cent overdue and so worn out they'll be worthless. The staff orders men around as if the central matter transform network were already stretched out over the whole universe."

"What's Kife doing now?"

"Getting ready to release a damper attachment that will cut out interference. Then people will be able to view other people even if those others have sets installed. Without the troops to back us up, it looks to me like our last chance; but I don't have any great hopes for it."

Stil nodded, then went back to work. He had the sensations of a man fighting a fire in his own back yard, and seeing the fire equipment rush directly past and vanish into the distance. As the days passed, new reports increased his uneasiness:

"Sets now widespread, sold all over the western bloc nations, and imported in huge quantities into the eastern bloc, largely to disrupt western reception."

"Kife is now marketing his interference damper in hopes people will be infuriated by sight of others invading their privacy."

"Extensive snooping has now convinced each big power bloc that the other did not originate the viewer. Both are now trying to find out who did."

"Damper is not having its expected effect. There is widespread anger over loss of privacy, but most violence is directed at sellers of dampers. As people using viewers are not generally interested in viewing other people using viewers, little trouble comes from that. Worse yet, there seems to be a considerable sprinkling of people who go their way regardless of viewers. The evident peace of mind of these people is starting to generate a certain amount of imitation, which is extremely bad from our viewpoint."

"A number of American and Russian viewers are now talking direct to each other on damper-equipped sets, using signs or interpreters to trade views, and meanwhile picking up each other's languages. Many violent disagreements; but what I don't like is, they are finding too many common interests. Too much mutual admiration is going on. If the leaders of the western and eastern blocs should stop being afraid of each other and start looking around for a new enemy, then we'll have the galloping nightmare after us."

Stil wiped his brow. He went to see Jad, and found him looking exceptionally sour.

"Listen," said Stil, "where are those troops now?"

"Just starting out again from Aret VI. Naturally, they won't get here in time.

"There are so many research groups and private individuals working on sets down there that we can't monitor them all. One of them has evidently discovered a built-in block in the sets. Now the block is a block no more. It used to jam reception, to keep Kife's underground headquarters out of view. But now we discover no less than eight sets tuned in on Kife and his headquarters. Pretty soon, they'll spot his various local branches, too."

Stil took a deep breath. "That ends it. Order Kife to evacuate."

"Kife has cracked up."

"Then put someone else in charge and bundle Kife out of there."

Jad shrugged and held out a spare headset. "Here, take a look."

Stil frowned, and settled the set on his head. A scene flared up before him. He recognized Kife's outer office, the screens untended, the office staff reeling around with half-empty bottles, or huddled around blankets to rattle little cups from which small, black-dotted white cubes shot out.

Stil took off the headset and said angrily, "We've *got* to get them and their records out of there. We'll have to use the ship's crew and guards, and we'd better get together as many volunteers as we can lay hands on."

Stil watched the forced evacuation on a big screen that showed Kife's headquarters in cross-section. The situation was made tense by the arrival aboveground of a monster earth auger on a huge truck trailer, followed by a motorized convoy bristling with American troops. While Stil tensely watched his men hustle Kife and his drunken crew into the matter transmitters, the gigantic auger rose up into drilling position.

Stil watched the auger eat into the ground. He stared at the discharged dirt piling up rapidly, and raised his microphone. "Never mind carrying out these files," he ordered. "Slag everything room by room and get out."

The men went from door to door, using guns on wide beam to destroy files and equipment.

The auger ate a big hole down to the top of the building with uncanny accuracy, then pulled out of the way. Two trucks trundled over carrying a metal frame between them, and stopped so the frame was right over the hole. From the frame, ropes and chain ladders with pipe crosspieces dropped into the hole, along with a cable bearing electric-light bulbs at intervals. Several long lines of troops wound over to the hole and started down, the lightly armed ones dropping fast down the ropes, the heavily-laden ones using the ladders.

Stil mopped his forehead. While his men were finishing up on the bottom floor, Earth troops were dropping in on the top floor. The end came in an exchange of ricocheting bullets and searing lines of light. An instant after Stil's men were through the matter transmitters, explosive packets were sent back the other way and blew the transmitters to pieces. But despite Stil's hardest effort, he was too late in reaching some of Kife's local branches.

When it was all over, Stil felt drugged from nervous strain and fatigue.

An aide now hurried over. "A call at Communications Booth I, sir."

Stil went to the booth, stepped in, and shut the door. The booth darkened, and a full-length screen flared to life. Directly before him stood a man in a neat dark suit, who now spoke in a low, hoarse voice.

"Every move you have made in the last hour, I have watched."

Stil forced himself to say, "Yes, sir."

"The net result of this operation is a disaster."

"Yes, sir."

"You may be interested to know what happened to the officer who sent Shock Group 68 back and forth through space to no purpose."

The screen flickered. Directly before Stil, a body hung on a rope.

The screen flickered again. Stil stiffened his knees. The low rough voice said, "Intelligent work is rewarded. Incompetence is punished."

"Yes, sir."

The screen went blank.

Stil swallowed. He mopped his brow and drew a deep breath. He stepped out of the booth, and the presence of people hustling about normally in the room surprised him. He stopped at Jad's desk. Jad had a screen set up before him, and motioned to Stil to take a look.

The screen was divided to show two scenes, each of a man in a laboratory jacket, standing before another screen with a disassembled viewer before him. Each man appeared on the other's screen. One held up a wire leading into a maze of circuits. The other nodded, drew rapidly on a pad, and held it up. The first man beamed, and pointed to part of another disassembled set.

Stil said, "What's *that*?"

"A couple of Earth's leading scientists in happy collaboration. They don't talk the same language—but nevertheless, they just got an idea to extend the range of these sets. I was hoping they wouldn't hit on that technique for a hundred years."

" 'Extend the range'?" said Stil. "Extend it *how far*?"

"They can reach from here almost to Aret VI, if they gang enough of those sets together."

Stil stood motionless as the meaning of this sank in.

Jad said, "If they set up relays at intervals, as we do, there is no theoretical limit. But even without that, they can reach a long, long distance."

"And transmission is practically instantaneous?"

"Yeah."

Stil nodded wearily. "Meanwhile, they have a heavily-populated planet geared for maximum production, already verging on space flight, requiring only a common enemy to channel their efforts, and a little more technical know-how to make them deadly. This place could make Aret VI look like a vacation. How long till those troops get here?"

"About fifteen days. They'll be in bad shape, of course, because they'll have traveled, all-told, a total of twice the distance under maximum boost, with hardly any rest at all."

"Any chance of reinforcements?"

"If Aret VI doesn't erupt again—which is problematical —we might get some from there. From anywhere else, the transportation problem is pretty tough."

"All right," said Stil. "Tell me if what I say is true. If we try to suppress this planet in its present state, using a comparative handful of worn-out troops, all we'll do is unite them permanently, and set them going on feverish preparation for interstellar war."

"Right."

"On the other hand, if we stay here and do nothing, they'll complete their long-range sets, spot us, go over our ship from one end to the other, record everything they see, and finish up with enough technical knowledge to build a fleet of their own."

"Right again. In fact, it will take so long for us to get out of range, that they'll probably do that."

"And then they'll be in a position to send shiploads of troops and viewers to Aret VI, for instance, and create a horrible situation.

"Or, if, to keep them from learning our secrets we blow this ship and everything in it, including ourselves, to little bits, that will temporarily unhinge the government of the whole sector, because all the plans, records, and strands of control are centered in this ship."

Jad nodded sourly. "Yeah. And with the unrest resulting from this Aret business, a lapse in sector government right now could be deadly. What is there left to do?"

Stil said sourly, "Practice smiling."

It was a week later that the big tender from the giant control ship landed on the planet. As the ramp slid down, and Stil stepped out, the cheering crowds waved and threw their hats in the air. A big loudspeaker boomed out a continuous commentary, of which Stil was able to make out occasional fragments:

" . . . Our galactic friends . . . wise and beneficent elder race from beyond the stars . . . bearer of wonderful gifts of science . . . partners . . . despite temporary unfortunate misunderstanding . . . one-hundred year trade treaty and mutual non-aggression pact . . . "

Stil beamed with determined friendliness as the leader of United Earth pumped his hand.

It seemed to Stil that the Earth leader ought decently to have waited a little longer before thrusting out his pen for Stil to sign the trade treaty.

But Stil was careful to smile and sign with no delay.

After all, a lot of eyes were watching him.

THE LAW BREAKERS

Stat yanked hard on the control bar, and slammed the antigrav pedal all the way to the floor.

A roar like that of a giant rocket grew loud below, shook the little scout ship with a tooth-rattling vibration, then dwindled into the distance.

Stat thrust the control bar forward, let up on the antigrav pedal, and—

"Look out!" shouted Vann. "Here comes another one!"

A huge silver aircraft with narrow swept-back wings grew large on the screen. Stat heaved back the control bar, and slammed down the antigrav. He glanced around in time to see a squat dark shape with stubby wings climb up on a pillar of fire, tilt, and streak past so close that he glimpsed the alien block letters that he couldn't read:

U.S. Mail

"For the love of heaven," said Vann, "set us down!"

Stat glanced around. To the north was the huge build-ing that was his landmark and eventual target. Around it, where he was supposed to land in "sparsely-settled farmland," a huge housing development was springing up.

On the screen, three needle-nosed aircraft with stubby wings and red-white-and-blue markings streaked in and out of view.

"Set down *where?*" said Stat. "Things have grown up since the maps were made."

"Set down *anywhere!*" said Vann. "Look out! *Here comes—*"

Stat took one glance, and thrust the control bar all the way forward. He yanked his foot from the antigrav pedal, and jammed the grav-assist almost through the floor. The ship plunged beneath him. The blood rushed to his head, and he saw through a reddish haze. There was a *whoosh* and a thunder overhead. A bell clanged. Stat jerked back the control bar, groped for the antigrav, pressed, and—

CRASH!

There was a dead silence. The ship sat still.

Vann got cautiously to his feet, and drew in a shaky breath. "Amen. We're down."

Stat looked around. "Yes, but where?"

"Never mind," said Vann, with feeling. "We're *down!*" He raised a hatch and leaned out.

Stat got up, and looked out over Vann's shoulder. They had landed in a thick evergreen forest, and the ship was strewn with small limbs, twigs, and bunches of green needles.

Stat ducked inside and glanced at several maps. He located a hilly, heavily-wooded portion, and decided it fitted in with his last hasty glance around before they came down.

Vann pulled back inside. "We're lucky those packs didn't blow up when we hit."

"Yeah, but we're not lucky about where we landed. We're too far from the target. If we start from here, we'll have an awful time getting there."

Vann bent over the map, and Stat put his finger on the wooded portion near the bottom. The target was well to the north, near the top.

Vann said, "If we could only bomb."

"It's been tried. This method is slow, but it ought to be sure."

Vann said nothing, and Stat, studying the map, thought back to the admiral's comments as he explained the mission to them.

"What I have to ask of you," the admiral had said, "is a hard and thankless job. A fighting man's duty requires him to kill others if his superiors give the order. But these others should, for his own peace of mind, be plainly ill-disposed persons, vicious savages, or loathsome aliens. Blasting the brains out of a blood-thirsty monster with teeth like bayonets isn't likely to bother anyone's conscience.

"But, unfortunately, there are times when the thing to be destroyed is not unattractive, is not vicious or ill-disposed, and is not even particularly alien. This is the kind of job I am now forced to give you."

The admiral turned to the map, and rapped the blue and green planet centered there.

"This planet first came to our attention some four hundred standard years ago, when our Controlled Expansion

Program called for the settling of another planet. This planet had abundant natural resources, suitable gravity and atmosphere, and many other desirable characteristics.

"Scout Teams roughly mapped the planet by air, then our Initial Exploration Teams landed to make their raw materials surveys.

"As you know, whenever you land on a new planet, you have to be ready for trouble. If you follow all the carefully tested procedures in the Manual, you'll be safe nine hundred ninety-nine times out of a thousand. But there is always that one chance out of a thousand that the standard procedures don't cover. The thing to remember about this planet is that that one exceptional case turns up here very often.

"To begin with, the dominant life form on this planet is no carnivore or insect, but an erect biped that looks just like us. The only way to tell the difference is to get its shirt off and see if there are any auxiliary joints in its arms. If there's nothing but shoulder, elbow, and wrist, and if it can't disjoint these at will, then it is not one of us. It is a human, as it would call itself. It is, in other words, just like one of us with a bad case of arthritis.

"And that's where the trouble starts.

"The humans are so much like us, in their appearance and their way of thinking, that our ancestors didn't follow the usual procedure. Instead of promptly exterminating this potentially dangerous life form, they called in the sociologists.

"The sociologists went down to the planet, came up goggle-eyed with their data, and ran up their projections. So far from being dangerous, they said, the humans were dead certain to wipe themselves out within the next three-and-a-half centuries. There were quite a number of reasons.

"First, their population-growth was uncontrolled. Snath's Law states that an uncontrolled population will increase much too fast for its food supply, and therefore starve.

"Second, the humans weren't rationing their raw materials, and it looked as if they didn't intend to. Krick's Rule of Exhaustion states that, unless strictly rationed, natural resources get used up at an ever-increasing rate, and finally give out entirely.

"Third, the humans were split up in groups with different customs and languages. They were already tied in knots by Gark's Principle of Mutual Interchange. Put in small words, Gark's Principle says that if you can't see what the other fellow is driving at, he will irritate you, and sooner or later you will have a big fight.

"Well, the humans had all this against them, and more, too. Our ancestors didn't have the heart to make it worse yet for them. They were so much like us, and anyway, in a little while they would wipe themselves out, and we could have the planet with a clear conscience.

"That was four hundred years ago.

"Since then, the humans have starved, run into scarcities, and fought each other tooth and nail all over the globe. For lack of applying Snath's Law, Krick's Rule, and Gark's Principle, the humans went through torture.

"But—for what reason we don't know—they failed to exterminate themselves.

"When the rockets first started coming up out of the atmosphere down there, the Watch Team got a little worried. The sociologists went down, took another look around, and said this was the crisis. Snath, Krick, and

Gark really had the humans by the throats and were knocking them senseless.

"A little while later, the humans burst out into our universe and got moving at a ferocious pace. What happened to Snath, Gark, and the rest of them, I don't know. The sociologists have all gone into their holes and won't come out to talk about it."

The admiral blew out his cheeks and loosened his collar. "That's what happened. Now the humans are roaring off in all directions setting up colonies. This has happened very fast. The Main Fleet is halfway around the system from here. As anyone acquainted with Bak's Theorem knows, nothing material can exceed the speed of light. By the time the Fleet gets here, the humans—who do not seem so restricted as we are by Bak's Theorem—will have their colonies well set up. The Fleet could settle this in short order, but you don't win wars with a force you can't bring to bear. Our only chance is to improvise, and somehow hamstring the human colonization program till the Fleet gets here." He looked intently at Stat and Vann. "Do you understand?"

"Yes, sir," said Stat and Vann.

"Good. Now, the humans are much like us. We don't *want* to hurt them. But at this rate, they are going to crowd us right out of the universe. "We've *got* to stop them. You see?"

"Yes, sir."

"Now, that planet is hard to scout. Mapping the important areas is like mapping erupting volcanoes. The features change too fast. And there are—difficulties." The admiral's gaze strayed toward a chart labeled "Accidental Deaths." He shook his head slightly, took a deep breath, and focused his eyes on Stat and Vann in turn.

"Nevertheless, I have excellent reason to believe the center of this web of colonization is"—he pulled down another map—"here in this huge building. It's just the size to house the mountains of files and armies of officials such a program would need. If we blow it up, it should disorganize the whole business."

The admiral went into minute details, and ended by saying, "We still, thank heaven, have the advantage of distorters, which the humans don't seem to have discovered yet. Your ship, and your packs containing the explosive, will be fitted with distorters of appropriate size and capacity. They will render you invisible to human eyes, but are synchronized so you will be able to see each other. This may seem to be an unbeatable advantage, but don't fool yourselves."

He glanced toward the chart labeled "Accidental Deaths," but looked quickly away. "Three times so far, I've sent men down to bomb that place. Each time, something's gone wrong. You never know exactly what is going to go wrong. Keep your eyes open. Be careful. On most planets, I could give you wise rules to guide your conduct. But on this place I will only say, good luck."

Stat heard again the admiral's warning to be careful as he and Vann looked at their present position on the scout ship's map. Stat said, "Much as I dislike to lift ship again, we need to get in closer. I'll try to stay low enough so we don't get knocked to pieces in the process."

Vann looked unhappy, but he closed the hatch.

Stat glanced at the screen, eased the control bar back, and pressed the antigrav.

Nothing happened.

Stat tried again. The ship didn't move.

Vann lifted up the cover of the floor well. Stat worked the controls with no result, frowned, and turned around. Vann was down on the floor, with one arm out of sight in the well. Stat got up and went over.

Vann looked up. "The control unit's sheared off."

Stat knelt down and reached in. He felt the loose control rods, groped around, and his hand came up against a thin sharp edge. He glanced at Vann. "The base plate's snapped off close to the converter housing. There isn't enough left to do anything with."

They digested this in silence. The ship had two antigrav units, one overhead, and one down below. Theoretically, either one could replace the other. But this would involve disconnecting a great number of wires, tubes, hoses, bolts, and mechanical linkages, as well as wrestling the heavy converters out of their wells. For a moment, Stat considered turning the upper unit completely over. Then he realized that even if it could be done, it would pass the narrow drive field right through the ship, and what would happen next was unpredictable.

As by common consent, Stat and Vann got up at the same time. Stat bent to close the cover of the floor well. Vann went for the packs.

As Stat straightened up, Vann dragged out the first pack. It bulged, its flaps stretched wide to hold even more than the usual load. The carrying harness was of woven cloth straps, fitted with a multitude of steel snaps, hooks and buckles.

Vann's face had a sober look. He crouched, grunted, and stood the pack up on end. He studied it a moment. "One of us better go outside, so we can pass these things out without jarring them again."

Stat climbed through the hatch and helped Vann get the packs outside.

Vann was climbing out after them when there came a thud of rapidly passing hoofs. A white tail flashed through the trees not far away.

Vann said in relief, "Just a wild animal. Help me on with this thing."

"Wait a minute," Stat went inside, and brought out the map. He pointed to their present location. "Now, it's a long way from here to that Colonization Center. But over here there's a highway that goes almost by it." Together, they crouched over the map, studying it. Carefully, they traced out the highway to make sure they made no mistake.

There was a crunching, snapping noise, and the sound of voices. Stat and Vann looked up sharply.

About fifty feet way, several pairs of boots came into view and stopped. Trousers of various shades of brown could be seen, and above that, through the trees, were flashes of bright red. The boots started to move and stopped again. Guns were now visible, thrust in various directions.

Stat jerked out his pistol. Vann did the same, then unclipped his holster, and slid it onto the pistol butt to form a rough stock that gave steadier aim.

From the direction of the boots and guns, there came angry voices, the words incomprehensible to Stat and Vann:

"We're going the wrong way, I tell you. The car's back down the hill, behind us."

"If it was, we'd have struck it just now. The road runs right along the ravine."

"There's more than one ravine in these woods. We hit the wrong one, that's all."

"*I* say we've got around on the wrong side of the mountain. At this rate, we'll waste all doe season trying to get home for lunch. The quickest thing from here is to go right up over the top and come down the other side. We're bound to strike the road."

"Man, are you out of your head? If we go to the top here, we land in the biggest windfall this side of Canada."

Arms shook and guns swung around. Stat and Vann eased back against the ship and separated. Soothing voices joined the angry ones. Eventually there was a silence, and gulping sounds. Something shiny landed at the base of a tree. The boots all turned around and tramped off downhill. Stat and Vann glanced at each other.

Stat said in a low voice, "I don't know what it was, but I'm glad it went away."

Vann nodded. "Me, too." He glanced around warily, and put his gun away.

Stat went off a little distance, studied map and compass, and came back.

Together, they pulled the packs away from the ship, and snapped on the distorters. The packs vanished. Stat helped Vann on with his pack. Vann vanished. Invisible hands helped Stat on with his pack, and then Stat could see Vann again.

"O.K." said Stat. "Let's go."

They started out.

The mountain rose gently but steadily before them.

***

The first few minutes, the ground was fairly level. The packs, however, strained at the cloth straps, which wrinkled up and pulled so tight they felt like wire cables. The buckles dug in. The chest straps made it hard to breathe. Then the steep uphill stretch started.

Several times, as they labored up the slope, there were shots, shouts, or the distant blasts of horns. They hardly heard them. Time was already stretching out in that process that lets a minute of pain seem to last forever.

Stat was discovering that no bending or pitching would shift the pack so it would dig in somewhere else than at a tender spot in the small of his back.

When the ground finally leveled out underfoot, they didn't know what had happened. Vann caught hold of a tree trunk to steady himself.

"Look. It's light ahead."

"Yeah. Might be a clearing."

They pushed through some small, close-growing saplings, parted the branches, and looked out.

A wilderness of jumbled wind-thrown trees stretched out into the distance before them. The trees lay crisscrossed with trunks, limbs, and branches interlocked. The spaces between them bristled with thorny brush. About a third of the way out, there rose what looked like a wisp of smoke. This resolved itself into a host of flying insects, which ranged all around, buzzing ill-temperedly.

Stat shut his eyes for a moment, and rested his weight against a nearby sapling. Vann grunted and swore.

The trees to either side made it impossible to tell for sure how far this spread out to right and left. But there was plainly only one thing to do.

Vann said, "We'll never get across that."

"I know. We'll have to go around."

* * *

For a long time, they picked their way around the edge of the windfall. In the distance, they could hear the high whine of ground-cars that came toward them, fell in pitch and faded away. Finally they had to stop for a rest. They struggled out of the packs, and shut off the distorters.

Vann lay down wearily and massaged his shoulders. After a long silence, he said, "We'll never make it at this rate."

Stat moved around carefully to try to ease his back. He glanced at some nearby saplings. "What if we cut down a couple of those and strap the packs between them?"

Vann eased himself to a sitting position and looked at the trees. "Anything's worth trying."

Stat went to his pack, absently brushed off some insects crawling over it in a long column, and got out his survival kit hatchet. He and Vann chopped down two saplings, trimmed off the branches and sharp stubs, and strapped the packs in place.

Vann slapped at his leg and swore feebly. Stat brushed some crawling bugs out of his way, put the hatchet back in the pack, and turned on the distorters. The packs and poles vanished. Beneath them was a kind of sizable crater in the dirt.

Vann groaned. "They have *ants* on this planet."

Stat said wearily, "Maybe they aren't so bad here."

They groped for the poles, picked them up, and started off.

The trip was not a cheerful one.

At intervals, there traveled down the invisible poles from the invisible packs, columns of invisible ants. These crawled off onto Stat and Vann, and went exploring.

Hot, tired, and miserable, the two invaders toiled their way through the forest, and down the hill through scrub trees and blackberry thickets, lurching and staggering under their invisible burden.

Twice, they had to take cover as shots tore through the brush around them. But there was so much shooting that they decided it must be a local affair having nothing to do with them. They were too tired to do anything, but merely got to their feet when the uproar died down.

About halfway to the highway, they passed within a hundred feet of a small group of humans in red coats, and never even saw them. The humans looked at Stat and Vann stumbling down the hill, and grinned knowingly. One of them gave a loud imitation hiccup as Stat and Vann staggered out of sight.

In due time, Stat and Vann came in view of the highway. They set down the poles, rubbed their shoulders and backs, and drew in deep breaths. Down below, long low shapes blurred past in a variety of bright colors.

"Pretty," said Stat.

"Yeah. But how do we stop them?"

Stat glanced around. There were a number of evergreens growing nearby. He selected two small pine trees. They cut them down.

"Now," said Stat, "we put the packs back on." He and Vann examined them carefully as they undid the poles. Vann said, "There shouldn't be too many left on them. I think about a hundred thousand came off my end of the poles."

They snapped the distorters back on, and helped each other on with the packs.

A few moments later, two small pine trees floated out over the moist soil at the base of the hill, leaving behind two intertangled tracks of footprints.

***

They struggled across a ditch up a bank to a wide dirt shoulder beside the highway.

Vann said, "Shall we throw the trees out on the road?"

"No. We might cause a wreck, and that's no good. What we want is a usable car, and a driver in the right frame of mind."

The two trees floated along beside the road.

Several ground cars of various sizes and shapes whizzed past in both directions. There came a high-pitched screech, and a long low car pulled off onto the shoulder in a great whirl of dust.

Stat held out his tree to Vann. "Can you carry this, too?"

"If I don't sink into the earth."

Stat glanced back to see that the road was clear, then stepped onto the hard surface and walked ahead fast.

The back of the car lit up brightly with red, then white, lights. It started to back, and Stat now saw that it was even more extreme than cars in recent photos the admiral had shown them. This one seemed to have barely room between it and the ground for a man to get his fist under it. Its top was around waist-high. A sort of periscope jutted up from the front of the top and was now swiveled directly back toward the two slowly-advancing trees.

A wing-shaped hatch in the left side of the car popped up and back. A hand appeared at the opening, and gripped the edge of the roof. A fierce grunting and puffing came from within.

Stat paused in alarm, and took another look at the car. What sort of creature, he asked himself, would fit into that kind of vehicle?

An elbow appeared above the edge of the roof. There was a repeated back-and-forth motion of wrist and elbow, coupled with hard grunting, then a red-faced figure of normal proportions levered itself up into view, and twisted around to stare at the two trees.

Stat stepped forward fast. The human turned his head sharply. Stat slowed so the human wouldn't hear his footsteps. The human frowned, and turned back to look at the trees. He blinked hard a number of times. With his gaze riveted on the trees, he shifted around to get a new perspective. He scowled, glanced down the road, and jumped off the car with a determined look. Stat hit him hard on the jaw.

Vann tossed the trees aside, glanced back at the road, and strode up as fast as his heavy pack would let him. Quickly, they carried the human out of sight at the base of the steep bank beside the road. They started eagerly back to the car, then involuntarily paused. They stared at the low rakish metal shape.

Vann said, "Do we lie down in there?"

Stat said, "Their cars seem to have developed some since the pictures we looked at."

Vann took a deep breath. "We'll have to try it."

"Lead the way."

"After you."

A severe struggle quickly showed that with all joints dislocated and moving freely, it was still not possible to get in through the hatch with the packs on.

They glanced around till there were few cars in sight, then Vann got out of his pack and crawled in head first. Stat handed in Vann's pack, glanced around, got out of his own, and handed it in.

He looked up to see the low bushes swaying at the edge of the embankment. Hastily, he climbed inside, reached up, and pulled down the hatch.

"Now," said Vann, "how do we run this thing?"

Stat listened to a muted throb from somewhere forward. "Evidently the engine's running." He leaned back in the seat till he was almost flat on his back, adjusted the periscope, whose screen hung directly in front of his face, then looked around. There seemed to be a great number of knobs and buttons to choose from. He reached for a likely-looking knob and pulled it.

A mighty hum of power told him he had hit the right knob. "There," he said triumphantly. Unfortunately, the scene in the periscope did not change.

Vann said exasperatedly, "It's getting awfully hot in here."

Stat hastily pushed the button back in, and tried another. Music swelled out from in front, in back, and from all sides. A quick succession of punches at various controls brought the loud blast of a horn, dancers jogging back and forth on a television screen, a wave of cold like the inside of an asteroid, and a blinking red oblong spelling out some word in the human alphabet that he couldn't read:

BRAKE

There now came a loud hammering at the hatch, and a muffled roaring noise. An oppressive, foreboding impression of almost physical rage reached through the closed metal hatch.

Stat jabbed, punched, and pulled at every control in reach.

There was a *snap!* And the car rolled forward. Hasty experiments revealed that the direction of motion could be controlled by moving the wheel that sat in Stat's lap.

***

The car now began to pick up speed. Stat braced his feet against the floor, and guided it out onto the highway. Immediately there was a loud screech, followed by powerful blasts on a horn, and from the side came a ferocious sensation of overpowering fury.

Their car, however, continued to pick up speed, and soon left this behind it.

Stat heaved a sigh of relief.

"*Now* we're moving."

Vann swallowed hard and said nothing.

The scenes in the periscope flashed by faster and faster. The traffic, most of which had been pulling away from them, now seemed to pause, then start flowing back toward them. A small needle on the dash in front of Stat crept steadily around its dial.

Stat braced both feet more firmly against the floor, and started to look around for some means of slowing the car down. He squinted at the knobs, switches, buttons, shiny rods and sliding levers. He had already tried most of them. But he couldn't remember which ones. Just in case he had missed something, he tried again.

Music played. Scenes flashed on and off the screen. Hot and cold air poured into the car. The seat gently massaged his back. A jet of water splashed on the front lens of the periscope, and a flexible blade wiped it off again. The seat grew soft, then extremely firm. The car continued to pick up speed.

A whining drone rose from the power plant, and the car began a trembling, pitching motion. Part of the scenery that now flashed past was a long low black-and-white-striped vehicle with a red light atop its roof near the periscope. As they streaked past this vehicle, Stat saw it give a sort of startled spurt of acceleration. There was the whining howl of a siren, which rapidly dwindled away to nothing.

Ahead, a barrier of little glass-and-concrete houses stretched across the road. It rushed closer, and Stat just had time to see some incomprehensible symbols spelling out "TOLL 1.50," which meant nothing to him. He barely had time to select an empty lane, aim for it, and streak through frozen to the wheel.

The small needle in front of Stat was now traveling up past "140." Various lights were flashing on and off, but Stat could see no more buttons to try. He glanced back and forth from the periscope to the controls. He spotted what looked like some kind of control in front of Vann.

He took one hand from the wheel for an instant and pointed. "Try that!"

Vann pushed it. It went in and stayed in. The car continued to roar ahead. There was a click. It popped out again. Vann leaned forward and squinted at it. He pushed it in. It popped back out. He pushed it. It popped back. He frowned, then his face cleared. He pulled it. It came off in his hand. Suddenly he let out a yell.

A sort of red-hot rivet with a handle on it flew through the air. It landed on Stat's lap.

Stat brushed desperately, got it off onto the floor, twisted in the seat and jerked his feet back out of the way.

Vann said, "It worked! We're slowing down!"

Vann's voice held a relief that Stat couldn't share. The road seemed increasingly crowded with cars. A series of important-looking signs that he couldn't read flashed past:

CAUTION
AT YOUR OWN RISK
SLOW
ONE-WAY TRAFFIC
NARROW ROADS
15MPH

Stat was driven to hairbreadth maneuvers to avoid the crowding cars. He glanced ahead and winced. Up ahead was a stretch of rough road. He had a vivid mental picture of the narrow space beneath the bottom of the car.

The needle on its dial was now edging down past "60."

The rough stretch of road rushed toward them.

"Brace yourself," said Stat.

Vann said, "That whine we heard a while ago is back again."

Stat suddenly remembered the black-and-white-striped vehicle with its red light.

The last stretch of smooth road went past and they hit the stony dirt. There was a jolt and a crash like a crate of loose metal hurled down from a height. The car bucked and slammed forward and back.

A cloud of dust swirled up and blotted out the view. All that could be seen was, every now and then, towering orange-painted machines that momentarily loomed into view, then vanished again.

The needle fell down the scale to "0."

Vann said shakily, "We're stopped."

Stat sucked in his breath and let it out again. "Don't touch anything."

"Don't worry," said Vann. He twisted around in his seat. "Let's get out. We can go the rest of the way on foot."

Stat took another deep breath. "I agree." He started to reach back for his pack.

A low wailing noise slid past the car and cut off. There was a snap and a bang of metal. Then there was the sound of heels crunching dirt.

"Now what?" said Vann.

A blast of unprecedented rage came through the metal shell of the car, and left them feeling like dried leaves in a hurricane.

Carried along with this blast of fury, like wreckage afloat on a flood, came a jumble of mental pictures that lit up in Stat's mind like the glowing images on a television screen.

One of these mental images was of vertical bars set in solid concrete. The other was of some kind of heavy chair with metal clasps and electric cables running to a switch on the wall. Stat did not know what these were, but he got the impression they were things to be avoided.

There now came a bang on the hatch, and a number of sharp words, including, "Open up in there!"

Enough of the sense of this began to get through to Stat to give him the general picture.

There was a creak of metal, and the car tilted slightly, as if someone had forced his fingers under the edge of the hatch and was trying to pop it open.

Outside, other sirens whined past and came to a stop.

Vann's face set in a look of grim determination. He loosened his gun in his holster.

Stat's numbed mind began to function again. He whispered, "Don't use the gun. Pull that pack onto your chest and hang onto it tight."

Vann scowled, reached back, felt around with both hands, and tugged hard. Abruptly, he faded out of sight.

Stat heaved a sigh of relief, and hauled his own pack over him.

There was a hard bang on the roof, and other voices outside:

" . . . Seventy miles over the speed limit anyway, when he passed me."

"OPEN UP IN THERE!"

"Give me a look through that periscope."

"How do we get into these sardine cans, anyway?"

"DO YOU HEAR ME IN THERE?"

"Go get that thin bar out of the trunk. We'll settle this bird in a hurry."

" . . . Can't see anything through this scope. He's got the whole roof opaqued, and on top of that, I think this job has an inside screen."

"OPEN UP!"

"O.K. Hand me that bar and shut your eyes for about two seconds."

There was a snap and a crash. Bright daylight shone in.

Stat, clinging to his pack with eyes shut felt a mental wave of astonishment wash over him.

Someone said, "Where's the transparency switch on these models? Edge of the hatch, isn't it?"

There was a click and a flood of light. Stat opened his eyes to see a crowd of men in uniforms squinting down through the now clear and transparent roof. The men outside glanced at each other blankly. One reached through, missed Stat by an inch, and extracted a set of keys. The faint throb of the engine cut off.

Stat heard the words, "This is one for the books."

"Couldn't be hiding somewhere in there, could he?"

"Where? Under the floor mat?"

"Let's open the trunk."

The crowd moved toward the rear.

Stat glanced at Vann. "Now or never."

Gingerly and with great pains, they worked themselves up through the hatch, clinging hard to the heavy packs. Only the energy of despair got them through, scraped and sprained.

One of the uniformed men looked up from the opened trunk lid.

"It doesn't seem to me we're causing all this jiggling around. Stand back a minute."

Vann jumped off onto the ground and hit with a puff of dirt. The car lifted slightly.

Someone said, "Now, what made that?"

Gingerly, Stat and Vann tiptoed away.

One of the uniformed men followed right along behind them, staring at the dirt.

Ahead, a line of cars was bouncing along over the rocky road. Two or three were raised up high on their wheels, and one was apparently supported on an air blast, as it tipped and bobbed and blew out clouds of dust.

Stat, glancing around desperately for some way to get away from his own footprints, headed for this last car and its clouds of dust. He went through the dust cloud behind it, hoping he and Vann could get across before anyone could follow. The next car, however, was fifty feet back, waiting for the dust to blow away. There was a blast on a whistle and it stopped.

Stat looked back and saw a small mob of uniformed figures coming rapidly along behind.

The packs had seemed heavy before, but never as heavy as this.

Vann said, "Look. Up ahead."

Stat glanced up, to see in the distance, beyond the place where the road work was being done, a valley dominated by a huge building set in a vast park of green grass and shrubs.

"That's it, all right," said Stat.

He looked back. The uniformed humans were spread out, examining the ground. One of them waved to the rest, and they all started directly toward Stat and Vann. Some of them spread out to the side and started to run. One turned around and headed back toward the parked cars.

Ahead, there was a steep bank, with a sparse woods of young second growth below it.

"Come on," said Stat. "If they catch us before we get off this dirt, we're finished."

He and Vann reached the bank about half a step ahead of a bunch of humans, and slid down. Two of the humans came right behind them. Stat put out a leg and tripped one of them. Vann hit the other over the head with his gun. Stat and Vann barely got into the woods as more humans came sliding down the bank.

Stat looked back, after he and Vann were well into the woods, and said, "For people who never saw a distorter in action before, they've got pretty fast reactions."

Vann took a deep breath. "Yeah." He set his pack against a tree. "Let's put these things on while we have time."

They stopped, and put on the packs, then peered through the trees to see if they could see the big building they'd seen from the road.

Stat said, "We can't see it from here, but if we go straight downhill, we're bound to come out somewhere near it."

They started out.

***

A long hike took them gradually away from the shouts of pursuing humans, and brought them in view of an enormous building set in a big green park, where large numbers of people walked or sat. Here and there, people took food out of containers, sat on benches, or spread cloths on the grass. Children tossed balls back and forth, and raced after each other in a variety of games.

Stat and Vann sank down wearily on the hillside above this.

Vann unfolded a diagram, and glanced back and forth from the paper to the building. He pointed at a black-topped drive where occasional cars moved by.

"We plant the first charge under that culvert, on the other side of that road."

Stat followed Vann's gesture, and saw near the culvert a group of children toss a ball to a brown furry creature that caught it, and darted back and forth amongst them.

Vann squinted and glanced around. "The next charge, we set up around the other side, right next to the building. You see that narrow moving stairway?"

"Where all the people are riding up into the big doorway?"

"That's it. We'll have to put the second charge right against the building there. The detonator we can set up back on that hillside. It works on line-of-sight, and it can set off both charges from there."

A wave of childish laughter reached Stat, and he glanced down to see the furry creature wagging its tail. The children tossed the ball again, near the culvert.

Stat swallowed.

Vann said, "We can set the remote up somewhere beyond the brow of that hill. We'll have to keep our eyes open for an any ditch or gully we can jump into." He studied the building with professional interest and added, "The air will really be full of flying junk when that place goes up."

The children ran back across Stat's field of view. "Yeah," he said. He glanced at the miniature bomb-and-fuse emblem on Vann's collar. He and Vann both wore the rocket and wings of Space-and-Air, but Vann was qualified in Bombs and Demolition, while Stat wore the head-thrust-into-the-jaws emblem of the Outplanet Scouts.

Vann struggled to his feet. We'd better get started." He reached down to help Stat. Stat got up.

They started down the hill, and Stat now noticed the marked variation amongst humans. They appeared to be all shades of pink, brown, and copper. Their manner of dress varied from one group to another. The more he looked, the more variety he saw.

He glanced at the building, and saw across the face of it, in huge incomprehensible human letters:

**UNITED WORLD
COLONIZATION
TEST
CENTER
12**

They crossed the road between two cars, and located the big culvert, where a trickle of water flowed out into a winding stream bed. They wrestled in the big container of explosive from Vann's pack. Vann artfully ran a thin wire up a crack in the concrete and set a pale pink button at the base of the guard rail by the edge of the road near the culvert.

The happy shouts of children grew loud behind them. Stat glanced around.

The furry brown creature raced in and out with the ball amongst the darting children. Stat looked away.

Vann took out a tin of pinkish gum, and carefully stuck the button in place. He wrestled the explosive further into the culvert, got out a slender rod and snapped a small telescope on top of it. He sighted through the telescope, first one way, then another. "Just right. The humans couldn't have set it up better for us."

Stat said, "Will the water hurt the explosive?"

"Not a chance. The cover's waterproof."

The children now sank down on the ground, talking excitedly.

Vann glanced critically at his handiwork. "That stuff has some funny properties. You have to get the angle just right, or you waste half the effect. Well, let's set up the other one, and get out of here."

They climbed up the bank, and started toward the building.

Behind them, the furry animal climbed to its feet, and ran with its tongue hanging out toward the water.

* * *

Stat and Vann carefully threaded their way through groups of humans and their occasional furry friends. They had almost reached the place they were headed for when a small jet-black creature with green eyes and vertical slit pupils trotted in front of them.

A burly human was striding toward them from the opposite direction. He stopped abruptly, and stared at the small black animal. He got out a big handkerchief and mopped his brow. He reached in his pocket and pulled out something that looked like a small white paw on a chain. He stroked it nervously, gripped it in one hand, and detoured warily around in front of the black creature, which had sat down to clean its fur.

Stat and Vann stopped dead still and stared at the animal. They looked at the grass the big human had carefully avoided. It *looked* all right. All the same—

Vann said, "You never know." They backtracked warily.

The black creature got up, stiffened, whirled around and streaked back in the direction it had come from. In the process, it passed in back of Stat and Vann, and blocked them in that direction.

Stat shut his eyes, and said in disgust, "Out the airlock with it. Come on."

"Wait a minute," said Vann. "What's *that*?"

The brown furry creature that had been playing with the children was snuffling along with its nose to the ground. It appeared to be headed straight toward them.

They paused to stare at it.

It came closer.

In the distance, the children had gotten up and were idly tossing the ball in the air, watching the furry creature.

Unerringly, it snuffled along the ground toward them.

Vann said nervously, "We'd better plant the rest of that explosive in a hurry."

"There won't be time."

Stat glanced around. There were various groups of humans around. The nearest seemed to be a group of strongly-built copper-colored humans by a tree. He said to Vann, "Listen, that thing is evidently a scent-tracker.

If we mingle with those humans over there, we'll throw it off the track."

"A good idea."

At this moment, the animal looked up and sniffed the air. It came warily forward, casting its nose around in different directions, and sniffed strongly. Its eyes lit as if there were a small flame behind each one.

"Whuff!"

It came closer. It bared a set of big teeth, and let out a spine-tingling growl.

Vann had turned to go off with Stat. The animal was now practically on his heels. There was a snap of teeth and a fierce barking.

Heads turned around. The children started running over.

Vann whipped out his gun. The animal lunged forward with a snap of teeth. Vann hit it over the head. It got up again. Vann hit it again. It got up with a low growl. Again Vann hit it. It lay still, but it had a certain stubborn look that suggested it would not be still long.

Stat glanced around and saw a number of humans staring in their direction. One or two started over. The children were running over fast. But Stat did not feel *really* alarmed till his glance took in the dark-haired copper-colored group near the tree. They were all standing up. Their faces were perfectly blank and expressionless, but they nevertheless had a look of extreme alertness. They looked athletic and fast on their feet.

A large, exceptionally well-built member of the group now raised one hand and pointed directly at Stat's feet.

Stat felt paralyzed. He raised one foot and saw, where his foot had been, that the grass was flattened out. It began to straighten up slowly. Of course, with his foot there, he couldn't see the grass. But to the humans he was invisible, and they *could* see the grass.

Vann had now noticed this group of humans. He glanced down at the grass and up at the humans.

Stat's thoughts were like water in a frozen stream. He struggled to clear his mind. He saw other groups of humans moving past on walks. Abruptly he came to life. "We've got to get onto a walk, where we won't leave any imprint."

At the same moment Stat and Vann started off, the whole bunch of humans started after them, their eyes intent on the grass.

Stat and Vann got onto a walk about two steps ahead of a tall sinewy human with a flinty look. They did their best to mingle with the humans moving along the walk, while not actually touching them. When they got close enough to the building, they stepped off the walk, placing their feet so as to take advantage of occasional rocks. Behind some evergreen shrubbery, they unloaded Stat's container of explosive, and put it close to the wall of the building. Vann ran his thin wire up the wall, and stuck the pink button below the molding of the window.

"That," said Vann, "should do it. Now, for the love of heaven, let's get out of this place."

They turned to go, and stopped in their tracks.

A crowd of men in uniform was coming across the park, their expressions watchful. In the lead was a big brown animal on a leash, its nose to the ground.

Stat said, "That one's bigger than the other one was."

"Yes, and it knows its business. Look at it travel."

The humans were having a hard time to keep up with it. It was headed straight for the spot where the other animal was now climbing to its feet.

Vann said, "We'll never outrun that thing." He reached for his gun. The animal vanished behind a group of humans.

"Listen," said Stat, "if we fire from here, they'll be able to tell the direction of the sound. Let's confuse the trail, then get in the building with that bunch of humans and out the back."

"We can't. In that crowd, they'll press against us, feel us and not see us."

"We'll snap off the distorters first. There are so many different kinds of dress here, they'll never see the difference."

"All right."

They stepped out, located the approximate spot where they'd stepped off the walk, and walked back and forth along it to make the scent stronger in the direction they now intended to go. They unclipped their holsters, dropped them in the packs, moved in back of a group of humans starting up the steps, and snapped off their distorters.

They glanced back and saw several of the uniformed humans conferring with the alert coppery humans. The boys were stroking their animal, which was looking around with an ugly expression on its face. The other animal was somewhere out of their line of vision. Then the moving steps swept them up into the building, along with the humans.

They found themselves in a long narrow hall packed with humans and filled with an air of crackling expectancy. The people seemed eager to go forward, and had none of that dull enduring look common to lines of people being sifted through a classification center. Stat looked around for the folders of forms, cards, and authorizations the people must have. He could see none anywhere.

Vann said in a low voice, "The first official that stops us, I'll punch in the nose. You snap on your distorter while I've got their attention. Then you can tip over some files, knock over desks, punch a few of them in the teeth and trip them up. In the uproar, I'll have a chance to snap on my distorter. Then we can get out the back way."

"O.K." To prepare himself, Stat visualized what would be waiting for them up ahead. His own experience assured him there would be long lines of people moving past innumerable desks, with placards bearing cryptic symbols stuck on poles beside each of the desks. At each desk would be an official glancing over forms and swiveling his chair around to pull out file drawers. The people who had reached this far were bound to have acquired the dreary look of those whose fate is in the hands of others, and who can do nothing about it but submit in silence.

They were almost at the end of the entrance hall, and Stat felt ready for anything.

Vann said, "Here we go."

"I'm right with you."

They were swept out of the narrow entrance hall and the humans dispersed in all directions.

Stat and Vann stopped in confusion. There were no desks or officials in sight. They were in a large, warm, dimly-lighted corridor. From this corridor, other corridors branched out. Some were on the same level, others led gently up and some sloped down. Each had, beside its entrance, lighted brass plaques in unreadable human languages. Directly before them stood a statue with more words they couldn't read at the base:

BUILD SO THE RIGHT
IS NATURAL

Stat and Vann looked at the statue, then at the various branching halls.

Vann said, "This isn't exactly what I expected."

"Me either."

"Still, if we're going to get out the back, obviously we should go straight ahead."

They started up a corridor, chose one of several branches, followed it a distance, then paused. They had seen no sign of an exit, and not a single window to the outside.

Vann took a deep breath. "Are you more tired, all of a sudden?"

"I didn't notice it before, but, yes, I am." Stat's feet felt heavy, and he paused to rest. Several groups of humans walked past. They all seemed to be rather short, stumpy types. They glanced at Stat and Vann curiously as they went by.

A glass door up the hall came open, and a tall human came out, passed a big handkerchief across his forehead, and staggered down the hall. As he passed Stat and Vann, he glanced at them ruefully, and said, "Not for me."

Stat couldn't understand the words, but some of the meaning came through in the human's tone of voice, and his rueful look.

Vann said, "The back of the building *must* be straight ahead. If we can get out there—" He started ahead, and Stat followed, wondering at his own weariness.

As Vann pulled open the door, Stat glanced up and saw more human lettering:

ULTRAHIGH GRAVITY

The door swung shut behind them.

Vann said, "I'm tired. I can scarcely lift my feet."

"I know it," said Stat. "So am I." He glanced around in puzzlement. His brain seemed to be full of fog. The atmosphere around him seemed to have thickened and grown dense. "Well," he heard himself say, in a dull voice, "we've been on the go since morning."

They moved slowly down the corridor. On either side, there were heavy doors, and beside the doors, miniature scenes behind glass. Stat looked at one of the scenes, and saw squat fur-clad humans making their way through a heavy snowstorm, guiding themselves by a rope stretched between two low buildings made of blocks of ice.

Vann said, "I don't see any windows ahead. Maybe in here—" He pulled open a door. There was a whistling roar and white snowflakes whirled out in a blast of cold. Snow lay a foot deep inside the room.

Vann let go the door in a hurry and it rammed shut with a solid crunch. The snow on the corridor floor melted in little droplets of water.

Vann and Stat stared at each other.

"What kind of place is this?"

"I don't know."

"We've got to get out of here!"

They headed up the corridor.

Their feet got heavier and heavier. They sagged, braced themselves, stumbled forward bent over. Their minds went gray. An unbearable numb weight dragged at them, as if their skin were made of lead. They gradually forgot what they were doing, stumbled, fell, and crawled on grimly. The pressure grew into agony, and all they could remember to do was to move.

There was a sound of feet and human voices. Someone said kindly, "You guys have got guts, all right, but you're not being very practical. You're not built for this stuff. Here, Phil, give me a hand with them. Don't lift. Just help me head them around the other way."

"You suppose they're doing this on a dare?"

"No, some guys just set their minds on some nice-looking planet, and they're going there, and that's that. But they wouldn't last two weeks once they got there. Now they see what it's like, they'll pick something they're suited for."

Stat felt big strong hands take hold under his arms. The world swung around him. He crawled grimly.

The pressure began to let up.

He and Vann staggered to their feet and looked at each other.

Without a word, they opened the glass door to the other section of the hall.

"Ye gods," said Vann, drawing a shaky breath.

The door swung shut behind them.

They looked around, and tried another corridor. As they neared its end, they found themselves under a steadily increasing blaze of light that hit them like a blow from a hammer. Several dark-skinned humans kindly led them out while they were still on their feet.

Stat could feel his skin prickling all over. Vann had turned a rather bright pink. They looked around dully. Other corridors opened in various directions. Some were lettered, "DESERT-TYPE," "HUMID," "LOW OXY-GEN." There was in the distance one lettered "CAFE-TERIA," and another further away labeled, "OUT." But

Stat and Vann could not tell one from another. Suddenly Stat's gaze settled on one he hadn't noticed. The indecipherable block letters there spelled: "KEEP OUT." But right beside was another notice.

Stat took Vann by the arm and pointed. "Look there!"

In their own language was one word:

ENTER

They stared at this for a moment, then glanced around. The way they had come in was blocked with a steady stream of entering humanity. There were other corridors in all directions, but Stat and Vann looked at them with a total lack of enthusiasm. They glanced at each other, looked back at the corridor marked, "ENTER," and went in cautiously.

This corridor was somewhat narrower than the others, and was dominated by three big pieces of statuary, one behind the other down the center of the hall.

The first one was of a brawny cave man with a skin wrapped around his waist. At his feet lay a powerful animal with long fangs, its skull bashed in. The cave man had one foot on the animal, and was gazing fondly at the stone axe that he held in his hands. Under the statue were the words, in Stat and Vann's tongue:

WHAT COULD BEAT THIS?

The next statue was of glass, shaped like a large barrel. The barrel was packed tight with large opaque spheres of all colors of the rainbow. The barrel's top cover bulged slightly. Below the barrel was the legend:

FULL

No sooner had Stat and Vann glanced at the legend and mentally agreed, than green-tinted water rose in the barrel. Fish swam freely in the spaces between the brightly-colored spheres. Small doors popped open in the sides of the spheres. Water plants drifted out. Little sea horses swam majestically past. Sand spilled from the bottom spheres to form a floor, and small creatures crawled through the sand.

Stat and Vann glanced at each other. Stat said, "We've been taken. There was no room for any more of those spheres. But the barrel wasn't *full*."

Vann said, "Do you get the impression someone thinks we maybe aren't too bright?"

Stat scowled back at the doorway they'd come in. It was still wide open.

"I don't know," said Stat. "Maybe they're trying to show us how they see things, and this is the quickest way to do it."

They looked at the last statue. It represented a road that wound several times around a mountain that grew steadily steeper. There was a long line of small human figures that stretched from a swamp at the base of the mountain and partway to its top. Something about the position of these figures looked odd, and Stat and Vann bent to look at them. They both gave a little jump.

At the beginning of the line of figures, the second man in the row had his fingers around the first man's throat, and was plainly choking him to death. This second man was himself being clubbed over the head by another man. This man was stabbed by the next in line, who was in turn killed by a man with a stone axe. A sixth man thrust a spear into the axeman and was himself shot with an arrow. So it went in a long line up and around the mountain to a place where two horrified figures looked down on the rest and clasped hands. The faces of these two figures looked somehow familiar. Stat glanced from them to the others. The same two faces were repeated over and over again, back to the beginning.

Under the statue was the word:

"VENGEANCE"

Vann straightened up slowly and glanced at Stat. "Maybe they aren't making fun of us, after all."

A door at the inner end of the hall opened up, and a white-haired strongly-built human glanced out at them. For the first time, Stat and Vann noticed the gilt lettering above the door. It read, "Chief of Outplanet Immigration."

The human smiled at them. Speaking their own language, he said, "Won't you come in?"

Stat had, for an instant, the impression that his feet had grown roots into the floor. He could not move forward or back. Suddenly he remembered the admiral's words:

" . . . The humans are much like us. We don't *want* to hurt them. But at this rate, they are going to crowd us right out of the universe. We've got to stop them."

Stat looked at the dignified human and felt no anger toward him. He felt respect, much as he felt for the admiral. But he reminded himself that he was a soldier with a job to do. He followed the human into the room with Vann right behind him. There was a window just across the room. He took one quick step forward as Vann shut the door. Then he stopped dead.

Half-a-dozen burly humans in khaki were standing against the wall. On their heads were helmets, and at their waists were wide belts holding big automatics in holsters. Every last one of these humans had a broad grin on his face.

Stat had an unpleasant tingling up and down his spine. Vann grunted, turned around again, and tried the door. It stayed shut.

Stat growled, "Distorters."

Simultaneously, he and Vann reached up over their shoulders and snapped them on.

At the same instant that they did this, the white-haired human banged his hand onto a button on the desk. There was a sliding noise. Stat had no idea where it came from, and didn't wait to find out. He sprang for the window.

Less than halfway there, he banged into an invisible wall. Dazed, he groped with his hands. A curved sheet of heavy glassy substance stretched from ceiling to floor.

Vann had his gun out and took a shot at it. A small nick appeared. Stat got out his own gun and took a shot at the door. A bit of paint flicked off to reveal what looked like a tool steel surface underneath.

Vann swore.

Stat whirled around. The line of human soldiers had vanished. As he watched, one of them shaded into view, his hand at his belt, turning a dial on a little box.

Shortly afterward, another one appeared. The white-haired human at the desk appeared, going through a similar process. In a moment, all the humans were back in their places, smiling cheerfully.

Vann growled, "*Variable* distorters!"

Stat said grimly, "Keep a hand on your side of that glass plate. We're in a box, but they have to get us out somehow."

Just then, a small nozzle in the ceiling overhead began to hiss.

***

Stat and Vann dizzily opened their eyes. They were seated in comfortable chairs before the desk of the white-haired human.

Stat sat up. The last thing he remembered was that hissing nozzle. He looked around and saw no soldiers. Of course, they could be standing unseen along that wall right behind him with their hands on their belts. If so, no doubt, they were all grinning cheerful invisible grins. He slowly sat back.

Beside him, Vann spoke up, "We're prisoners?"

"No. You're immigrants."

"*Immigrants?*"

"Of course. You have to consider our customs in this matter." The white-haired man smiled in a friendly way. "As a hypothetical case, say that you came down here to blow up this building, thus murdering all the helpless women and children around it. Once word of that got around, public opinion might require that we boil you in hot lead for punishment. On the other hand, if you had merely decided to ditch your heavy explosive, in order to get into our new installations here and select a planet, then, obviously you are immigrants."

The white-haired human bridged his fingers and said with an air of regret, "Gentlemen, I am sorry to have to tell you that we unfortunately have no new openings available for you as yet on our colony planets. You will have to settle on Earth."

Stat blinked. "Here?"

The human nodded and pressed a switch on a box that sat in one corner of his desk, and leaned slightly forward.

"Miss Dana, will you call the shop and ask Mr. Kakk to come up, please?"

A feminine voice came out of the box. "Yes, sir."

The human leaned back and looked at Stat and Vann in a friendly way. Stat analyzed the human's expression, and decided it was not exactly friendly. Or rather, it was friendly, plus another quality. He puzzled over this, and decided that the human looked like a man who has just completed a highly profitable business arrangement.

Stat said suddenly. "I don't understand this."

"Ask anything you want."

"You seem glad to see us."

"I am. We lose a great many potential immigrants through carelessness coming down through the airlanes, in traffic accidents, and so on. We're glad you made it."

"You *knew* we were coming down?"

"Not you personally. We knew *someone* would be coming down."

"Then you know our plans?"

"We know the situation your superior officers are in. We deduce what we would do in a like situation, making full allowance for your lower level of technical knowledge. This gives us a good idea which one of the limited choices your superiors will decide to choose."

Stat sat back with a feeling of deep depression. "In other words you see way ahead of us, because you're a superior race."

"No," said the human, sitting up straight. "Absolutely not."

Vann said, "You must be. In a short time you've surpassed us in practically everything."

The human frowned. "What you say may be true, but not in the way you mean it. We may be, compared to you at the present time, a superior *race*. But we've tested many of you who have come down here, and we consider your average intelligence to be about the same as ours. Moreover, the distribution of superior intelligence among your people follows about the same curve as it does among ours."

Stat said, "That can't be. It's nice to try to spare our feelings; but in that case, there's no explanation."

"There is. The cave man who develops a stone axe may think he has the last word on weapons. His admiring tribe may agree. If, later on, some unknown in the same tribe tries to suggest something better, he will be shut up in no uncertain terms. Who is *he*? This pattern repeats itself over and over again in history. Hosts of men with superior ideas have been ground to powder by this simple mechanism. New ideas are not given a fair trial. Progress comes about *despite* this."

Stat thought of the lives of great men he had read. Some of them had certainly experienced this very thing. "Yes," he said grudgingly, "I suppose that's true."

"All right. Now, we've talked to your people who came down before. Tell me, what was it that led your sociologists to decide we wouldn't last?"

Stat named the admiral's two first reasons, then said, "And besides, you were split up into groups with different customs and languages. This made for all kinds of confusion and disagreements."

"Whereas," said the human, "*your* race was pretty nearly alike in language and customs?"

"Certainly."

"There's your answer," said the human. "Whoever is on top tends to get hidebound. Why change anything? The stone axe works. As likely as not, it will take the neighboring tribe to demonstrate the fact that spears are good for something. Now, humanity has been split up in quarreling groups for a long time. We have certainly suffered from this. But there were gains, too. As each group developed, a few great men fought their way to the top, built systems, and the systems hardened. Soon it came about that no one dared open his mouth against them. *That* group became hidebound. But note this:

"All humanity never got hidebound together.

"Your race did. If, for instance, some scientist in your race put forth a hypothesis and it got generally accepted as a natural law, there was the end of the matter for a long, long time. In our race, there was still the chance that someone in some other group might take an irreverent look at this so-called 'natural law', or even not know it was supposed to be a natural law, and break it. Thus proving it was only a hypothesis after all."

Stat frowned, and thought about this. Behind him the door came open. The human glanced up, smiled, looked back at Stat and said, "It isn't always the *race* that's superior. It's the *method* the race uses. He got up, and said, "Mr. Kakk, this is Mr. Stat, and Mr. Vann. Mr. Kakk will show you around and help you get acquainted with our ways of doing things, and hm-m-m—help place you in our scheme of things."

Vann said suddenly, "What's the point of that glass barrel outside?"

The human said courteously, "Although our planet is crowded with *us*, there is room and opportunity for *you*."

"Oh," said Vann.

***

Stat and Vann followed Mr. Kakk into the hall. Vann stopped suddenly. "Wait a minute. How can that be?"

Stat was noticing the way Mr. Kakk bent his arm as he shut the door. Stat said to him, "You're one of us? I mean, you're a . . . an immigrant, too?"

Kakk looked faintly offended. "I *was*," he said. "I'm a *citizen*, now."

"Un-m-m," said Stat. He began to wonder exactly how the admiral was going to stop these humans. They didn't kill their enemies; they converted them.

Kakk said, in a more friendly tone, "I hear you tried to blow the place up. I tried to bomb it." He shook his head. "There's some kind of shield up there, I suppose, to keep stray planes and missiles away. I hit the thing, slithered down it, and came to in a human hospital. Then the Air Police caught up with me." He opened a door leading into an empty shaft. "Step right in behind me. A wide-beamed gravitic field will catch you."

Stat and Vann stepped off queasily after Kakk, and floated to the floor below.

"What," said Stat uneasily, "did the Air Police do to you?"

"Oh, they got me for a restricted airspace violation, and the judge sentenced me to two weeks working on the police machines. After that, I got a steady job here." He stepped out the shaft and pointed into a big, brightly-lit room.

"Lots of machinery in this building. Gravitors, heaters, air conditioners, generators. Something wrong with all of them. Plenty of work to do. Then there's a garage over there where the humans keep their cars. Want to see?"

"Well," said Stat dubiously, "we've already had a little experience—"

Vann said, "We'll *look* at them. But we won't get in."

Kakk led the way into a big room with bright overhead lights, air hoses dangling down at intervals, and cars standing around all over, some with their front ends jacked up in the air, others with all four wheels off the ground on gravity lifts, and a vast number with hoods up and blue-overalled mechanics practically out of sight within them.

Stat stared. "These are all out of order?"

"Every last one of them. There are more outside ready to go out of order any minute."

A vast weight of inferiority lifted from Stat's shoulders. "These humans can't be so smart after all."

"Oh," said Kakk, "they're smart enough, all right. That's where the trouble comes from. Instead of settling down with something nice and reliable, what do they do but keep making improvements in the things. Naturally, the improvements aren't proven yet, so something goes wrong, and by the time they get that figured out, something else goes wrong, and then they're out with a brand-new improvement, and they have the whole thing to go through all over again."

Stat looked at all the raised hoods in undimmed amazement.

Vann said, "Not for me. There's trouble enough with that in space. When I set down on a planet, I want something reliable. Give me a nice coal-fired steamer any time."

Kakk said, "Well, these humans see it differently. There, isn't that a pitiful sight?"

A human in blue overalls raised his head and shoulders out of the engine compartment of a car. His face had a look of rage, and what he said, even in the unfamiliar tongue, was a fearful thing to hear. The human's hair hung down in his eyes, and he was smeared here and there with grease. His face set in a grim expression, he pulled a light on a long cord into a new position, and bent into the hood, banging his elbows and cursing steadily.

"You see they have only one joint in the middle of their arms," said Kakk, "and they can't dislocate *it* except by accident. That fellow is after the starting motor, I'd be willing to bet. Pretty soon, he'll probably give up and try from underneath. But on *that* model—" Kakk shook his head and made a clucking noise.

Stat said, "Why do they build them like that?"

"Well, you see, they're after mechanical perfection. They make them low so they can go fast without turning over. But that squashes the engine down into that flat space. And, of course, they aren't satisfied with just an engine. They've got radio, television, air conditioning, heaters, massaging seats, power windows, power steering, power brakes—you've got to fit all that stuff in there somewhere. And if you think *these* jobs are bad, you should see the ones with the new antigrav drive. *Whew!*"

Vann made a choking noise. "How do they fix them?"

"There you see it right before you," said Kakk.

The grease-covered man in blue overalls rose from the engine compartment and looked around. He opened his mouth and shut it again. Clearly, he was past the point where words would do any good. He rolled a big jack over and slid it under the front of the car. He cranked the handle up and down and crawled underneath.

"They have," said Kakk, "the same problem on their spaceships. At the beginning, you can imagine, they tried to keep free of that. But now they're up to their ears in superfluous complications. They have little robots that crawl in to do some of the work; but, of course, *they* are complicated, too."

Stat and Vann looked thoughtfully at the feet thrust out from under the car.

Kakk said, "It happens that a great number of them *like* this work. Some of them are unusually good at it. But things break down so often there aren't enough of them to go around. Let me tell you, there are plenty of jobs for people with the right qualifications."

A big, genial-looking man with "Manager" on his gray overalls came striding over. His eyes were focused hopefully on Stat and Vann. Kakk looked around, and the manager talked to him a few minutes, then glanced around, took out a cigar, stripped off its wrapper, and lit it with a judicious look.

Kakk said, "He wants a demonstration. Put your right hand up over your head and reach down your back into your left side trousers pocket."

Stat did so. Vann did, too.

The manager's eyes lit up. He made an obvious effort to keep a poker face, and spoke briefly to Kakk. Kakk said, "He offers you one-fifty an hour and you learn on the job. You'd be foolish to take it. Insist on four, and maybe you'll get three. Once you learn, you'll get more."

Stat hesitated. All this had happened very fast. He still felt a firm loyalty to the admiral. On the other hand, the humans could easily have shot him. Instead, they were friendly, and were even willing to welcome him as one of their own.

Kakk said, "He offers you two-and-a-quarter. Hang on. I think he's worried."

Stat was now thinking that since the humans knew about the explosive, they had no doubt removed it. What could he do at best but kill a few humans who had never hurt him, and what good would that do anyone? Next, could he get the ship back to the admiral and tell him what he knew?

"He offers two-seventy-five," said Kakk. "I think that's his limit till you learn."

Stat grunted and looked away indifferently. He was wrestling with the problem of repairing the ship. The floor unit was sufficient for ship maneuver near the planet. But they would need both out in space. Worse yet, the admiral by that time would have given them up for dead, and changed the phase of his distorters, as a safety measure in case their ship had been captured. There would then be the problem of finding him.

But, thought Stat, suppose Vann and I *do* get back. Suppose by some miracle we don't blunder into another ship and wreck us both in the process. Next, I give the admiral this fantastic information. And suppose he even believes it. What good will that do?

The manager's face was undergoing a severe struggle. "Three-and-a-quarter," he said, as if the words were torn out of him with hooks, "But not a cent more!"

Kakk translated.

"O.K.," said Stat. In his mind, everything fell into place. He would work for the humans, giving them good value for their money. He would learn all he could from them. He would try to find out the secrets of their progress, and apply them himself. And—who knew what might happen? Meanwhile, he and Vann could make themselves a small, safe, self-propelled coal buggy in their spare time.

He was just deciding this when the manager, turning from Vann with a satisfied expression, looked at something back of Stat and Vann, stared, and slowly took his cigar out of his mouth.

Stat, his future still rosy in his mind, glanced around.

About half-a-dozen men in uniform were coming across the room behind a large sad-eyed animal with its nose to the floor.

"Ah-hah," said one of them, using the human tongue, and glancing at Stat and Vann triumphantly. "Here we are at last. Let's see your driver's license, and after that we want a peek at your registration. And you went through a toll booth without paying toll, did at least seventy miles over the speed limit, and resisted an officer." He whipped out a large pad and pencil, and from his self-contented look as he took another breath, he had hardly scratched the surface as yet.

Kakk translated gloomily.

The manager shook his head in disgust, threw down his cigar, and carefully ground it out. He walked away, then turned back.

"Remember," he said, "there's a job waiting for you when you get out. I offer three twenty-five to start. Remember that. Don't let those crooks keep you for less."

The uniformed human paused in mid-sentence at the word "crooks." He glanced up with an offended air.

The manager turned away. The uniformed humans grilled Stat and Vann, using Kakk for an interpreter. Kakk's face took on a stupefied look as he translated the long list of offenses. At length, they came to an end.

Stat looked at Kakk.

Kakk shook his head gloomily. "Before you get loose after doing all that, you'll repair every car they've got. And, oh boy, wait till you see them. Moreover, as I remember, they pay you about twelve cents an hour. A cent is one one-hundredth of a dollar."

The uniformed men looked at each other cheerfully, and spread out in a protective circle as they moved off with their valuable prisoners.

Vann glanced sourly at Stat.

Stat looked sourly back.

Vann said, "This reminds me of another eternal truth. They ought to make a statue of it and put it upstairs."

"What's that?"

Vann glared at the cheerful officers. "In every worldly paradise, there's a snake."

COMPENSATION

Sten and Ral looked the new planet over with the casual superiority of long experience.

"No roadblocks or checkpoints," said Ral, tilting his head toward the cloverleaf with cars streaming up and around it.

Sten tossed a curd of muggum into his mouth and smiled faintly. "Pushover," he said.

Ral cast around mentally. "And not a telepath among them."

"Nope," said Sten. "Nothing but static."

"Why look further?" said Ral in wonderment. "They aren't putting out on a single frequency. Their security is nonexistent. They're wide open from here to home and back."

Sten stirred uneasily. "Yeah. But maybe we better drift around a little. You know—pad the report."

"I suppose," said Ral. "If we send them back anything less than a first-class brain-splitter, they'll think we're asleep." He looked at the whizzing harmless cars. "But, if we sent them just one thought on this place, they should be happy. It only takes one thought to describe it."

"What's that?" said Sten.

"Pre-slave," said Ral.

They smiled and started for the highway.

The city was there almost before they realized it. As they watched from the speeding car, the houses thickened beside the road, the lots grew smaller, separate buildings gave way to buildings with a common front and the buildings grew taller. The car slowed, and their host turned halfway around in his seat to face them.

"You guym rana ledout here?" he said, his forehead faintly wrinkled.

Ral moved his lips and cast a strong questioning thought at the native: "What?"

The man in the front seat squinted, "Want to get out here?"

"Oh. Yeah."

"Whaddat? Spee glub, mizzer. I'm a liddel ef."

Ral frowned, squinted. "What?"

"You want out?"

Yes."

"Oh."

The car pulled in toward the curb at a corner. Ral and Sten got out. The car pulled away.

Sten looked at Ral. "I wonder if they're *all* like that?"

"I don't know. I wouldn't be surprised. Their output is so low the static would practically hide it. And their sensitivity is practically nil. Yet that one seemed to get along with his fellows, and look what his sensitivity was."

"Poor characteristic for slaves," said Sten sourly. "A man doesn't like to wear an amplifier just so his slaves can hear him."

"That's true," said Ral. "but they might be good for household slaves. They couldn't eavesdrop and spread gossip, at least."

Sten nodded. "That's something."

As they talked, the two of them were looking around at the city.

"Don't see a single monitor station," said Ral finally.

"No," said Sten. "Nor a watchtower."

"There weren't any gates the way we came in."

"Nor a single checkpoint."

"Funny place," said Ral. "They must never have had any wars or difficulties. I feel a little sorry for them."

"Don't start that," said Sten. "A slave's a slave. You start feeling sorry for them, and there's no end to your troubles."

"True enough," said Ral, looking around. He smiled faintly. "Look over there."

All the cars in the street were halted, and right across the street was a store, its windows plastered with signs, and the display cases behind heaped with piles of harmless merchandise. "Typical," said Ral. He started out.

"Watch that overhead signal," growled Sten. "When it changes color, these cars rush forward. I saw a woman almost get hit."

"Visual signal control," said Ral, crossing the street. "Maybe that's how we can get around their lack of sensitivity."

"May be," said Sten.

With a roar, the cars started up behind them.

Sten and Ral looked in the store window.

"These devices are for measuring time," said Ral. "You see how that little pointer swings around. Apparently they only divide the day into twelve main units. That indicates they're easy-going."

"They don't *look* easy-going," said Sten. "See how they rush along."

"Hm-m-m," said Ral. "That's a point."

"Something screwy about this place," said Sten. "I don't know what it is, but something doesn't seem right."

Ral scowled and looked around. "Yes, I see what you mean. Something—"

A policeman wearing a gun and a belt of bullets, and swinging a club, strolled past.

Ral nudged Sten, who jumped.

"There's your missing piece," said Ral.

They watched the policeman vanish in the crowd, then looked at each other blankly.

"Screwier than ever," said Sten abruptly. "How come he *mingled* with them?"

"I was overhasty," said Ral, frowning. "That's another piece, all right, but it doesn't fit. It just makes things worse. I didn't get a single thought from him. Some of those people around him had faint fear thoughts, and some had assurance thoughts. I could swear one of them wanted to hit him. But at least two others liked him."

"Funny reactions," said Sten, his face all twisted up. "It just doesn't fit for master and slaves."

"Well, what else *could* it be?" said Ral. "That thing on his hip was a hand weapon, an explosive-powered slug-thrower if I ever saw one. And, for that matter, a man doesn't walk around with a bludgeon is his hand unless he thinks he's going to need it."

"Yeah," said Sten. "Well, it doesn't fit no matter how you twist and squeeze it. We'd better admit it and settle in for a full-length stay."

"I suppose so," said Ral gloomily.

Sten and Ral hunted around for a place to stay while they studied the city. They finally decided on a hotel as the most anonymous place to live, and as the place where they could best observe a large number of the natives at one time. Right at the beginning, they had a few uneasy moments.

The clerk shoved a register and a pen across the desk. Ral, thinking fast, deduced that the pen was designed to produce a wavy line such as the wavy lines above it on the paper. He tried first one end of the pen, then the other, then, scrawling rapidly from right to left, produced what looked to him to be a very satisfactory wavy line with a few decorative spatterings of ink around it.

The clerk looked blank, spun the book around, stared at it, looked at Ral—who stared back at him radiating thoughts of friendly assurance—blinked, and spun the book around for Sten.

Sten picked up the pen and drew it rapidly from right to left, giving a close imitation of Ral's performance.

The clerk pulled out a handkerchief and wiped his forehead, upper lip, and neck.

Sten and Ral radiated friendliness and assurance at him.

"Hm-m-m," said the clerk. "Blew guyd Arabd dor zumthig?"

Ral made a mighty effort to increase his sensitivity. He leaned forward radiating curiosity.

"I said," said the clerk, "are you guys Arabs, or something?"

Ral caught the significance of the question. "Something like that," he radiated.

A tall man in a brown suit detached himself from a pillar in the shadows to one side and came forward quietly, his gaze intent on Ral's lips.

Ral detected suspicion and intense curiosity.

"Sten," he thought, "hold that other native off."

Sten turned toward the tall man and radiated confusion, forgetfulness, and sleepiness.

The clerk unhooked a set of keys.

The tall man yawned, blinked, scowled, came forward and stood uncertainly.

Ral took the keys and followed Sten to an elevator. They got off at the third floor, wandered out onto a fire escape and stared around in a sort of daze.

"Well," said Ral, "apparently we made it through the first checkpoint."

"Maybe, but now what do we do?"

"These things here are plainly keys."

"Keys to what? This is a big building."

"Let's go back in and look around."

After about five minutes, Ral said, "The faces of the doors here have some kind of symbols on them. This tag hooked to the keys has symbols on it. Apparently we have to find a door with symbols on it that match the symbols on the tag."

"Well," said Sten wearily, "let's start hunting."

Half-an-hour later, they were in their room. Another half hour passed while they lay exhausted and tried to clear up several points about the system of symbols on the tag.

"These people," Ral concluded, "have been handicapped by their lack of telepathic faculties. Obviously they have had to adopt substitutes. Where one of us would merely visualize the entrance of the room and the route to it, these people must first *mark* the room, then refer to it by the mark. It's easy to see how their handicap has thwarted them."

"Wait a minute now," said Sten, scowling. "Which is easier? Visualize the whole thing? Or just refer to a mark?"

"Well—But they have to *go* there first, and *mark* it."

"All right. We have to go there first and *see* it."

"Well—" Ral blinked. "Wait a minute, now. We can get it from someone *else* who's seen it."

"*If* he's a good observer."

"Well, sure—"

"How many of *them* are there? You remember that escaped prisoner on Gulmatz? The officer on the spot relayed his appearance mentally through sixteen passengers on sixteen different ships that happened to make an extended circuit from Gulmatz to Srin, where the prisoner was supposed to be headed. Then the official set off for Srin. Five minutes after he stepped off the ship he was locked in irons. It took him a week to talk his way out of it."

"Well, yes. But *sixteen*—"

"The officer sent out a description of the *prisoner*. By the time it reached Srin, it was a good description of *himself*."

"Yes, all right, but *sixteen*—"

"They never *did* catch that prisoner!"

"A relay through *sixteen* people is too many!"

"I bet you could relay something like this symbol through sixteen people."

Ral glared at the little number on the tag. He shook his head fiercely. "All right. Considering they aren't telepathic, they've compensated pretty well."

"And now I think of it, those surface cars of theirs are quiet, smooth and fast."

"So are ours."

"We don't have that many. And I would like to know, just how do these nontelepaths get complex ideas across to each other, anyway? Making a surface car is no simple matter. Who controls the sub-groups of workers to see that they co-ordinate properly? We've seen development like this before, but *not on a nontelepathic planet*."

Ral scowled, "I don't know. Anyway, does it matter? The important thing to remember is: These people are soft, spoiled. How many people have we seen that could possibly stand up to a master?"

"That's true," said Sten, thoughtfully. "Yes, that's so. Just one. Or," he frowned, "possibly two. The man that came over while we were downstairs had something dangerous about him."

"True. Well—" Ral shook his head. "I admit I'm a little uncertain how we're finally going to decide this; but I still have to file my initial report."

Sten nodded gloomily. "There's no getting away from that."

Ral lay back and thought intently. After a long time, an answering flicker reached out to him. Slowly, forming each thought fully and carefully, he sent home his report. Time passed. Beads of perspiration stood out on his forehead. His collar grew limp and flaccid. His breath came hard and heavy. He writhed like a man caught in the grip of a giant snake, then shivered and lay limp.

"Your turn," he said in a dull, hollow voice.

Sten began to sweat.

At the end, they stared at each other.

"Well, misbegotten thought!" snarled Sten. "They don't believe us!"

Ral sat up, bared his teeth, and made a gargling sound deep in his throat. For a moment, he sat red with anger, then ran his hand through his hair, groaned, and lay back on the bed. After a moment, he said, "I thought they'd believe me when you told them the same thing."

"They didn't believe a thought I sent them."

"Did they spring the same explanation on you they did on me?"

"I can only stand so much," said Sten. "I made myself as unreceptive as possible while you were sending. What they told *me* was that it was impossible. Quote: Civilization as we know it can't exist without telepathy. Coordination of large-scale enterprises would be impossible. End quote."

Ral sat up and looked out the window at tall buildings, and ranks of distant smokestacks belching clouds of gray and black.

"Yeah," he said. "We aren't seeing that."

"Mass-hypnosis," said Sten with a sour smile. "Obviously if it can't be so, and we see it, somebody has us under illusion."

"I don't think that idea improves the situation," said Ral angrily. "If it's a choice between having some one strong enough to beat you up, and having someone suggestive enough to convince you you're beat up—down to the point where you spit out pieces of clinking tooth—which is worse, anyway?"

"Don't blame me. I didn't say it."

"Well—" Ral glared around the room. He jumped up, banged the wall with his fist, whirled, snatched up a blanket on the bed and felt its texture. He strode into the bathroom, gripped the bar of soap, seized a glass, dropped it, heard the crash, bent over and felt the pieces. He gathered them together, looked around in disgust, and dropped the pieces in the sink. He went back into the bedroom. "It's the most real illusion *I* ever saw," he said. "When an illusion gets *that* real, what's the difference?"

Sten tossed a curd of muggum into his mouth and shrugged helplessly.

Ral sat down again. "This is going to ruin our standing."

"It sure is."

"Every time they think of our names from now one, there's going to be a fuzzy aura of unreliability around them." He got up and paced.

"Yep," said Sten.

"You going to just *sit* there?" said Ral.

"Can you think of anything better?"

Ral sucked in a deep breath, frowned angrily, blew out his cheeks, and shook his head. "No."

"Let's go to sleep. This is bad enough without thinking about it."

Ral went into the bathroom and threw the broken glass out the window. Then he washed up and got ready for bed.

The next day was beautiful, but neither Sten nor Ral could appreciate it. They sampled the native food, and found it strange but edible, got into a tangle with a waiter over "pay," which the native insisted on receiving in return for the food, ended up radiating charm and good will at the manager, and nevertheless soon found themselves in the kitchen up to their elbows in soapy water.

Sten made the situation worse by radiating images of giant fungoid monstrosities, and Ral enlarged on that by putting in mental pictures of loathsome creatures all teeth, claws, and stinging spines. Sten's funguses immediately snaked out strangling tentacles. Ral's monsters promptly writhed around and sank their teeth in them.

As Ral and Sten left the place, the manager leaned against the cashier's desk grinning. The cashier was blushing a bright pink.

Ral turned his receptivity to the highest point, then looked sourly at Sten.

"They think they *heard* us. At least we were able to get across to them somehow."

"That's nice," said Sten. "Now let's go somewhere where it's peaceful and figure out this 'money' business."

They radiated happy friendliness past the hotel clerk's desk, got up to their room, and lay down exhausted. They discussed the matter a while, then cast out mentally. It was a hard job, but gradually a few weak bare images came to them, from one part of the city, then another. They kept at it with dogged persistence, extracting all the pertinent information they could. Finally they looked at each other sourly.

"The stuff is changing hands all over the city."

They lay back and stared at the ceiling.

"Well," said Sten, "I hate to say this. But this 'money' system is better than having to remember every item you've ever bought from anybody, and then having to trade mental images till it balances out."

Weakly, Ral answered, "It's crude. Clumsy. It's— physical."

"It works," said Sten doggedly.

Ral let his breath out with a sigh. "Wait till we try to explain *this*."

"It isn't only that that worries me," said Sten. "I'm getting hungry again. I don't want to have to go through what we went through this morning every time we want a meal."

Ral rolled over on his face and didn't say anything for a long while. He cast around mentally for the needed information, then muttered, "We're going to have to get a job."

Job," said Sten. "What's that?"

Ral explained.

Sten angrily created a fantasy so monstrous that Ral had to turn his sensitivity down to its lowest level. At last Sten lay back shaking.

"No," he said grimly, "there's a better way."

"You name it," said Ral.

"There's a lot of this 'money' around. Everybody seems to have it. All right. Let's *take* some. How will *they* know? They aren't telepathic."

"Hm-m-m," said Ral, turning the idea over in his mind. "Yes. That's *right.*" He sat up. "Of *course* they won't know. How could they? At home, of course, somebody would be sure to know the minute we so much as thought of the idea, but *here*—" Ral let out a sigh of relief. "I'm glad you thought of that."

"The idea just came to me," said Sten modestly.

"It's very original," said Ral. "Well, let's not just lie here. Let's go out and do it."

They got up and went downstairs. On the way past the desk, they had to exert their powers to the limit.

"That clerk," said Sten angrily, "seems to get more untrusting all the time."

"It's these clothes," said Ral. "We should have made three or four sets of them before we left the ship. As it is, they're a little—Well, all those dishes and everything—"

"We'll settle that," Sten growled, "as soon as we get a store of this 'money.'"

They paused outside the hotel, and cast around in thought. The mental images from the people in the city were, as usual, relatively few and scanty. But where large amounts of "money" was concerned, the images seemed somewhat more numerous and clearer. In a few moments Sten and Ral were headed toward a place where a large stock of money was being transferred.

"It's in a ground-vehicle," said Sten. "They're putting it inside a building. I got that much perfectly. It stands to reason there's bound to be a few stacks of it sitting around forgotten for the moment."

"Sounds ideal," said Ral.

They reached the spot where the transfer was taking place.

A squat armor-plated truck sat at the curb. The long snout of a gun stuck out of a turret on top. A man with a gun at his side stood at the rear of the truck. Two men, wearing guns, carried bags into a nearby building. The building had heavy bars on the windows, massive metal doors, and walls so thick the place looked as if it were built to withstand a siege. At the door of the building stood another man with a gun.

Ral and Sten looked at each other, hesitated, then turned around and headed moodily back toward the hotel. On the way they stopped to look in store windows.

"Some of this stuff looks sort of nice," growled Sten, looking in the display window of a big department store.

"Yeah," said Ral. "But that doesn't help us any."

Sten scowled. "Let's go in and just see how they work it. I mean, how they transfer this 'money' for these goods. Maybe we could think of something."

"It's worth a try," said Ral. "We couldn't be much worse off than we are now."

They strolled around inside for a while, watched people being waited on, fought off several remarkably persuasive attempts to sell them refrigerators, dining-room suites, portable drills and sanders, and new, guaranteed puncture-proof, no-bump tires.

Ral finally found himself staring at Sten outside the store.

"I just barely got you out of there," said Sten. "Another couple of instants and you'd have had us loaded down with a set of no-bump, easy-cushion, self-sealing tubeless tires—whatever they are."

Ral blinked. "I remember I wanted them, Sten, but I don't know why."

"Me either. I was sort of interested in that big red drill you could switch around into a lathe."

Ral scratched his head. He seemed to have the beginnings of an idea, but he couldn't quite get hold of it. He scowled and shrugged. "Well, now we have a better idea how that money works. Let's look around some more."

They found themselves outside a jewelry store. Brilliant overhead lights shone down on flashing rings, necklaces, earrings and bracelets. They moved around toward the doorway, and abruptly Ral felt as if he had come to for a moment. Sten, his expression somewhat vacant and staring, was just opening the door. Ral glanced up and saw a man, inside, look Sten's clothes over with pursed lips, study Sten's face, then come forward, beaming, his eyes riveted on Sten. He put an arm around Sten and led him off to a counter. With another hand he beckoned to a girl rearranging necklaces in a showcase. The girl came over. She smiled at Sten, all attention.

With a sort of horrified fascination, Ral watched the girl lead Sten off to another counter, where she modeled bracelets, dangling earrings, and necklaces that flashed like the milky way on a string.

Meanwhile the first man signaled to a second, who whipped out a large pad and came forward to watch Sten and the girl closely, then slide in behind the counter. The girl, still talking, slid out smiling as the man slid in smiling. The man put down the pad and drew out a pencil. Sten was holding a thing that sent out blinding flashes of light as he turned it.

Ral rushed inside, heard the man with the pad say " . . . And just how much did you plan to pay on this per week, sir? How much—May I ask? Just what is your salary?"

Ral grabbed Sten by the arm, wrenched the blazing stone from Sten's grip, and heaved him backwards toward the door. One of the men in the store started toward them staring. Ral sent a blast of friendliness at him, followed it up with an overwhelming jolt of sleepiness, and hastily backed Sten out the doorway. Then he turned him around and walked him fast back toward the hotel.

"What hit me?" said Sten.

"You almost bought a big jewel."

"What in space would I want *that* for?"

"I don't know. But I just got an idea."

They walked rapidly into the hotel past the desk, pouring friendliness and trust at the clerk, made it to their room and lay down.

"This place may not have telepathy," said Sten, "but it certainly has something."

"I know it," said Ral, "but the point we've got to hang onto is that these people are *soft, vulnerable*. Their stuff may be good, and they certainly seem to be able to make people want it, but nevertheless, they're *weak*. We've got to hang onto that fact. They're weak. Soft and weak."

"Yeah," said Sten.

"If we can remember that, we may be able to get our reputations back yet."

"How do we live meanwhile?" said Sten.

"When we were in that department store, I noticed there were people who sold things and people who bought things. Now we can't buy anything. No money. But why couldn't we *sell* things? Maybe that's their strong point, but did they ever try it with *telepathy*?"

"Hm-m-m," said Sten.

They lay back to comb the city for every available scrap of information on salesmanship. Then they washed, carefully combed their hair, cleaned their teeth, examined their fingernails, went over the spots on their clothes with a moist towel, polished their shoes as best they could, and set out to look for jobs.

Sten found a job selling washing machines in a department store, and Ral located a job in a used-car lot.

Sales of Jiffy-Swish washers and Double-A-Plus used cars boomed all week.

Unfortunately, Sten and Ral were not satisfied.

They sat on the front porch of the rooming house they'd moved into, and petted the landlady's cat.

"In the first place," said Sten, "the people back home simply don't believe a word of it. Maybe they thought it was funny at first, but now they're getting scared. They say the illusion is too consistent."

"I know," said Ral. "I'd give up if it weren't that these people are so soft. Soft as this animal, this what-do-you-call-it?"

" 'Cat,' " said Sten.

"Yes, 'cat.' All fur and love for luxury. Well if it weren't for that, I'd quit. But there's got to be *some* way—"

"Yes," Sten agreed, looking a little glassy-eyed, "that's the way I feel, too. If it weren't that I haven't quite got the down-payment for my lathe—and of course the natives are so weak—I'd quit, too."

Ral stopped stroking the cat, which continued to purr, and stared at Sten. " 'Down payment,' " he said. "I thought we agreed not to buy any—"

"Well, we work so hard all the time. Radiating friendliness and fascinated interest all day long is *hard* on a man. I need a little relaxation."

"Well, sure, so do I, but—that stuff may be all right for the people who live here, but it's pretty powerful for us." Ral pulled out a handkerchief and wiped off his brow. "Just this afternoon," he said, "the boss almost sold me a three-tone late-model car."

Sten sat up straight. "What in space do we need a *car* for? The bus goes right past here. The ship is well hidden not over two hours away."

Ral shrugged helplessly. "What do we need a lathe for, either? I tell you, if they weren't such a natural pushover—"

From overhead came an uncanny reverberating crash and thunder. A track of white vapor was drawn across the sky, high up. A group of boys walking past with a bicycle stopped to look up.

"Boy," came their thought, "there goes one of them Sky Slashers. I heard where one of them can carry a city-buster under each wing."

The cat suddenly decided to get up. Ral didn't let go. The cat put forth eighteen claws and got up.

Sten and Ral glanced at the cat, looked up at the track in the sky, and stared at each other.

A chronological report on unidentified flying objects lists for that night a flash of extraordinary brilliance, which traveled from low on the horizon, zoomed skyward, and vanished quickly. The best expert opinion is, it was a lighted weather balloon.

MERRY CHRISTMAS
FROM OUTER SPACE

☆ ☆ ☆ ☆ ☆ ☆
—SUBGRAM—

FROM:
   Q. Sarul, Chief, Unit 28
   Bureau of Outplanet Sabotage
   Block 262,498 Level 18
   Aldebaran 4(2) QZ66:722:14

TO:
   J. March, Agent
   Branch Office Terra

   Message: March—I am sending, as soon as the Chute
stabilizes, an improved-model thought-disruptor which

you should find very useful in implementing our policy of frustrating and delaying the attempts of the Terrans in North America to make serious space progress.

Let me somewhat belatedly congratulate you on that beautiful job you did on the cameras in their previous moon-rocket. This equaled the job your opposite number in North Asia performed on the communications system of that planetary shot that went the distance—in silence.

Keep up the good work. The idea is to never let them know they are being sabotaged, but gradually make them so sick of the mounting expense and so weary of the unexplainable flops and failures, that they will voluntarily give up their space programs. The Fleet can't be everywhere at once and it is much easier to control isolated planets than it is to put them down after they start spreading out over the whole solar system.

You should find the new thought-disruptor highly useful. Full instructions will, of course, be included with it. My suggestion is that you plant it in some research installation governing their long range space-exploration program. The effect should be beautiful.

Yours in anticipation,
Q. Sarul

STUPENDOUS PUBLICATIONS
Interoffice Memo
7/1/64

Liz—

I have to be out of town for several days, but hope you will sift the incoming mail for anything that looks at all promising. We seem to be going through some kind of writer's drought. That, plus the heat, and the noise as the monster JPN Cybernetic Research outfit moves in next door, has made this the worst summer yet.

What's wrong with J. A. Catherton? Why don't we hear anything from him?

R. B. Jones
Editorial Director

☆ ☆ ☆ ☆ ☆ ☆

STUPENDOUS PUBLICATIONS
Interoffice Memo
7/1/64

R. B.—

I'll do my best, but if you can't squeeze anything usable out of this pile, I just can't make any promises.

J. A. Catherton's literary agent says Catherton made three successive sales to *Playboy*, and has now gone off to Bermuda. At last report, he was seen riding around the island in a carriage with three blondes.

The agent expects it will take Catherton two months to go through his money, and one month to recover. We therefore can't expect anything from him till sometime in October.

Have a good trip.
Liz

☆ ☆ ☆ ☆ ☆ ☆
—BY HYPERWARP—
2074B14

TO:
G12, Centauran High Command
04618 Central MM10001AAA
Centaurus Prime

FROM:
Jones A1A Terra

RE: Countersabotage

Sir: This is to report successful deactivation of the source of an Aldebaranian-type remote-handling-machine signal; deactivation was carried out by resonant tracer-wave apparatus. No countertracing operation was detected. It is to be assumed that the Aldebaranian-type signal resulted from a flaw in the shielding of the source. Total burn-out of this source's A and M circuits appears probable from analysis of filtered-signal characteristics during deactivation.

Let me say again that handling two jobs at once is not ideal, particularly if the Aldebaranians are on this planet. I repeat that in my opinion they are.

I again request assistance to enable me to carry out at least one of my two assignments with maximum efficiency.

Jones

☆ ☆ ☆ ☆ ☆ ☆

—BY HYPERWARP—

2074B16

TO:
  Jones A1A, Terra
  ZZ6074BZA

FROM:
  G12, Centauran High Command
  Centaurus Prime

RE: Report and request

Sir: Your report of deactivation of Aldebaranian-type signal-source highly satisfactory.

Your request for assistance refused, due to prior commitments of higher priority.

Keep up the good work.

J. Schnock, Stf. Col.
In-Charge

Branwell, Ohio
R.F.D. #1
7/2/64

Mr. R. B. Jones, Ed.
Stupendous Publications
4622 East 42nd St.
New York, N.Y.

Dear Mr. Jones:

I have long read your publications with great interest, but, just between us, I think your latest issues are not up to your usual high level. I think I could do better for you myself.

I am, therefore, enclosing a novelette, titled "Break of Day."

When you send the check, please note I am not your prize author J. A. Catherton, who is no relative of mine. If he were my own brother, I would not talk to him after the way he ended that novel in the December issue. To avoid confusion, I want to use the pen name, Lance Burnett.

Sincerely,
J. C. Catherton

—SUBGRAM—

FROM:
  J. March, Agent
  Branch Office Terra

TO:
  Q. Sarul, Chief, Unit 28
  Bureau of Outplanet Sabotage
  Block 262,498 Level 18
  Aldebaran 4(2) QZ66:722:28

Message: Chief—The Chute has yet to stabilize enough to let your new sabotage gimmick through.

I hope you will also send through a new remote-handling-machine control-unit. This one gave a weird hum and blew up in a shower of sparks the other night, just as I was getting set to have a little fun with the second stage of an Atlas Agena rocket.

I can't sabotage anything without this remote-handling-machine control-unit. Also, please send a new viewfinder, as the eyeplates of this one are fogged and starred.

—There aren't any Centaurans on this planet, are there?

Yours in frustration,

J. March

☆ ☆ ☆ ☆ ☆ ☆

—SUBGRAM—

FROM:
  Q. Sarul, Chief, Unit 28
  Bureau of Outplanet Sabotage
  Block 262,498 Level 18
  Aldebaran 4(2) QZ66:722:32

TO:
  J. March, Agent
  Branch Office Terra

Message: March—Indications here are that the Chute will stabilize momentarily, to be followed by a long interval of instability.

Unfortunately, our credit-allocation is about used up for this budgetary period, so you will have to position the disruptor manually.

—Yours in adversity,

Q. Sarul

STUPENDOUS PUBLICATIONS
Interoffice Memo

Liz—

I'm taking Catherton's story, "Break of Day." Make out a check for $500.00. The address is RFD #1, Branwell, Ohio. Note, please, that this is J. C. Catherton, penname Lance Burnett. *Don't* send the check to J. A. Catherton, as this is not the same man.

R. B. Jones

—SUBGRAM—

FROM:

J. March, Agent
Branch Office, Terra

TO:

Q. Sarul, Chief, Unit 28
Bureau of Outplanet Sabotage
Block 262,498 Level 18
Aldebaran 4(2) QZ66:722:34

Message: Chief—The disruptor got through the Chute the day before yesterday, about the same time as your incredible message. Do you have any idea what you're asking me to do when you say, first that I should plant this device in a "research installation governing their long-range space-exploration program," and then, in a later message, you drop the suggestion that I will have to do this "*manually?*"

Fortunately, I found that the instructions for this thought-disruptor itself were clear. I can see that, what with its projecting a wide-angle cone-shaped beam, at random intervals, that interrupts mental activity, and creates confusion, memory lapse, and short-range subjective quasi-temporal jumps, this would be an effective device to sabotage high-level local space-planning. I was glad to see that this was a practical gadget.

But I can tell you I have no intention of trying to plant this device by hand, and thereby wind up shot, in prison, under questioning by the FBI, or giving testimony before a Senate committee. You don't seem to realize what I am up against.

Luckily, just as I was examining the gadget, I had a brain wave.

There is a big important organization called JPN Cybernetics Research, which has the lion's share of the supersecret design-computer market, and is, I believe, starting to supply these computers to the military and the space program.

Well, suddenly I could see exactly what to do. JPN Research is just moving into new offices, and I immediately went there, landed a job as janitor, and in the bustle and confusion succeeded in planting the disruptor behind a louvered panel in the back of a big RECONVEN-666 SUPERTRON computer.

As you can see, the disruptor is bound to affect the action of the 666, and this, in turn, will throw the JPN program off-base, which, by an inescapable chain of events will then react on the local space program, since JPN Research is integrally bound into this program.

I was in a somewhat exhilarated frame of mind, thanks to this coup, and, thus keyed up, I was unable to avoid grabbing a shapely secretary I met in the hall, and dancing a little jig with her, along with giving her a brotherly local-style "kiss" for good measure. Unfortunately, she turned out to be the wife of some stuffed shirt who immediately fired me. This does not matter, however, since the disruptor is already in the 666, doing its work. I enclose a diagram to show where I planted it.

I think I deserve a medal for this job, don't you?

Incidentally, you didn't answer the questions in my previous message: There aren't any Centaurans on this planet, are there?

—Yours in triumph,
J. March

☆ ☆ ☆ ☆ ☆ ☆
—SUBGRAM—

FROM:
Q. Sarul, Chief, Unit 28
Bureau of Outplanet Sabotage
Block 262,498, Level 18
Aldebaran 4(2) QZ66:722:35

TO:
J. March, Agent
Branch Office, Terra

Message: March—One more job like this, and the medal you get will be a size twelve nuclear grenade wrapped around your neck on a length of high-voltage cable.

In the first place, putting the disruptor inside a *computer* is plain stupid. How do you know it will work on an electronic device? This disruptor was designed for human-type organic nervous systems. Maybe it will work on this 666 you mention, but how do you *know*?

In the second place, what if the 666 does act up? What if they then run a test problem through it and get a wrong answer? Then they will examine it and *find* the *disruptor*, right?

In the third place, what you say about your frame of mind when you had this disastrous stroke of genius suggests that you had inadvertently brushed against the switch, turned the device on, and gotten a high-power jolt at short range. This is the only explanation I can think of for your catastrophic series of blunders, which is capped by a classic error evident in the diagram enclosed with your message.

In this diagram, you show a distinct bump on one side of the little rectangle you use to represent the disruptor. Apparently you believe that this side with the bump is the front of the case. No. This is the *back* of the case. The cone of mental disruption is projected at random intervals out the *other* side of the case, which is a plain flat plate of electromagnetically-transparent plastic.

You have, then, got this device in the wrong place, and you have got it in there *backwards*.

Now, reference to your diagram reveals one additional, purely-gratuitous element of disaster.

This device is now aimed through two walls into the adjacent building; that is, according to your diagram, into an office of Stupendous Publications, Inc.

Now, in reply to your question whether the Centauran Technocracy has any agents on this planet, we do not actually *know*. But subject-matter analysis of material put out by Stupendous Publications suggests a strong Centauran bias. Intensive probing operations have failed to prove a thing, but we positively do *not* want to complicate both our space-sabotage program and our investigation of possible Centauran involvement by tangling the two together.

To correct this chain of errors, we are sending you, as soon as the Chute stabilizes, a beam-projector that can be aimed at the appropriate spot in the JPN Cybernetics building, and it will positively burn out every circuit in the disruptor.

Until this time, the cone of confusion, will, at random intervals, be projected through the two walls, somewhat attenuated by such a thickness of matter, into an office of Stupendous Publications.

—Well, if they *are* Centaurans, they will deserve what happens. But they may get suspicious.

Keep a close watch for the beam-projector, which we will send as soon as the Chute stabilizes. We want to get rid of that disruptor before anyone finds it.

—Yours in catastrophe,
Q. Sarul

☆ ☆ ☆ ☆ ☆ ☆

STUPENDOUS PUBLICATIONS
Interoffice Memo
7/9/64

R. B.—

I have just sent out a check for $500.00, for "Break of Day," by Lance Burnett, penname J. C. Catherton. I've been careful not to send the check to J. A. Catherton.

Liz

☆ ☆ ☆ ☆ ☆ ☆

STUPENDOUS PUBLICATIONS
Interoffice Memo
7/9/64

Liz—

I'm afraid you've somehow got this backwards. "Lance Burnett" is the penname of J. C. Catherton, not the other way around.—However, I'm sure the check will reach him, as he lives in a small town, and probably they know his penname. And if it doesn't, he will let us know. This is much better than sending it to J. A. Catherton and having to extract it from him afterward.

R. B. Jones

☆ ☆ ☆ ☆ ☆ ☆

U.S. POST OFFICE
BRANWELL, OHIO
7/10/64

Sam Barnet
R.F.D. #2
Branwell, O.

Dear Sam,

I have an envelope here from Stupendous Publications, Inc., addressed to "Lance Burnett," R.F.D. #1, Branwell. Do any of your relatives spell their names

"Burnett"? This name doesn't sound like anyone else who lives around here.

T. Stubbs
Postmaster

R.F.D. #2
Branwell, Ohio
7/11/64

T. Stebbs
Postmaster
Branwell, Ohio

Dear Ted,

No relative of mine—Imagine the letter has the wrong address, and should be sent to Branvill, not Branwell.

Sam Barnet

U.S. POST OFFICE
BRANVILL, OHIO
7/18/64

Miss Lucy Barnett
R.F.D. #1
Branvill, O.

Lucy—

We have an envelope here from Stupendous Publications, Inc., addressed to "Mr. Lance Burnett." Is this anyone visiting you, or could it be a misspelling of your name?

Edna R.

R.F.D. #1
Branvill, Ohio
7/21/64

Mrs. Edna Ramsey
Postmistress
Branvill, Ohio

Dear Edna:

No, Tom and Alice are going to visit us later, over Labor Day; but there's no "Lance" in the family, and I have never had any business with the company you mention.

Possibly this was intended for Larry Barton.—Or the letter *could* have been meant to go to Oregon.

Lucy Barnett

☆ ☆ ☆ ☆ ☆ ☆
—SUBGRAM—

FROM:
   J. March, Agent
   Branch Office Terra

TO:

    Q. Sarul, Chief, Unit 28
    Bureau of Outplanet Sabotage
    Block 262,489 Level 18
    Aldebaran 4(2) QZ66:722:98

Message: Chief—I am still watching the Chute for that beam-projector, but the Chute is still unstable.

The thought disruptor is still in the 666, unless they've found it.

—Yours in gloom,
J. March

STUPENDOUS PUBLICATIONS
Interoffice Memo
10/29/64

Liz—

Every so often lately, all hell breaks loose around here. Exactly how did it come about that this cover illustration by Beame, with the big "B" down in the corner, plain as day, is credited to Hoxmeyer on the contents page?

We now have about a hundred thousand copies of this issue moving out all over the country, and what do you suppose is going to happen when Beame gets a look at that contents page?

R. B. Jones

STUPENDOUS PUBLICATIONS
Interoffice Memo
10/29/64

R. B.—

I don't know *how* that Hoxmeyer thing in the current issue came about, but right now I am going through a stack of letters in response to your answer to the letter from Mr. Larry J. Prendergast in the previous issue. As you remember, you said, "Light travels at up to twelve times the speed of sound (in space), so that Fizeau's experiment did not prove the relativity of c in interplanetary travel."

I am trying to arrange these letters for your convenience in considering them.

Liz

STUPENDOUS PUBLICATIONS
Interoffice Memo
10/30/64

Liz—

Obviously, my reply to Prendergast must have been a joke.

On page 65 of this current issue containing the Hoxmeyer error, however, I find that kind of thing popping up too often.

Whose bright idea was it to run three streams of type down through this illustration, in the background, so that text and illustration are mutually fouled up?

R. B.

—SUBGRAM—

FROM:
  J. March, Agent
  Branch Office Terra

TO:
  Q. Sarul, Chief, Unit 28
  Bureau of Outplanet Sabotage
  Block 262,498 Level 18
  Aldebaran 4(2) QZ66:723:14

Message: Chief—That beam-projector has yet to come through the Chute, and the Chute is just as unstable now as earlier.

I have tried to get at the disruptor by less drastic methods, but that part of the JPN building is sewed up tight.

—Yours in weary patience.
J. March

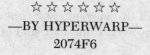

—BY HYPERWARP—
2074F6

TO:
 G12, Centauran High Command
 04618 Central MM100001AAA
 Centaurus Prime

FROM:
 Jones A1A Terra

RE: Suspected Aldebarian harassment

Sir: I enclose a full report covering what I believe to be mental harassment aimed at disrupting the efficiency of this operation.

I have warned you repeatedly that it is too much to expect two such jobs of one individual.

Now I request that you study the enclosed report, and then send me at once one Model C rapid-keying beam-thrower with attached direction-finder so that I can end this business.

Jones

☆ ☆ ☆ ☆ ☆ ☆
—BY HYPERWARP—
2074F8

TO:
 Jones A1A Terra
 ZZ6074BZA

FROM:
 G12 Centauran High Command
 Centaurus Prime

RE: Report and request

Sir: I fully appreciate your irritation at this low blow by the Aldebaranians, who have, however, thus revealed their presence definitely. We are preparing measures to localize them precisely.

We must now avoid revealing our own hand. You must, therefore, bear up under this frustrating experience.

J. Schnock, Stf. Col. In-Charge

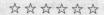

STUPENDOUS PUBLICATIONS
Interoffice Memo
11/27/64

R. B.—

Yes. I know we had things straightened out for a while there, and I honestly don't know how we came to buy "Weeping I Through the Ship Chandlery." As I remember, you, I, and the business manager were standing in a corner of the room with one of us laughing and reading it out loud, and all of a sudden we just realized it was great.

I believe you are right that this was written by splitting a page of Dickens' "Old Curiosity Shop" down the middle, and joining the left half of this page line-by-line with the right half of a page from Bowditch's "Practical Navigator."

I am very embarrassed not to have noticed this before. I certainly agree that it should be suppressed.

Liz

☆ ☆ ☆ ☆ ☆ ☆

R.F.D. #1
Branwell, Ohio
12/10/64

Mr. R. B. Jones, Ed.
Stupendous Publications
4622 East 42nd St.
New York, N.Y.

Dear Mr. Jones:

On July 1st of this year, I sent you a novelette titled "Break of Day," under the penname, "Lance Burnett."

I have yet to receive any word about this novelette.

I realize that long delays are customary in the writing business, and I am prepared to be patient. But you have now had this story for six months.

I hope you will either accept, or send it back to me so that I can send it somewhere else.

I understand editors complain that there are not enough good magazine writers around nowadays.

Obviously, they have all died of starvation.

Truly yours,
J. C. Catherton

☆ ☆ ☆ ☆ ☆ ☆

STUPENDOUS PUBLICATIONS
Interoffice Memo
12/11/64

Liz—

Make out a check for $500.00 to J. C. Catherton, and send it to him at RFD #1, Branwell, Ohio. Take care of this at once, and see that it goes out as quickly as possible.

R. B. Jones

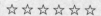

STUPENDOUS PUBLICATIONS
4622 East 42nd St.
New York 58, N.Y.
12/11/64

Mr. J. C. Catherton
R.F.D. #1
Branwell, Ohio

Dear Mr. Catherton:

I want to express my sincere regret for the minor clerical error that has prevented our check for $500.00 from reaching you in payment for your novelette, "Break of Day."

This check was mistakenly sent to "Lance Burnett," your penname, and apparently was lost in the mail.

I want to thank you for your very fine work on "Break of Day." Another check is being sent you at once.

Cordially,
R. B. Jones
Editorial Director

☆ ☆ ☆ ☆ ☆ ☆

R.F.D. #1
Branwell, Ohio
12/11/64

Mr. R. B. Jones, Ed.
Stupendous Publications
4622 East 42nd St.
New York, N.Y.

Dear Mr. Jones:

Please accept my apology for my hasty letter of Dec. 10th.

Shortly after sending it, it occurred to me that you could possibly have written to me under my penname. I inquired at the post office, and sure enough, there was an envelope addressed to "Lance Burnett."

Thank you very much for the check.

I am currently working on a new novelette and I intend to send it off to you around the end of this month.

Sincerely,
J. C. Catherton

☆ ☆ ☆ ☆ ☆ ☆

STUPENDOUS PUBLICATIONS
Interoffice Memo
12/12/64

Liz—

. Don't send that check to J. C. Catherton. Let me know at once that you haven't sent it.

Jones

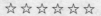

STUPENDOUS PUBLICATIONS
Interoffice Memo
12/12/64

R. B.—

The check went out last night, as you told me. I mailed it from the central post office, Air Mail, Special Delivery.

Liz

STUPENDOUS PUBLICATIONS
4622 East 42nd St.
New York 58, N.Y.
12/12/64

Mr. J. C. Catherton
R.F.D. #1
Branwell, Ohio

Dear Mr. Catherton:

I have your letter of Dec. 11th.

As we have just sent your second check, to replace the check which you have now received, I think I should warn you that we have been in touch with our bank, and payment on this second check has been stopped. So that there will be no misunderstanding—the first check will go through, but the second check will not.

Do not deposit this (second) check. Do not cash it. Do not try to use it in any form. This check is no longer valid.

Return this second check to me at once.

Sincerely,
R. B. Jones
Editorial Director

☆ ☆ ☆ ☆ ☆ ☆
—SUBGRAM—

FROM:
Q. Sarul, Chief, Unit 28
Bureau of Outplanet Sabotage
Block 262,498 Level 18
Aldebaran 4(2) QZ66:723:47

TO:
J. March
Branch Office Terra

Message: Dear March—Please be patient. We are trying to get the beam-thrower to you, but severe instability continues to block our efforts. No, use of explosives is not justified in this case, as it would not destroy the disruptor circuits with the certainty we require.

Q. Sarul
Chief, Unit 28

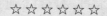

R.F.D. #1
Branwell, Ohio
12/14/64

Mr. R. B. Jones, Ed.
Stupendous Publications
4622 East 42nd St.
New York 58, N.Y.

Dear Mr. Jones:

I have just received your replacement check for "Break of Day," and your letter explaining the mix-up over the checks.

Thank you very much for this second check. I hope you will excuse my depositing this additional check at once—for the purpose of knocking the look of superiority off the face of the frustrated social arbiter who serves as teller at the bank here. I am enclosing herewith my own check for five hundred dollars, so you see it comes out right in the end.

Thanks very much for your kind words about "Break of Day." I am working hard on the new novelette, and hope you will like it just as well.

Cordially,
J. C. Catherton

STUPENDOUS PUBLICATIONS
4622 East 42nd St.
New York 58, N.Y.
12/16/64

Mr. J. C. Catherton:

I am dumbfounded by your letter of Dec. 14th, which has just reached me.

Thank you for your check.

I have, of course, gotten in touch with our bank, and instructed them to pay our check when it is presented.

Please disregard my previous letter. It is always easier to give authors money than it is to get it out of them again, as you would know if you gave advances, as we do in our book division.

However, I am sure we will have a most harmonious business association.

We are looking forward to your new novelette, and will give it a very careful reading, as we do all material of real merit submitted to us.

Cordially,
R. B. Jones
Editorial Director

☆ ☆ ☆ ☆ ☆ ☆

R.F.D. #1
Branwell, Ohio
12/16/64

Mr. R. B. Jones
Editorial Director
Stupendous Publications
4622 East 42nd St.
New York 58, N.Y.

Dear Mr. Jones:

I am astonished at your letter of Dec. 12th.

If you want men to write for you, not frightened mice, you should treat your writers like men. You will never get decent stories from the kind of people who will accept the treatment laid down in your letter of Dec. 12th.

Why should you stop payment on the second check?

I have sent my *own* check. That you stop payment on your second check means that I have received *no* payment for this story, as my check now cancels out your first check. This is the height of callous disregard for the rights of others.

Do you propose that I write for you for nothing?

Perhaps you would like me to send you a check for $500.00 along with my next story.

I can assure you that until this matter is straightened out, and until you stop using a manner of speaking which suggests that I am operating some kind of racket by expecting payment for my work, you will see no more of my work.

I am stopping payment on my check forthwith.

Truly yours,
J. C. Catherton

☆ ☆ ☆ ☆ ☆ ☆

—BY HYPERWARP—

2074J5

TO:
  G12, Centauran High Command
  .04618 Central MM10001AAA
  Centaurus Prime

FROM:
  Jones A1A, Terra

RE: Continued harassment

  Sir: I enclose a new report on continued Aldebara-
nian activity.
  You had better hurry up those countermeasures or I
am going after this bird with a trace meter and photoplas-
mic homogenizer.

                                                    Jones

                    ☆ ☆ ☆ ☆ ☆ ☆
                  —BY HYPERWARP—
                        2074J6

TO:
  Jones A1A Terra
  ZZ6074BZA

FROM:
  G12, Centauran High Command
  Centaurus Prime

RE: Harassment

  Sir: Don't do it. We now have their installation bugged
with a thousand percent overlap in all directions, and are
taking out valuable information by the bucket.

They are just as anxious to close out this operation as you are.

If this gets to be too much, take a Z-capsule and hold your breath for a moment. This will give the temporary outward effect of apoplexy, which is exactly what the Aldebaranians would expect of a Terran in this spot.

J. Schnock,

Stf. Col. In-Charge

☆ ☆ ☆ ☆ ☆ ☆

STUPENDOUS PUBLICATIONS
4622 East 42nd St.
New York 58, N.Y.
12/19/64

Mr. J. C. Catherton
R.F.D. #1
Branwell, Ohio

Dear Mr. Catherton:

I am writing to you in place of our editorial director, Mr. R. B. Jones, who was taken to the hospital yesterday with a mild heart attack.

I have gone over your correspondence with Mr. Jones, and agree that some injustice has been done here. Mr. Jones, as you know, is one of the old "tough" breed of editors, and is inclined to be a little harsh, even—perhaps especially—with his favorite authors. He expects a very high standard of performance.

Now, as for this difficulty about the checks. I have here your letters, dated December 10th, and 13th, and copies of Mr. Jones' letters which seem to make clear that your story "Break of Day," due for publication in January, has in effect not yet been paid for.

I am enclosing herewith our check for $500.00 to make good this error.

Sincerely,
Richard R. Manning
Publisher

☆ ☆ ☆ ☆ ☆ ☆

STUPENDOUS PUBLICATIONS
Interoffice Memo
Dec. 21, 1964

Richard—

I have word from the bank that payment has been stopped on this check from J. C. Catherton. If I understand these vouchers correctly, Catherton has now been paid $1500.00 for this one novelette, "Break of Day." This is already 50% over our top rate. But what worries me is that there seems to be no end in sight. Every few days, another check goes out to Catherton. We'd better draw the line somewhere.—Let me know if you want me to take a crack at straightening this out.

Harold Halliburton
Business Manager

☆ ☆ ☆ ☆ ☆ ☆

STUPENDOUS PUBLICATIONS
4622 East 42nd St.
New York 58, N.Y.
Dec. 21, 1964

Mr. J. C.. Catherton
R.F.D. #1
Branwell, Ohio

Dear Mr. Catherton:

Our bank informs us that you have deposited check No. 6428 to your account, and that this check has been duly paid. We have accordingly stopped payment on checks No. 6998 and 7002.

As you have stopped payment on your check No. 289, I sincerely trust that this solves the problem of paying for your story "Break of Day."

Very truly yours,
Harold J. Halliburton

R.F.D.. #1
Branwell, Ohio
12/21/64

Mr. Richard R. Manning
Publisher
Stupendous Publications
4622 East 42nd St.
New York 58, N.Y.

Dear Mr. Manning:

I have received your letter of December 18th, and am very grateful for your kindness.

I was very sorry to hear of Mr. Jones' illness, and certainly hope that this mix-up over the checks was in no way responsible.

It appears to me that the matter is still not entirely straightened out. Apparently, you did not see my letter of Dec. 16th, in which I said that I was stopping payment on my check, owing to a slight misunderstanding with Mr. Jones, who I thought was stopping payment on his checks.

If I understand this correctly, I will now have one thousand five hundred dollars for this story, and this is three times your standard rate. All I should get is five hundred dollars.

Accordingly, I am sending you a check for one thousand dollars.

This is the difference between $1500.00 and $500.00. and should straighten the matter out entirely.

Cordially,
J. C. Catherton

STUPENDOUS PUBLICATIONS
12/23/64

Harold—

I have just received a $1000 check from J. C. Catherton, to make up the difference between the $1500 I was giving him, and the $500 that was his payment for "Break of Day."

It appears to me that your stopping payment on the two latest checks means that he will suffer severely for selling us the novelette. If I understand this correctly, we are now $500.00 ahead. In effect, he has paid us $500 for the story.

Richard

STUPENDOUS PUBLICATIONS
12/23/64

Richard—

I have a terrific cold, and am not sure I am thinking any too clearly, but this matter is certainly so elementary that it can be straightened out.

Now, as I understand it, we owe Catherton five hundred dollars, over and above the five hundred for the story.

Accordingly, I am sending him air mail two checks for five hundred dollars. The first nullifies the debt and the second pays him for the story.—Now we have that out of the way.

Next to counteract the $1000 check Catherton sent you, I have instructed our bank to pay the two $500 checks you and Jones sent Catherton. Thus these two checks cancel out the $1000 check from Catherton.

Now, on top of this cold, I have a blinding headache, so I am going home, have a hot toddy, and start the Christmas season early.

I would advise you to do the same.

Harold.

☆ ☆ ☆ ☆ ☆ ☆
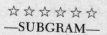
—SUBGRAM—

FROM:
  J. March, Agent
  Branch Office Terra

TO:
  Q. Sarul, Chief, Unit 28
  Bureau of Outplanet Sabotage
  Block 262,498 Level 18
  Aldebaran 4(2) QZ66:723:51

Message: Chief—On returning from successful performance of my mission, I got drawn into a local celebration, but assuming I can focus long enough, I want to report that I finally got the beam-thrower through the Chute, and am happy to say that I put it into action—successfully, since the red tell-tale light lit up bright when I fired at the disruptor.

The natives on this planet have a saying that "Every cloud has its silver lining."

If so, I would like to know where it is in this mess.

—Yours in hung-over relief,
J. March

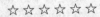

R.F.D. #1
Branwell, Ohio
January 1, 1964

Mr. Richard R. Manning
Publisher
Stupendous Publications
4622 East 42nd St.
New York 58, N.Y.

Dear Mr. Manning:

I am belatedly writing to you today because for the past week I have been waiting to be sure that I am caught up on all the letters coming in from your wonderful Stupendous Publications.

As you may imagine, I was absolutely dumfounded to receive two more checks for $500.00. Especially so, since upon receiving Mr. Halliburton's very cold letter of December 21st, I had immediately stopped payment on my check for $1000.00.

You may imagine my further astonishment when the two previous checks which Mr. Halliburton said he had stopped payment on, were also paid.

This means that I have now received five checks for five hundred dollars, two sent by Mr. Jones, one from you, and two from Mr. Halliburton. This is a total of two thousand five hundred dollars for this one story.

I have thought of sending back to you a check for two thousand dollars, but I am afraid of what might happen. This way we know where we stand.

I am enclosing a new story, and I am happy to tell you that you can have it free, as you now have a credit on account with me of two thousand dollars.

Don't worry that I am going to give up writing. I see there is real money in it, and I will be working at it day and night.

But I don't expect to have another Christmas like that one for a while. Happy New Year!

Cordially,
J. C. Catherton

THE PLATEAU

Iron-shod heels clanged in the streets of New York and Moscow.

In a one-hundred and twenty mile arc from Yinkow to Antung, along the base of the Kwantung Peninsula, the Chinese dead lay mouldering in windrows.

In the wreckage of the northern half of London, the fight dwindled away, amidst smoke and radioactive debris. South of the line of the Thames, no human moved from Portsmouth to Margate.

Earth was conquered.

At no place on the globe was there a well-equipped body of human combat troops larger than a platoon.

▌▌

Dionnai Count Maivail studied the final reports of the Invasion Group commanders, and sent for his Executive Staff Chief.

Kram Baron Angstat came in, and halted with a click of the heels and a stiff bow from the waist.

"Excellence?"

Maivail inclined his head slightly toward the reports. "I am quite satisfied. Phase Military is complete. My compliments to you, the Staff and the Group Commanders."

"I am honored, sir. I shall relay your words. On behalf of the Executive Staff, I thank you."

"We now begin Phase Industrial. Just as our initial blows came as a complete surprise, following without warning two years after their attainment of the first real interplanetary capability, so our next blows must come with the greatest shock, at that moment when they begin to feel themselves recover from the first blow."

Angstat nodded his head. "Understood, Excellence."

"I need not remind the Chief of the Executive Staff that on such a planet as this, agriculture is to be considered an industry."

"It shall be so designated, Excellence."

"The centralized production of electrical power, and its transmission, is to be considered an industry."

"Understood, Excellence."

"Such miscellany as dams, bridges, ships, air and ground transportation centers, hospitals, schools, wire and wireless electromagnetic communications centers—such as these are to be considered industries."

"They shall be so treated, Excellence."

"Now that this first phase is over, I shall want a more thorough, personal report from our principal resident agent."

"He shall be sent in."

"Good. Withdraw the troops into the cleared zones and begin scanning at once."

Angstat clicked his heels and saluted.

Dionnai Count Maivail straightened in his seat and returned the salute sharply.

※ ※ ※

On the conquered Earth, from Britain to China, from the Soviet Union to the U. S., the victorious invaders began to withdraw into their strongholds.

III

Richard Holden, dizzily surveying the glistening, faintly-milky surface through a pair of binoculars, then lying back to look up at the silver forms that blurred out in endless streams, branching north and west, then branching again in the far distance, and finally returning from the south, shook his head.

"How can we ever beat that?"

His companion, Philip Swanbeck, was a strongly-built man in khaki, with a single silver star at his collar.

"Can't give up," he growled. "They'll never beat us."

"Save it for the troops," said Holden. "They've already whipped us."

Swanbeck murmured, "It pays to learn from the enemy. In the second world war, there was a German pilot who had a pretty good philosophy. I don't suppose he originated it. But he put it in one sentence. Want to hear it?"

Holden stared through the binoculars at the glistening, semi-transparent surface that had resisted a direct hit by a Naomi missile with fifty-megaton warhead. "Sure. Go ahead. What's the harm?"

"Listen carefully."

"I'm listening."

" 'He alone is lost who gives himself up as lost.' "

Holden thought it over as he studied the barrier. Whatever that glistening surface was, it barred human entrance to the valley as absolutely as if it were made of armor steel a mile thick. And yet, the bright wingless aircraft passed through it as if through fog. Holden shook his head and lowered the glasses.

"He should have seen this. But I can give you the philosophy, more condensed yet."

Swanbeck was scowling as he studied the milky surface, sighted his compass, and made notes on a small pad. He glanced at Holden in surprise. "In fewer words than that?"

"Easy. Listen."

"I'm listening."

" *I still live.* ' "

Swanbeck blinked, then slowly smiled. "Yes, that's it. Exactly. Who said that?"

Holden grinned. He pulled the camera free of its case, and aimed it so that it focused directly on the place where the shining wingless aircraft passed through the barrier.

"Ever hear of John Carter?"

"The name's faintly familiar. Who's he?"

"An immortal Earthman who became Warlord of Mars."

Swanbeck looked at Holden sharply, then smiled, "—A fictional hero?"

"Who knows? We haven't explored Mars very thoroughly, you know. And *this* crew"—He nodded toward the glistening barrier—"obviously came from somewhere more distant, or we'd have seen some sign when they took off."

Swanbeck smiled. " 'I still live.' That's pretty good." He closed his notebook. "Got the pictures?"

"Got them." Holden slid the camera carefully back into its case.

Swanbeck put his compass away, folded up a thing like a transit, set on short legs and with angled eyepiece, and twisted open a thick tube from his pack. He pulled out a brown oval-shaped object with a spike at the bottom, glanced around, pulled loose a pin near the base of the spike, and stabbed the spike into the ground.

"Okay. Our people will see that when it goes off, and recheck our position by it. Now let's get out of here."

Carefully, they wormed their way backwards, then stumbled to their feet and ran down the hill.

IV

Dionnai Count Maivail nodded impersonally to resident agent Sumer Lassig.

"Yes. Your reports have been thoroughly scanned, Agent Lassig. You were quite right to recommend reduction of this folk. Your reports have been received with the highest approbation by the Supreme Determinative Council. I have, of course, myself perused them."

Lassig bowed. "I am honored, your Excellency."

"Now, however, I want to hear it first hand."

"Yes, sir." The transparent membranes slid down briefly over Lassig's eyes as he thought back, then they flicked away. "To begin with, sir, I arrived here only four months ago, local time, to find that my predecessor had grossly neglected his duty. He was evidently a scholarly individual, not suited to the task."

Maivail nodded with interest. "What had he done? In what condition did you find him?"

"As for what he had done, he had sent back rather confused reports, suggesting at first the possession of unusual skills by the local folk. Under hard questioning from home, he confessed error, excused himself on the basis of language difficulties, and sent back innocuous reports that were duly accepted as valid, until the locals sent up that first sizable interplanetary expedition, which was, of course, picked up on the monitor. This negated the picture he had created. When I found him, he was surrounded by translations of local documents. He was muttering to himself. 'It can't all be true. But which is which? I'm going insane.' He was hopeless, sir. I shot him."

"Excellent. What about his staff?"

"It soon became evident that they too were infected. Some had taken to solacing themselves with local narcotics. The rest were even more incoherent. They blabbered about 'multiple skills,' talked about a 'ladder of achievement,' said the locals had 'nearly all the rungs, not just the upper rungs,' and so on, and to cap the climax, they presented me with a list of things they claimed the natives had that we did not have."

Maivail looked interested. "Have you this list?"

There was a crackle of paper. "I thought you might want to see it, sir."

Maivail took it, and looked it over.

"H'm. *Humor. Chemistry. Fiction. Sense of smell.*" Maivail looked up. "What *are* these things?"

"On the chance that there might be some validity to this after all, I questioned the staff most carefully. Their answers were heretical gibberish. To prevent the infection from spreading to my own staff, I flash-bombed the lot of them immediately."

"Good, good. But, now—Take this first word, '*Humor.*' What's that?"

"This is a local word, sir. We have transliterated it, but cannot translate it. We have no corresponding word. According to the staff, it is a peculiar sense which causes the locals to *laugh.*"

"What?"

"Sir?"

"Laugh. What does *that* mean?"

"A spasmodic contraction of the diaphragm, coupled with reddening of the face, and choking noises."

Maivail settled back. "I see. Now, look here, Lassig. Kindly don't use one local word to define another. This could become quite difficult to follow."

"I'm sorry, sir. I'll try to avoid that. Now, this peculiar sense, this *humor,* causes the natives to choke and gag in certain situations."

"It sounds to me as if '*humor*' should translate as 'dust in the air-tubes.' Obviously, the spasmodic contractions of the diaphragm must be intended to eject the dust."

Lassig nodded. "Exactly, sir. But the staff had got off on some sidetrack, and claimed it was psychological."

"*Psychological.*"

"Yes, sir."

"M'm. Spasmodic contractions of the diaphragm. Choking. Gagging.—And this is *psychological?*"

Lassig spread his hands. "*Their* word for it, sir. They said that someone else's sudden fright, or hurried narrow escape from danger, would often cause the locals to choke and gag."

Maivail turned it over in his mind. "What's the causal connection?"

"According to the staff, this—this 'sense of humor,' sir."

Maivail squinted. "This explanation has a certain tinge of lunacy."

"Exactly, sir."

"What about this next item on the list, 'Chemistry'? What might that be?"

Lassig took on the look of a man confronted with the job of lifting a large heavy object having no handle.

"Well, sir—ah—it's supposed to be a—ah—Well, a form of *Science*—"

"There is only one true Science. That is the control of *mer*, or matter-energy."

Lassig looked uneasy. "Yes, sir. Of course, you're right, sir. The staff went into this business about the ladder, and claimed that *mer*-control originally came in two parts, the control of matter, and the control of energy. *Chemistry* was the control of matter."

Maivail stared. "Why, any fool knows that matter and energy are basically the same. Matter is condensed energy. Energy is, in effect, highly rarified matter."

"Yes, sir."

"How did the staff get around *that*?"

"They claimed, sir, that to *attain* scientific knowledge was a very slow, laborious, and gradual thing, whereas—"

Maivail snorted. "This is fantastic. It takes exactly three years to learn the whole business."

"Yes, sir. Precisely what I said to them. But the staff argued that there was a time, before the schools—"

"*Before* the *schools*?"

"Yes, sir."

"Who, then, would have taught the youth?"

"They claimed the—ah—the people of that day had to teach themselves."

"Teach themselves! But—Great merciful—See here, surely the members of the staff had seen a hydrofuser. How the devil could you *build* one, if you didn't already *have* one?"

Lassig shook his head, and said glumly, "They claimed the people on this planet were gradually working their way around to *making* one."

"*How*?"

"That I couldn't possibly hope to explain, sir."

"The basic tool in *mer*-control is the hydrofuser. And you can't *make* a hydrofuser unless you've *got* a hydrofuser. You can't construct a hydrofuser from nothing, any more than you can breed *slergs* without a parent *slerg* to start with. But when you *do* have a hydrofuser or a parent *slerg*, then it's easy."

"Yes, sir. They were far gone, sir. You couldn't talk to them."

"What about this next thing? 'Fiction.' What might that be?"

"The staff were pretty confused about that, sir. It seems that the locals—Ah—Frankly, sir, I don't know *what* fiction is. That was what my predecessor was trying to figure out when I got there. He claimed that some of the local's reports were unreal.—No, not that, synthetic."

"Synthetic reports?" Maivail's eyes momentarily bulged. "You mean these locals *falsify their own reports*?"

Lassig blew out his breath. "That's the beauty of it. The fellow claimed it wasn't actually *falsification*."

"Not falsification? But—If it's synthetic—"

"He claimed that the locals *knew* the reports were synthetic, so that they weren't fooled." .

Maivail swallowed hard. He could feel his poise slipping away by the instant.

"Look here, Lassig. *If* the locals *know* the report is false, how does the falsifier *profit*?"

Lassig looked hopeless.

Maivail said exasperatedly, "Let's assume for the moment that I am a supply-inspector. You are, we also assume for the moment, a cheating contractor. You have delivered six and nine-tenths gluts of smollonium ore .006 fine. You contracted to deliver seven gluts .008 fine. You make out your affidavit and present it to me, labeled 'False.' Now. You know it's false. I know it's false. Where are we? What's the point?"

Lassig could find no answer.

Maivail said, "Either these locals are a very involved race of people, or the entire staff was falsifying its *own* data. And yet, who would believe them? What's the purpose? There's something peculiarly out-of-focus about this. Now, let's try just one more of these things. What might 'sense of smell' be?"

Lassig nervously rubbed his hand across his breathing-duct orifice.

"Well, sir—Ah—As to that—"

Maivail watched him flounder, and squinted at him coldly—This was a man selected for his ability to absorb, evaluate, and explain alien cultures.

Despite the perfection with which the military operations had thus far gone off, Maivail could not escape the impression of something unpleasant, looming just outside the range of his vision.

In the underground command center, it was dim and quiet. The papers were spread out under the cool glow of the fluorescent lights.

"Okay," said Swanbeck, "we've finally got it, then."

Holden glanced at the composite drawing. The precise place and angle at which the stream of exiting aircraft passed out through the barrier, and the corresponding place and angle at which the returning vehicles re-entered, were clearly shown.

Holden shook his head. "It's going to be quite a problem to get a Naomi to hit that barrier at precisely that angle. Moreover, it's got to get there at exactly the right moment, or it will catch up and collide with one of those vehicles. The Naomi's going to be moving at around eighteen thousand miles an hour, remember."

"Don't worry about that. Thanks to this lull, we're in touch with Denver again. There are half-a-dozen launchers on the way with the new-type Raquet. If Naomi can't do it—"

"Raquet has a chemical warhead."

"Not this bunch."

Holden thought it over. "You know, Phil, I just had a thought."

Swanbeck smiled. "Don't be modest. Let's hear it."

"Look, now, if this doesn't work—"

Swanbeck winced. "Then we're no worse off than we were. We'll try another approach." He turned away.

"Wait a minute," said Holden.

"There's no point worrying about *failure*, Dick. Drop it." Swanbeck started to walk away.

Holden raised his voice. "All right, but the point is, what if it *does* work?"

Swanbeck turned, frowning. "We're in."

"And *they're* warned."

Swanbeck blinked.

Holden said, "We're too busy thinking how to *make* it work, to think, what next, if it *does* work? How many chances like this are we going to get?"

"What are you thinking?"

"Half-a-dozen simultaneous *failures* wouldn't hurt us. That's just more of the same. But if we have half-a-dozen simultaneous *successes*—"

Swanbeck nodded slowly. "That's a point. We'll see if Denver can spread the word."

VI

Dionnai Count Maivail put down the new staff reports. "Very good, Angstat. These are most complete. What is *your* impression of the local reaction?"

"Fast and flexible, sir. I must say that their recovery, militarily speaking, is a good deal above what we might have expected. I notice particularly that they are very careful to remain dispersed. Another noteworthy factor is their avoidance of vain effort. Following their initial abortive strikes against the cleared zones, there's been nothing but very light reconnaissance. But their organization is obviously knitting together rapidly."

"They could have been a most dangerous adversary."

Angstat nodded. "Once they adapted sufficient of their hydrofuser power to interplanetary, then interstellar uses, they could have been extremely dangerous. As it is, of course, their base—just one planet—is too restricted, and hence vulnerable. Their delay at achieving a broad base has cost them dear. One wonders at their reasons."

Maivail nodded thoughtfully. "I suppose we'll never know for certain. Lassig's report shows an incredible mental confusion on their part. Possibly some religion, or some 'little-planet,' mind-our-business-and-turn-our-back-on-the-galaxy philosophy was the real cause of the trouble. You remember our own back-to-nature fanatics?"

Angstat snorted. "Who could forget them? Throw away their hydrofuser, smash their correctors, go off naked to some hole somewhere, and squat by a mess of smoldering mulch eating scorched meat, with the bugs around them in clouds, and tell themselves they're *really* living. There, they say, that's what Nature *intended*. By the Great—" He caught himself, and cleared his throat. "They can *have* it. When *I* get pains in the knees, or an attack of galloping scrombosis, I want to be where I can get in a corrector, and no delay."

Maivail nodded. "The only reasonable interpretation of Lassig's data seems to be that this planet is overrun with all kinds of these back-to-nature fanatics. And, of course, our scanners have brought back actual pictures of them in action.—Incredible."

"It doesn't speak well for their general level of intelligence."

"No. It doesn't. Yet, their *military* reaction—"

Again, there was that peculiar sense of something looming, something just outside his range of vision.

Angstat cleared his throat, and straightened.

"About the beginning of Phase Industrial, Excellency?"

Maivail dropped his informality and sat straight, considering it. "Their recovery seems well started. Their hopes should once again be reviving. All reports indicate a marked recovery in surface transport and wireless electromagnetic communication. Very good. At the next turning of the watch, order the scanners in. Secure the opened lanes. Phase Industrial will begin one watch later."

Kram Baron Angstat clicked his heels and saluted.

Dionnai Count Maivail sat straight, and returned the salute.

VII

Swanbeck held the phone to his ear as he made rapid notes.

"Yes, all right . . . Okay, but we don't want any delay beyond that time. We have no way to know how long this opportunity will last . . . No, but there may be something similar to closing a gate. Otherwise, I don't see why they go in and out, all at the same places . . . Yes . . . Yes . . . Okay . . . Yes, sir. We'll do it. We'll delay again till 1630 . . . Yes, sir . . . Good-by."

Scowling, he set the phone back in its cradle, and snapped orders to a doubtful-looking colonel, who saluted and hurried out.

Holden said, "What is it this time?"

Swanbeck delivered himself of a string of profanity. "Now the Chicom aren't ready."

Holden shook his head. "This close reconnaissance isn't going to last forever. Sooner or later, they're going to pull the last of those aircraft inside and plug the holes."

"I know it. But Denver wants to hit as many as possible all at once. Damn it, the way they've got it set up, it's going to be all or nothing."

Holden smiled sourly. "Not necessarily. Somebody could jump the gun."

Swanbeck's face hardened.

Holden said, "Denver couldn't be so busy, could they, that they didn't think of this?"

"We'll find out." Swanbeck picked up the phone.

VIII

Dionnai Count Maivail selected a delicate-stemmed slender goblet, and contemplated the pale-violet liquid within.

"Excellent hue, Choisoiel."

Ferrard Choisoiel, Maivail's steward, dipped at the knee and bobbed his head in gratitude. "Thank you, sir."

Maivail flicked the edge of the goblet with his fingertip, and turned his head to listen.

Kram Baron Angstat smiled, as he held up his own goblet.

"Fine timbre and resonance, Your Excellency."

"It has indeed."

Choisoiel was all but overcome.

Angstat heard a silver bell chime.

"The turning of the watch, sir. The signal to return the scanners."

"Ah. Soon Phase Industrial will begin."

"Exactly, sir."

Maivail raised the slender goblet.

"The success of all our plans—"

Angstat replied "—and the obstruction of all our enemies!"

They sipped the liquid.

IX

Swanbeck put the phone back in its cradle and smiled.

"Denver has already told the Chicom there are twenty-five Naomi missiles with their fuses burning, just in case they doublecross us on this."

"What's the Chicom reaction?"

"Very cooperative. They've apparently had enough from the outworlders to blunt their taste for seas of blood drowning seas of flame."

"Then we're spared that." Holden glanced at his watch. "If 1630 would only hurry up."

"Not too long, now."

A young lieutenant hurried in, saw Swanbeck and saluted.

"Sir, the Bugs have stopped sending out scouts. They're pulling the rest back in pretty fast."

Swanbeck glanced at his watch.

The lieutenant added, "What do we do? Wait for 1630?"

Swanbeck glanced at the phone, and back at the lieutenant.

Holden let his breath out in a sigh of weary disgust.

Swanbeck said roughly, "Hit them."

X

Dionnai Count Maivail put his neatly-booted feet on the footrest.

"Superb, Choisoiel."

He selected a pale-blue mint with little silver flecks, and settled back contentedly.

Angstat sighed, and munched delicately.

Choisoiel gratefully thanked Maivail for the compliment, and began to clear away the remains.

Maivail and Angstat beamed upon each other. Both had the same thought, and they spoke at once.

"The perfect end to a—"

The *boom* started loud and grew louder fast. Their chairs rose and tipped as the floor heaved, and the wall across the room bulged toward them.

Ferrard Choisoiel threw himself between Maivail and the wall.

Maivail and Angstat sprang to their feet, their hands at the hilts of their weapons.

The wall burned through, and a white glare looked in upon them.

As it burned away exposed flesh, Maivail stood facing it, a bright white lance of destruction leaping from his weapon into the chaos.

XI

Swanbeck lowered the glasses.

"Whew! They won't survive that."

Before them, the gleaming wall remained unbroken, but from one side reached out a huge dazzling-white plume of gas, smoke and debris, that made a roar like a rocket at lift-off.

Holden nodded. "That's the end of *that* bunch. But what about the others?"

"Damn it. If we'd had *time*, we could have cleaned out the three-fourths of them in reach of modern weapons-teams."

"Maybe we did—If the others reacted in time—"

"*Maybe*. Well, that's that. We've gained, even if this is the only knockout."

"Yes," said Holden. "We know they're vulnerable. And that we aren't necessarily powerless."

He put the filter over the glasses to look briefly at the huge flaming jet. "As you expressed it. 'He alone is lost who gives himself up as lost.' "

Swanbeck nodded, and studied the enemy base.

" 'I still live,' " he said.

XII

Maivail saw flashing red and green lights. His body burned from end to end. Wrapped in flame, he spun like a whirl-wind amidst a dazzling drift of stars. Then he seemed to slip, slide, the cosmos around him began to waver as if seen through water—A voice spoke and while Maivail understood it at the time, what it said slipped away, and for the moment he retained only the sense of a single comment: "The present home of your soul is again ready for you."

Dizzily, Maivail opened his eyes.

He was lying in a corrector, the padded cushions softly supporting him. Framed in the opening above him, Angstat looked down.

Maivail swallowed.

"That was close."

"Close enough," said Angstat.

"What happened?"

"Evidently they got a hydrofuser in through an opened lane, and then destabilized it."

Maivail considered what this meant in terms of speed and control of trajectory.

Angstat said, "The thing over-powered the secondary screens, and the excess radiation burned right through the exposed sides of the ships. We'd have been finished if a technician hadn't thought, earlier, to install an excess-radiation switch. The switch kicked over the potential-control in the energy-bank circuit. The banks reversed polarity, and absorbed enough of the excess energy so the screens could recover. The heat and pressure slowly blew out through the exit lane. The ships themselves are in terrible shape."

"Whew," said Maivail. "Keep back. I'm coming out." He hauled himself out of the corrector, and briefly considered the shape he must have been in when he was put into it. "How long was I in there?"

"Four days."

Maivail reminded himself that half-a-day would cure any ordinary illness, and one day would correct a severe case of overall long-term cumulative fatigue and deterioration. Two days would take care of the average victim of an explosion, provided he was not actually blown to bits. Soldiers suffering from serious wounds were in and out in less time than that. And he had been in for *four days*. He flexed his arms, bent, and straightened. He felt fine.

Angstat handed him a fresh uniform.

Maivail dressed rapidly. "How many men were we able to salvage?"

"About a third, sir." As Maivail winced, Angstat added, "I'm happy to say, sir, that your steward, Ferrard Choisoiel, was among them. He acted heroically at the moment of disaster, throwing himself between you and the wall as it began to buckle inward."

Maivail nodded. "Award him the Order of the Copper Sun, with twelve rays." He glanced around. "Where are we right now?"

"Level B of the below-ground base that was under construction at the time of the attack, sir. The ships are under repair. All but three of them are holed, and every one of them has suffered severe external damage."

"Well, we can fix that." Maivail told himself that, whatever he felt, he must bear himself unflinchingly. But he had some of the emotional sensations of a person who has taken on a bear, and lost an arm and a leg in the first exchange of blows. "What damage to the—the locals, in the past few days?"

Angstat was leading the way down the corridor. He paused to open a door freshly blazoned with the emblems of the Commander and of the Executive Staff. "—Damage to the *locals*, Excellency?"

"My orders," said Maivail, "were to commence Phase Industrial one watch following the return of the scanners."

"Unfortunately, sir, out of a total of eighteen cleared zones, each protected by a heavy screen, *six* underwent exactly the same thing that happened to us."

Maivail felt the room spin. "How severe was the damage?"

"Two-thirds to almost total."

Maivail's voice seemed to come from far away. "When I give an order, I expect it to be obeyed. Regardless of losses."

"Yes, sir."

"Why wasn't that order obeyed?"

"Because the mechanism of command was temporarily destroyed, above the level of the Invasion Group commanders. For a day-and-a-half, the entire Executive Staff was out of action. Even later on, there was delay, because the external portions of the communications equipment had been vaporized. The result was immediate cessation of the higher functions of control and coordination. The remaining group commanders found themselves unable to raise headquarters. Six of the eighteen Invasion Groups had apparently ceased to exist. At that point, no-one knew what had happened."

"Yes. Yes, I see." Maivail felt himself come back to reality. He found a door with his emblem blazoned on the outside, walked in and sat down wearily. He had a strong urge to crawl back in the corrector, but suppressed it. "What's the overall percentage of loss?"

Angstat pulled out a paper covered with figures. "Close to twenty-five percent, sir."

Maivail dizzily pictured what would happen when word of this got back to the Supreme Council.—Well, there was nothing to be done about that. He groped for something positive. "The scanner photos, maps, data, and classification lists.—Did any of them survive?"

"Happily, sir, the filed data was only slightly damaged. The heat and associated stresses did create drifting instability in some of the memory banks. But we've overcome most of that."

"Ah, good.—And with that data, we can reconstitute the models and classification lists?"

"Yes, sir. We've started work on it."

"Good. And we again have communication with the group commanders?"

"Yes, sir."

"All right. Have them fabricate new shielding generators, and set up an external screen around each screen already existing. Use a number of cleared lanes, in this new *external* screen, and block and unblock them, directing outgoing and incoming traffic to the various lanes at random. And I *mean* at random."

"Yes, sir."

"Moreover, each set of cleared lanes in the outer shell is to be changed at the end of the day, and a completely new set used the following day."

"Yes, Excellency. And shall we shift our forces to balance the strength of all the Groups?"

Maivail thought a moment, then shook his head.

"No. The full-strength groups, once they've protected themselves, will carry out Phase Industrial in their regions. The understrength groups will go back to Phase Military. When the full-strength groups finish the job in their regions, they will join the understrength groups in *their* regions, and carry out Phase Industrial, and absolutely obliterate the industrial resources of those regions."

Angstat clicked his heels and saluted. "It shall be done, Excellency."

XIII

Swanbeck put the phone gently back in its cradle, and looked at Holden curiously.

Holden was frowning as he studied several diagrams, each showing an object partly merged into a surrounding doughnut-shaped structure. From different points on the doughnut-shaped structure, short lines projected, with a set of angles written along the lines, and with times jotted down nearby.

Swanbeck cleared his throat. Holden looked up. Swanbeck said, "They just wiped out the dummy command-post west of Centerville. And Higgins and Delahaye have been captured."

Holden winced. "How did that happen?"

"They went up by way of the ravine, and got into the observation-post early this morning. Since the trees have leafed out, actual observation from there has been worth-less. They crawled out in the dark, and dug themselves a hole in a sizable clump of brush further down the hill, dragging the dirt back into the forest on shelter-halves, to get it out of sight."

"Why didn't they just dig their hole at the edge of the forest?"

"The slope is gradual there, and there are so many small poplars out in the field that from ground-level you can't see a thing. From this clump of brush, though, they figured they'd be safe from observation from any direction, would have a good view of the barrier, and could pass the information back using a directional handset."

"What happened?"

"The Bugs have a habit of setting off flares at odd times in the night, and they have aircraft up to patrol within a mile or two of the barrier. Anything suspicious, they fire on. This clump of brush was fifty feet out from anything else you could call cover, and not wanting to be caught on their feet in the open when a flare went off, Higgins and Delahaye *crawled* back a number of times, with the dirt. When the sun came up this morning, they discovered that a lane of shiny straw was bent back where they'd crawled out dragging the dirt. It was like a fifty-foot path leading direct to where they were hidden."

Holden swore. "Then what?"

"They sent back reports till the sun reached the right angle, and some alert Bug happened to spot the bent straw. Then a troop-carrier and several floating forts came out, and heavily-armed Bugs dropped down on all sides of them. Higgins and Delahaye were loaded down with range and direction finders, cameras, and that contraption that's supposed to see through the Barrier—"

"Did it work?"

"No." Swanbeck shook his head in disgust. "But in consequence of lugging that stuff along, all they had between them was one .45. They got off a few shots, then the Bugs had them trussed up, and threw them into the troop carrier."

Holden blew out his breath. "Higgins and Delahaye were two of our more intelligent men."

"For what it's worth, Higgins grabbed the directional handset at the last minute, and shouted 'I still live' into it. They picked it up back at the observation post. But they didn't know what had happened till Schmidt, who'd been at the edge of the forest trying to see something through all that mess of poplar leaves, got back to tell them."

Holden frowned. "That's funny. *We've* been talking about that very expression. Why did *he* use it?"

Swanbeck drummed his fingers on the table. "Did Higgins read a lot?"

"He'd get streaks where he was a terrific reader. He'd go through shelves of books like a mining-machine through a coal vein. For a couple of fanatical health-enthusiasts, they both had a lot of brain-power to the ounce."

"Maybe Higgins had run across that saying, and it just occurred to him as a gesture of defiance."

"Maybe."

"What makes you think it might be something more?"

"I don't know. But Higgins and Delahaye both had a fiendish sense of humor. This just seems—" Holden shook his head.

Swanbeck frowned, then finally shrugged and said dryly, "If they've got humor, they'll need it. Every bit.—Now, what do you think about the Bugs' improved Barriers?"

Holden scowled at the diagrams. "We've got a small chance of getting a missile in through one of these holes. But it isn't going to do much damage. They've obviously built a kind of antechamber. Their returning ships pass into this antechamber first, then the outer entrance is closed, and a passage is opened through the inner barrier. If we get a missile through the outer barrier, all it will hurt will be whatever happens to be in the antechamber."

"Not good enough. We almost put that outfit out of business the last time. This time we want to finish them."

"There's just a *chance*—It's slight, though."

Swanbeck's eyes came to a focus. "What are you thinking?"

"You're familiar with the idea of 'limpet mines'?"

XIV

Dionnai Count Maivail studied the latest reports with the grim satisfied look of a champion boxer who has been knocked flat by an upstart, and who has spent the following rounds lambasting the challenger all over the ring. The military reports were splendid. Maivail scowled, however, at some lengthy items at the end of an intelligence report, then turned back to the front to see if he had missed something.

The report was headed, "Interrogation of Prisoners —A Summary of Conclusions."

The first section described the methods used:

"Prisoners were detained in groups of medial size, as most conducive to free discussion amongst the prisoners. Each cell was equipped with concealed communication heads. The interrogation proper was usually carried out singly or in pairs, and the resulting discussions when the prisoners returned to their cells were carefully analyzed. This paper contains a summary of the conclusions derived from these discussions and interrogations, carried out in various locations over a large portion of the surface of this planet, amongst various ethnic, linguistic, and cultural groups of the local populace."

Maivail nodded to himself. Save for the use of three long words where two short ones would do, that part seemed clear enough.

He glanced over the bulk of the report, and located a section that seemed to summarize the rest:

"These people are, therefore, divided into many religious, racial, and cultural groups. They are fad-ridden to an almost incredible degree, yet an underlying sameness and mutuality may be observed at times.[3,4] It is particularly to be noted that the populace is evidently divided into two primary groups: 1) Those educated in Science; 2) Those not educated in Science. The warrior-caste is evidently made up of those not even slightly educated in Science, as no single individual prisoner manifested any knowledge of the hydrofuser—the basic scientific tool—and, in fact, such individuals did not recognize hydrofusers when confronted with them. Yet the existence of scientific knowledge is inescapably demonstrated by the technology manifest on nearly all sides. One wonders at the absence of effective shielding equipment, but can only suppose that the hydrofusers in use are somewhat crude, and suffer from some unknown defect, possibly a periodic fluctuation in output which creates lag and/or some kind of overlapping envelope effects . . . "

Maivail squinted at this for some time. He could not escape the impression that the person who had prepared this report was missing something, or distorting something to fit his own preconceptions. The trouble was, whatever the difficulty might be, Maivail did not seem to be able to get a grip on it, either.

This was bad enough, but worse yet was that set of facts presented modestly in the body of the report as: [3,4]

Turning to the next to the last page, Maivail found:

[3] Gavik, Major K. Baron: "Report Intel. S63. Anomalous Remarks . . . Conversation Between Prisoners. Hdq. Inter. Co-ord. Cmd." This report, itself a summary of many other reports, states that various prisoners from widely-separated localities, in expressing perplexity over the events surrounding the invasion and their interrogation, have referred to a formidable individual who remains, apparently, aloof from the fight. This sentiment is usually expressed by some variant of the following statement:

"Well, it would take Shurlok Homes to figure this out."

This widespread belief that this entity, Shurlok Homes, would solve the problem, yet does not apparently choose to interest himself in it, when it amounts

(from the local viewpoint) to nothing other than the conquest of the home planet, is in itself amazing. (Does the
word Homes—plural of 'home'—have any significance
in this respect? Does Homes have more than one
home?—More than one home planet?) Even more
amazing is the apparent lack of any feeling of resentment
that the entity Shurlok Homes does not enter the field
with his formidable powers, whatever these may be. (If
Homes is elsewhere, situated on another home planet,
possibly as yet unaware of events here, it would explain
the lack of resentment over his failure to intervene in
the present struggle.)

Maivail could feel the beginning of a headache, and
resolved to go into the corrector at the first opportunity.
However, having finished [3] he now had to go on to [4]:

[4] Sarokel, Lieutenant K. "Report Intel. 12438. The
Higins-Delahi Conversations. Hdq. Inter. Unit 1." The
report states, in detail, the conversations in their cell of
Andru Higins and Stefin Delahi. These two captives are
apparently not warriors, but seem to be members of a
local technical organization acting in cooperation with
the armed forces. It is necessary to emphasize the qualification "seem" because the in-cell conversations of these
two prisoners, unlike the usual case, are totally at vari-
ance with their out-cell responses to direct questioning.

It is worth noting that these two men apparently are
members of different races. Higins is of a light skin-
coloration, Delahi is very dark. Outwardly (toward their
interrogators) they firmly supported each others' state-
ments to the effect that they were local technical personnel. Higins spoke to Delahi as "Steve," Delahi spoke to
Higins as "Andi." Once alone, however, their manner
changed drastically. Higins and Delahi, once the guard

withdrew from the corridor, addressed each other by different names. Delahi became "Dottor Sojak." Higins was now "Odwor Jaf Kalas." Their behavior toward one another became noticeably more ceremonial, less informal. Their principal topics of conversation fell into two categories: 1) What they would do to the invaders (that is, to us) if they had the opportunity 2) By what practical means they might inform some being referred to as, among other things, "the Warlord."

It seems impracticable to meaningfully summarize the conversation of these two individuals. However, the following brief excerpt from the record seems representative:

Dottor Sojak: "If only we'd never let that scoundrel Tovas talk us into this. All it is to him is an experiment."

Odwor Jaf Kalas: "We'll get back. Don't worry. As soon as the time's up, he'll bring us back."

Sojak: "Meanwhile Barzum goes unwarned."

Kalas: "And how would we warn them, Dottor, if we had never been here? Let us think what we will do to these calotts, not waste our time worrying."

Sojak: "The first problem will be to get word to the Warlord. If he has gone off on another expedition, it may be no simple matter to locate him."

It would, perhaps, be premature to draw firm conclusions from these two reports, but a connection suggests itself: *Might not the entity Shurlok Homes be the Warlord, who is difficult to locate but terrible in action?*—Further study may clarify this problem.

* * *

Dionnai Count Maivail looked up dizzily. His headache was now well-developed. He got up, and was about to head for the nearest corrector when Angstat came in, looking concerned.

"Sir, two prisoners are missing."

Maivail looked blank. "How can *that* be?"

"No-one knows, sir. They've just vanished."

Maivail started to speak sharply, then suddenly picked up the report he'd just been reading, and thumbed through it hastily. There, staring up at him were the words:

Odwor Jaf Kalas: "We'll get back. Don't worry. As soon as the time's up, he'll *bring us back*."

Maivail looked tensely up at Angstat. "Do you have the names of these prisoners?"

Angstat pulled out a slip of paper.

"Andru Higins and Stefin Delahi."

XV

Swanbeck, Holden, and half-a-dozen others were around the table, cigarette butts smouldering in an ash tray in the middle, pencils, erasers, and slide rules lying here and there, crumpled papers littering the table and the surrounding floor.

"Okay," said Swanbeck, looking up from a drawing, "Now, we've got the design, and, as you say, the thing ought to fit close up against the front of the tailwheel housing. *Maybe* they won't notice it."

"Use a bright aluminum shell," said a slender, sharp-eyed man with a pencil over one ear, "and it ought to be a perfect match. They've got at least three designs of these aircraft. That one with a slanted set of doors to let the tail-wheel out should look just about the same, if we fit this on the kind with *fixed* tail-wheel."

"In flight, maybe," said Swanbeck. "But when it lands, the tail-wheel is going to stick out at a different angle, and there'll be no doors."

"The chances are, they won't notice. We can rig up something that will look like doors."

Holden said exasperatedly, "Look, though, this thing is too far aft. The weight is going to pull the tail down."

Swanbeck said, "Where else can we put it? We can't move it forward. Two models of these aircraft have forward wheels that fold up to the sides of the ship. The other model has fixed forward wheels. But either way, this would stick out like a sore thumb anywhere except in front of that tailwheel."

"I can't help it, Phil, it's *still* going to weight the tail down. If we put it there, we've got to do something to give them some logical reason to explain the sag of the tail."

"That's a thought. But what?"

Holden frowned. "Maybe we could fit it in with that little problem of getting the thing attached in the first place."

Swanbeck nodded. "I'm sure we can think of something. What we need is something to attract their attention and get them to land. Or some way to *force* them down."

The man with the pencil over his ear said, "This may be beside the point, but has it occurred to anyone that these aircraft have a peculiarly simple design?"

Holden said, "What do you mean?"

"Why, look at them. Obviously, it took technical know-how to make them. The things are *wingless*, and made out of some metal so tough that what blows up *our* aircraft merely *dents* theirs. And yet, here's one with *fixed landing gear*. The thing gives me the impression of a hybrid cross between an advanced technology and a simple technology—as if a patched-up World War I Spad mated with the Marsship and here's the offspring. Or as if we were invited to the launching pad of some great technical race, and when their countdown reached 'ignition,' some guy in an asbestos suit tore out to the rocket, and threw a lighted match down a hole. Like you should open up the hood of a car, and inside where the power plant ought to be, there's half-a-dozen squirrels in a treadmill, if you see what I mean."

Holden, scowling, said, "Let's see those photographs again."

Someone slid them up the table, and Holden and Swanbeck bent over them.

Holden used a magnifier on the photo. "That *is* a damned crude landing gear."

Down the table, someone said, "Of course, a great many so-called improvements actually bring their own disadvantages. Maybe these people just like to keep things simple."

"Yes," said someone else. "But the trouble with simple things, is, they make your *procedures* slow and complicated. They're good to fall back on, but if you use them as a mainstay, you're like a man with hammer and handsaw trying to compete with power tools. It just doesn't stand to reason that a race so advanced would use such a simple landing-gear."

"Why not? It's got fewer parts. It's—"

The man with the pencil over his ear said impatiently, "Because the thing is *crude*, that's why. Can you think of any engineer who could see that and leave it as it is? Ye gods, man, can you yourself sit there and look at that big flat washer, with the monster cotter pin to keep it from falling off the end of the shaft, and honestly tell me things have got to be *that* simple?"

Swanbeck glanced at Holden and said hesitantly, "What do you think?"

Holden put the photographs back on the table. "The inescapable fact is, they *do* use them."

"Yes," said someone, "but *why*?"

Frowning, Holden picked up the photograph. "Why should a race so advanced that it can produce supertough metals, force-screens and, apparently, anti-gravity, be so crude when it comes to a landing-gear?"

Swanbeck said wonderingly, "When you get right down to it, that's not the only thing they're crude about. Their strategy and tactics are crude, when you stop to think about it."

"They flattened us."

"Who couldn't, with their superiority? Their procedure has been nothing other than to divide Earth into so many regions, put an expeditionary force down in each region, and methodically pound us flat. All this shows is superiority of *force*."

Holden exasperatedly tossed the photograph back on the table. "Yes, but how did they *get* this superiority of force? They've solved problems we'd have thought impossible. That presupposes a level of technical ability that *couldn't* be maintained by boobs." He looked at the photograph lying in front of him on the table and as if of its own accord, his hand reached out and picked it up.

The crude disc wheel, with its flat rubber tire, looked up at him blandly.

XVI

Maivail studied the guard intently.

"Let me be sure I understand this," said Maivail. "You were ordered to take the prisoners to Lieutenant Sarokel for questioning?"

The guard, pale and trembling, stood at attention.

"Yes, sir."

"You approached the cell door, drew your pistol, and ordered the prisoners to stand back from the door?"

"Yes, sir."

"Did they obey?"

"Sir, I don't know. Something seemed to explode in my breathing passages. There was a coldness, a sense of—like heavy fog—then a—I just don't know. When I could see again, I was on the floor. The prisoners were gone."

Maivail frowned.

"All right, then. You distinctly remember that, when you approached the cell, the prisoners *were there*?"

"Oh, yes, sir."

"Did they make any threatening move toward you?"

"None that I can remember, sir."

"Did you see anyone else around?"

"No, sir. No-one at all, sir."

"Did you hear any movement behind you?"

"No, sir."

"Does your head hurt?"

"No, sir."

Maivail scowled. "When you woke up, the prisoners were gone, but the cell door was closed and locked?"

"Yes, sir."

"The cell door, in other words, was just as it had been when you approached to let the prisoners out?"

"Yes, sir. Exactly."

Maivail glanced at Angstat, who was frowning at the guard. Angstat said, "What of your keys? Had they been removed?"

"They were in the clip at my belt, sir.—The same as before."

Maivail said, "How close were you to the cell door when you lost consciousness?"

"Very close, sir. I was almost ready to open it."

Maivail glanced inquiringly at Angstat, who shook his head. Maivail looked back at the guard.

"You may go."

The guard saluted stiffly and went out.

The Dispatcher of Aircraft marched in, halted, saluted, and stood straight as Maivail and Angstat focused their attention on him.

"Now then," said Maivail, "as I understand your report, no aircraft are missing?"

"No, sir," mumbled the dispatcher.

Maivail said angrily, "Speak plainly."

The Dispatcher stiffened up, increasing his height another quarter of an inch. "Sorry, sir. I mean: 'that is correct, sir. No aircraft are missing, sir.'"

"*No single aircraft is unaccounted for?*"

"That is correct, sir."

"What chance is there that any aircraft could have been boarded by the escaped prisoners?"

"Sir, it's possible. If they got to the loading docks unseen, and if they were careful, they could enter the aircraft without too much trouble. There are always at least a dozen aircraft being loaded. The loading crews aren't particularly vigilant—there's no need for it—and it would be a simple job to get into an aircraft that had just been towed in from Maintenance. Then too, the flying crews always wait till the last minute, and only board the aircraft after the Dockmaster signals that loading is complete. The crew naturally would have no reason to search the cargo section. When they reached the target area, they'd just crank the conveyer and send someone back to keep the 'fusers on the belt and trip the levers as they went by. Also, of course, if the conveyer got stuck, they'd all rush back to heave out the tripped hydrofusers, since a lot of them are set for air-burst, and that cuts the time-margin pretty thin."

"When would the prisoners be spotted?"

"Sir, if they crawled back over the tail wheel and kept their mouths shut, they *wouldn't* be spotted."

"All right. Put three men down there to search each and every aircraft as it comes back in."

"Sir—Since they hit us a while back, we've been short-handed. The only way I can get three men is to take them from the Dockmasters' gang or from a flying crew."

"Take them from a flying crew, then. If you take them from the Dockmaster, it will slow down the whole procedure."

"Yes, sir."

"I want those prisoners."

"Yes, sir."

"All right. That's all."

The Dispatcher saluted and went out.

Maivail glanced at Angstat. "What do you think?"

Angstat shook his head. "It's beyond me, sir. What, actually *did* happen to the guard? If they'd gotten him in close and hit him over the head, I could understand it. But they didn't."

"Well, we've had the whole cleared zone searched, and they just aren't here, so far as it's possible to find out. That means they *must* be outside. No aircraft are missing; therefore they did not steal one, overpower the crew, or otherwise get control of one. That means they're either hiding on board, or—"

Maivail picked up the summarized report of one Lieutenant K. Sarokel, and read, " . . . As soon as the time's up, he'll bring us back." Maivail looked up exasperatedly.

"Get Sarokel up here."

XVII

Swanbeck listened dazedly to the weary voice coming over the phone. Finally, Swanbeck said, "Yes, sir . . . Yes, I understand, sir . . . Yes . . . Yes, sir . . . " Gently he put the phone down.

The room was silent as Swanbeck looked up.

Holden started to ask him what had happened, but, seeing Swanbeck's expression, said nothing.

Swanbeck looked emptily across the room for a long moment, then his eyes came to a focus.

"That was Denver. They've finally gotten enough reports in to piece together a picture."

Holden said hesitantly, "Pretty bad?"

Swanbeck nodded. "You remember, there were eighteen of their invasion forces. We hit six of them pretty hard. They all went into their shells, and nothing much happened for several days. Then they all built these huge doughnut-shaped chambers to protect against another attack like our first one."

"Then," said Holden, "here, at least, they took up where they left off, only with reduced force."

"Yeah. Well, at the six places where they were hit hard enough, they've done just as they've done here. But at the *other* twelve places, they've changed their tactics. Now, instead of attacking troops, missile-launching sites, and other military installations, they're attacking productive facilities of all kinds. One of their aircraft comes over a target, bobs around through a maze of fire from anti-aircraft guns and rockets, then lets go a carpet of bombs. Every last one is a hydrogen bomb. The target and defense facilities disappear. The plane turns around and goes back for another load. What can anyone *do*?"

Holden said in puzzlement, "Even *that's* crude."

Swanbeck looked blank.

"Sure," said Holden, "it's what we were talking about. Their methods are effective, but only because of their overpowering force."

Swanbeck had the expression of a man hit in the stomach.

"I know. It's my own argument. But what's the difference? Sure, they're using their force clumsily. They're laying down a dozen H-bombs when one would do the job nicely. But what of it? They've got H-bombs running out of their ears. What does it matter if your opponent is wasteful of his strength, *if his strength is unlimited*?"

There was an undertone of despair in Swanbeck's voice, and Holden said softly, "He alone is lost who—"

Swanbeck blinked. "Sorry. But this is like fighting a duel with someone who has impenetrable armor, a blade that cuts steel like cheese, and such perfect health that he never tires, and his wounds heal before your eyes. What do you *do*?"

Down the table, the thin man with pencil over his ear gave a dry laugh. "There's a standard answer to that problem. You can't win it *his* way. Instead, squirt tobacco juice in his eye."

Swanbeck started to make an angry retort, then blinked, as did Holden. For an instant, something seemed to quiver in the air, and both men tried to grasp it.

At length, Swanbeck said, "This limpet-mine idea. There's something missing."

"I know it," said Holden, puzzled by his sense of having been close to a solution. "But, aside from the fact that we have to attach the thing—"

"Yes, but look. It's not a *general* solution. Even if we knock out three or four of their bases, what's to prevent the rest from finishing up where they are, then moving over to polish us off? Meanwhile, if only *one* of these invasion forces spots the trick, it can notify the rest. What if, then, they just put an inspection team into action to check incoming planes?"

"It will stop us."

Swanbeck nodded. "Now look. We're in a terrible spot. We've got to beat them fast, because time is on their side. Yet they've got almost an absolute defense. The only place where you can get through that barrier is the spot where their own planes go through. But they're crafty. They've fixed it so there are a number of entrances, open just briefly. And even then, we don't hit their *inner* base."

Holden nodded. "That's why we thought of the limpet mine. If they don't see the mine, and pass the plane through to the interior, *then* it blows up—"

"Yes, but there are too many *ifs*. The first plan we used offered us the possibility of knocking out two-thirds of them. *This* plan only offers us a chance to hit two or three of them. After this they will increase their precautions to the point where we will never be able to get another thing through."

Holden drew a deep breath. "You've got a point."

There was an intense silence as they groped for another solution.

A startled-looking sergeant stepped in.

"Sir, Mr. Higgins and Mr. Delahaye are out here."

Swanbeck and Holden stared at the sergeant.

"Send them in."

XVIII

Dionnai Count Maivail glared at Lieutenant K. Sarokel.

"Do you mean to tell me *they* interrogated *you*?"

Sarokel spread his hands. "Your Excellency, my purpose was to get information from them. A good intelligence officer can learn much from the questions the prisoner *asks* him."

"But meanwhile, you are giving him information."

"But what can he do with the information, sir? A *prisoner*, inside the shield, totally cut off from contact with the outside—"

"This pair seems to have gotten out."

"Sir, as soon as I heard them make that comment about being gotten out, I ceased to give them information. The possibility of their escaping had never occurred to me before."

"I suppose the information you gave them was *true* information?"

"Sir, to give them falsehoods would have complicated the matter hopelessly. These locals were not fools, sir. They were very sharp."

"Are all the prisoners intelligent?"

"Not as intelligent as this pair."

"So, naturally, you gave information to those who are most dangerous."

"The most intelligent are the most dangerous, your Excellency, but they are also the ones from whom the most can be learned, and who can help most if their cooperation is gained."

"Did you gain the cooperation of these two?"

"Not yet, sir. Though I believe I *had* succeeded in dulling the edge of their enmity."

Maivail straightened in his seat. "—In, that is, making friends with and comforting the enemy?"

"Prisoners under interrogation are in a special category, sir. The comfort which they receive is intended to react to our benefit. If they incidentally are made to feel better for the time, this does not harm us. They will speak more freely if they feel that they are speaking with a friend."

"You would as readily shoot one you were friends with, then, as one you had interrogated strictly according to standard procedure?"

"Not at all, sir. I would regret the necessity. But I would do it anyway. My superior would, however, be unlikely to order me to do it, as it would react on future interrogations. I would be less likely to make friends if I knew I might later have to execute the prisoner. My job, sir, is strictly and solely to get information. I may be removed any time, but so long as that remains my job, I do it to the best of my ability,"

Maivail nodded. "Nevertheless, Lieutenant, these prisoners escaped."

Sarokel looked regretful but firm. "Guarding the prisoners is not my job, sir."

Maivail sat back. "Very true. Now, you say you can learn from what questions the prisoners *ask*, as well as answer. And of course, you learn from what you *overhear*?"

Sarokel hesitated. "That depends on circumstances, sir."

"Such as what?"

"Well, sir, prisoners are not always truthful."

"I am speaking now of their conversations while alone in their cells."

"Yes, sir. Since there is a presumption that what is said alone, away from the interrogation room, is unforced and therefore true, it follows that it is exactly there that highly-intelligent prisoners would be most likely to try to deceive the listener."

"Do you mean," said Maivail angrily, "that you *told* them there were concealed receptor heads in their cell?"

"Certainly not, sir. I told them no such thing. And they never asked. I only mean that these were highly-intelligent individuals, and they *may* have guessed the presence of those listening devices."

Maivail drummed his fingers.

"Then you don't believe that conversation you reported?"

Sarokel looked acutely uncomfortable. "I neither believe nor disbelieve, sir."

"You reported it."

"For evaluation by higher authority."

Maivail finally nodded. "All right, Lieutenant. You have defended your actions very creditably. Moreover, I have the impression that you must have formed some sort of coherent picture of this folk, its customs and capabilities. I would like to ask you a few questions."

"Certainly, sir. I'll tell you whatever I can."

XIX

Swanbeck and Holden stared at the two ex-captives. Higgins had his left arm in a sling, and Delahaye was on crutches. Both were grinning.

Swanbeck said, "Do I understand correctly that you have been *inside that barrier*, and nevertheless are now out again?"

Higgins said, "We were inside *both* barriers. They've got one inside the other."

Delahaye added, "The cells we were in were inside a kind of underground building within the barrier."

Swanbeck said, "Did you get to look around in there very much?"

"Sure," said Higgins. "We not only got to look around, but we had things interpreted for us, and explained to us."

Delahaye said, "We interrogated our interrogator. It was a highly worthwhile experience, though a little boring toward the end."

"However," said Higgins, "it seemed worthwhile to stick around. It was educational. Moreover, it seemed a shame to hurt Sarokel's feelings."

Delahaye nodded. "It would have been interesting to bring him out with us. Only fair, too, after he'd shown us around."

"It would have confused the issue, however," said Higgins.

Swanbeck looked around helplessly at Holden. Holden leaned forward. The first problem, he told himself, was to somehow split them apart. He asked solicitously, "How's that leg, Steve?"

"Not bad," said Delahaye. "All considered."

Higgins said, "Those trees only *look* soft."

Holden glanced pointedly at a man down the table, and at the empty chair beside him. He looked back at Delahaye. "Hurt to stand on it?"

"Well—"

Toward the other end of the table, someone cleared his throat. "Come on down here, Steve. We've got an extra chair."

Higgins and Delahaye glanced at each other. Delahaye grinned and walked to the other end of the table, where he was immediately surrounded by eager questioners.

Holden centered his attention on Higgins. "They're pounding most of the civilized centers of this planet to bits."

"Naturally."

"Why? What did *we* do to *them*?"

"Well," said Higgins dryly, "we sent up a pretty good-sized planetary exploration team. What else?"

"Why should that hurt them?"

"Obviously, it made us a potential rival. It proved we had—ah—'hydrofusers'—and so were dangerous."

"What's a *hydrofuser*?"

"The basic tool of Science."

"The *what*?"

"There is no Science without hydrofusers. Hydrofusers are the basic tool of Science. Science is the knowledge of what you can do with hydrofusers, and how to do it. You can only make hydrofusers when you already *have* hydrofusers. When you *have* hydrofusers, and know how to use them, then you have endless power, can control atomic and molecular structure, process metals, set up impenetrable barriers, create contragravity, build correctors, and make *more* hydrofusers. If you have an enemy, you make lots of hydrofusers, pull back a special switch on one side, and dump them on him. When they go off because of instability, that's that."

Holden was leaning forward, gripping the table. "Are you saying they've got some one master tool—Wait a minute. This is a controlled *hydrogen-fusion reactor*?"

"How should they know? And if *they* don't know—"

"Wait a minute. If they *make* such a thing, they *must* know!"

"Why? Can't I use a hammer without knowing the composition of steel?"

"Yes, but you sure can't make *another* hammer without knowing how to do it."

"Oh, *sure*, I've got to know how to *do* it. What you do is, you take four *hydrofusers*, and look up the settings in the Manual, under the Reprostruct Heading. Then you get or make the stated quantities of materials, and using one *other* hydrofuser as a model, you place it in alpha-focus of the other four hydrofusers. Now, you check the settings of the other four hydrofusers, and move the assemblage so the materials are in the beta focus. Then you set the four for cycling instability, and go away for a while. When you come back, most of the materials are gone, and you've got *six* hydrofusers instead of five. Now you run off an extra Manual to go with the new hydrofuser, and there you are. It's easy. That lesson comes in Science 6."

Holden and Swanbeck glanced at each other. Swanbeck looked at Higgins, and said dubiously, "How do you *know*—"

"That we were told the truth?" said Higgins innocently. "Of course, we *don't*. Possibly they planned to let us go after pumping us full of lies, and actually *helped* us to escape."

"Well," said Swanbeck, "it seems surprising that you *did* manage to escape."

Holden, knowing Higgins' distaste for authority, settled back and said nothing. There was a side of Higgins that Holden tried to avoid.

Higgins was now smiling pleasantly at Swanbeck, and let his gaze rest admiringly on the silver star of Swanbeck's rank.

Swanbeck's neck reddened. His hand tightened reflexively into a fist, then relaxed. Abruptly he said, "Go get it."

Higgins looked at him ironically. "Get what?"

Swanbeck made a gesture of disgust. "While you enjoy yourself, the Bugs go on with their plan."

Higgins looked off at a corner of the room, then stood up, and went out without a word.

Swanbeck glanced at Holden. "What started that?"

"He doesn't like authority. Moreover, you doubted his word."

"I had to."

"What does that matter? Just watch yourself, or you may wind up as Exhibit A in the damnedest farce you've ever experienced."

Swanbeck, his face perfectly blank, watched Higgins come back, carrying a dark brown box about the size of a desk dictionary. He set it down directly in front of

Swanbeck, and turned it so that a slot in the brown surface was faced toward Swanbeck. This slot was about half-an-inch wide by two inches long. Beside it to the right was a long orange triangle pointed down, with what roughly looked like Greek letters at the base of the triangle. To the left of the slot was a similar green triangle, pointed up. One corner of the box was torn, crumpled, and stained.

"Now," said Higgins, eyeing Swanbeck alertly, "I'll tell you how we got out of the Bugs' prison." He reached into his pocket and pulled out a small flat toy pistol, and pointed it at Swanbeck. Swanbeck eyed it without a flicker of expression.

"This," said Higgins, "is a squirt gun. Right now, there's a little piece of wax over the nozzle." He covered the end of the gun briefly with one hand, and then held out the hand.

Swanbeck's facial expression didn't change. "Ether," he said.

Higgins nodded. "We went to the base of the ravine, when we left, by Jeep. I'd had trouble starting the engine earlier, and brought this out to try squirting ether in the carburetor. But Andy had already found what was wrong, and so we didn't have any trouble. I stuck this toy gun in the top of my boot when the Bugs got us and they didn't find it. Now, the Bugs have bigger eyes, but look a lot like us. Only they have one peculiar feature. Where you'd expect a nose, they have something that looks for all the world like the intake of some kind of air duct, complete with grille. They not only breathe through this thing, but sounds come out of it. As nearly as we could discover, it isn't equipped with anything corresponding to our sense of smell. There's been terrific devastation in there, and the stench almost knocked us out. Now and then, the Bugs seemed to choke a little, but they were nowhere near as conscious of it as we were.

"Well, to find out if they could smell or not, I put some ether on my handkerchief one time, and whipped it out when the guard came in. He didn't comment, but he lost his balance and looked dazed. When it came time to escape, we gave him a good squirt in the air duct and he passed out. We let ourselves out, hid in a plane, and as we passed low over some pines, we threw this box here out and jumped for the trees. Now, *I* say this is a hydrofuser, which they use to make things, and which they convert to a bomb by a process that puts a little lever here under this slot in the box, where usually there's a blank space."

Higgins looked intently at Swanbeck.

"Now, maybe they fooled us. Maybe we're suckers. Pull the little lever and find out."

XX

Maivail listened attentively but with a deep frown as Lieutenant Sarokel summed up.

"To put it as briefly as possible, sir, I can't escape the impression that these people have a fundamentally different approach from ours. To draw a comparison —Are you familiar with the Great Plateau of Sanar?"

"Where the vacation resort is located? Certainly. I've been there several times."

"Well, sir, you may remember what the approach to it is like. The bulk of that section of the planet is a swamp."

Maivail smiled reminiscently.

"Yes, and the back-to-Nature faddists ride self-powered wheels from the spaceport across the causeway over the swamp, then they climb up the side of the cliff to the Plateau." He laughed. "When I was a boy, I got drawn into a nature-faddist group, and went over the causeway on a wheel. The bugs all but ate us up on the way. Then we arrived at the bottom of a steep cliff, and I looked up, and up, and up. I was tired, hot, and miserable. Around me, the faddists were getting ready, without any delay, to start the climb. Way up the side was a little ledge where we'd spend the first night. The cliff wall in front of us was vertical, like the side of a building.

"Just as we were about to start, there was a shout, then a scream, and I looked up to see several climbers silhouetted against the sky, tied together with a long rope. They plummeted down behind a shoulder of rock, and then I couldn't see them, but I could still hear the scream. There were several of the climbers, but it sounded like just one scream. Then there was this *crump* sound.

"Our own party stood there, looking pale. Some of them were trembling. Then the leader, a burly fellow, said in a matter-of-fact tone, 'That approach never *was* any good. Okay, hook up. Best we start.'

"About that time," said Maivail, "an air-taxi hovered to one side, and the driver called out without much hope, 'Anyone for the top?' I got in that taxi so fast it went sidewise for a while. Well, all the way up, we passed cliff face, and more cliff face, and as that flat vertical wall dropped down past us, I was giving thanks for the one sane impulse that had put me inside the taxi, instead of on a rope with two or three people shaking and trembling in front of me, and that long drop gaping underneath.

Then for some reason, I started to accuse myself of cowardice, and was almost fool enough to go back down again. But fortunately it occurred to me that I was going to the Plateau for a *vacation*, not as part of a combat-infantry training program. I went on up to the top, and had three days vacation more than I'd have had if I'd climbed up and down the side, and I'll tell you, I enjoyed that extra time. I like the Plateau. But not that business of climbing up the side."

Sarokel was listening intently. "Yes, sir. That is exactly the way it is. The land below is flat, but it is bug-infested, soggy, miserable. The land atop the Plateau is also mostly flat, but except for the lakes and pools, it is dry, firm, and smooth. But to get to the Plateau, if you don't have an air-taxi ride, is quite a steep climb, even if you pick the gentlest possible approach."

Maivail nodded. "Not worth it. Unless, of course, you had no other way up."

"And that's it, sir."

Maivail scowled. "What do you mean?"

"That's the comparison. We are *on* the Plateau. These people here are either on the ground below, or climbing up the cliff to the Plateau."

Maivail thought it over. "This sounds fanciful."

"I admit it, Your Excellency. It *is* fanciful."

"But you think it's true?"

"Yes, sir."

"Can you back this up? Can you connect your comparison to actual facts?"

"I believe so, sir."

"Go ahead." Maivail waited tensely.

XXI

Swanbeck and Holden stared at the smooth, olive-green device with its little knobs and dials, at the depleted pile of iron nails at one end of the device, and at the little shiny ingot at the other end.

Holden hesitantly reached out, and picked up the ingot. It felt warm, and very heavy for its size.

Swanbeck, frowning, said, "*Is it—*" He studied Holden's face, glanced at the device, then at the depleted pile of iron.

Holden took out his pocket knife.

"It's comparatively soft," he said. "Not iron. And it's heavy. *Very* heavy. If it *isn't* platinum, it's something just as good."

"Then," said Swanbeck, "are we to assume that this—device—*turned iron into platinum?*"

Holden looked at him quizzically. "*Assume* it?"

"Right. How do we *know* this isn't some kind of shell game? This is the kind of thing people are always falling for. Higgins, here, has been in the hands of these highly-advanced aliens for long enough to have been brain-washed, hypnotized, and programmed to believe anything they choose to tell him. Sure, we see the little barriers form on each end, and we wind up with less iron and this chunk of platinum. Very convincing. What if there's a stack of these platinum samples in there. If we fall for this, our best scientists go off after this red herring, and waste time that should have been spent figuring out how to smash the invaders."

Holden frowned. "Bill?"

A heavy-set man stepped forward. "More nails?"

Holden nodded and picked up the brown case the "hydrofuser" had been in. "Get enough to fill this."

"Sure thing."

Holden beckoned to another of his men. "Hunt up a Geiger counter, will you?" He turned to Swanbeck. "We'd hate to wind up with a home-made, alien-style atom-bomb here."

Swanbeck, who had been examining the little ingot, set it down in a hurry.

Higgins looked blank for a moment, then got up and pulled Delahaye out of a huddle of spell-bound questioners. Higgins' blank look now appeared on Delahaye's face. Both of them, looking serious, pulled over pads and pencils, sat down, and began to sketch the "hydrofuser." Their faces were intent.

Swanbeck glanced at Holden, and nodded, frowning, toward Higgins and Delahaye. Holden studied their faces, then glanced back at Swanbeck. "They've just thought of something. They think maybe they've overlooked something, and they're trying to find out.—That's my guess."

"They look worried to me."

Holden shrugged. "If so, it's their problem. They're conscientious, and we can trust them."

Swanbeck looked unconvinced, but said nothing.

One of Holden's men came in and set down the brown box, filled with nails. Another came in with a Geiger counter, tried it on the little ingot, and shook his head. "Nothing doing."

Holden tried it and nodded. "My wrist watch is a lot worse than this ingot."

Higgins and Delahaye traded drawings, studied them intently, closed their eyes briefly as if giving thanks, and got up simultaneously.

Swanbeck's face remained totally blank and expressionless.

Higgins said, "You had a point there, all right. We *could* have been brainwashed. But if we'd been hypnotized, and taught how to use this thing under hypnosis, it strikes me our memory of it ought to get better than if we'd only learned by seeing it demonstrated.—Well, it isn't so."

Higgins and Delahaye handed Swanbeck their sketches. Swanbeck compared them with the hydrofuser and with each other. In both, the general proportions of the device were good, and the relative positions of most of the dials and knobs were right. But some of the knobs were misplaced, the sizes of the knobs weren't clear, and while the *relative* positions of most were right, the actual positions weren't. The sketches were about what might have been expected from two careful observers who had watched to see how a strange piece of equipment was used, but had had no opportunity to study it repeatedly.

Swanbeck nodded, and handed the sketches to Holden. "But why," he said, glancing from Delahaye to Higgins, "did they show you how this was used?"

Higgins said, "We had a clever interrogator. Why *not* show us? He might guess from our reaction whether we had the thing ourselves."

"Beside," said Delahaye, "as far as he knew, we weren't going anywhere."

Swanbeck glanced at Holden, who said, "They think *we* have it?"

"What *else* could we have slung in through the—ah—'cleared lane' that would have done so much damage?"

Holden looked at the device, then glanced at Swanbeck. "This might explain the crude construction features of their planes. If they have the capacity to produce very tough metals, but not the skills to form and process them—after all, when possible, you finish the surface of stainless steel *before* you heat-treat it—"

"So they make their things in the easiest, simplest shape to form?"

"I'd think they'd *have* to." Holden glanced at Higgins. "Are these people scientists?"

Higgins said dryly, "Sure they are. Science is, 'How to use hydrofusers.' "

Delahaye added, "They have no word for 'research.' "

Swanbeck said, "What about medicine?"

"Correctors," said Delahaye.

"What's a corrector?"

"You get in, it puts you to sleep, and when you wake up, you're better."

Higgins said, "I got a pretty bad cut on my wrist when they captured me. They put me in a 'corrector.' " He held out his wrist. "It doesn't prove anything, because you didn't see the cut. But there's no scar."

Holden said, "Wait a minute. You remember that time you jabbed a length of glass tubing into your thumb? Let's see that hand again."

Higgins came around the table, and held his right hand out. The left arm was in a sling, but the hand was unbandaged. Holden studied both thumbs. "Which one was it?"

"The right, I think."

Swanbeck said, "This was a bad cut?"

"It was deep," said Higgins.

Holden said, "It wasn't dangerous actually, but it left .a distinct scar." He turned Higgins thumb over, then shook his head. "No sign of it now."

Swanbeck scowled. "When did you hurt your arm?"

"Getting out of their plane.—Or rather, in reaching the ground afterward."

Swanbeck said, "I can accept the reality of this— 'hydrofuser'—more readily than I can believe in a thing that automatically cures sicknesses."

Holden scratched his head. "I can't help it, Phil. There was a distinct scar there, and it's gone now." He glanced at Higgins. "How does it work? What's the principle?"

Higgins looked doubtful, and glanced at Delahaye. Delahaye in turn shook his head, and glanced off across the room. Higgins said, "Trying to get theory out of that crew was like trying to squeeze water out of a rock."

Delahaye said, "We tried." He looked at Higgins. "What was the explanation? There was something about an alpha-current, but I think that had to do with how you hooked it up. What was that other—"

Higgins frowned. "I think I remember the gist."

Holden and Swanbeck leaned forward alertly.

Higgins quoted slowly, " 'The device detects by examination a state of affairs which is not healthful, and corrects it.—Naturally, because this is its function.' "

Holden swore.

Swanbeck smiled sourly, then said, "Wait a minute, now. Higgins, did you have any fillings?"

"Yes, of course."

"Any teeth pulled?"

Higgins frowned. "Sure." His face took on the peculiar expression of one using his tongue to feel around the inside of his mouth. Then he said, "This is silly."

Holden frowned. "The device could hardly take out fillings or grow new teeth."

"All right," said Swanbeck exasperatedly. "But let's put some limit to the thing. I'm up to my ears in wonders and mysteries. Find something they *can't* do."

Holden got up. "Okay, Andy, take my seat."

Higgins, scowling furiously, said, "What for?"

"So I can bend your head over the back of this chair.—Just imagine it's time for your dental check-up."

Glowering, Higgins sat down. Delahaye grinned. Holden bent over Higgins, and Swanbeck leaned out across the table with a flashlight. There was a considerable silence.

Holden straightened up, his face showing awe. Swanbeck looked totally blank. Higgins shut his mouth with a click, and looked around anxiously.

Holden said, "That *doesn't* limit them." He glanced at Swanbeck. "You don't think they did *this* with hypnosis?"

Swanbeck shook his head.

Delahaye, grinning, said, "The suspense is killing him. What's he got in there?"

"Thirty-two perfect teeth," said Holden.

Swanbeck sat down. "It isn't going to be enough to *beat* them. Somehow, we're going to have to *capture their equipment*."

XXII

Dionnai Count Maivail felt dazed. "No correctors, either. What do they do when long-term fatigue hits them?"

"They eventually cease to exist physically. As with us in a violent accident. As with savages, animals, and diehard Nature fanatics."

"All of them?"

"Apparently, sir."

"*Whew.* And for sickness and injuries?"

"Specific cures and treatments. Different ones for different troubles."

"How, considering all this, do you explain their managing to put up such resistance?"

Sarokel said cautiously, "They've been climbing for a long time. They haven't quite reached the plateau, but they aren't bog-dwellers, either. They have almost the know-how they need to *build* the things that we rely on as basic."

Maivail looked at Sarokel. "You don't choose to draw any conclusion from that?"

Sarokel stiffened. "No, Your Excellency."

Maivail said, "Then I will have to ask you. You say you think that they are almost ready to make, for instance, hydrofusers?"

"Yes, sir."

"And make them *without already having them*?"

"Yes, sir." Sarokel looked tense.

Maivail leaned forward. "Can *we* make hydrofusers, without first having them?"

Sarokel drew a slow breath. "No, sir."

"Then *they can do what we cannot*?"

"The conclusion, unpleasant as it is, seems inescapable, sir."

Maivail nodded, and settled back. "That's heresy. You remember your teachings:

" '1) In the Beginning was Man, and his hydrofusers, and the Manual, and above all the Ruling Spirit.

" '2) And by command of the Ruling Spirit, Man was taught to use his hydrofusers, and to read the Manual.

" '3) And the use of the hydrofusers according to the Manual is Science, and it is taught that Science sets Man above all other worldly creatures.

" '4) And the use of Science destroys hunger and sickness, and clothes and shelters Man, and defeats his enemies . . . ' "

Maivail paused, then repeated, " '1) In the beginning was Man, *and his hydrofusers* . . . '—How do you get around that?"

"That," said Sarokel uneasily, "may hold for *us*, sir. But these creatures have apparently not yet reached what we look upon as the beginning."

"But they are getting close to it?"

"Yes, sir. Speaking on the basis of what I have deduced from questioning a great many of these people, listening to their secret conversations, and studying the available translated literature, I see no other reasonable conclusion."

"All right. Now then, that brings up two points. First, if they *should* develop our devices, what then? Who will be more powerful then?"

"Well, sir—it's weighted in our favor now. Our base is much broader. But they are no push-over. With our devices added to theirs—It doesn't appeal to me, sir. It looks clear that they would have a considerable local edge. For instance, think what the ability to screen their defenses would mean to them. They would block our attack. Another question that occurs to me is, is our Plateau the highest possible peak of attainment? I hesitate to go on lest I fall into heresy. Yet, even without considering that, it seems clear that if they should somehow acquire our devices while retaining their own—which have already sufficed to damage us severely—"

"—They might win?" said Maivail.

"—In time. It certainly seems reasonable, sir."

Maivail nodded. "If A is only moderately bigger than B, then it follows that A plus B is much bigger than A alone. This is certainly logical."

"Yes, sir."

Maivail nodded, his expression that of a man who bites down on a succulent mouthful, and finds a pebble.

"Very well," he said. "That bring us to the second question." He glanced at a report, then pinned Sarokel with his gaze. "The Warlord."

"Sir," said the lieutenant plaintively, "I have admitted that I simply don't know about that."

"Then relieve your mind of the uncertainty," said Maivail, pulling out a thick wad of reports. "Here are the fellow's memoirs, translated. They came in a little while ago."

Sarokel stared at the top report, which was headed:

—A Translation—
WARLORD OF 12Q2(2P6)11–4
—Personal Reminiscence—

Sarokel looked up. "Why that's the next planet out from this one."

"Exactly. But the description doesn't match our survey report."

"I think I can explain that, sir. After all, if this Warlord *is* a reality, then it follows that the conversations of Higins and Delahi are probably true.—It's the work of a camouflage device made by two scientists of

12Q2(2P6)11–4. I don't remember their names, but it's all down in a report somewhere. The two prisoners were talking about it one day. I remember it very clearly. One of them commented about the heavy gravity on this planet. The other remarked that for that reason the Warlord might better not come direct to here with his forces, but entice us to attack the home planet. His words were 'It will be much handier to kill them there.' But the first said that, of course, this camouflage device Tovas—that was one of the names—had made, would keep us from invading, as it would cast the wrong image on our minds and instruments. Then the second said, in that case, exactly how were they to get their swords into us? The first said not to mention it, but the Warlord some time ago had commissioned one of these scientists that had been mentioned—I think it was the other one—to start his 'automatic factory'—I take it this is an assemblage of a great many hydrofusers, timed by clockwork—to start this huge assemblage turning out space-warships. With these, he said, it would be simple to cut our communications with home, and they could have a colossal space-battle with us when we tried to take off, and *that* would afford everyone ample opportunity for glory. All they would have to do to start this battle would be to locate the Warlord. About this time one of them spoke of the 'wizardry' of the scientist who'd sent them here, and asked the other if he'd noticed what tongue they'd been speaking. That was the end of the information, sir. The other gave an answer that started off something like 'Raj dia Dotor, sij haed . . .' We weren't able to match it up with any of the local languages, and before we could get much more of it down on tape, they disappeared."

Maivail was wide-awake. "They didn't say any more about the timing of their attack, or their tactics or weapons?"

"Nothing, sir. I gathered that all the decisions would be made by this Warlord. We'd have to take into consideration his character."

Maivail had already spent considerable time doing exactly that. It was obvious that the fellow liked nothing better than a good battle. Anxiously, Maivail leaned forward. "Listen, Sarokel, how long do you suppose it will take them to locate him?"

"I have no idea, sir."

With an effort, Maivail suppressed his anxiety, and nodded. "Well, you've been very helpful, lieutenant."

"Thank you, Your Excellency."

Sarokel went out. Maivail sucked in a deep breath, and reminded himself that they didn't *know*, on the basis of actual physical observation that the Warlord was a reality. But, if he wasn't, what was the fellow writing his memoirs for?

Frustrated and angry, Maivail cursed under his breath. What was *he*, Marshal-General Dionnai Count Maivail, Supreme Commander Combined Invasion Force 12, wallowing around in this bog of pestilent half-facts for? Why should *he* have to evaluate these mysteries?

Then he remembered that the cause of the trouble was nothing else than that the original chief resident agent on the planet, who had run into the mess first, had been shot by that second resident agent, Lassig, and the original staff, that had more or less figured out the situation, had then been flashbombed out of existence by this same Lassig. And Lassig's *own* staff naturally had been careful not to arrive at the same solution.

Maivail for an instant saw dancing spots before his eyes. There passed through his mind, with grisly satisfaction, the realization that he would certainly be perfectly justified in taking Lassig, and—

But then it dawned on Maivail that he *couldn't* do that, considering that he had already awarded Lassig a silver nebula for those self-same actions that now caused all this mess.

Maivail's clenched fist struck the desk. With his attention no longer fixed on concrete problems, he became conscious of a rasping sensation in his throat. He seemed, now that he thought of it, to be swimming in some kind of a gaseous sea. The bobbing of this sea caused the distortion of objects in the room. As he watched dazedly, the thing got worse. The desk stretched out like a space-port. The opposite wall shrank into a little thing no bigger than a piece of paper.

Maivail groped amongst the gigantic objects on his desk, and reached out with an arm the size of a spaceship toward the button that would summon his Executive Staff Chief, Kram Baron Angstat.

However, to hit the big button was no easy job. The motion of Maivail's huge arm had to be coordinated with precision, or it would miss the button. As he watched in frustration, the arm cruised past the button well to one side, and when he sent out his mental orders to correct the error, the arm was sluggish in coming back so he could make another try. Worse yet, as was only natural, an arm *that* size was heavy, and it was pulling him off-balance.

Maivail's next attempt, however, landed his gigantic thumb smack in the middle of the enormous button, and then it vaguely occurred to Maivail, as a little, barely-perceptible figure appeared in the tiny door across the room, that something was not right.

Angstat's voice reached him clearly enough. "Sir, there's a new report on this 'Shurlok Homes.' The—*Sir*—Your Excellency! What's wrong?"

Angstat's voice, toward the end, was like booming thunder in Maivail's ears.

"You damned little ant," he said, eyeing the miniature figure that wavered before him on the steeply slanting floor. "Get your voice down to normal or I'll drop a finger on you."

The tiny figure of Angstat registered alarm as Maivail menaced it with a space-fleet-sized hand. Then abruptly, Angstat rushed forward, enlarging enormously as he came.

The room went into fantastic vibrations, with everything in sight changing shape, proportions, and relative position. The enormous desk inverted itself, an incredible feat for an object nearly the size of a planet, and it carried with it the monster chair, still attached to the tiny, far-away floor.

Angstat was urgently saying something, in a voice like ten hydrofusers gone unstable at once, but it suddenly was all too much for Maivail. The whole miserable scene suddenly dwindled and faded—sight, sound, touch, balance—everything—and then he was free of the mess.

XXIII

Swanbeck put the phone down carefully. "Denver thinks we've got damned little time. The Bugs are starting to switch their heavy forces into new territory. Denver can get the ether to us; but to get it inside of warheads, rigged so it will escape into the air, and not flash into flame—"

Holden said, "The only way to get it in there is to *take* it in there on one of those planes."

"How do we do *that*?"

There was a tense silence around the table. Holden glanced at Higgins. "You *jumped* out of their aircraft, and lived to tell about it. How low was it?"

"This one," said Higgins, "was maybe ten feet above the tops of the pines when it slowed and changed course."

Swanbeck said, "That's a rarity. But at night, when they protect the approaches to the Barrier, at times they drop to fifty or seventy-five feet above the ground."

Holden nodded, and turned back to Higgins. "You were *in* the aircraft. Were there any unusual features about the way it was built?"

"Sure. The walls were hard as steel, and about three inches thick."

"The planes have windows. What's the glass like?"

"Like thick armorplate."

Holden exasperatedly moved the stack of heavy shiny ingots to get at the photographs underneath. He studied the plane with fixed landing gear. The crudity of the thing now stared him in the face.

"All right," he said, "what about this undercarriage? Could we shoot an arrow with fishline between the axle and fuselage?"

"H'm," said Swanbeck.

Higgins said, "With fishline attached?"

He glanced at Delahaye, who nodded, then sorrowfully tapped Higgins' arm and his own crutches. Higgins looked momentarily crestfallen, then straightened up. "We can bring them down low. We can probably even get back in, ether and all."

Holden said, "How?"

"We watched them while we were in there. They've got so much power, the average Bug just doesn't need to think very much."

"Go on."

"Well, while we were in there, our interrogator casually asked us about Sherlock Holmes. Was our morale suffering because he hadn't gotten into the fight and helped us?"

Holden blinked, stared at Delahaye, then back at Higgins. "Why did he ask *that*?"

"There's only one conceivable reason. They believe he's a real person."

Swanbeck shook his head, and glanced at his watch. "Time's flying."

"Wait a minute," said Holden. He glanced at Higgins. "What's the connection?"

"We planted the idea that there is an *actual Martian civilization*. If they'll believe the one, why not the other."

"Why should they believe *either*?"

"Because by routine, they've got teams working through our literature—our so-called 'Planetary Records.' Their habit of thought is different from ours, and they haven't got things sorted out yet."

"What's the advantage of fooling them?"

"At best, they're going to think an army of Martians is all set to descend on their rear. At the least, they're going to waste time trying to figure out what's going on."

"And so," said Holden, "how does this help us bring them down?"

Higgins said, "We've got access to ground-effects machines, and the facilities to form medium and small pieces of metal quickly, right?"

"Yes, if we don't get blasted off the map before you get to the point."

"Okay," said Higgins. "That should do it." He pulled over a piece of paper, sketched rapidly, leaned forward, and began to talk in a low earnest voice.

XXIV

Dionnai Count Maivail opened his eyes to see Angstat looking in the opening of the corrector.

Maivail, feeling like himself again, climbed out. "How long was I in, this time?"

"Nearly two days, sir."

They started down the corridor.

Maivail said, "*That long?*"

"Yes, sir. I've been in and out myself. There's some kind of sickness going around. We've had to triple the number of correctors to keep up with it."

"What's the cause?"

"The usual sir. It's something in the food, or the air, or something. The details don't matter."

They stepped around the mouldering odds and ends of a corpse lying in a cross-corridor, where the earlier blast had burned away a ramp leading to the surface.

Maivail said, "This ought to be cleaned up."

"I know it, sir. But there have been so many more important things to do—" Angstat spotted a technician idling along down the corridor. The fellow looked as if he had all the time in the universe. "You there!" bellowed Angstat.

"Sir?"

"Come here a minute . . . You see that. Shovel it into the corner with the rest, and polish up this space on the floor here."

As the technician leaped to obey, Angstat rejoined Maivail. "You're right, sir. It's bad for morale to let our standards down. I'll see that the policing of the area is kept up to regulations from now on."

Maivail nodded approval. "Now," he said, "to more important matters."

"Yes, sir."

"Have we located those two missing prisoners?"

"No sign of them, sir. They've vanished into thin air."

"Any indications of—ah—hostilities—from the fourth planet?"

"Not a solitary thing, sir. They probably haven't managed to locate this Warlord."

"How's the conquest of the locals coming along?"

"Well, sir, there's this sickness, but, on the whole, it's coming along splendidly. We've got production facilities in two-thirds of the districts reduced practically to rubble." He hesitated. "However—in the rest of the districts, sir—I regret to say that there have been untoward incidents."

"Such as what?"

"Well, for one thing, every place where the locals' original counterattack hurt us, there's been some variation on this sickness. Everybody is, has been, or will be, a good deal below par. Up to two-thirds or even more of the personnel have been knocked out at a time, and we were already well below strength—"

"Get to the point," snapped Maivail, "what's happened?"

"Due to overfatigue and sickness, sir, the Traffic Controllers have evidently gotten a little careless at times, and have varied the order of opening the cleared lanes according to a pattern, instead of by pure chance. The locals have promptly figured out the pattern and shot things in."

"How much damage?"

"Base 4 got hit with what must have been half-a-dozen destabilized hydrofusers, and lost twenty aircraft and their crews. The lanes through the inner barrier were closed, however.

"Base 6 had some kind of big local aircraft flash in, and pile up against the inner barrier. Fortunately, nothing happened.

"Bases 8 and 11 were bombarded with drums that burst apart to let out swarms of flying insects. These insects sting, and they have proved extremely troublesome. We've switched Groups 14 and 17 into the cleared zones of Bases 8 and 11, and set them down under protection of the 8 and 11 shields. The men, however, refuse to debark, because of these flying insects."

"Are the insects inside the inner barrier?"

"Unfortunately, sir, they are. The inner lane was opened up according to rule, as soon as the outer lanes were all closed. The bugs came through.—It's chaos in there."

"Well—We should survive that, even if it *does* keep the correctors busy. Is that all?"

Angstat scowled. "Not quite, sir. There's still Base 9."

"What happened there?"

"Well—They were hard hit by the sickness." Angstat brushed away flies as they passed a cross-corridor. "And

I suppose they got pretty careless. The Traffic Controller was found stiffened up with a horrible grin on his face, and it took six days in the corrector to bring him around."

"*Six days!*"

"Yes, sir. It's unprecedented, sir. Well, while they were in this state, with everyone either getting in or out of a corrector, they forgot the cleared lanes completely, and a party of locals came in on a rope. Things got pretty ugly in there, sir."

Maivail moodily turned this event over in his mind. "They threw the locals out, didn't they?"

"*They* didn't. We shifted Group 15, and Group 15 threw them out."

"Then that's taken care of."

"Yes, sir. Except that now Group 15 has apparently caught the sickness. They're fabricating extra correctors at top speed, and they can hardly keep up with the demand."

Maivail thought it over. The enemy productive and war-making capacity was now pulverized in two-thirds of the war zones. However, roughly a quarter of the overall invading force had been knocked out in the initial enemy counterattack and the result of the various sequels was to tie up an additional three full Invasion Groups, plus various odds and ends. The effect was to reduce him to about fifty percent of his strength.

"Oh," said Angstat. "There was one other thing. I was about to tell you, sir, when you got sick."

"What's that?" said Maivail, frowning as he stepped over a thick stream of ants crossing the floor.

"We've found out more about Shurlok Homes."

Maivail had forgotten that. He ducked a large greenish beetle winging down the corridor, then opened the door leading to his office.

Inside, several staff members were brushing away clouds of flies as they ate their lunch. There were flies in the air and on the table, flies landing on the regulation biscuit, flies swimming around in the regulation soup. The staff ate on stoically.

Maivail dismissed the triviality from his consciousness, reminding himself that warriors must be prepared to endure such irritations. He focused his thought on more important matters.

"Is this Homes the same as the Warlord?"

"No, sir. They are separate individuals. But we now have proof positive that the locals *do* have correctors, though evidently in limited numbers."

Maivail sat down at his desk. "How so?"

"Well, sir, we've calculated that this Homes is around a hundred years old, or possibly more. On this planet, seventy years is about the average life-span. Yet the comments of the locals show that they regard Homes as being possessed of full vigor and all his faculties. It follows that he must possess the use of a corrector, to overcome the long-range cumulative fatigue."

Maivail brushed away a gnat. "Aren't we being excessively clever, Angstat? Why not simply *ask* the locals about this fellow?"

Angstat shook his head gloomily. "We've tried it. That brings on these choking fits. Then, afterward, when we listen to their conversation, first they talk as if he didn't really exist, then they talk as if he *does* exist. The best the interrogators have made out of that is that he's away on a long trip. We haven't got anywhere with that approach, sir."

Maivail said exasperatedly, "Listen, we've never *seen* this Homes. *We've never seen* the *Warlord*, either, though at least there has been *some* proof of his existence. Now, we've got trouble enough without complicating the situation with these mysterious beings, who haven't declared themselves, anyway. Let's forget this Homes, entirely. As for the Warlord, what we need to do is just keep an eye on the fourth planet. Once we have *these* people *here* conquered, then we can handle *him*." Maivail, still feeling fresh from his stay in the corrector, added decisively, "The devil with all these unseen entities." He waved away circling flies. "If you can't even see a thing, how can it hurt you?"

"Now, Angstat, we'll want to shift these remaining Invasion Groups to new cleared—"

The door burst open. "Sir! General Angstat!"

Maivail looked up in astonishment.

A staff member, spoon in hand and a haze of flies around him, pointed urgently into the other room. "Sir, an alien airship—"

Maivail snapped, "Exactly what is unusual about that?"

"This one, sir, matches the projections for the aircraft of that 'Warlord!'"

Maivail and Angstat catapulted into the next room and hurled staff members in all directions to get at the screen. Sure enough, there, gliding behind a nearby hill, was a fantastic airship, with short masts, rigging, weird guns fore and aft, a cabin amidships, and copper-colored warriors in steel and leather on the deck and at the guns.

"All right," snapped Maivail, glaring around at the apprehensive staff. "Now finally we'll get to the bottom of this. Order up Groups 2, 5, 16 and 18 to guard the planet against external attack. Groups 7 and 10 are to stand by in immediate reserve. Now, get every troop carrier and combat aircraft we can man out there, and bring me in as many of those soldiers as you can get your hands on!"

"Sir," quavered a staff member, "might it not be more prudent—"

Maivail lashed out and knocked him over a desk into the corner.

"Groups 3 and 13," said Maivail, "will act as reserve for Groups 4, 6, and 12, which will reconnoiter the planet for any further sign of these intruders. Headquarters Group will devote itself entirely to capturing these soldiers. *Move!*"

The staff sprang into action.

"Sir," said Angstat, as soon as they were alone in Maivail's office. "We may end up with two wars on our hands."

"That matter isn't exclusively up to me. And if it happens, I intend to find out about it before we get maneuvered into a nutcracker. Get the Planning Staff at work on the quickest route out of here."

"Yes, sir."

Maivail sat down and drummed his fingers on the desk. What if there *were* a Warlord, in control of the fourth planet. What if Shurlok Homes *did* exist, at the peak of his powers through possession of his own corrector? There across the room in a file case was a report that listed other formidable entities that seemed to live a charmed life. Some of these beings possessed their own armies. Some lived on distant planets but might roar in anytime with a space fleet. Some could change their form at will, others had peculiar powers that it stopped the thought-processes to merely think of. What would he, Maivail, do if his men ran into a being that whizzed through the air under his own power, could not be dented by explosives, and squashed steel in his bare hands?

"Well," he told himself, "this is the acid test. We'll just see what this Warlord can actually do."

Maivail settled back, noticed a new report in the "In" square on his desk, and picked it up. The title read: "Latest Conclusions on the Social Structure of the Local Inhabitants of 12Q2(2P6)11–3." Scowling, Maivail glanced through it, then straightened up hopefully. The report was written in fairly plain language, did not generally use four long words when one short one would do, and, on the surface, at least, gave no sign of that cold rebuff to the intruder upon the sacred mysteries. It appeared possible to *read* it, not decode it, and it even had an introduction at the beginning, and a summary at the end.

Eagerly, Maivail read: "From the facts given, namely: 1) The very high level of technical skill evidenced by the locals; and 2) The apparent existence of recognized 'Immortals' such as the famous Homes, and the self-admitted Immortal known as 'The Warlord,' it becomes evident that this planet logically *must* have hydrofusers and correctors.

"But it is equally clear, from the short lives of the average citizens, that these correctors are not generally distributed. Their existence is, in fact, not widely known, and the long lives of the Immortals are apparently explained away under one pretext or another.

"Why?

"This report concludes, from a careful study of the available translated documents, that a small group of exceptionally competent citizens maintains these devices for their own use, elects new members to join the group, and withholds knowledge of the device from all unqualified outsiders.

"This conclusion harmonizes obvious local facts with a basic proven rule of Science: *A hydrofuser cannot be made except by those already in possession of hydrofusers and skilled in their use.* Also, correctors cannot be made save by the use of hydrofusers.

"The question immediately arises: 'Why are hydrofusers and the devices based upon them withheld from the bulk of the local inhabitants?'

"Two answers present themselves:

"1) The Immortals wish to gather the fruits of diversity which the lack of these ultimate tools forces the local inhabitants to develop.

"2) More basically, the nature of the bulk of these inhabitants is so chaotic, undisciplined, divided, violently ambitious, and short-sighted, that the possession of these ultimate basic tools would create chaos. To avoid disorganization, the Immortals restrict the ultimate tools to their own use, but permit the wide-spread use of secondary group-sources of similar but lesser potency.—Thus a degree of organization and harmony is maintained. If the ultimate tools were to be generally released by the Immortals, they would put into the hands of innumerable diverse, mutually jealous factions the means for each other's destruction and their own aggrandizement. Chaos could be expected to follow in a very brief time.

"We submit that this explanation is simple, logical, in accord with the known facts, and is therefore right."

Maivail felt a great wave of relief, which vanished with a shout from outside.

Angstat ran into the room.

Into the outer office burst copper-hued warriors in metal-and-leather, the cut ends of cords still fastened to their wrists, their holsters and scabbards empty, but small pistols in their hands. There was no noise, no flash, but the staff and a few desperate guards went down right and left.

Maivail got over his moment of paralysis. "*Lock that door!*"

Angstat slammed it shut and locked it.

Maivail smashed a glass plate over a red button inset into his desk. He jabbed the button twice, and the blare of a horn resounded in an intricate pattern that commanded: "Retreat, fighting, to the ships."

There was a heavy crash against the door.

Maivail yanked a desk drawer open, tossed an extra gun to Angstat, jammed one under his own belt, picked up a hydrofuser from a little stand, swiftly reset it, and cut a hole through the wall into the corridor.

There was another heavy crash against the door, but now Maivail and Angstat were in the corridor.

Throughout the underground command center, the call resounded, and around Maivail and Angstat, the men were retreating, clutching guns, captured swords, broken chair legs, anything. At every cross-corridor, they shouted, "Look Out! *The Warlord!*" Halfway to the ships, there was a panic as someone sighted a tall figure and screamed "There's Shurlok!"

Cursing savagely, Maivail and his officers finally got the disorganized horde into the usable ships. Before anything else went wrong, Maivail slammed down the switch that relayed the order to open a lane in the outer screen. The relay performed its task, and Maivail ordered, "Lift ships!"

Then they were up and out of the chaos.

Angstat said, "Now what, sir?"

"I won't fight two planets at once," said Maivail, "but we aren't beaten yet."

"Wouldn't it be better to get out of here before that space fleet turns up?"

"Not yet. We have to land one final blow."

XXV

Swanbeck stumbled out into the open air.

"Ye gods, what a stench! How did they live in that slaughterhouse?"

"With no sense of smell," said Holden, "and a universal cure on hand, I suppose it's about what you'd expect."

The two men walked a long distance off, and looked back at the huge glistening doughnut-shaped barrier. Swanbeck cleared his throat.

"Here, at least, is one impregnable defensive position that *we* own. Complete with power-source, controls, cylindrical flying warships, and dozens of 'hydrofusers,' 'correctors,' and other fantastic devices, plus enough prisoners so we can wring the information out of them, and find out how to *use* these things."

Holden nodded. "What a pesthole it is, though."

Back at the Barrier, a big bundle was being lowered down on the end of a rope. It was easy to imagine the grisly load within. Several men dropped out and staggered off several hundred yards to get a breath of air.

"Okay," said Swanbeck, "now let's get the news back to Denver." He faced up the long slope, beckoned, and pumped his arm up and down.

There was a roar, and a Jeep came down the slope. They got in, and heaved and crashed up the hill, down the other side, and along a long dusty road, with empty scabbards clattering, and metal ornaments digging into their flesh. On the way, Swanbeck said with relief, "Those boys are on the run. We're over the worst of this."

Holden struggled to pinpoint just what it was about the statement that bothered him. When they got out of the Jeep, Swanbeck was confident, and Holden had his fingers crossed. They walked away from the road along the rocks, careful to leave no trail that would give away their hiding place. The Jeep drove on.

They were no sooner inside than a worried corporal hurried up to Swanbeck.

"Sir, Denver's on the line. They got a hot coal down their neck."

Swanbeck, scowling, picked up the phone. "Hello . . . Yes, it came off beautifully . . . No . . . No, sir. Perfect . . . They've what? Lifted ships? . . . Yes! Yes, sir . . . What? . . . What's that, sir?" Swanbeck's buoyant tone faded into incredulity. "What do they expect to gain by *that*? . . . Yes, sir . . . Well, what can we . . ."

Holden waited for the worst. Swanbeck put down the phone.

Holden said, "Now what?"

"Let's go outside. Maybe it's started here now."

"Maybe what's started here now?"

"Their damned clincher."

Holden swallowed. He was afraid to ask anything more.

Once outside, Swanbeck gazed up at the sky. "There's one."

Holden squinted. Forty or fifty feet overhead, a little white piece of paper drifted down.

They watched it descend, then Swanbeck picked it up. "Yes. That's it."

He handed it to Holden, who read:

—Fellow Creatures—

For ages you have been victimized by your leaders, who have possessed, unknown to you, marvelous tools capable of making each of you healthy, rich, and powerful beyond your dreams.

They have suppressed these tools.

We have invaded, not to conquer you, but to smash the murderous grip of these leaders at your throat. *We are determined that these marvelous tools shall be yours . . .*

To prove what we say, we have left on your planet many of *our own* tools, and we are preparing simplified Manuals in your own languages to show you how to use them.

We are your friends.

We make no charge, we put no price on these precious gifts.

You can be forever healthy, you can make what you will, you can conquer gravity, go anywhere, have perfect privacy, amass riches in quantities you have never dreamed of.

Only, you must see that treacherous leaders do not again take away from you what is yours.

***

Holden looked up dizzily.

Another paper was drifting down a hundred feet away.

Swanbeck said sourly, "Look there."

An olive-colored case, apparently degravitized to make it light and buoyant, drifted to the earth near the road, and tumbled slowly along in the wind.

Swanbeck and Holden caught it, opened it up, and found the familiar device inside, complete with Simplified Manual.

Holden opened the Manual, and read aloud, "How to Create A Privacy Shield, How to Make Gold, How to Reproduce Food Without Work, How to Make a Corrector and Be Forever Healthy, How to Defend Yourself, How to Make *More* Hydrofusers, and How to Blow Up your Enemies . . ."

Dizzily, Swanbeck and Holden looked at each other.

XXVI

Dionnai Count Maivail, moving slowly at high altitude as the stream of hydrofusers poured out of his ships, explained the situation to Kram Baron Angstat.

"Offer a man, long deprived, his fondest wish, and will he refuse it? First, there will be fighting because there aren't enough hydrofusers to go around. Then there will be all kinds of private sanctuaries where they can do whatever they want, because of the shield, and can escape the most obvious consequences, because of the correctors. Only after ages of working at cross-purposes, and after exhausting all manner of appetites and delusions, will they begin to see the flaws. Meanwhile, they will forget their other skills. The result, Angstat," he said enthusiastically, "will be utter stagnation."

A sudden thought occurred to Maivail. He didn't voice it. But a glance at Angstat's blank wondering look showed that it had occurred to him, too.

Dumfounded, Maivail thought, "Could something like this have happened long ago to *us*?"

XXVII

Swanbeck, Holden, Delahaye, and Higgins, crouched over the instruction books. Off to one side, a bilingual captive with a gun in his ribs eagerly poured out a flood of information from the full-sized, unsimplified Manual.

Half-a-mile away, a few iridescent small-sized half-globes wondered off across the valley, momentarily flickering out from time to time as their owners paused to look around.

Swanbeck glanced up and swore. "Look at them! Over the hill in broad daylight! Unpunishable desertion!"

Holden pointed to the Manual. "How do we figure *this* out. Less talk and more thought."

Swanbeck subsided angrily, took a final cold look at the walking AWOL's under their privacy shields, and returned to the instructions with a will. What had to be done, he reminded himself, was to somehow figure out roughly just what was inside that case, and build the thing into the system of accumulated knowledge before it turned into a craze and *replaced* that knowledge.

And, he told himself, no matter how rough the road, *never give up*.

XXVIII

Dionnai Count Maivail squinted at the stacks of trans-lated human documents. The fleet itself was well out now from the dangerous planets, but Maivail could see that the permanent superiority of his people would be assured only when they added the captured know-how of the earthmen to their own Science.

Somehow, when he got back home, Maivail was going to have to put this idea across without getting disassembled for heresy in the process.

For now, his problem was just to absorb the substance of a few dozen of these translated documents, so he could get a general picture of what passed for science on this planet. That would enable him to present his argument logically when the time came. Surely, he told himself, there should be nothing hard about *that*.

He massaged his throbbing brow, closed this latest report, shoved it aside, and selected a fresh one.

Time crept by.

Isolated fragments of information from various reports swam through Maivail's consciousness:

" . . . elevated to 350° F, with agitation to maintain a uniform temperature throughout. This produces first-settle plaster. This is the half-hydrate $CaSO_4$, $1/2H_2O$. The anhydrous second-settle plaster is produced by . . . "

" . . . a low-pass filter for the noise, assuming, that is, that the signal can be satisfactorily approximated by the expansion $K_0 + K_1t + K_2t_2 + \ldots K_nt^n$, in which . . . "

" . . . 4,000 to 5,000 psi. The 70–30 mix can be fired under-watered, or cake to . . . "

" . . . the heavier type of these two kinds of mesons has a mass 273 times that of the electron; this is the *pion*. The lighter *meson* has a mass 207 times that of the electron; this is the *muon*. The *pion* and the *muon* may be both either *positively* or *negatively* charged. Spontaneously, a charged *pion* (if, that is, it is not previously captured by an atom) changes into a . . . "

Maivail looked up dizzily. He promised himself that if this headache got any worse, he would head for the nearest corrector. In fact, it might not be a bad idea to have one set up right here in his office, where it would be handy.

Doggedly, Maivail pulled out the next report, and opened it at random:

"... *if* f(x) is finite and single-valued in the interval pi>x>-pi and has only a finite number of maxima, minima, and discontinuities in this interval, *then* ..."

Maivail's head suddenly threatened to blow wide-open, and he lurched to his feet.

He knew the predicament he'd created for the humans was tough. Managing things on the Plateau was no easy job.

But something told Maivail that relearning how to climb was worse yet.

CAPTIVE LEAVEN

In the dripping blackness, Dane turned slowly till the sliding sound grew loud in his earphones. He heard the faint hum that told him he was facing the source of the sound directly. Gently he squeezed the trigger.

There was a hiss that dwindled fast, then grew loud again in the phones.

Dane heard a dry cough and the clatter of equipment. He felt the magazine of the gun, and the three little studs told him there were three shots left. He moved his head, heard the slap of branches and the faint sounds of men moving through the brush out of range behind him.

Nearby in a fan tree, a nightwatcher began its liquid warbling.

Dane dropped to the ground and crawled away through the brush toward the distant roar of the surf.

A buzzing whir circled and criss-crossed behind him. Back in the forest, someone shouted impatiently. A bat-like flitting sound went past overhead, and Dane flattened himself against the earth.

There was a brilliant flash. The ground jumped under him, and there was a blast that hurt his ears. He lay still as dirt pattered down.

A voice shouted, "To your left! *There!*"

Dane pressed himself flatter.

There was another flash, farther away.

Dane turned slightly to glance up at the sky. He pried the face of his watch away from his wrist, and the glowing, slowly-turning numerals told him he had five hours left till dawn.

He listened carefully, then rose on one knee.

There was a sliding slipping sound in the brush in front of him.

He turned his head slowly, and rested his forearm on his bent knee as he carefully centered the gun on the sound and squeezed the trigger.

This time there was a gagging, and a wild thrashing that came to him in full detail before the cutout left him with only normal hearing. He took a shaking breath, then froze as a brilliant flash lit the brush and dead tree-limbs in a brief white glare.

The light died away, and Dane listened carefully to the darkness ahead of him. There was no sound of motion. He rose carefully and listened behind him. A multitude of men were rustling and clinking through the brush.

Dane turned again, felt of the two little studs on the magazine of his gun and started carefully in the direction of his last shot.

Overhead, the loud cry of a sea skimmer swept past, repeated over and over with the last note off key.

Dane dropped to the ground, his heart beating fast.

A pinpoint of light grew overhead, casting its pale glow over forest and wasteland. A glider swooped past, headed inland from the sea.

Dane counted ten slowly as he unclipped a bird's-egg grenade from his belt, pulled the safety pin with his teeth, and lobbed the grenade out into the open.

There was a bright yellow flash.

From inland came shouts, the blast of a whistle, and scattered bursts of firing.

Dane tightened the strap of his light pack, put his gun flat on the ground, put grenade belt and listening apparatus on it, then forced back a plate on the side of the stock. He felt for a lever underneath, and waited tensely.

A second glider swooped down.

Dane thumbed back the lever, dodged through the brush, and sprinted for the glider.

A curved hatch on the glider swung open.

Dane swung a leg over, dropped inside and lay flat, gasping for breath.

There was a sharp blast as his equipment blew up.

Something whined past overhead.

The hatch dropped and latched.

There was a low roar. The glider rocked, rushed forward and up.

Through a transparent plate by his face, Dane could look down and see shadowy running figures on the ground below.

Then the dim light faded behind them and they were over the sea.

A voice spoke urgently, and for an instant, Dane didn't understand the words, "Did you get it?"

"Two," said Dane carefully. "In my pack."

"Good work."

Dane lay still, wondering that he had been away so long that his own tongue sounded strange to him. Then the blackness outside seemed to merge with a bone-weariness in Dane's limbs, and he fell through layers of darkness into a deep exhausted sleep.

He gradually became conscious of a low throbbing roar that grew, then faded, and of a rushing swooping motion like that felt by a man on skis. He drifted, half-asleep, till someone shook him by the shoulder and pointed out a double line of dim blue lights in the darkness below.

"There's a bimarine down there. We're going to try to land on it."

"I see."

"If we don't make it, they'll light the underside of the middeck. Swim toward it. They'll have boats out."

"All right."

"Here we go."

The glider seemed to hang motionless, then the row of lights tilted and grew larger. They slid past below. Then there was a roar in his ears, a moment of swirling blackness, and the lights were rushing toward him, flashing past on both sides. The glider tipped, bounced, and whirled to a stop. An instant later, the hatch was snapped open, and strong hands lifted Dane out.

There was a chill breeze in his face. The blue lights dimmed and faded out. Someone spoke out of the darkness, "Did you get him?"

"Yes, sir."

"I can't see a thing in this gloom. Hello, Dane?"

"Right here," said Dane.

"Put out a hand. We've changed the design of these ships since you left. You don't want to go over the side after you've lived through that."

Dane reached out, found a rough, calloused hand, and let himself be led past a place where the sound of rushing water came up from below. They went across a swaying gang-plank, along a deck and into a dark corridor. Then a door opened into a small well-lighted room lined with books and maps. Two men at a round table to one side looked up as he came in. One man wore the uniform of a general. The other was a civilian, a man Dane recognized as Hoth, little changed from his appearance eight years ago, when Dane had seen him last. Both of the men looked tense.

Dane's guide, a bearish man in the uniform of a naval captain, said to Dane, "Here I leave you to a fate worse than life with the Flumerang—An interrogation by experts."

The general said, "Don't go, captain."

"I have to. Half their navy may be after us." He went out.

Dane glanced at Hoth, saw the suspense on the man's face, and wordlessly unbuckled his pack. He swung it free of his shoulders, set it on the table and loosened the straps. He pulled out a roll of khaki-colored clothing, and carefully spread it out. Four small metal boxes were inside. He opened them and took out the soft cloth padding.

In two of the boxes were pairs of thick, plastic-rimmed spectacles. In the other two lay what looked like large beetles. One of these beetles was dull brown and ordinary in appearance. The other was blue and gold, with large strong jaws, as if for fighting.

The general carefully picked up the big-jawed beetle. He touched an edge of curving jaw with his finger. The flesh cut neatly, and a drop of blood oozed out.

Hoth said, "Where did you get them?"

"At the factory where I worked. I short-circuited a power line to get into the shipping section unnoticed."

"What was your job there?"

"I was in final assembly."

Hoth leaned forward. "Then you know how to put them together?"

"These two types. There may be others."

"Have you ever used one of them?"

"I stole one earlier, and practiced with it."

"The control unit is in the glasses?"

"Yes."

Hoth studied one of the pairs of glasses. Inset in the plastic were tiny bright oblongs. "Do you know how this works?"

"I know how to use it. But that's all."

"Can you show us?"

Dane nodded and sat down by the table. He took the heavy, plastic-framed glasses and slid them on. For a moment, there was a distortion due to the slight curvature of the lenses. Then he tipped the brownish beetle out of its case and saw two superimposed scenes, as in a double exposure. One scene was his normal view of the two men before him. The other was an image of a sort of dark rolling plain.

Dane held his attention steadily on the second scene. His normal vision faded, and the rolling plain grew distinct and clear. He felt an instant's fear, and an urge to draw back. He held his attention steady. Then he seemed to be in the midst of the rolling plain. He willed himself to rise. The unfamiliar scene fell away, and came into perspective as the unrolled khaki clothing from his pack. For an instant, Dane hovered before the general and Hoth, his vision much the same as it normally was except that things seemed flatter, and the details unnaturally clear. There was no sound, and little sense of effort, so that it all seemed dreamlike.

He flew up, over the heads of the men, glanced at the shelves of books, circled the room like a swimmer gliding through a huge tank of clear water, then swung back over the desk and dropped down onto it.

Now, he reminded himself, came the end of the pleasant part and the beginning of the tricky part.

He turned to face a comparatively dim and featureless corner of the room, and tried to shift his attention back to his normal vision.

Nothing happened.

He tried steadily and firmly to will his attention back to his normal vision.

He couldn't do it.

He flew up to go to a darker corner of the room, and found himself facing a motionless figure wearing a pair of glittering plastic-framed glasses. This figure had a look of waxy immobility, its gaze remote and trancelike.

Dane fought off panic, dropped into a dark corner and waited tensely.

There was a total stillness, and after a long time a faint glimmer of light in the darkness. Dane held his attention firmly on that glimmer. The glimmer grew to a patch of light, then to vague forms huddled together. Dane focused hard on these forms, trying to make them clear and distinct. He could vaguely see two men seated at a table. Slowly his vision cleared, sharpened, and he saw them plainly and saw nothing else.

Dane's hands and feet tingled. He drew in a long deep breath, took off his glasses, stooped and found the beetle. He put it in its box and looked up.

Hoth said, "Is it all right for us to try it?"

Dane explained what he had just been through, and Hoth nodded. "We'd better try that later." He glanced at his watch, and said sympathetically, "You must be tired out."

The general said, "I would like to ask just one question." He looked at Dane intently. "*When?*"

Dane thought a moment. "I'd guess about a year."

"Why not in a month?"

"I can only judge by the way they're expanding their productive facilities, and by the fact that they've only begun to prepare the attitudes of their people for a war with us. Then too, they're bound to think that their production of these devices will make them much stronger in a year than us."

The general nodded. "That's how we figure it."

Hoth said, "I'll show you to your cabin. Tomorrow will be strenuous, so you'll need plenty of sleep."

Dane lay down and promptly fell asleep listening to the throb of the ship's engines. He was soon jarred awake by a violent concussion. He heard a howl of machinery and a creak from steel deck and bulkheads. He gripped the cot with both hands and hung on as the ship swerved sharply.

The blast and shock seemed to go on forever. When it ended, Dane found himself worn out, but unable to sleep. His thoughts drifted to the last time he had seen

Hoth, in a coastal trader working toward the southwest peninsula of Flumerang. Hoth had been urgent in explaining to Dane that his job was an important one.

"Remember, Dane," said Hoth earnestly, "each year we slip ashore at various points on the globe, two-to-three-hundred men and women whose only purpose is to act as potential probes. Many of these people we don't hear from for years. They settle down in an identity prepared for them by our people already established. When they're sure of their dialect and local background, they drift inland. If nothing happens, they become part of the population they're assigned to. Traders, merchants, technicians—even local government officials. It then seems like a pointless waste of effort on our part. But if they scent something, or if we do and call for action, then all the time and work pays off."

"I understand," said Dane.

"Good. And bear in mind, it's a wearing thing to feel that your life is ticking away while you wait for something that may never happen. *Don't* wait. Live your life and make yourself useful. Remember, the people of Flumerang are just as human and worthwhile as our own. But in case you sense anything, or if we call for you, *keep yourself ready*."

Lying in the blackness of the cabin on the ship headed for home, Dane thought over his experiences in Flumerang and was surprised to realize that what Hoth said had been exactly true. Regardless of what the official propaganda of both sides would say in a few weeks or months, the people of Flumerang were much like his own people. There was, it was true, a certain combination of earthiness and innocence that differed from the dry realism he had grown up with; but even in this there were similarities.

Dane remembered walking one evening across a meadow with a dark-haired girl who suddenly stopped to look up at the stars. "I wonder what's up there?"

"Who knows?" said Dane.

"My grandmother says there are people like us, just like on the other side of the world. Even the priest says the *Fiery Ship* sailed from a star."

The back of Dane's neck tingled. The legend of the *Fiery Ship* was one he had often heard at home. Unbidden, a rhyme Dane had learned as a child sang itself in his head:

"A ship of fire sailed the sky
To bear its gifts to you and I
From a star far away,
For that ship, dear God, we pray."

Dane was trying to phrase the rhyme in the Flumerang tongue to repeat it to the girl, when she gripped his hand. "Priest says the crew of the *Ship* is still living with us, and some day we'll all be children of the ship and they will take us back to the star with them. Do you believe that?"

Dane rolled over in the dark cabin and sat up.

After a long moment, he lay back down again, and finally fell into a troubled and restless sleep.

He woke up with a feeling of impatience and dissatisfaction. He washed, dressed, and moodily walked out onto the middeck to watch the ocean rushing back between the twin bows. Hoth led him off to a hasty breakfast, then they got started.

The first part of the day passed in an interrogation that narrowed from generalities to key particulars, and brought Dane to the limits of memory. That afternoon, he was questioned in a state of drug hypnosis about details he couldn't consciously recall. That evening, the three men sat around a table and went over the results.

"I think," said Hoth, "that we can build copies of this device. But we won't have time enough to come anywhere near the Flumerang rate of production."

The general nodded. "In that case we're in a mess. This thing will revolutionize reconnaissance. It can be plainly be fitted for use as a weapon. It·could be issued as standard equipment for spies to infiltrate our research centers. And, as usual, we can't oppose it directly."

Hoth said, "The production of this device seems to have started in their western province and moved from there to the capital. The only hopeful sign is that they are apparently restricting the device to a small elite."

"If," said the general, "we can get at that elite, and its source—"

Hoth nodded. "I think we're going to have to use a complex cutting-out operation, and use it on a grand scale."

Dane tapped the box containing the blue-and-gold beetle. "These things are going to make that approach even trickier than usual."

Hoth nodded. "I know it. But the only alternative is a ruinous war. A war *may* follow, anyway; but if we judge the Flumerang government correctly, it will follow immediately. If so, they'll be fighting blind and off-balance, so we should win quickly."

"Which," said Dane dryly, "should give us time to get ready for the next one."

The general shrugged. "We're the dominant power, and we can count on being disliked, distrusted, and sniped at, for just as long as we stay on top. Afterwards, they'll spit on us."

Hoth growled, "And that knowledge is a powerful stimulant."

"That's true," said Dane, "but what puzzles me is this—individually, they're nice people."

"Sure," said the general, "and the executioner may be a nice fellow socially. It's when you meet him in his official capacity that the unpleasantness comes."

"Maybe that's it," said Dane. "We always come up against other nations in their official capacities."

Hoth shrugged and looked at the blue-and-gold device with its curved, razor-sharp jaws. "I don't care to meet this thing in its official capacity."

Dane and the general followed Hoth's gaze and nodded.

***

The following months passed in grueling work. Dane struggled to develop counter-measures, and was repeatedly called on to help solve production difficulties in turning out a unit similar to that of the Flumerang. He was able to help with practical problems, but could only shrug when frustrated engineers told him, among other things, that the electrical circuits of the device defied understanding, and appeared to include the electrical properties of the unit's mechanical parts. But despite the theoretical difficulties, production gradually got under way.

As the first of their own units were produced, Dane practiced hour after hour, and when he was satisfied with his own skill, he helped train a crew of operators.

By this time, Hoth had a big board in his office covered with stolen samples of the Flumerang device. He showed them to Dane one day, pointing out samples bearing small drills and cutters, little tubes of explosive, miniature torches, sharp double-edged blades, and mechanical stings capable of injecting narcotic drugs or poison.

"Look," said Hoth, "at this thing." He pointed to a beetle with the bristly appearance of a burr. "That's the latest type. It's designed to cling to clothing. It contains a small explosive charge and blows up if the shell is distorted. The natural instinct of any man with a burr stuck on him is to pull it loose. In this case, that is likely to lose him his hand."

Dane said, "Exactly how are we going to run a cutting-out operation in a country swarming with these things?"

"At night," said Hoth. "They don't have anything yet that can see at night, and I am not going to wait till they invent something that can." He pulled out a big map and spread it on his desk. "Our main trouble is here, in this industrial town south of the capital. That is where the people live who design these things. But the main source of this nest of geniuses is further west, in the teachers of one outstanding technical school in this town near the coast. Happily, we've put quite a number of probes into Flumerang over the past few decades, so we've been able to get pretty close to their organization."

"All the same," said Dane. "I don't see how we are going to get a sizable force into those cities. The streets are lighted at night, and some intersections are floodlit. There is a continuous surveillance of all movements. I don't see how we can do it that way, night or no night."

Hoth nodded. "It will be tricky. But you have to remember, Flumerang is still ruled by the bunch that ruled it before. The device is a striking technological development. But the genius is in the Flumerang scientists and technicians, not in their government. Their government is using the device in a strictly conventional way, for purposes of war and internal control."

"True," said Dane, "but why should that help us?"

"Because," said Hoth, "war and internal control require stronger centralization. And that gives us an opening."

Hoth explained his plan, and ended by saying, "You see what that involves. Do you think we can do it?"

Dane thought it over. "Just let there be enough time for practice."

Dane lay in the blackness on the hillside, looking down on the lights of the town below. He carefully wormed his way between several low shrubs, then pried the face of his watch away from his wrist, and took a container from his pack. He unrolled a band of cloth, and set a small object outside the shrubs on the sparse dry grass. Then he carefully slid the band of cloth over his head, feeling till it fit smoothly at his forehead. He lay face down and shut his eyes.

All was darkness and intense silence around him. Then he saw a faint reflection, rose and turned, toward the lights of the city. He soared straight out over it, watching rectangles of darkness come into focus between lanes and pools of light. He looked down, circling slowly toward a lighted avenue that passed an angled block of darkness lit brightly at each corner.

As he dropped closer, he could see details in the avenue. He hovered and watched as a lone bent figure shuffled forward into the pool of light.

At the edge of the city, there was a bright flash and the streetlights below Dane went out. The lights at the building below faded out, then came on more dimly. Dane slipped down toward the light.

The bent figure was that of an old woman, talking through a grille to a scowling guard.

A small black shadow flicked from her outstretched hand. The guard stiffened. Dane watched the shadows on the old woman's face. She seemed to be talking steadily, persuasively.

The guard pressed a button, and spoke into a phone. The old woman shuffled toward a door of the building. The door opened. A frowning guard stepped out. At that moment, the clapper of a bell above the doorway blurred. Several small vague forms dropped into the light and clung to the woman's shawl. The cloth moved as she turned her head. There was a bright flash, then another and another.

As she fell, small shadows like darting minnows flicked away from her toward the open door. The guard there toppled forward, and there were two forms lying motionless in the pool of light.

Dane dropped fast, and streaked through the doorway and down a hall. He shot up a broad staircase, and saw a man before a closed door, his eyes wide behind a pair of heavy, plastic-framed glasses.

Dane streaked for the man.

Three blue-black streaks blurred up the staircase toward the door.

Dane struck the man at the base of his neck. He stumbled, his expression suddenly vague. Then he lost his balance, and toppled at the head of the stairs.

There was a bright flash, then another.

The door sagged on one hinge.

Down the hall, streaked a small blue-and-gold blur that swerved and dove at Dane with a sharp silvery glitter.

Dane dove, then climbed fast toward the doorway.

Another blue-and-gold streak shot past him, then another. Tangled blurs whizzed down the hall, whirled and dove after him as he flashed past the door.

In the room, tense men lay on bunks, each wearing the heavy glasses. Little blue-black forms dove at one after another, and each in turn lost his look of intense concentration.

Dane dove at several of the remaining men, each hard contact triggering the release of a minute quantity of quick-acting narcotic.

He streaked upward, and saw that the blue-and-gold Flumerang devices were all scattered on the floor.

Dane circled, waiting. Without hearing, he had no way to tell if the sirens of captured police trucks were sounding outside or not. He was painfully aware that part of the plan could have failed completely, and then all the rest would be for nothing.

He waited in growing anxiety.

Then the door flew back, and tough-looking men in the uniforms of the Flumerang National Police burst in. They seized the unconscious men from their cots, carried them out, and down the stairs into waiting trucks.

Dane swung up fast into the night, circled to get his bearings, then climbed toward the distant hills.

Dane and the rest of the men were back on the ship before dawn. As the captives were taken below, Dane reported to Hoth.

Hoth listened carefully, then said, "Good work. With the other reports I've had, this means we've got the key scientific personnel, and the bulk of their elite of operators. Just in time, too." He tossed across a bulky sheaf of papers.

Dane glanced through diagrams, charts, and orders in the Flumerang tongue. He studied with particular care a map showing his homeland divided up into occupation districts.

Hoth said, "Now they can either attack us, in which case they fight disorganized, or they can wait, in which case our own production will outstrip theirs."

"But in any case," said Dane, "we can expect another upheaval sooner or later, here or elsewhere."

"Yes," said Hoth, "and we can hope our probes sense it before it gathers momentum." He looked at Dane intently. "We stop most of them before they get to this stage, you know."

"Yes," said Dane, "but I wonder about the whole thing. Suppose, as some people say, there are other planets which have human life. Say there are thousands of these planets. I wonder if even one of them has a nation like ours?"

"What do you mean?"

"Well, other countries have spy networks, to snoop out secrets. *We* have individual probes, alert to sense any ferment of ideas, then locate the source. It seems natural, because I'm used to it. But when I stop to think of it, then it seems odd."

"It works."

"Yes, but *why?* Why is there this cleavage between the average person or situation and the dangerous one we're trained to sense? Why is it we usually find someone—or at most just a few—individuals at the center of a sort of whirlwind of ideas, which speedily develops into a hurricane if we don't get to it when it's little? I realize, experience shows it works this way, but experience doesn't tell *why.*"

"Maybe," said Hoth, "our situation is unusual."

"How so?"

Hoth grinned. "When I was a young man, filled with natural conceit and a keen awareness of my own superiority, my long-suffering superiors assigned me to Tongobokku—I think to take some of the edge off. Tongobokku had a climate like the inside of a steam boiler. The place is infested with land crabs, carnivorous trees, man-eating lung spiders, leeches, stinging and biting insects, and parasites of all varieties. In short, a real hell hole. The chance of anyone having leisure to get an idea in this place seemed negligible to me. But while I was there I heard what might be an answer to your question."

"What was that?" said Dane, leaning forward.

"A sort of song the children used to chant. I can only suppose it has to do with the *Fiery Ship*, but from a different angle than usual." Hoth leaned back, glanced into the distance for a moment, then began to repeat in a singsong voice:

> *Strangers come in big canoe*
> *   That float up in the sky.*
> *They come down, step out here*
> *   Though I cannot say why.*
> *Ask me much, lips tight shut*
> *   And glare me in the eye.*
> *You got water catch on fire?*
> *   No.*
> *No? You got air that burn?*
> *   No.*
> *No! You got stone that light like sun?*
> *   No.*
> *No. You know how we get out of this place?*
> *   Me no know.*

O.K. You got thin-fine very-strong bend-easy?
  No.
You tell us where we get?
  Me no know.
Everybody else this place all the same like you?
  Me no know.
You ever see canoe like this?
  No.
You see man fly in air?
  No.
You see big hut swim in sea?
  No.
Carramba sun a beach!
Same as the rest.
Now we had it.
Start from the bottom and work up.
So long, Bud. You'll be seeing us around."

Hoth paused, and Dane stared.

"There," said Hoth, "we have a possible answer."

"The *Fiery Ship* got *stuck* here. Ran out of fuel or some necessity—?"

Hoth smiled. "The production of a little precise part can require a whole worldwide technology to support it."

"What a fate," said Dane. "To have to uplift a whole planet in order to get off it."

"It's worse than that," said Hoth. "We don't know if we're dealing with people having a supernatural life span or with their descendants, or what. It's nice of them to inspire us and to prod our technology along. But we're keeping a close watch on things, and the price they have to pay runs higher."

"What's that?"

"When they lift," said Hoth, "*we* lift with them."

Dane grinned. He thought of the Flumerang girl who wanted to join the people of the *Fiery Ship* in the stars.

"Who knows?" he thought.

SINFUL CITY

Hubertus Van Mock, the Earth delegate, was the last member of the tri-racial committee to arrive at Badron City. The fame of the place had spread all the way around Carlson VI to Headquarters-Earth, on the planet's opposite side, but Hubertus still wasn't prepared for the sight when he saw it.

Daurek and Fsslt, standing beside him, had seen Badron City before, and had passed the stage of amazement. Daurek, the Centaurian delegate, stood with four of his six arms crossed on his chest, with the other pair set indignantly on his hips, and with his handsome, silver-thatched head thrust forward belligerently.

Fsslt, the tall, thin, many-armed, multi-jointed delegate from the Probity Council of T'ng, stood like a teepee of writhing black sticks, his big eye glaring malevolently down the street, his whole posture suggestive of destruction and slaughter, barely restrained.

"Well," said Daurek, turning to Hubertus, "there it is. Now what do you say?"

Hubertus shut his eyes for an instant, then opened them. He was staring down a long narrow street lined on each side by shops lettered *Bakery* and thick doors with plaques marked *Dentist*. In solemn procession, on either side of the street, candy-striped barber poles turned in unison as far as the eye could see.

"To read the signs," said Daurek, "there are more bakery shops, barbers, and dentists, in this one place, than we need on the whole of Carlson VI."

"I still can't believe," said Hubertus, "that they're—Well, that they're—"

Daurek snorted. As they watched, drunken figures lurched in and out of the bakeries, bottles in hand. Husky rocketeers hurried into dentists' offices, to emerge arm-in-arm with short-skirted women, many of whom had faces hard enough to scratch diamond. Rather dopey-looking individuals drifted in and out of barber shops, their hair just as long when they came out as when they went in.

"Well," said Hubertus. "This is quite a problem."

"You're only beginning to see it," said Daurek. "The T'ng and I have been working on it for a week-and-a-half, and I think we'd supernova the place if we thought we could get away with it.—Look there!"

Down the street, a barber-shop door flew open. A tall Centaurian ran out, flung all six arms to the skies, and leaped into the air, clicking his heels and shouting "Oloo! Oloo! Oloo-looloo! Qloolooloolooloolo—"

Several men of various races, wearing white barber coats, rushed out to hustle him back inside. Hypodermics gleamed in the hands of some of them as the tangled mass rushed across the street back into the building.

"Another case of the dancing jeebees," said Daurek angrily. "There goes another rocketeer. Three more months of this, and half the Centaurian Sector VIII Fleet will be grounded."

Fsslt, the T'ng, raised a kind of small black box on a stick, with a hole in one side, then stopped as his attention was caught by a partly-clad Earth woman who raced across the street. One of Fsslt's country-men was close behind her, with a multitude of thin black arms grasping tattered pieces of clothing.

Fsslt spat a little bright-red ball out of what was anthropomorphically called his "mouth." The ball shot into the black box on a stick that Fsslt was holding, and the box spat out "Miscegenation!" in a flat, grating tone of voice.

"Electrocution would be closer to it," said Daurek. "The T'ng reproduce electrically."

"Whatever it is," said Hubertus, "it's got to come to a stop. It's in places like this that the epidemics get started."

"Agreement," said Fsslt, the little red ball slamming back and forth to the translator. "But how?"

"How? Slap an off-limits on it. Raid the place. Close it up. Fine them. Deport them. You name it, we can do it. I'll bet there isn't a law or ordinance on the planet they haven't broken. What do you mean, 'how'?"

Daurek laughed dryly. "We'll show you. Come on." They started down the street.

"Wait a minute. Look there," said Fsslt, putting out five or six limbs to hold them back. "There's that six-armed Centaurian pick-pocket we ran into the other day."

"Sure enough," said Daurek.

Directly in front of them, a scrubby-looking Centaurian had appeared from an alleyway. Two of his hands were rubbing briskly together, and the other four were floating around aimlessly as he made believe he was stretching himself. His eyes were running over their clothes greedily, plainly assessing the items of value that might be found within.

"Cross the street," growled Daurek.

Fsslt spat his ball into the translator, and the translator gave off a threatening rumble.

When they crossed the street, the grubby Centaurian drifted along behind them, flexing his half-dozen hands. As they walked, their ears were assailed with moans, cries, low screams, and incoherent babblings from the various places of business. Fleeting whiffs of strange odors subjected Hubertus and Daurek to sudden gusts of exhilaration and depression. As they passed a "dentist's office," a six-armed Centaurian woman, lavishly built according to the pattern of six-armed Centaurian women, stepped down, slid one arm around Hubertus' waist and one around Daurek's. "Muffla minnen, Moddy?" she murmured to Daurek.

Daurek's face twisted in revulsion, so she turned quickly to the stupefied Hubertus.

"Have a tooth pulled. Buddy?" she said. "The sweetest, longest, loveliest tooth-pull you ever—"

Whack!

Hubertus whirled around to see the grubby Centaurian pickpocket sink to the earth. As his hands opened up, there spilled out of them Hubertus' wallet, cigarette lighter, and wrist watch, and a number of exotic items that had apparently been filched from the distracted

Daurek. Fsslt was rising from over the pickpocket, the translator box gripped like a club in one of his appendages.

Daurek thrust the dentist's assistant, now giggling hysterically, back into the doorway. Hubertus swiftly put the valuables into his pockets. The enraged Fsslt swore furiously into the translator, from which there emerged an outrush of garbled abuse, ending up " . . . iseramable ously bod-gammed don-of-a-sitch, tlash bim, anyway!"

The Centaurian delegate turned back to Hubertus to get his valuables, and Fsslt shook the translator and looked at it intently.

"Say, Buddy," mumbled a thick-tongued Earth pilot weaving across the sidewalk. "You didn't do right by that little spider-girlie. Boy, they're the greatest—"

"*Spider* girlie!" snapped Daurek, pausing as he stuffed a thing like a small gold-plated hedgehog back into his pocket.

"Tooth-pull, Honey Baby?" said the dentist's assistant, emerging again from her doorway.

"Tooth-pull? Say, will I!" The pilot lunged around and started for the door. He vanished inside with three arms around him, one ruffling his hair, and another going through his left hip pocket.

"What a place!" snarled Daurek.

"Let's get going," growled Fsslt; he then held up the translator, glared at it, and raised two or three arms to point down the street.

"Why can't we go around this rathole?" demanded Hubertus. "Isn't there a less-traveled side-street, or preferably a country road we could use?"

"This is the only street in the place," said Daurek. "The town dump is spread out on both sides where you might expect side-streets to be. If you want to go through the dump and fight rats, slikes, and gang-beetles, you're welcome to it."

They moved on in silence, past a pale-faced barber with tiny pupils who mumbled, "Haircut, buddy? Give you the closest shave from here to Polaris."

"Thanks, no," snarled Hubertus, shouldering past.

As Hubertus passed, the barber took his arm. "Just a little nip will give you an idea—"

Whack! The barber sank to the earth, a hypodermic needle projecting from the half-closed fingers of the hand.

Hubertus glanced at Fsslt, whose big black eye was roving around with an ugly glint in it as he passed the dented translator from one appendage to another.

The two motionless bodies spread out on the sidewalk behind them seemed to have some influence on the other residents of Badron City. Patrons came to the doors of the shops to eye the trio speculatively, but no one else tried to force his wares on them.

Two-thirds of the way down the street, Daurek halted by a man-hole cover. "Feel that rumble?"

"Underfoot?" said Hubertus. There was a faint, steady trembling of the pavement. "Yes, what is it?"

In answer, Daurek reached down with all six arms, and after a brief tussle got the heavy cover loose and rolled it aside. A sound like Niagara flowing through a sewer pipe came up to them. Tiny droplets of spray wet the pavement about the hole.

"So much for that," said Daurek, tossing the cover back on the hole. "Come on."

At the end of the street was a rail like that at the stern of an ocean-going ship. Hubertus blinked and started.

Beyond the rail was a moderately wide river, flowing, flowing, flowing, steadily toward them, only to disappear with a deafening roar.

"Look down," yelled Daurek.

Hubertus leaned far out over the rail, and saw a honeycomb of pipes and conduits of various sizes and shapes, into which the water swirled and vanished. As he watched, water backed up out of one large pipe, as if the pipe had suddenly filled. Some ten or twelve feet away a turbulent stream of water suddenly gushed down into a large culvert.

Hubertus straightened up, frowning. He looked around. Fifty feet upstream, a line of steel posts embedded in concrete swept out in a protective arc. Between the pipes and the foot of the rail where Hubertus stood, a heavy mesh fence stretched down at an angle from the roadbed into the stream, and vanished underwater in a line of foam. He glanced around again, then climbed down onto the fence. It trembled slightly under him as he examined the pipes and the shifting flow of water.

Shortly before coming to Badron City, Hubertus had received a sheaf of documents on the legal aspects of the subject, and he had fully intended to study them. However, one of his minor assistants chose that exact time to elope with a pretty Centaurian girl, and in the three-ring hullabaloo that followed, Hubertus never did get to the papers. They now lay unread in a briefcase in his hotel room. Hubertus shook his head and climbed back up the fence with a feeling of bafflement and frustration.

As Hubertus reached the top, some sixteen to twenty hands, nippers, and tentacle-tips seized him, and hustled him, horizontal and facedown, across the street into a big silent building, and hurled him into a heap with Daurek and Fsslt. A door clanged and they were left in the dark.

"Birthless wasterds!" cried a grating voice and Hubertus realized Fsslt still had his translator. He disentangled himself as well as he could, and got to his feet. Beside him, Daurek was saying something that sounded like "muggermuggermuggermugger *mugger*." This was exactly what the Centaurian girl's father had said about the elopement.

Then the door opened, and a bright light came on overhead. Daurek broke off his monologue. Hubertus saw two heavily-armed Centaurians and a tough-looking Earthman carrying an electric whip.

As these three came in, Hubertus could see Fsslt out of the corner of his eye. The T'ng was passing the translator from one limb to another, apparently to keep it out of the line of vision of the gunmen. A faint twitching in one of Fsslt's larger limbs gave a clue to what he had in mind, and made Hubertus nervous.

"In the back!" barked the Earthman, waving his whip. Behind him, a tall, crafty-looking T'ng came in, his various arms folded together in a look of smug superiority. Hubertus looked at him and instantaneously wanted to batter him against the wall. There was a moment's silence as the T'ng seemed to relish the situation. Then he raised an enameled blue translator with gold trim. In languid tones, the translator said, "I am ready, Slits. Put your questions to the beastlings."

"All right," snapped the Earthman. "What you snooping around here for? Who you think you are, anyway? You spies or something? Give me one good reason I shouldn't put you through the chopping machine and throw you out to the slikes and gang-beetles."

Fsslt's arm gave a big twitch. Hubertus felt his stomach muscles tense.

Daurek raised three hands, palm out. "Suppose I tell you gentlemen, we are higher-ups from Earth, Centaurus, and T'ng. That our cops will come in here and wipe the floor up with you guys if you have the cheek to dare interfere with us in any way? How about that? What's to keep them—I mean, what's to keep *us* from shooting a fleet of torps down that puddle and really blowing this dump sky-high? How dare you detain us like this? Where's your security?"

The Earthman blinked and looked around at the T'ng. Two or three of the T'ng's arms came loose and moved around vaguely, then he raised the enameled translator.

"Obviously, they are *not* officials, or they would not state that they *are* officials. Moreover, they talk as if they might be friends of yours, Slits."

"May be," said the Earthman, trailing his whip on the ground. "But I don't trust them; they look like they got class."

"It is easy to give the exterior a thin coating of culture," said the T'ng. "If you will look at your countryman closely, Slits, I think you will see what I mean."

Slits looked hard at Hubertus. Hubertus bared his teeth slightly, evaded Slits' gaze, and let his glance dart around the room.

"Yeah," said Slits. "I see what you mean. All right, Buddy, let's hear *you* say something."

Hubertus jerked his head toward Daurek. "He can talk for me."

Slits looked back at the T'ng. "Now what?"

"Inquire the business of these gentlemen, obviously. If there's profit in it—"

Slits turned around again. "What's your racket?"

Daurek scratched his head, sides, back, and hip with five of his hands, and took Hubertus' arm with the sixth. "Listen," he said in a low voice, "I think we can do business with these boys. There's room for us. We'll just fit right in. The only thing is, suppose something happens to this river trick they got . . . Then what?"

Hubertus, who had only the haziest idea what was going on, grunted noncommittally.

"Okay," said Daurek, turning back to the tough-looking Earthman. "We don't tell you *nothing* till we get the word on this river trick. Suppose we come in here, sink a lot of capital in a little place, and the cops clean us out? Then what?"

Slits turned dispiritedly back to the T'ng for more instructions.

The T'ng had his arms all folded, and was holding his head tilted calculatingly. He appeared to have the situation reduced to the question whether to kill Hubertus and Co. first and then cut them up, or the other way around. "We have already," he said, in icy tones, "entirely as many shops as we need."

A look of decision came to Slits. He opened his mouth to bark orders.

"Aw, go on," Daurek interrupted, "there's not a pick-me-up on the place."

Slits stuck the butt of his whip in his mouth and bit on it. He turned back to the T'ng for new orders.

The T'ng looked confused. "A pick-me-up?" he said, forgetting to talk through his intermediary. "Isn't that just a—a—"

"Sure, sure," said Daurek, looking eager and alight with enterprising genius. "See, you got all these—ha, ha—bakeries, and so on. All right, a guy goes into one of these places, and first thing you know, he's had all he can use. Right? Well, what then? Maybe he's still got part of his roll stuck in his shoe." Daurek looked outraged, and stepped forward as he slammed three fists into three open hands for emphasis. "You going to let him get away while he's still got some money?"

"Well—" said the T'ng.

"You're not going to let *money* get away from you, are you? So—" he beamed—"that's where we come in—A pick-me-up. A step-uppery."

He pointed a hand at the confused Slits, who was chewing idly on the whip handle. "Right? Am I right? You got limits, you know what I mean? You go out for a good time; after a while it isn't good any more, am I right? Okay, you come to our little pick-me-up, and we set you up for the next round. We refresh you. That's what you need around this place. *Everybody'll* make more money."

By this time, Daurek had Slits by the arm in his eagerness. Daurek paused for a moment, looking benign and fatherly. "You better take that out of your mouth," he said, gently removing the whip. "Hurt your teeth." With another hand, he was feeling Slits' arm. "Boy, you got a muscle. Any time you want to drop around to our place for a free shot—"

Slits nodded, looking vaguely agreeable. The two guards seemed ready to go to sleep on their feet from boredom. The T'ng vaguely raised an arm, as if for attention. The whip leaped across the room, letting out long white sparks. *Whack!*

Fsslt was gone from Hubertus' side.

Hubertus dropped low, and charged for the one guard still on his feet.

The guard had six arms, but Hubertus concentrated on the little finger of the hand at the end of one of those arms. There was a loud yell, and a sound like thirty pounds of scrap being dumped on the floor. Hands seemed to take hold of Hubertus from all over. He lay on the floor and bent a newly-captured wrist back sharply.

Whack!

The guard went limp.

Hubertus got up to see Fsslt returning his attention to the other T'ng. The various limbs of the two T'ngs were so hopelessly intertangled that it made Hubertus dizzy to watch it.

Daurek was using a couple of hands to flail the other guard with the electric whip, and had Slits by the throat with his remaining two pairs of hands. Hubertus picked up a gun with a heavy handle and knocked out Slits. A moment later, Fsslt rose, leaving the other T'ng on the floor. Fsslt had the little blue-enameled translator in his hand.

The three of them left the place, Fsslt sporting the flashy translator, Daurek waving half-a-dozen of the captured guns, and Hubertus with the whip tucked under his arm, the lash trailing on the ground behind him as he walked.

The street cleared magically before them, and they arrived back at their hotel without incident.

Fsslt gave the translator to a bellboy, made signs that it was to be thoroughly sterilized, then led the way to their suite. The hotel was in T'ng territory; but the suite had been fitted out to accommodate all of them, so Hubertus sank down on a big soft couch with a sigh of relief. Daurek settled back in an easy chair with three tiers of arm-rests, and began grumbling,

"*Muggermuggermuggermuggermugger . . .*" Fsslt sat down on a little stool and started to spin, his arms flailing out loosely as he went around and around, faster, and faster, relaxed and more relaxed. Hubertus looked away dizzily.

They rested awhile, then had dinner in a peaceful atmosphere. Hubertus ordered thick steak and french fries; Daurek ate a meal that was a fantasy of tiny servings in innumerable dishes, finished off with a brightly-colored cake of many layers. Fsslt, on the other hand, went to work on a bowl of dull gray objects about the size and shape of marbles. His various limbs lined up between this bowl and a slot in his chest, and the gray marbles began to climb single file from limb to limb to limb to limb to limb out of the bowl and into the slot. It took a while before the first marble made it to the slot. Then there was a loud *crack*, then a crunching, popping, snapping sound that made Hubertus sit up straight and run the tip of his tongue over this teeth and stop eating.

Across the table Daurek put his fork down and was waiting with the look of wincing patience that Hubertus felt forming on his own face. The splintering, grinding noise rose to a dull roar and was joined by a low vibration and a high-pitched hum. The effect was like having a tooth filled while a crew with pneumatic drills worked on the walls of the room. Hubertus felt thankful to see the bowl empty rapidly. Then Fsslt pulled over a small side-dish of bright red, green, and white marbles, and began to eat them one at a time, with relish. These seemed to have a soft core, and the noise was, compared to what had gone before, almost like silence.

At last, Hubertus and Daurek leaned back, while Fsslt finished the meal off with a little bright yellow marble that tinkled as he ate it.

"Now," said Daurek, "to business."

"Right," said Hubertus, "and I may as well admit right now that I never got briefed on the legal aspects of this. One of my assistants ran off with a little Centaurian girl, and that put sand in the machinery for a week."

"Well, *mugger*," growled Daurek, "what did she see in—"

"Suppose you infants try to control yourselves," said Fsslt coolly. As Daurek and Hubertus turned to stare at him, Fsslt held up the blue-enameled translator with gold trim and looked at it suspiciously. Then he tried again. "Before I decide on the correct approach to this problem, you gentlemen will find it advisable to keep your mouths closed."

Daurek turned a dull red.

Fsslt put the translator on the table, left the room, and came back with a duplicate of the black box on a stick he'd used earlier. He tossed the blue-enameled translator down a disposal chute. Then he pulled out his stool. "Okay."

Daurek let out his breath with a hiss.

"It was the translator," said Fsslt. "No offense."

"As I was saying," Hubertus put in, "I never got to find out the legalities of this mess."

Daurek turned back. "It's all legalities. That's the trouble."

"An Earthman founded it," said Fsslt dryly.

"Name of Jaxon Badron," said Daurek. "He picked the one spot on this side of the globe where Earth, T'ng, and Centaurian territory come together."

"Oh, oh," said Hubertus, "as I remember, Centaurus has one side of the river, and Earth and T'ng have the other."

"That's right. Centaurus to the west of the Sendyou, Earth and T'ng to the east."

"But at Badron City," said Hubertus, "where's the river?"

"That's it," said Daurek. "Where is it? Jaxon Badron put it underground."

"Well—" Hubertus scowled, remembering the roar and the pipes.

"Don't forget," advised Fsslt, "Fix Creek is in there somewhere, too."

"That's right," said Daurek. "It seemed like a nice simple boundary when they made it. Centaurus west of the Sendyou, Earth and T'ng to the east. Earth north of Fix Creek, T'ng south of Fix Creek. The only trouble was, they didn't make any law against moving the river. So now, *nobody can claim jurisdiction, because nobody can locate the boundary.*"

Hubertus grappled with the problem. "Maybe we could claim that, inside those culverts, it's not a river any more. Then, quick, we shut the place down."

Fsslt showed no enthusiasm. "If it's not a river, then what is it?"

"H'm . . . Ahh . . . A sewer?"

"I don't think so," said Daurek. "Badron City has lawyers."

"Me, either," said Fsslt. "The lawyers will split rocks down into grains of sand, count the specks and we'll all wind up paying Badron City an indemnity."

"All right, then," said Hubertus, "take the line of the old channel."

"We can't," said Daurek. "The treaty specified the *river*, not the channel."

"Well, revise the treaty."

"No thanks," said Daurek, "that means a conference."

"Well, all right," said Hubertus. "Why not? I mean, have a conference."

Daurek groaned.

"Not me," said Fsslt. "One more conference, and I drown myself in the Sendyou River."

"I see what you mean," grumbled Hubertus. "All right, average the flow."

"How?" said Daurek.

Fsslt added, "They switch it around pipe to pipe."

Hubertus hesitated. "Maybe we could clog the pipes?"

Daurek nodded. "We've been working around toward that."

"Personally," said Fsslt, "I favor blasting the place clean off the planet. Float enough spun plutonium down the stream and let it pile up on that wire screen they've got in front of those pipes—"

Hastily, Daurek said, "We've been over this."

"I know," said Fsslt. "On mature consideration, I can see this would leave a hole where Badron City was, and until the river filled the hole up and flowed on, we'd have a boundary mess from here to the sea."

Hubertus was watching Fsslt in fascination. Turning to Daurek, he said, "The idea has its attractions."

"It's more of this damned T'ng direct action," said Daurek. "Once the city went up in smoke, Centaurian reporters would claim it was Centaurian territory; T'ng reporters would say the sneaking Centaurians had made off with a piece of T'ng territory; *Earth* reporters—"

"Never mind," said Hubertus hastily, "I get the point."

"Personally," said Fsslt, "I resent that about 'Damned T'ng direct action.' "

"Well," said Daurek, "I apologize."

"But," said the Centaurian, "on another hand, I think it's perfectly true."

Fsslt's translator box let out a dangerous hiss.

"Men—" said Hubertus, uneasily.

"Listen," snapped Fsslt, "we've got to close this rat's nest *soon*. Last week, another rocketeer came back with the orange mold. He infected half-a-dozen more before they got him into the chambers. Then all seven had to go. The Admiral swore he'd blow the place off the map if it happened again."

"More direct action and simple solutions," said Daurek. "What do you want, a war?"

"No," said Fsslt. "I just tell you we're going to have a real incident here next time. Before you bang and hammer on us T'ng for being simple, show us what you subtle, complicated Centaurians have got done."

Daurek looked down at the floor and grumbled, "I got us out of that cell they had us in."

Fsslt hesitated, then spat the little ball into the translator. "Truth," said the translator, grumpily.

"That's right," said Hubertus. "We owe you a lot for that. And you and I owe Fsslt a lot for getting us past that pickpocket and the so-called barber."

Daurek looked up. "Yes, that's true. Well, Fsslt's simple solutions will get us in a worse mess on this problem, and my complicated ideas can't even get a grip on the thing. The trouble is, it's a complexity—the mixed channels—hidden, under a simplicity—the surface that hides the channels' courses and amounts from us."

"Well," said Fsslt hesitatingly, "if we could somehow strip off that surface—"

"No," said Daurek, scowling, "that would be violence. Maybe if we, say, dyed the stream—"

"But," said Fsslt, "the stream course would still be hidden under the ground—now maybe if we put acid in to eat out the pipes—"

"Only," said Daurek, "that would make trouble further down stream. Say, though, what about a radioactive solution, then fly above the city and plot the channel—"

"Pest on it," growled Fsslt, "they switch the water from channel to channel so by the time we figure it out—"

"Damn," grumbled Daurek.

Hubertus suddenly sat up straight. "Wait a minute. I think I've got it!"

"What!" Fsslt and Daurek looked at him pessimistically. "Remember," said Daurek, "they switch all that water around, so even if we—"

"Never mind that," said Hubertus, "you wait and see." He got up in excitement. "All I want is your agreement, and we can start right now."

"Well, you've got my agreement," said Daurek.

* * *

Fsslt and Daurek were standing with Hubertus a week later, when the last of the big bulldozers stopped working. From the hill where they stood they had a splendid view of Badron City and its surroundings. Hubertus studied the scene for a moment, then spoke into the microphone: "*NOW.*"

To the north of Badron City, a big water-gate fell into place. The river backed up momentarily as if dammed. There was the sound of a soft explosion that heaved an earth embankment, then the river flowed through into its new artificial channel, a big ditch which flowed completely around Badron City, well to the west. To the east of the river, another water gate closed and Fix Creek flowed through a new channel to rejoin the river well to the south.

Badron City was now completely in T'ng territory.

From the northwest, a black column, as thick on the road as ants, could be seen approaching the city. Watching the column through field glasses, Hubertus could make out a number of the T'ngs' famous Mangler tanks, each consisting of one motorized six-inch gun with a heavy sheet of metal wrapped around it. Following these came a T'ng housewrecking machine, a thirty-foot steel club mounted on a massive motorized platform.

Behind these came a large mass of outraged T'ng citizenry, from which were occasionally raised aloft large clubs, mallets, and mauls. Pulled along behind the crowd came a gallows on wheels, portable electric chairs, chopping machines and dessicators, each with its own generator mounted beside it ready for use.

From Badron City, meanwhile, a horde of barbers, dentists, and bakers, could be seen fanning out for the river. No one stopped to argue. In a situation like this, the T'ngs' simple methods were unbeatable.

Fsslt turned to Hubertus. "The stinking pesthole is cleaned out," he said with satisfaction.

"Thank heaven," said Daurek. "Now maybe we won't have a war or an incident for another year."

Notables of various races were coming toward Hubertus in groups, all looking, after their fashions, pleased and congratulatory.

"While we stick together," said Fsslt, "what problem can't we solve?"

"But," said Daurek, "for this one, Earth deserves the credit."

Suddenly Hubertus was surrounded with happy Admirals, mayors, and directors of health, and Hubertus was shaking their hands. More hands, incidentally, then he would have cared to count.

BEHIND THE
SANDRAT HOAX

I

Redrust Northeast Bunker, New Venus, July 17, 2208. Sam Mathews, missing converter technician from the Kalahell Solar Conversion District, was today admitted to Redrust Medical Center. Mathews's sand-buggy overturned May 17, in the middle of the Waterless Kalahell Desert.

☆ ☆ ☆ ☆ ☆ ☆

Date: July 19, 2208
From: Robert Howland, Director, Kalahell Conv. Dist.

To: Philip Baumgartner, Director, Redrust Med. Cen.
Subject: Sam Mathews
Recode: 083KCrm-1

Phil: Hope you will patch Mathews up and get him back to us as soon as possible. We are eager to learn how Mathews survived two months in the Kalahell, starting with two one-quart canteens of water.

Date: July 20, 2208
From: Philip Baumgartner, Director, Redrust Med. Cen.
To: Robert Howland, Director, Kalahell Conv. Dist.
Subject: Weak Patient
Recode: 083kcRM-2

Bob: Sorry, there's no question of getting Mathews back to you quickly. With a sheet and a blanket over him, you still see his ribs. Besides, he's incoherent.

July 22, 2208
Howland to Baumgartner
083KCrm-3

Phil: I hope you will listen carefully to every incoherent word Mathews speaks. Please bear in mind, we found his overturned sand-buggy, with water tank burst, *three hundred miles* from Redrust Northeast Bunker. There is no known water in between, and the vegetation is dry as dust from April to Ocnovdec. *How did he do it?*

☆ ☆ ☆ ☆ ☆ ☆

I August 24, 2208
Baumgartner to Howland
083kcRM-4

Bob: Sorry this reply is late. Our supply ship cracked up on its last trip, with a crew of four and nine offworld tourists. We suddenly had eleven badly burned men to care for, and little time for Mathews. However, we will see if we can learn anything for you.

I August 30, 2208
Baumgartner to Howland
083kcRM-5
Subject: Pure Lunacy

Bob: Sorry, but we're sending Mathews to Verdant Hills Medical Center. Their facility is big enough to handle his case, I think. If not, they will send him to Lakes Central. Too bad, but he went through quite an experience, as you realize.

Purgatory 2, 2208
Howland to Baumgartner
083KCrm-6
Subject: Nut Stunts

Phil: Yes, I realize what Mathews went through: *He crossed three hundred miles of desert on two quarts of water.* That's what I'm trying to find out about. From the heading of your message, I take it Mathews has gotten "mentally unbalanced" now it's time for him to go back on duty. Look, Phil, try to remember, Mathews is a case-hardened "sandrat" of long experience. This is not your average patient. You let a sandrat get his chosen angle on a situation, and he will stand it on its head. *Don't send Mathews to Verdant Hills. Hold him till the cyclone pack goes through here, then send him to us.* And Phil, will you tell me what Mathews said about his experience? This is important to us here.

Purgatory 16, 2208
Baumgartner to Howland
083kcRM-7

Robert: In dealing with my own patients, under treatment at this facility, I rely on my clinical judgment, balanced by the professional opinion of my staff, and not on sandrat amateur psychology. Mathews had been released, for observation at Verdant Hills Medical Center. And I am not at liberty to divulge confidential details, from the closed files, on this case. *Note, please, that this communication is the 3rd transmission of a series, repeated periodically over land-line central cable, and by semaphore across fault-gaps, crush-zones, and landshifts, and that transmission between remote peripheral stations may be delayed during periods of intense meteorological or seismic activity.*

Hell 14, 2208
Howland to Baumgartner
083 KCrm-8

Dear Doctor: I wonder if, in the full wisdom of your clinical judgment, balanced by all the professional personnel on your staff, any of you qualified people had the wit to try to put yourselves in the place of your lowly sandrat patient, and see how things looked to *him?* What does your clinical judgment tell you about someone who has spent years in the dustbowl of this poverty-stricken sandpit planet? How will this sandrat react when he gets the chance to be sent, free of charge, to a comparative Garden of Eden, provided he can just *prove he's nuts?* I won't waste breath describing the stunts some of these birds have staged, just to get back to Bonescorch for a week. And far be it from me to pry into the confidential privileged communications between you and one of my best technicians on a matter vital to the Kalahell Conversion District. No. Better that my men should die of thirst when their vehicles give out than that you should open your closed files. Sorry if my message seemed unprofessional, Phil. Forgive me for presuming on our former friendship. *Note, please, that this communication is the 6th transmission of a series . . .*

☆ ☆ ☆ ☆ ☆ ☆

Date: Hell 30, 2208
From: Philip Baumgartner, Director, Redrust Med. Cen.
To: Quincy Cathcart, Chief of Medical Services
Subject: Interservice Friction
Recode: 082RMmc-1

Sir: I am sending separately a record of my recent correspondence with Mr. Robert Howland, Director of the Kalahell Solar Conversion District. As the correspondence will show, a difference of opinion regarding medical treatment of one of my patients has caused some friction between us. I call this matter to your attention because of recent failures in certain electrical facilities at the Redrust Medical Center. These power failures, of precisely thirty and sixty-second duration, have formed a pattern which it seems to me could not be random. I do not accuse Director Howland of being the cause of this serious interference, but I feel that this matter should be investigated without delay. I would appreciate your assistance in this matter. *Note, please, that this communication is the 2nd transmission of a series, repeated periodically.*

☆ ☆ ☆ ☆ ☆ ☆

Date: Salvation 6, 2208
From: Quincy Cathcart, Chief of Medical Services
To: Philip Baumgartner, Director, Redrust Med. Cen.
Subject: Ego Reduction

My boy, if I were a purely conventional Chief of Medical Services, I would have your jackass hide drying in the breeze this minute; but it is your great good fortune that I have a large capacity for suffering fools gladly, and also am somewhat short of replacements for you at the moment. You have committed three really outstanding stupidities. First, you have "pulled rank" on an equal. You may regard yourself as enormously superior, mentally, socially, and professionally, to Director Howland, but kindly observe that Director Howland is *Director* Howland. Kindly do not increase my difficulties by your ineffectual efforts to snub those to whom you are not superior. Second, if you *do* try it, show the forethought not to commit the additional stupidity of voluntarily doing it in fully documented form, where anyone may see your ego, complete with scalpel, stethoscope, and halo, spread-eagled in all its glory. Third, when you *have* done it, do not expect me to get you out of the mess. Just exactly what do you propose that I do? Suppose I should take this matter up with the Chief of Power Production? As he is just as busy as I am, or almost so, he will be in an equally irritated mood after examining the records. Certainly, he will request Director Howland to check this power interruption. However, you may count on it, the field of power-supply zionids, or the theory of tertiary trilovolt transmission zone interactions, or whatever may happen to be involved, will be so abstruse and complex that neither you nor I will have any idea whether what follows is justice, persecution, or the operations of someone's sense of humor. Kindly note that I am not interested in becoming involved in this, particularly since this power interruption obviously does not risk your patients' well-being, or you would plainly and unequivocally say so. All it is doing, therefore, is to sweat your ego, and far be it from me to interfere. Permit me, however, to make a suggestion. You, obviously, have two main alternatives: a) You may demand in an authoritative way that Director Howland come to heel like a chastised dog. In this case, I strongly suspect that the Director will suddenly discover that your difficulty shows the danger of incipient overload of the flarnitic leads of the intercontinental power net or something equally nice, and a disaster team will descend on you and make your present discomfort look like heaven; b) Alternatively, you might send a simple manly note of apology for your highflown missive of Purgatory 16th, explaining what is doubtless the truth, that you were overtired. Express your willingness to help solve the problem. I fully authorize your opening the files for this purpose. I await with interest the results of your joint investigation of the matter, as I frankly would like to know how any human could cross three hundred miles of the Kalahell Desert alone on foot, starting with just two quarts of water, and with nothing between him and his destination but dried-out vegetation and dust. I am setting additional inquiries in motion on this matter and advise you to start your investigation promptly, if you wish to receive credit for the solution. *Note, please, that this communication is the 4th transmission of a series, repeated . . .*

▮▮

Date: Salvation 14, 2208
From: R. Stewart Belcher, Director, Verd. Hills Med. Cen.
To: Quincy Cathcart, Chief of Medical Services
Subject: Sam Mathews
Recode: 081mcVN-2

Sir: In answer to your inquiry, yes, we had a patient by the name of Sam Mathews here. He arrived from Redrust Med. Cen. in a special reinforced straitjacket, and we shipped him out in a padded cocoon. As for his condition—well—if you will permit me to drop the usual lingo, this fellow was stark raving nuts. I would hesitate to try to pin it down any closer. We sent him straight to Lakes Central. He got here Purgatory 16th, and we got rid of him on the 18th. *Note, please, that this is the 4th of a series . . .*

☆☆☆☆☆☆

Date: Salvation 15, 2208
From: Martin Merriam, Director, Lakes Cen. Med. Cen.
To: Quincy Cathcart, Chief of Medical Services
Subject: Sam Mathews.
Recode: 082mcLM-2

Sir: Yes, we do have a patient here named Sam Mathews. Mr. Mathews is under treatment at our Outpatient Clinic. His case is highly interesting, and I think, offers many insights into the nature of religious fanaticism. You see, Mathews was employed for years as a technician, tending solar-conversion units out in the Kalahell Desert. One day, while far out, an unexpected tornado hit, his sand-buggy overturned, his water tank burst, and he found himself isolated in this waterless desert. The psychic shock must have been formidable. Tchnudi, who is handling his case, is slowly bringing the infraconscious symbolism to the surface; but, of course, the process cannot be hurried. Subjectively, Mathews evidently experienced a vision, which left him convinced he was under the care of a being called the Prophet Awashi. Tchnudi, by the way, finds an intriguing symbolism in the name of this prophet. By the time Mathews emerged from the desert, the whole thing was quite real to him. However, his latent fanaticism only burst to the surface when he was told that he was to be sent *back* to the Kalahell. Instead, he insisted that he go on to the "promised land," as the Prophet had commanded him. This incident, I think, offers many possibilities for theoretical insights. Tchnudi is treating the psychosis by what might be called "psychiatric hydrotherapy." The patient is encouraged to swim and boat and is responding quite well, despite occasional relapses. We have high hopes of achieving an eventual cure. *Note, please, that this message is the 6th . . .*

Salvation 23, 2208
Cathcart to Baumgartner
081rmMC-3
Subject: Sam Mathews

   Well, my boy, I would like to know the results of *your* investigations thus far. *Note, please, that this message is the 4*[th] . . .

☆ ☆ ☆ ☆ ☆ ☆

Salvation 24, 2208
Baumgartner to Cathcart
081RMcm-4

   Sir: I can only say that Mathews was incoherent when he arrived here and insane when he left.

   He appeared to be progressing nicely, but our treatment was interrupted by the crash of a supply ship, so that we necessarily may have neglected Mathews to some extent. *Note, please, that this message is the 9*[th] . . .

Salvation 20, 2208
Cathcart to Baumgartner
081rmMC-5
Subject: Evasion

   Dear boy: You may not believe it, but there are worse places on this planet than Redrust. Specifically, let me call to your attention Medical Outpost 116, located in a spot picturesquely named "Ssst," from what happens when you spit on the sand. Outpost 116 is situated in the center of a kind of natural bowl. When the sun reaches the zenith over this bowl, it is possible to be burned simultaneously on all exposed surfaces of the body, whether the said surfaces happen to face up, down, north, south, east, or west. Owing to the really excessive seismic activity in the region, this is a *surface station*, of the type mounted on very large skids designed to flex with the waves when the quakes hit. Unfortunately, the elastic-rebound qualities of the skids sometimes react unfavorably with the seismic waves, so that you are going up when the ground is going down, and vice versa. The mechanical qualities, insulation, *etc.*, of the station have suffered accordingly. Permit me to point out that this outpost has been untenanted for some time, as I have been unable to find anyone with the unique qualities desirable in the occupant of this station. Let me point out, it would be of great value for the Service to know *how Mathews survived so long without water*. Of course, you need not trouble yourself with this problem if it bores you. *Note, please, that this message is the 6*th . . .

II August 3, 2208
Baumgartner to Cathcart
081RMmc-6

Sir: I send separately complete copies of all records of this Center pertaining to former patient Samuel Mathews. I realize that it may be of some interest that this patient survived severe exposure over a relatively long period. However, determination of the cause of this anomaly is not possible with the facilities available at this Center. We lack sufficient advanced computer backup to correlate the data. In any case, data-sifting, data-analysis, and theoretical synthesis is not the function of this Center.

II August 6, 2208
Cathcart to Baumgartner
081rmMC-7
Subject: Reassignment

Sir: Effective on receipt of this message, you are removed as Director of Redrust Medical Center, and reassigned to Medical Outpost 116. You will report to Medical Outpost 116 on the next supply ship, traveling by way of Kalahell Water Extraction Center and South Bonescorch Junction. Your assignment is: a) to repair and render fit for occupancy Medical Outpost 116; b) to occupy Medical Outpost 116 until further notice, maintaining it in optimal condition, and duly operating all recording equipment relating to solar radiation, temperature, humidity, atmospheric pressure, wind-speed, incidence and severity of sandstorms, cyclones, groundslips, seismic tremor, *etc.*, *etc.*; c) to render medical assistance to the occupants of the Equatorial Conversion District. To facilitate your medical-assistance patrols, Medical Outpost 116 will be equipped with one (1) Model STV-4 sand-buggy. You are cautioned to operate this vehicle with due care, as vehicle malfunction, especially in the prolonged dry season, is a major factor in the mortality rate of the Equatorial Conversion District. Bear in mind that, due to electromagnetic disturbances, and violent meteorological and seismic activity, outside help is not to be anticipated.

☆ ☆ ☆ ☆ ☆ ☆

Date: II August 14, 2208
From: Quincy Cathcart, Chief of Medical Services
To: Robert Howland, Director, Kalahell Conv. Dist.
Subject: Desert Survival
Recode: 081MCkc-1

Sir: I am sending, separately, recordings of Sam Mathews' conversations at Redrust Medical Center. It would appear that he expected to die and was passing along information he considered important. For instance, there is the following:

Attendant: Don't overtire yourself, Mr. Mathews. Just settle back.

Mathews: No. I've got to tell—

Attendant: Not now.

Mathews: It's for my buddies. Look—

Attendant: Lie back, please. Don't overtire yourself.

Mathews: Who cares? I know I won't make it. Somebody else can make it. Listen—

Attendant: Of course you'll make it. Now, I've got to give you this—

Mathews: Write this down, will you? The rat story's right. You can eat grass and all. You can eat dry scratchweed. You can—

Attendant: *Sure* you can.

Mathews: You've got to get one *alive*. You can't cook it.

Attendant: Just lie back.

Mathews: Are you going to write it down?

Attendant: Sure. Let me just pull your sleeve up.

Mathews: *Then* you can eat anything. Even scratchweed. It turns to water in your stomach.

Attendant: Just lie still while we get the hypogun . . . *There*.

Mathews: Are you going to write this down? Do you follow?

Attendant: Sure. You don't cook the scratchweed. Now—

Mathews: No! *You don't get it!* It's the *rat* you don't cook!

Attendant: Sure. Sure. You cook the weed, you don't cook the rat. Lie back.

Mathews: It's not . . . you eat it raw . . . the weed . . . you wouldn't, anyway . . .

Attendant: Lie down, now.

Mathews: No . . . But the rat . . . you . . . important to remember . . . the rat . . .

Attendant: Sure . . . Whew! He's under. *Finally.*

Dr. Hinmuth: Try to keep your reassurances more general. Avoid specifics.

This conversation seems to show Mathews trying to get *something* across. I would value your opinion as to what this something might be.

☆ ☆ ☆ ☆ ☆ ☆

Date: II August 18, 2208
From: Robert Howland, Director, Kalahell Conv. Dist.
To: Quincy Cathcart, Chief of Medical Services
Subject: Desert Survival
Recode: 081mcKC-2

Sir: Many thanks. I've wanted these records for a long time. As for Mathews's "rat story"—that's a kind of legend. The basis is a creature called a sandrat that burrows at the base of the larger chalaqui weed and sunrustle stalks. This creature is active while other local life is estivating. The legend is that if a man will catch a sandrat, cut out its digestive tract and eat it raw, he will be able to live in the desert without water. This is supposed to have been the secret of "Desert Bill," an early settler renowned for his ability to survive the desert. I've never taken the story seriously, and considering what you have to do to test it, I don't know anyone who *has* tested it. But I'm calling for volunteers.

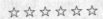

September 17, 2208
Howland to Cathcart
081mcKC-3

Sir: Well, it took work to find volunteers, and I had to offer a week's leave in the worst fleshpot in the hemisphere. But we have now tried it out. Don't ask me how it could be, but one volunteer went almost three weeks without water, and another went sixteen days. This won't convince everyone, but I'm notifying all the conversion districts. Now, if a man gets stranded, he has a chance.

September 19, 2208
Cathcart to Howland
081MCkc-4

Sir: Congratulations. I now have a cage of sandrats myself, but no volunteers. What's the name of that fleshpot? Once I have volunteers, I intend to impose controls so stringent no one in his right mind can question the results. Of course, that won't include everybody.

▌▌▌

Princeps, New Venus, Ocnovdec 30, 2208. Dr. Charles de P. Bancroff, Director-in-Chief of the Interscience Federation today rebuked Dr. Quincy Cathcart for his "sandrat hoax."

In an unprecedentedly severe public statement, Dr. Bancroff charged: "This absurd parody of an experiment exposes New Venus Science to the ridicule of more mature scientific bodies everywhere. Numerous palpable errors in this widely publicized—I might almost say widely advertised—report qualify it as a treatise on 'What to Avoid in Science.'

"To begin with, the sample employed *was not pure.* Assuming the results to be as stated, no one could say what agent or agents were responsible.

"Second, it is absurd to suggest that such results *could* be possible; obviously, digestive action would destroy the ingested tissue, and with it its presumed magical power to change food into drink.

"Third, even assuming the ingested tissues were *not* digested, peristaltic action would reject it from the body.

"This should give some suggestion of the flaws in this 'experiment.' Even laymen can understand such fallacies.

"However, to the scientist, other flaws are at once evident. This experiment is not 'elegant.' It lacks the sense of 'form' which gives the conviction of validity. Moreover, there is nothing quantitative about it.

"There can be no excuse for such an imposture.

"I call upon Dr. Cathcart to publicly admit that this so-called experiment is nothing more nor less than a hoax. This may, at least, permit New Venus Science to regain some shreds of scientific credibility."

Operations Central, New Venus, Janfebmar 4, 2209. Dr. Quincy Cathcart, Chief of Medical Services, today replied to the criticism of Dr. Charles de P. Bancroff. Referring to Dr. Bancroff as a "pedant laboriously mining his rut," Dr. Cathcart stated:

"In the formal organization of which we are both members, Dr. Bancroff is an administrator, not a scientist. As a scientist, I decline to accept any judgment based on Dr. Bancroff's opinions. That his statement is unscientific is easily shown:

"1) He bases his argument on the grounds that my experiment might cause 'New Venus Science' to lose caste in the eyes of others. This is suppression of data for fear of unpopularity.

"2) He states that the experiment cannot be correct, because it disagrees with his presuppositions. This is the attempted refutation of physical facts by favored theories.

"3) He objects that the experiment is not 'elegant,' and hence cannot be true. This is the subordination of Science to Esthetics.

"4) He complains that the experiment is not 'quantitative.' Note that *each* volunteer ate *one* sandrat digestive tract and then, while carefully and continuously supervised, existed for stated days, hours and minutes without drinking water. All that is required of an experiment is that it proves a point, and that the facts be so reported as to be capable of independent check. It is unscientific to include irrelevant data and superfluous charts and calculations merely to make the experiment 'look scientific.'

"My learned colleague's objections are those of the scholastic pedant, not of the scientist.

"In science, theories are based on *facts*, not viceversa."

Princeps, New Venus, Janfebmar 6, 2209. By 8–4 vote, the Personnel and Appointments Committee today fired Dr. Quincy Cathcart, Chief of Medical Services. By unanimous vote, the Committee on Professional Conduct formally censured Dr. Cathcart for "unprofessional conduct."

Rathbone, New Venus, Janfebmar 8, 2208. Dr. Quincy Cathcart, former Chief of Medical Services, in a brief statement commented on his expulsion from office and the formal rebuke delivered by the Interscience Federation. Dr. Cathcart said:

"By these measures, the governing bodies of the so-called Interscience Federation reveal themselves as composed largely of sycophants, obsequious to an administrator who, as I have demonstrated, does not know what science is. These people may, of course, take their stand with whoever they wish. I will stand with Galileo."

Princeps, New Venus, Janfebmar 8, 2209. By 7–5 vote, the Committee on Accreditation today placed Quincy Cathcart on "indefinite suspension of professional status." A spokesman explained: "This means Cathcart cannot practice, and further that no paper or presentation of his may be considered by any accepted medium for the dissemination of professional information or opinion."

The action was taken "to avert harmful public controversy."

IV

Rathbone, New Venus, April 16, 2209. Two magnetic-sieve prospectors reached here today, haggard from exposure and lack of rest, to tell of a waterless trek across the Salamari Waste. They attribute their survival to "travel by night, an accurate map, and two raw sandrats."

Flarnish, New Venus, May 1, 2209. Doctors here are puzzled by the case of a fourteen-year-old boy who eats grass, refuses to drink water, and apparently suffers no harmful effects. He insists he ate a sandrat.

Bonedry, New Venus, May 26, 2209. Hank J. Percival, proprietor of the Last Chance Supply Mart, reports a brisk sale of sandrats to prospectors, surveyors, and cable riggers, setting out across the Bonescorch Plateau.

Princeps, New Venus, May 29, 2209. Experiments carried out under the auspices of the Interscience Federation "demonstrate that the effectiveness of sandrat ingestion in preventing dehydration is a myth. Careful experimentation with measured quantities of crushed digestive tissues of laboratory sandrats shows no statistical increase in resistance to dehydration."

South Bonescorch Junction, New Venus, June 10, 2209. Philip Baumgartner, from Medical Outpost 116, collapsed shortly after arrival here this morning. Baumgartner explained that his sand-buggy broke down "ten to twelve days ago" and he'd been on foot ever since. A small wire cage lined with sunrustle stalks, and now empty, was found secured to his pack straps. Such sandrat kits are sold locally for use in case the purchaser gets lost without water.

Princeps, New Venus, June 22, 2209. By order of R. Q. Harling, Planetary Food and Drug Administrator, all sales of "sandrats or related rodents, for use in preventing dehydration," were today forbidden as "dangerous to the public health, both directly in light of possible infestation by possible indigenous intestinal parasites and indirectly because of the mistaken belief that sandrat internal organs are a specific against dehydration. This myth has been thoroughly exploded by controlled scientific experimentation."

Bonedry, New Venus, June 26, 2209. Hank J. Percival, proprietor of the Last Chance Supply Mart stated today he is continuing sales of sandrats, "as pets."

Broke and Ended, New Venus, June 27, 2209. Sandra Corregiano, a missing tourist on the Trans-Desert Safari, was today brought out after an extensive search around Mineral Flats. Miss Corregiano explained that she had caught a sandrat. "I hated to kill the poor thing," she said, "and I nearly died with the—you know—what you have to do with them. But then I was all right."

Princeps, New Venus, July 6, 2209. Planetary Food and Drug Administrator Harling today warned that he will "proceed to the courts" in all cases wherein sandrats are sold contrary to law. Administrator Harling added that he will prosecute offenders "vigorously, to the full extent of the enforcement resources at my disposal."

Princeps, New Venus, July 8, 2209. The Planetary Food and Drug Administration today released results of chemical analysis of the sandrat digestive tract, by an independent and analytical laboratory "of recognized standing." No cause for protection against dehydration was found.

Bonedry, New Venus, July 10, 2209. The bodies of two Planetary Food and Drug Administration field agents were found near here this morning. Evidence seems to show that the two PFADA agents shot each other in a gun battle. Cause of the fight is not known.

South Bonescorch Junction, New Venus, July 14, 2209. A PFADA agent was found dead in the wreckage of his sand-buggy this morning. Evidence thus far uncovered appears to indicate that the sand-buggy's engine exploded.

Slag Hills, New Venus, July 19, 2209. The body of a PFADA field agent found here the day before yesterday was today shipped back to Princeps. Cause of death was a large bullet hole in the left chest.

Princeps, New Venus, July 20, 2209. PFADA administrator Harling today announced that enforcement of his sandrat-sales policy is being "temporarily suspended, pending completion of a massive public-education campaign."

Princeps, New Venus, July 22, 2209. Dr. Charles de P. Bancroff, Director-in-Chief of the Interscience Federation, today unveiled results of a new experiment "to determine the possible effects of sandrat ingestion." The intestinal tracts of sixteen sandrats, raised at the PFADA laboratories nearby, were "thoroughly macerated, divided into one hundred portions, and each weighed portion mixed with a weighed sample of a specific local plant. *In no instance was the proportion of water significantly increased by admixture with sandrat intestine.*"

Dr. Bancroff stated: "I am amazed that superstition can persist in the face of repeated consistently negative experimental evidence."

Dry Hole, New Venus, July 28, 2209. Sixteen inmates of the Dry Hole Correctional Training Institute have disappeared in the last month. It is believed the prisoners are getting away as fast as they can catch sandrats. Owing to the isolated location of the Institute, and the local lack of surface water, it was never thought necessary to use an escape-proof outer wall.

Princeps, New Venus, I August 4, 2209. Officials of the Interscience Federation today announced new measures to "eradicate the sandrat superstition." A concerted effort will be made to coordinate teaching materials of all types, to render this superstition psychologically distasteful. Special mention was made of the trideo film, *Disaster in the Desert*, which, said a spokesman, "illustrates, step by step, the chain of causation leading from acceptance of the myth to the ultimate test, when the family sand-vehicle malfunctions in the desert. Then there is this distressing scene with the sandrats, and afterward we experience the deterioration of the family, physically and mentally, and the horror as they try to eat sunrustle stalks and other things of that type, and realize that they *don't* turn into water. We got Peter de Vianhof and Celeste Silsine for the principal characters—the stars of our show—and we think they've done a really superb and convincing job for us. It's one thing to just be *told* an old wives' tale is false. It's something else to actually *experience* it this way, right before your eyes." Another official stated, "We're going to pull out all the stops. We're going to crush this superstition."

V

Date: Frigidor 26, 2212
From: Presley Mark, President, New Earth Research
To. Col. J. J. Conrobert, C. O., Stilwell Base, New Earth
Subject: Dehydrated Water?

Con: Sorry this reply is late, but we've had a little trouble here. Some jackass greased the liquid air machine. Regarding your query as to whether there is any way to solidify water without freezing, I would certainly say, "No." But some vague memory keeps circulating through my mind.

What's your problem?

☆ ☆ ☆ ☆ ☆ ☆

Date: Frigidor 27, 2212
From: J. J. Conrobert, C. O., Stilwell Base, New Earth
To: Presley Mark, President, New Earth Research
Subject: Outposts

Pres: The problem is, I've got eighteen detached observation posts in this freezebox, and supplying them is driving me nuts.

I've tried to explain through channels that these outposts serve no useful purpose, that anything incoming—aliens, bootleg spacecraft, planetary raiders, you name it—will show up on the screens. The generals tell me screens can be fooled and visual observation is a useful backup. That's that.

Well, we've got pretty rugged terrain. These observation posts are at high elevations, sunk into windswept crags overlooking wide sweeps of territory. We can't provision them from the air, because of dangerous winds and violently unpredictable meteorological conditions in general. We supply them *from the ground*. There's no vehicle or pack animal that can handle this. *We* do it. Every time we supply these outposts, it's like a battle. What gets us worst is water. In summer, it sloshes and shifts. In winter, the snow is contaminated by spores of the parasite of a solitary overgrown wolf that gets moisture by gulping snow. This parasite will infest humans, which complicates everything from the first snowfall to the middle of summer.

Yes, I realize waste can be purified, but kindly think over our budget, our conditions and the unscientific viewpoint of the troops.

Incidentally, I might add that this solitary powerful wolf finds our isolated snow-melting water-boiling shelters ideal for winter headquarters.

Now, these difficulties are samples. They don't exhaust the list. All these things interlock; you can't do this for one reason, or that for another reason. But if we could eliminate this water-delivery problem, with its complications of liquidity, freezing-point, spores, melt-houses, snow-wolves, *etc.*, it would simplify things enormously.

Could you work up some kind of gelatin, and when it cools it's a powder. Then when it's eaten, the water is released? Never mind if it weighs twice as much. We would gladly trade complications for some straightforward drudgery.

☆ ☆ ☆ ☆ ☆ ☆

Date: Frigidor 29, 2212
From: Mark, New Earth Research
To: J. J. Conrobert, Stilwell
Subject: Nonliquid Non-Ice Water

Con: Am onto a weird track that may solve your problem—a discovery made on our sister planet. True to form, they ganged up on the discoverer, who showed some originality. Will let you know what I find out.

☆ ☆ ☆ ☆ ☆ ☆

Date: September 16, 2212
From: Mark, New Earth Research
To: J. J. Conrobert, Stilwell
Subject: Waterless Water

Con: My investigations into New Venus "science" disclose that there is a creature there called a "sandrat" that lives on dry stalks while the other creatures sleep out the hot weather. For years, the local people have known this, and it appears that someone, stranded without water, decided that if he ate the creature, maybe he could do it, too.

Obviously, this couldn't work. But he tried it, and it *did* work.

Our experiments show that, in this particular animal's digestive system, there's a culture of microorganisms that breaks down cellulose. These microorganisms are passed on from generation to generation, when the mother sandrat feeds the baby pre-chewed food.

When the human eats the sandrat, the human's digestive juices naturally tend to kill the microorganisms. But the human is hoping against hope that he too can now process dried weeds and make water out of them. He promptly chokes down dried weed. The microorganisms go to work on it and produce among other things, a kind of porous charcoal dust, and water. The cellulose, you see, is $(C_6H_{10}O_5)$, or $[C_6(H_2O)_5]$, provided you remember the hydrogen and oxygen are not actually joined as water to form a hydrate. The microorganism takes care of this problem. Don't ask me how just yet. It will take us a while to figure this out. But here is your dry water, if you don't mind the weight penalty.

Evidently, the New Venus authorities fed their laboratory sandrats on starchy food and water. This microorganism, for some reason, doesn't like starch, and dies for lack of cellulose. Hence, their experiments demonstrated that the actual facts were imaginary. By means of a propaganda campaign, they rammed this revelation down the throats of the populace. Nice, eh?

To get back to our problem, we've tried cultures of the microorganism and find they will work on sawdust, amongst other forms of cellulose. Am sending cultures and live sandrats for your own use.

Don't know if this solves your problem, but it's a start. Incidentally, we find we get the best results with the raw digestive tract of the sandrat. Let me know how military discipline solves this problem.

We are also interested to see how New Venus "science" will explain the dilemma created by our report. We are releasing it in a special way.

☆ ☆ ☆ ☆ ☆ ☆

Rathbone, New Venus, II August 16, 2212. Quincy Cathcart, a seed salesman here, today made public the text of a communication from Dr. C. J. Horowitz, Director of Research at the prestigious New Earth Research Corporation. Dr. Horowitz's message reads, in part:

" . . . We wish to publicly acknowledge the prior date of your investigations into this important matter and to acknowledge further that your conclusions have been found to be entirely accurate.

"Owing to your researches, our efforts have been greatly facilitated.

"Mr. Presley Mark, President of the Corporation, has suggested your name for our Mark Medal and accompanying cash award. As you may know, this prize has not been awarded for three years, so that the award money has accumulated. We will be in touch . . ."

☆ ☆ ☆ ☆ ☆ ☆

Princeps, New Venus, II August 18, 2212. P. L. Sneel, spokesman for the Legal Staff Section of the Interscience Federation, today warned that Quincy Cathcart, Rathbone seed salesman, "cannot legally accept any payment, emolument, reward, prize, or other recompense for performance of services which he is legally debarred from rendering. Under Sections 223, 224, and 226, Cathcart must refuse such payment or suffer the full legal penalties."

Rathbone, New Venus, II August 20, 2212. J. Harrington Savage, prominent Princeps attorney visiting at the home of Dr. Quincy Cathcart, today announced that "this allegation of the Legal Staff Section of the Interscience Federation is in violation of Section 6, which specifically prohibits *ex post facto* laws. Dr. Cathcart may be rewarded, to any extent and without limitation, for *past* services, rendered at a time when his outstanding qualifications were fully accredited. Any attempt of the Interscience Federation to enforce this ruling will be met with legal action on whatever scale may prove necessary."

Princeps, New Venus, August 22, 2212. R. J. Rocklash, of the law firm of Savage and Rocklash, today announced that he represents the relatives of one hundred sixty-two exposure victims lost in desert localities. Mr. Rocklash charges, "These people are victims of the propaganda of the Interscience Federation, which struck from their hands the obvious remedy and thus killed them."

Princeps, New Venus, II August 23, 2212. P. L. Sneel, of the Interscience Federation's legal staff, revealed today that the Federation, "as a gesture of reconciliation toward a former colleague fallen from grace," will not insist that Quincy Cathcart refuse payment for past services; "but Cathcart must be exceedingly careful to remember that he is debarred from undertaking to render any services, now or in the future, for which he is professionally disqualified."

Rathbone, New Venus, August 24, 2212. J. Harrington Savage, attorney for Dr. Quincy Cathcart, today warned the Interscience Federation that, "no gesture of reconciliation has any legal standing whatever in this matter. The Interscience Federation statement of II August 23, 2212 presupposes that the Federation may grant or withhold prosecution as an act of favoritism. This calls into question the propriety of Federation policy and its legal validity under sections 66, 67, and 68, governing the relations of governmental authorities and the citizens of New Venus. We are examining the very serious implications of this statement. If need be, a broad legal attack will be instituted to crush the evils inherent in such arbitrary and unprincipled behavior."

Princeps, New Venus, II August 26, 2212. Byron T. Fisher, well known popular author, arrived here today on the spaceliner *Queen of Space.* Mr. Fisher has come "to do research on my new book, *The Martyrs and Tyrants of Science.*"

Dry Hole, New Venus, II August 29, 2212. Three tourists stumbled out of the desert here at first light this morning and attributed their safe arrival to "sandrats and chalaqui weed." They displayed official Interscience Federation Tourist Guide pamphlets warning that "the quaint belief that ingestion of sandrats digestive organs will obviate the need for water is simply an old wives' tale. Scientific experimentation demonstrates that the sandrat is as dependent upon liquid water as any other creature." All three tourists stated that this pamphlet was what nearly killed them.

Princeps, New Venus, September 6, 2212. In chaotic sessions of the governing bodies of the Interscience Federation the following actions were today taken: Dr. Charles de P. Bancroff stepped down as Director-in-Chief, citing reasons of health. By unanimous vote, the Committee on Accreditation reversed its former decree, to restore the full qualifications of Dr. Quincy Cathcart, former Chief of Medical Services. The Committee on Professional Conduct narrowly defeated a motion to overturn its formal rebuke of Dr. Cathcart, whose name, however, was returned to the active roster. In a further upheaval, the Legal Staff Section was drastically overhauled. So far, the Board has proved unable to select a successor to Dr. Bancroff, and is reportedly split into violent factions.

Princeps, New Venus, September 8, 2212. Dr. Sherrington Shiel was today named Director-General of the Interscience Federation. Dr. Charles de P. Bancroff resigned from the Board of Directors, to become head of a special Internal Procedures Study Group. Dr. Shiel's elevation vacated the post of Chief of Medical Services, and the Personnel and Appointments Committee unanimously approved Dr. Cathcart as Chief of Medical Services. An inside observer who asked not to be identified observed that, "Now we have Justice. Whether we get Truth out of it remains to be seen."

Date: September 12, 2212
From: Quincy Cathcart, Chief of Medical Services
To: Philip Baumgartner, Medical Outpost 116
Subject: Reassignment
Recode: 121MC-m116–1

Sir: Owing to retirements and promotions, the position of Director of Redrust Medical Center is now open. If you wish to accept this position let me know at your earliest convenience. I appreciate that you may encounter some difficulty in leaving your present post until the rains subside, in view of the surrounding bowl-shaped terrain. As I recall, the station has waterproof seals, and a cable-and-drum device to allow it to float up off its skids. I trust you have kept the cable well greased.

Date: Ocnovdec 26, 2212
From: Quincy Cathcart, Chief of Medical Services

To: Robert Howland, Director, Kalahell Conv. Dist.
Subject: Science Wipes Out Superstition
Recode: 121MCkc-1

Sir: I quote, for your edification, the following from the newly published Pamphlet 2P-103 of the Interscience Federation Press, titled, *Rusty Learns About Biotechnology*:

"Yes, Rusty, for years people died in the desert, when a plentiful supply of water was as near as the nearest vegetation—dry and useless though it seemed. At that time, the organized research facilities of the Interscience Federation had not yet created Biaqua. But there *was* a way—by ingestion of the common sandrat—to avoid the more harmful effects of extreme solar exposure."

"Gee, Doctor! Didn't the people know about it?"

"No, Rusty. Opinion Research instituted in April, 2211, showed that 92.65% of persons responding believed ingestion of the internal organs of the sandrat would have *no* effect on dehydration; 4.17% believed it might have *some* effect; 2.49% did not mark their ballots correctly; and only 0.69% believed it would *prevent* dehydration, and most of these lived in primitive outlying regions and believed it purely on the basis of superstition and folklore.

"Today, we instruct all travelers to carry Biaqua, and in emergency to overcome their squeamishness and rely on this simple biotechnological means of obtaining water from dry plant tissue . . ."

Pamphlet 2P-103 goes on in this vein for many pages.

Incidentally, I have informed the New Earth Research Corporation that you carried out the first formal experiments on this subject. The credit belongs to you, not me.

☆ ☆ ☆ ☆ ☆ ☆

Date: Ocnovdec 28, 2212
From: Robert Howland, Director, Kalahell Conv. Dist.
To: Quincy Cathcart, Chief of Medical Services
Subject: Sandrats
Recode: 121mcKC-2

Sir: No, you are the one who risked your neck. Anyway, it appears to me the credit would ultimately go to Desert Bill, but how do you get it to him?

If you'd like to do something for me, I am chronically short of trained personnel. As you recall, some time ago, one of my converter technicians, Sam Mathews, turned up at Redrust Medical Center, tried to explain the plain truth and finally decided that if he was going to be thought nuts, he'd be nuts in the most profitable way. He is still enjoying a free vacation at Lakes Central.

Not long ago, one of my assistants went there on business and had a talk with Mathews. Mathews complains that when he goes to bed at night, the cot seems to be bobbing up and down. He walks with a rolling gait, as if he had spent his life on the water. Dr. Tchnudi, who is analyzing him, is trying to get at his basic subconscious mechanisms, and he is straining Mathews's powers of invention. Mathews thus has hydrotherapy coming out of his ears, and he hungers and thirsts after some place where he can "look anywhere, and not see more than one canteen of water at a time."

I hope you will take care of this, as I have just the spot for him.

☆ ☆ ☆ ☆ ☆ ☆

Ocnovdec 30, 2212
Cathcart to Roberts
121MCkc-3

Sir: I am happy to say that Tchnudi willingly let go of Mathews, stating that he believed he, Tchnudi, had effected a complete cure. Mathews is on his way back to you, and if you will just hang him up for a week or so and let the water drain out, I imagine he will be all right.

Meanwhile Tchnudi, elated over the "cure," is elaborating his sessions with Mathews into a gigantic tome that doubtless will make his reputation, will very possibly found a school of thought and perhaps make him "immortal."

This Mathews case has certainly been illustrative of the continuing conquest of uninformed prejudice by the rational forces of science.

The only trouble is, there are times when it's a little hard to tell which is which.

NERVES

The Martian paused at the doorway and looked in. Bathed in the light of Mars' two moons, he saw her, locked in the arms of the Earthman. Her face was that of his wife. He turned, and his tall slender form moved away from the building, casting two shadows in the light of the moons.

He saw the Earthman next at breakfast. But before he saw him, he saw his wife. And she did not come to breakfast.

"Where's Rita?" asked the Earthman.

"Reeta is indisposed," said the Martian pleasantly. "Perhaps she will go with us to the spaceport, but I cannot tell. When she wakes with a headache, it sometimes lasts all day."

"Too bad," said the Earthman. He tapped absently on the bare wood of the table.

"Here," said the Martian, holding out a dish of curled reddish flakes, "do you like *berra* meat?"

"No. Thanks, I don't care for any." The Earthman frowned. "Rita said she'd be here for breakfast."

"Ah?" said the Martian. "When did she say that?"

The Earthman opened his mouth and closed it. He had been about to say, "Last night."

"The reason I ask," said the Martian, taking a curl of *berra* meat delicately in his finger, "is because of Reeta's extraordinary memory. We Martians do not make a statement of future intent, and then not carry it out. It is a point of courtesy with us. Surely you know this."

"That's right," said the Earthman, remembering.

"Therefore, if she said she would be here, even with a headache she would be here. With myself," the Martian shook his head regretfully, "it is often different. My memory is often at fault." He crunched the *berra* meat with relish.

"I think I would like some of that," said the Earthman. He took some of the meat. "I guess I was wrong about Rita. I probably heard her wrong."

"Most probably " said the Martian.

The Earthman looked at him intently, but the thin Martian face was pleasant. "You know," said the Earthman, "it's been pleasant here. Before I left home, I didn't know. You hear so many stories about Martians. You know, about how tricky and subtle Martians are. But what the heck, Martians are just like anyone else." He smiled a sudden secret smile. "Yes, sir, just *exactly* like anyone else. Taller and thinner, is all." He took a handful of the *berra* meat and crunched loudly. "Good stuff," he said.

The Martian winced faintly, then smiled. "Yes, it is surprising. We have much the same physical form, much the same mental capacity. There is probably more variation among two races on Earth than between Earth and Mars. We can eat the same food and have the same diseases. It is surprising."

"Sure is," said the Earthman. He settled back and signaled to the manservant for some more of the strange mint-flavored coffee.

The Martian was leaning back, smoking an aromatic cigarette. His eyes looked into the distance as he spoke. "Yes, it is strange, the similarity in us. The same emotions,—Love, hate, jealousy. Tempered, perhaps a little more by the passage of time and the aging of the race. Carried out, perhaps a little more in the sphere of the mind than in that of the body. We are the same in body, though."

"Yes," the Earthman put in, grinning with half of his face.

"Yes," agreed the Martian, still looking off into space. He breathed out twin plumes of the aromatic smoke. "There is, however, a danger there, which we so far have held in check."

"What's that?"

"Disease." The Martian's hawk-like eyes touched impersonally on the Earthman and then glanced away.

"Why's that?" asked the Earthman, feeling strangely chilled. "What about disease?"

The Martian hesitated. "Well," he said finally, "we are an older race." He ground out his cigarette.

"So?" said the Earthman. "What of it?"

"Disease which have become benign in us, due to an immunity acquired over the ages, might become virulent in your race."

"Oh. We haven't got the immunity yet. But our scientists—"

The Martian rose. "We must not stay chatting till you miss your ship. Excuse me a moment," He left the room and the Earthman heard him speaking in low, considerate tones, but could not make out the words.

"Reeta is still sick," said the Martian coming back into the room. "It is one of her headaches. She will be over it tomorrow. I asked her of her promise to be with us this morning. She remembered nothing of it.—Curious."

"My mistake," said the Earthman, laughing a little unnaturally.

The Martian shrugged. "My own mistake as well. If we had not gone to the fireshow last night, she would have no headache, and be with us today. Oh well, let us go. I have had Fernand see to your goods. You have the contract with you, I suppose?"

The Earthman frowned, patted his breast pocket absently and heard the crinkle of paper. He accompanied the Martian through the short central hall with its latticed screen to the outside. The air was brisk but the sun was warm.

"A pleasant day," said the Martian. "A little hot, perhaps." He crossed to the peculiar, many-wheeled vehicle the Martians used for traveling, and slid up a door. He motioned the Earthman in, then sat down beside him. The machine jolted into motion and something clattered to the floor.

"What's this?" said the Earthman, picking up a small metal disc. He accidentally touched a stud, and it flew open, showing a small blue-tinted mirror, and something that looked like rouge.

The Martian glanced over at it. "Rita's compact," he said. "I suppose she forgot it at the fireshow last night. Your women use those too, don't they?"

"Yes," said the Earthman, frowning. The fireshow. They had offered to take him there. That is, his host had offered to. But he thought that he saw something else in the eyes of his hostess, something far more worthwhile than the fireshow. He had said he thought he would go to bed, since he had to leave the next day. He had seen the promise in Rita's eyes. And she had kept that promise. Then how could his host talk of the fireshow? Rita could not be two places at once.

The vehicle was crawling forward at what the Martians considered a good speed. The Martian was admiring the scenery. "Beautiful," he was saying. "this is the best time of the year."

"Yes," said the Earthman. "Uh, about the fireshow. What time was that last night?"

"As always at midnight," said the Martian. "Are you regretting that you missed it?"

"Sort of," said the Earthman. He was thinking that it had been shortly before midnight when he went for his short walk. She had been waiting at the flowering shrubs. They had gone back together, wordlessly. Midnight. This was impossible. "How long did the show last?"

"About three hours," said his host. "We didn't stay to see the end, though. We'd only been there an hour-and-a-half when Reeta complained of a pain over her eyes. The fireshow will do that to some people, you know.

But the Earthman was staring out the window. They passed a small Martian house surrounded by flowers. Rita, looking strangely pale was standing among the flowers, putting some in a slender vase. She waved good-bye. "Why, there's Rita!" cried the Earthman.

His host turned slowly and glanced back. He shook his head. "I tell you frankly," he said, "I am glad you are leaving."

The Earthman stared at him.

"That," said the Martian, "was not Reeta. You may have noticed the difference in complexion."

"Why, she *was* pale. But, who was it?"

"I have never told you. Perhaps I should have. That was Reeta's twin."

The Earthman felt as if his head were spinning. "Why didn't I ever meet her?"

"It is a story I do not want to get out. You must agree not to tell."

"Well, sure, if you want me to."

"Very well. Reeta's sister, is well, somewhat wanton, She was brought up with her sister, they are like each other in appearance, but Neena had some unfortunate experiences as a girl. She is overly friendly with men,"

"Oh." It crossed the Earthman's mind that perhaps the mixup about the fireshow was not so strange after all. "Well," he said, "I won't repeat it."

"It was not that I wished you not to repeat." The Martian was looking straight ahead at the road.

"Oh? What was it then?"

The Martian seemed to speak with some difficulty. "On Earth, you have the common cold, as it is called. We are, you know, immune to that here."

"Yes, I've heard that."

"You may not have heard that we have other diseases which are to us as your common cold is to you. They are irritating while they last, but they pass and we, with our acquired immunity, recover. While they last, however, we must avoid contact with Earthmen.. The diseases are more violent with them."

A chill seemed to have entered the vehicle.

"Neena," the Martian went on, "came down with a mild case of one of these Martian colds. This was what I did not tell you. Perhaps I should have. Suppose you had chanced to come down this way, and she in her thoughtless carelessness had spoken to you?" The Martian shivered.

"What," asked the Earthman hollowly, "did she have?"

I do not know the name. My memory is not good. On Earth it produces sores—hideous. I have been told limbs drop off."

Terrified, the Earthman sat up straight.

The Martian glanced at him. "Come," he said comfortingly. "Relax yourself. She will get over it. It is not so severe here. I told you, with us it is like a cold. But you see, I do not wish this to get round. Our trade with Earth is mutually profitable. A misunderstanding on this could ruin it."

Yes," said the Earthman in a haunted voice. "You don't—you don't remember the name of this disease?"

"Ah, my memory is not too good. Reeta would know. It is a shame she could not come.—Headaches are not catching."

"That's good to know," said the Earthman. "Look, this 'cold'—would a person from Earth be likely to catch it? I mean—the odds?"

"We have not experimented," said the Martian dryly. He swung the many-wheeled vehicle onto the edge of the landing field. "I must leave you here. It has been a pleasure having you, my friend. I hope the contract will be satisfactory to everyone."

"Yes," said the Earthman faintly. "I'm sure it will." He looked off at the ship that was to carry him home.

But he did not look happy. He looked as if he had gone hollow inside.

On the way back, the Martian stopped at the small house surrounded with flowers. He called inside.

"Why," demanded the slender, pale-faced woman who came to door, "did you make me come down here just now? Why did you make me wear this horrid chalky face-whitener?"

Her husband spoke with a softness that was like velvet over a sword. "I know about last night, Reeta."

His wife caught her breath.

Her husband turned to the smiling woman who walked out to greet him. "I am sorry, Mohain," he said gently, "We must go home, now. Perhaps you will come up tonight with your husband?"

"Ah, he only takes me out once a week," the woman laughed, "and last night it was to the fireshow. Did you see it?"

"Alas," said the Martian with a faint tinge of a smile, "unfortunately, we did not."

With a heavy rumble, the Mars-Earth spaceship passed overhead.

THE GENTLE EARTH

Tlasht Bade, Supreme Commander of Invasion Forces, drew thoughtfully on his slim cigar. "The scouts are all back?"

Sission Runckel, Chief of the Supreme Commander's Staff, nodded. "They all got back safely, though one or two had difficulties with some of the lower life forms."

"Is the climate all right?"

Runckel abstractedly reached in his tunic, and pulled out a thing like a short piece of tarred rope. As he trimmed it, he scowled. "There's some discomfort, apparently because the air is too dry. But on the other hand, there's plenty of oxygen near the planet's surface, and the gravity's about the same as it is back home. We can live there."

Bade glanced across the room at a large blue, green, and brown globe, with irregular patches of white at top and bottom. "What are the white areas?"

"Apparently, chalk. One of our scouts landed there, but he's in practically a state of shock. The brilliant reflectivity in the area blinded him, a huge white furry animal attacked him, and he barely got out alive. To cap it all, his ship's insulation apparently broke down on the way back, and now he's in the sick bay with a bad case of space-gripe. All we can get out of him is that he had severe prickling sensations in the feet when he stepped out onto the chalk dust. Probably a pile of little spiny shells."

"Did he bring back a sample?"

"He claims he did. But there's only water in his sample box. I imagine he was delirious. In any case, this part of the planet has little to interest us."

Bade nodded. "What about the more populous regions?"

"Just as we thought. A huge web of interconnecting cities, manufacturing centers, and rural areas. Our mapping procedures have proved to be accurate."

"That's a relief. What about the natives?"

"Erect, land-dwelling, ill-tempered bipeds," said Runckel. "They seem to have little or no planet-wide unity. Of course, we have large samplings of their communications media. When these are all analyzed, we'll know a lot more."

"What do they look like?"

"They're pink or brown in color, quite tall, but not very broad or thick through the chest. A little fur here and there on their bodies. No webs on their hands or feet, and their feet are fantastically small. Otherwise, they look quite human."

"Their technology?"

Runckel sucked in a deep breath and sat up straight. "Every bit as bad as we thought." He picked up a little box with two stiff handles, squeezed the handles hard, and touched a glowing wire on the box to his piece of black rope. He puffed violently.

Bade turned up the air-conditioning. Billowing clouds of smoke drew away from Runckel in long streamers, so that he looked like an island looming through heavy mist. His brow was creased in a foreboding scowl.

"Technologically," he said, "they are deadly. They've got fission and fusion, indirect molecular and atomic reaction control, and a long-reaching development of electron flow and pulsing devices. So far, they don't seem to have anything based on deep rearrangement or keyed focusing. But who knows when they'll stumble on that? And then what? Even now, properly warned and ready they could give us a terrible struggle."

***

Runckel knocked a clinker off his length of rope and looked at Bade with the tentative, judging air of one who is not quite sure of another's reliability. Then he said, loudly and with great firmness, "We have a lot to be thankful for. Another five or ten decades delay getting the watchships up through the cloud layer, and they'd have had us by the throat. We've got to smash them before they're ready, or *we'll* end up as *their* colony."

Bade's eyes narrowed. "I've always opposed this invasion on philosophical grounds. But it's been argued and settled. I'm willing to go along with the majority opinion." Bade rapped the ash off his slender cigar and looked Runckel directly in the eyes. "But if you want to open the whole argument up all over again—"

"No," said Runckel, breathing out a heavy cloud of smoke. "But our micromapping and radiation analysis shows a terrific rate of progress. It's hard to look at those figures and even breathe normally. They're gaining on us like a shark after a minnow."

"In that case," said Bade, "let's wake up and hold our lead. This business of attacking the suspect before he has a chance to commit a crime is no answer. What about all the other planets in the universe? How do we know what they might do some day?"

"This planet is right beside us!"

"Is murder honorable as long as you do it only to your neighbor? Your argument is self-defense. But you're straining it."

"Let it strain, then," said Runckel angrily. "All I care about is that chart showing our comparative levels of development. Now *we* have the lead. I say, drag them out by their necks and let them submit, or we'll thrust their heads underwater and have done with them. And anyone who says otherwise is a doubtful patriot!"

Bade's teeth clamped, and he set his cigar carefully on a tray.

Runckel blinked, as if he only appreciated what he had said by its echo.

Bade's glance moved over Runckel deliberately, as if stripping away the emblems and insignia. Then Bade opened the bottom drawer of his desk, and pulled out a pad of dun-colored official forms. As he straightened, his glance caught the motto printed large on the base of the big globe. The motto had been used so often in the struggle to decide the question of invasion that Bade seldom noticed it any more. But now he looked at it. The motto read:

Them Or Us

Bade stared at it for a long moment, looked up at the globe that represented the mighty planet, then down at the puny motto. He glanced at Runckel, who looked back dully but squarely. Bade glanced at the motto, shook his head in disgust, and said, "Go get me the latest reports."

Runckel blinked. "Yes, sir," he said, and hurried out.

Bade leaned forward, ignored the motto, and thoughtfully studied the globe.

***

Bade read the reports carefully. Most of them, he noted, contained a qualification. In the scientific reports, this generally appeared at the end:

" . . . Owing to the brief time available for these observations, the conclusions presented herein must be regarded as only provisional in character."

In the reports of the scouts, this reservation was usually presented in bits and pieces:

" . . . And this thing, that looked like a tiny crab, had a pair of pincers on one end, and I didn't have time to see if this was the end it got me with, or if it was the other end. But I got a jolt as if somebody squeezed a lighter and held the red-hot wire against my leg. Then I got dizzy and sick to my stomach. I don't know for sure if this was what did it, or if there are many of them, but if there are, and if it did, I don't see how a man could fight a war and not be stung to death when he wasn't looking. But I wasn't there long enough to be sure . . . "

Another report spoke of a "Crawling army of little six-legged things with a set of oversize jaws on one end, that came swarming through the shrubbery straight for the ship, went right up the side and set to work eating away the superplast binder around the viewport. With that gone, the ship would leak air like a fishnet. But when I tried to clear them away, they started in on me. I don't know if this really proves anything, because Rufft landed not too far away, and he swears the place was like a paradise. Nevertheless, I have to report that I merely set my foot on the ground, and I almost got marooned and eaten up right on the spot."

Bade was particularly uneasy over reports of a vague respiratory difficulty some of the scouts noticed in the region where the first landings were planned. Bade commented on it, and Runckel nodded.

"I know," said Runckel. "The air's too dry. But if we take time to try to provide for that, at the same time they may make some new advance that will more than nullify whatever we gain. And right now their communications media show a political situation that fits right in with our plans. We can't hope for that to last forever."

Bade listened as Runckel described a situation like that of a dozen hungry sharks swimming in a circle, each getting its jaws open for a snap at the next one's tail. Then Runckel described his plan.

At the end, Bade said, "Yes, it may work out as you say. But listen, Runckel, isn't this a little too much like one of those whirlpools in the Treacherous Islands? If everything works out, you go through in a flash. But one wrong guess, and you go around and around and around and around and you're lucky if you get out with a whole skin."

Runckel's jaw set firmly. "This is the only way to get a clear-cut decision."

Bade studied the far wall of the room for a moment. "I'm sorry I didn't get a hand at these plans sooner."

"Sir," said Runckel, "You would have, if you hadn't been so busy fighting the whole idea." He hesitated, then asked, "Will you be coming to the staff review of plans?"

"Certainly," said Bade.

"Good," said Runckel. "You'll see that we have it all worked to perfection."

* * *

Bade went to the review of plans and listened as the details were gone over minutely. At the end, Runckel gave an overall summary:

"The Colony Planet," he said, rapping a pointer on maps of four hemispheric views, "is only seventy-five percent water, so the land areas are immense. The chief land masses are largely dominated by two hostile power groups, which we may call East and West. At the fringes of influence of these power groups live a vast mass of people not firmly allied to either.

"The territory of this uncommitted group is well suited to our purposes. It contains many pleasant islands and comfortable seas. Unfortunately, analysis shows that the dangerous military power groups will unite against us if we seize this territory directly. To avoid this, we will act to stun and divide them at one stroke."

Runckel rapped his pointer on a land area lettered "North America," and said, "On this land mass is situated a politico-economic unit known as the U.S. The U.S. is the dominant power both in the Western Hemisphere and in the West power group. It is surrounded by wide seas that separate it from its allies.

"Our plan is simple and direct. We will attack and seize the central plain of the U.S. This will split it into helpless fragments, any one of which we may crush at will. The loss of the U.S. will, of course, destroy the power balance between East and West. The East will immediately seize the scraps of Western power and influence all over the globe.

"During this period of disorder, we will set up our key-tool factories and a light-duty forceway network. In rapid stages will then come ore-converters, staging plants, fabricators, heavy-duty forceway stations and self-operated production units. With these last we will produce energy-conversion units and storage piles by the million in a network to blanket the occupied area. The linkage produced will power our damper units to blot out missile attacks that may now begin in earnest.

"We will thus be solidly established on the planet itself. Our base will be secure against attack. We will now turn our energies to the destruction of the U.S.S.R. as a military power." He reached out with his pointer to rap a new land mass.

"The U.S.S.R. is the dominant power of the East power group. This will by now be the only hostile power group remaining on the planet. It will be destroyed in stages.

"In Stage I we will confuse the U.S.S.R. by propaganda. We will profess friendship while we secretly multiply our productive facilities to the highest possible degree.

"In Stage II, we will seize and fortify the western and northern islands of Britain, Novaya Zemlya, and New Siberia. We will also seize and heavily fortify the Kamchatka Peninsula in the extreme eastern U.S.S.R. We will now demand that the U.S.S.R. lay down its arms and surrender.

"In the event of refusal, we will, from our fortified bases, destroy by missile attack all productive facilities and communication centers in the U.S.S.R. The resulting paralysis will bring down the East power group in ruins. The planet will now lay open before us."

Runckel looked at each of his listeners in turn.

"Everything has been done to make this invasion a success. To crush out any possible miscalculation, we are moving with massive reserves close behind us. Certain glory and a mighty victory await us.

"Let us raise our heads in prayer, then join in the Oath of Battle."

***

The first wave of the attack came down like an avalanche on the central U.S. Multiple transmitters went into action to throw local radar stations into confusion. Stull-gas missiles streaked from the landing ships to explode over nearby cities. Atmospheric flyers roared off to intercept possible enemy attacks. A stream of guns, tanks, and troop carriers rolled down the landing ways and fanned out to seize enemy power plants and communications centers.

The commander of the first wave reported: "Everything proceeding according to plan. Enemy resistance negligible."

Runckel ordered the second wave down.

Bade, watching it on a number of giant viewscreens in the operations room of a ship coming down, had a peculiar feeling of numbness, such as might follow a deep cut before the pain is felt.

Runckel, his face intense, said: "Their position is hopeless. The main landing site is secure and the rest will come faster than the eye can see." He turned to speak into one of a bank of microphones, then said, "Our glider missiles are circling over their capital."

A loud-speaker high on the wall said, "Landing minus three. Take your stations, please."

The angle of vision of one of the viewscreens tilted suddenly, to show a high, dome-topped building set in a city filled with rushing beetle shapes—obviously ground-cars of some type. Abruptly these cars all pulled to the sides of the streets.

"That," said Runckel grimly, "means their capital is out of business."

The picture on the viewscreen blurred suddenly, like the reflection from water ruffled by a breeze. There was a clang like a ten-ton hammer hitting a twenty-ton gong. Walls, floor, and ceiling of the room danced and vibrated. Two of the viewscreens went blank.

Bade felt a prickling sensation travel across his shoulders and down his back. He glanced sharply at Runckel.

Runckel's expression looked startled but firm. He reached out and snapped orders into one of his microphones.

There was an intense, high-pitched ringing, then a clap like a nuclear cannon at six paces distance.

The wall loud-speaker said, "Landing minus two."

An intense silence descended on the room. One by one, the viewscreens flickered on. Bade heard Runckel say, "The ship is totally damped. They haven't anything that can get through it."

There was a dull, low-pitched thud, a sense of being snapped like a whip, and the screens went blank. The wall loud-speaker dropped, and jerked to a stop, hanging by its cord.

Then the ship set down.

***

Runckel's plan assumed that the swift-moving advance from the landing site would overrun a sizable territory during the first day. With this maneuvering space quickly gained, the landing site itself would be safe from enemy ground attack by dawn of the second day.

Now that they were down, however, Bade and Runckel looked at the operations room's big viewscreen, and saw their vehicles standing still all over the landscape. The troops crowded about the rear of the vehicles to watch cursing drivers pull the motors up out of their housings and spread them out on the ground. Here and there a stern officer argued with grim-faced troops who stared stonily ahead as if they didn't hear. Meanwhile, the tanks, trucks, and weapons carriers stood motionless.

Runckel, infuriated, had a cluster of microphones gripped in his hand, and was pronouncing death by strangling and decapitation on any officer who failed to get his unit in motion right away.

Bade studied the baffled expressions on the faces of the drivers, then glanced at the enemy ground-cars abandoned at the side of the road. He turned to see a tall officer with general's insignia stagger through the doorway and grip Runckel by the arm. Bade recognized Rast, Ground Forces Commander.

"Sir," said Rast, "it can't be done."

"It has to be done," said Runckel grimly. "So far we've decoyed the enemy missiles to a false site. Before they spot us again, *those troops have got to be spread out*!"

"They won't ride in the vehicles!"

"It's that or get killed!"

"Sir," said Rast, "you don't understand. I came back here in a gun carrier. To start with, the driver jammed the speed lever all the way to the front shield, and nothing happened. He got up to see what was wrong. The carrier shot ahead with a flying leap, threw the driver into the back, and almost snapped our heads off. Then it coasted to a stop. We pulled ourselves together and turned around to get the cover off the motor box.

"*Wham!* The carrier took off, ripped the cover out of our hands, threw us against the rear shield and knocked us senseless. Then it rolled to a stop.

"That's how we got here. Jump! Roll. Stop. Wait. Jump! Roll. Stop. Wait. On one of those jumps, the gun went out the back of the carrier, mount, bolts, and all. The driver swore he'd turn off the motor, and fangjaw take the planet and the whole invasion. We aren't going to win a war with troops in that frame of mind."

Runckel took a deep breath.

Bade said, "What about the enemy's ground-cars? Will they run?"

Rast blinked. "I don't know. Maybe—"

Bade snapped on a microphone lettered "Aerial Rec." A little screen in a half-circle atop the microphone lit up to show an alert, harried-looking officer. Bade said, "You've noticed our vehicles are stopped?"

"Yes, sir."

"Were the enemy's ground-cars affected at the same time as ours?"

"No sir, they were still moving after ours were stuck."

"Any motor trouble in Atmospheric Flyer Command?"

"None that I know of, sir."

Bade glanced at Rast. "Try using the enemy ground-cars. Meanwhile, get the troops you can't move back under cover of the ships' dampers."

Rast saluted, whirled, and went out at a staggering run.

Bade called Atmospheric Flyer Command, and Ground Forces Maintenance, and arranged for the captured enemy vehicles to be identified by a large yellow X painted across the top of the hood. Then he turned to Runckel and said, "We're going to need all the support we can get. See if we can bring Landing Force 2 down late today instead of tomorrow."

"I'll try," said Runckel.

***

It seemed to Bade that the events of the next twenty-four hours unrolled like the scenes of a nightmare.

Before the troops were all under cover, an enemy reconnaissance aircraft leaked in very high overhead. The detector screens of Atmospheric Flyer Command were promptly choked with enemy aircraft coming in low and fast from all directions.

These aircraft were of all types. Some heaved their bombs in under-hand, barreled over and streaked home for another load. Others were flying hives of anti-aircraft missiles. A third type were suicide bombers or winged missiles; these roared in head-on and blew up on arrival.

While the dampers labored and overheated, and Flyer Command struggled with enemy fighters and bombers overhead, a long-range reconnaissance flyer spotted a sizable convoy of enemy ground forces rushing up from the southwest.

Bade and Runckel concentrated first on living through the air attack. It soon developed that the enemy planes, though extremely fast, were not very maneuverable. The enemy's missiles did not quite overload the dampers. The afternoon wore on in an explosive violence that was severe, but barely endurable. It began to seem that they might live through it.

Toward evening, however, a small enemy missile streaked in on the end of a wire and smashed the grid of an auxiliary damper unit. Before this unit could be repaired, a heavy missile came down near the same place, and overloaded the damper network. Another missile streaked in. One of the ships tilted, and fell headlong. The engines of this ship were ripped out of the circuit that powered the dampers. With the next enemy missile strike, another ship was heaved off its base. This ship housed a large proportion of Flyer Command's detector screens.

Bade and Runckel looked at each other. Bade's lips moved, and he heard himself say, "Prepare to evacuate."

At this moment, the enemy attack let up.

* * *

It took an instant for Bade to realize what had happened. He canceled his evacuation order before it could be transmitted, then had the two thrown ships linked back into the power circuit. He turned around, and his glance fell on one of the viewscreens showing the shadowy plain outside. A brilliant flash lit the screen, and he saw dark low shapes rushing in toward the ships. Bade immediately gave orders to defend against ground attack, but not to pursue beyond range of the dampers.

A savage, half-lit struggle developed. The enemy, whose weapons failed to work in range of the dampers, attacked with bayonets, and used guns, shovels, and picks in the manner of clubs and battle axes. In a spasm of bloody violence they fought their way in among the ships, then, confused in the dimness, were thrown back with heavy losses. As night settled down, the enemy dug in to make a fortified ring close around the landing site.

The enemy missile attack failed to recover its former violence.

Bade gave silent thanks for the deliverance. As the comparative quiet continued, it seemed clear that the enemy high command was holding back to avoid hitting their own men dug in nearby.

It occurred to Bade that now might be a good time to get a little sleep. He turned to go to his cot, and there was a rush of yellow dots on Flyer Command's pilot screen. As he stared wide-eyed, auxiliary screens flickered on and off to show a ghostly dish-shaped object that led his flyers on a wild chase all over the sky, then vanished at an estimated speed twenty times that the enemy planes were thought capable of doing.

Runckel said, "Landing Force 2 can get here at early dawn. That's the best we can manage."

Bade nodded dully.

The ground screens now lit in brilliant flashes as the enemy began firing monster rockets at practically point-blank range.

Night passed in a continuous bombardment.

At early dawn of the next day, Bade put in all his remaining missiles, and bomber and interceptor flyers. For a brief interval of time, the enemy bombardment was smothered.

Landing force 2 set down beside Landing Force 1.

Bade ordered the Stull-gas missiles of Landing Force 2 exploded over the enemy ground troops. In the resulting confusion, the ground forces moved out and captured large numbers of enemy troops, weapons, and vehicles. The captured vehicles were marked and promptly put to use.

Bade spoke briefly with General Rast, commanding the ground forces.

"Now's your chance," said Bade. "Move fast and we can capture supplies and reinforcements flowing in, before they realize we've broken their ring."

Under the protection of the flyers of Landing Force 2, Rast's troops swung out onto the central plain of the North American continent.

***

The advance moved fast. Enemy troops and supply convoys were caught off guard on the road. When the enemy fought, his resistance was patchy and confused.

Bade, feeling drugged from lack of sleep, lay down on his cot for a nap. He awoke feeling fuzzy-brained and dull.

"They're whipped," said Runckel gleefully. "We've got back the time we lost yesterday. There's no resistance to speak of. And we've just made a treaty with the East bloc."

Bade sat up dizzily. "That's wonderful," he said. He glanced at the clock. "Why wasn't I called sooner?"

"No need," said Runckel. "It's all just a matter of form. Landing Force 3 is coming down tonight. The war's over." Runckel's face, as he said this, had a peculiar shine.

Bade frowned. "Isn't the enemy making any reaction at all?"

"Nothing worth mentioning. We're driving them ahead of us like a school of minnows."

Bade got to his feet uneasily. "It can't be this simple." He stepped out into the operations room and detected unmistakable signs of holiday jubilation. Nearly everyone was grinning, and gawkers were standing in a thick ring before the screen showing the map room's latest plot.

Bade said sharply, "Don't these men have anything to do?" His voice carried across the room with the effect of a shark surfacing in the midst of a ladies' swimming party. Several of the men at the map jumped. Others glanced around jerkily. There was a concerted bumping of elbows, and the ring of gawkers evaporated briskly in all directions. In every part of the room there was abruptly something approaching a businesslike atmosphere.

Bade looked around angrily and sat down at his desk. Then he saw the map. He squeezed his eyes shut, then looked again.

In the center of the map of North America was a big blot, as if a bottle of red ink had been thrown at it. Bade turned to Runckel and asked harshly, "Is that map correct?"

"Absolutely," said Runckel, his face shining with satisfaction.

Bade looked back at the map and performed a series of rapid calculations. He glanced at the viewscreens, and saw that those which would normally show the advanced ground troops weren't in use. This, he supposed, meant that the advance had outrun the technical crews.

Bade snapped on a microphone lettered "Supply, Ground." In the half-circle atop the microphone appeared an officer in the last stage of sleepless exhaustion. The officer's eyes twitched, and his skin had a drawn dull look. His head was slumped on his hand.

"*Supply?*" said Bade in alarm.

"Sorry," mumbled the officer, "we can't do it. We're overstretched already. Try Flyer Command. Maybe they'll parachute it to you."

Bade switched off, and glanced at the map again. He turned to Runckel. "Listen, what are we using for transport?"

"The enemy ground-cars."

"Fast, aren't they?"

Runckel smiled cheerfully. "They are built for speed. Rast grabbed a whole fleet of them to start with, and they've worked fine ever since. A few wrecks, some bad cases of kinkfoot, but that's all."

"What the devil is 'kinkfoot'?"

"Well, the enemy have tiny feet with little toes and no webs at all. Some of their ground-car controls are on the floor. There just isn't much space so our men's feet get cramped. It's just a mild irritation." Runckel smiled vaguely. "Nothing to worry about."

Bade squinted hard at Runckel. "What's Supply using for transport?"

"Steam trucks, of course."

"Do they work all right, or do they jump?"

Runckel smiled dreamily. "They work fine."

Bade snapped on the Supply microphone. The same weary officer appeared, his head in his hands, and mumbled, "Sorry. We're overloaded. Try Flyer Command."

Bade said angrily, "Wake up a minute."

The man raised his head, blinked at Bade, then straightened as if hauled by the back of the collar.

"Sir?"

"What's the overall supply picture?"

"Sir, it's awful. Terrible."

"What's the matter?"

"The advance is so fast, and the units are all mixed up, and when we get to a place, they've already pulled out. Worse yet, the steam trucks—" He hesitated, as if afraid to go on.

"Speak up," snapped Bade. "What's wrong with the trucks? Is it the engines? Fuel? Running gear? What is it?"

"It's . . . the water, sir."

"The water?"

"Sir, there's that constant loss of steam out the exhaust. At home, we just throw a few more buckets of water in the tank and go on. But here—"

"Oh," said Bade, the situation dawning on him.

"But around here, sir," said the officer, "they've had something called a 'severe drought.' The streams are dry."

"Can you dig down?"

"Sir, at best there's just muck. We *know* there's water here somewhere, but meanwhile our trucks are stalled all over the country with the men dug down out of sight, and the natives standing around shaking their heads, and *sure*, there's *got* to be water down there somewhere, but what do we use right now?"

Bade took a deep breath. "What about the enemy trucks? Can't you use them?"

"If we'd started off with them, I suppose we could have. But Ground Forces has requisitioned most of them. Now we're spread out in all directions with the front getting farther away all the time."

***

Bade switched off and got in touch with Ground Forces, Maintenance. A spruce-looking major appeared. Bade paused a moment, then asked, "How's your workload, major? Are you behind schedule?"

The major looked shocked. "No, sir. Far from it. We're away ahead of schedule."

"Aren't these enemy vehicles giving you any trouble? Any difficulties in repair?"

The major laughed. "Fangjaw, general, we don't repair them! When they burn out, we throw them away. We pried up the hoods of some of them, pulled off the top two or three layers of machinery, and took a good look underneath. That was enough. There are hundreds of parts, all shapes and sizes. And dozens of different kinds of motors. Half of the parts are stuck so they won't move when you try to get them out, and, to top it all, there isn't enough room in there to squeeze in an extra grain of sand. So what's the use? If something goes wrong with one of those things, we give it a shove off the road and forget it. There are plenty of others."

"I see," said Bade. "Do you send your repair crews out to shove the ground-cars off the road?"

"Oh, no, sir," said the major looking startled. "Like the colonel says, 'Let the Ground Forces do it.' Sir, it doesn't take any skill to do that. It's just that that's our *policy*: Don't repair 'em. Throw 'em away."

"What about *our* vehicles then? Have you found out what's wrong?"

The major looked uncomfortable. "Well, the difficulty is that the vehicles work satisfactorily *inside* the ship, and for a little while *outside*. But then, after they've been out a while, a malfunction occurs in the mechanism. That's what causes the trouble." He looked at Bade hopefully. "Was there anything else, sir."

"Yes," said Bade dryly, "it's the malfunction I'm interested in. What *is* it that goes wrong?"

The major looked unhappy. "Well, sir, we've had the motors apart and put back together I don't know how many times, and the fact is, there's nothing at all wrong with them. There's nothing wrong, but they still won't work. That's not our department. We've handed the whole business over to the Testing Lab."

"Then," said Bade, "you actually don't have any work to do?"

The major jumped. "Oh, no sir, I didn't say that. We . . . we're holding ourselves in readiness, sir, and we've got our shops in order, and some of the men are doing some very, ah, very important research on the . . . the structure of the enemy ground-car, and—"

"Fine," said Bade. "Get your colonel on this line." When the colonel appeared, Bade said, "Ground Forces Supply has its steam trucks out of service for lack of water. Get in touch with their H.Q., find out the location of the trucks, and get out there with the water. Find out where they can replenish in the future. Take care of this as fast as you can."

The colonel worked his mouth in a way that suggested a weak valve struggling to hold back a large quantity of compressed air. Bade looked at him hard. The colonel's mouth blew open, and "Yes, sir!" came out. The colonel looked startled.

Bade immediately switched back to Supply and said, "Ground Forces Maintenance is going to help you water your trucks. Why didn't you get in touch with them yourselves? It's the obvious thing."

"Sir, we did, hours ago. They said water supply wasn't in *their* department."

Bade seemed to see the bursting of innumerable bubbles before his eyes. It dawned on him that he was bogged down in petty details while big events rushed on unheeded. He switched back to the colonel briefly and when he switched off the colonel was plainly vibrating with energy from head to toe. Then Bade looked forebodingly at the map and ordered Liaison to get General Rast for him.

***

This took a long time, which Bade spent trying to anticipate the possible enemy reaction if Supply broke down completely, and a retirement became necessary. By the time Rast appeared on the screen, Bade had thought it over carefully, and could see nothing but trouble ahead. There was a buzz, and Bade looked up to see a fuzzy picture of Rast.

Rast, as far as Bade could judge, had a look of victory and exhilaration. But the communicator's reception was uncommonly bad, and Rast's image had a tendency to flicker, fade, and slide up and down. Judging by the trend of the conversation, Bade decided reception must be worse yet at the other end.

Bade said, "Supply is in a mess. You'd better choose some sort of defensible perimeter and halt."

Rast said, "Thank you. The enemy is in full flight."

"Listen," said Bade. "Supply is stopped. We can't get supplies to you. Supply can't catch up with you."

"We'll pursue them day and night," said Rast.

"Listen to me," said Bade. "Break off the pursuit! We can't get supplies to you!"

Rast's form slowly dimmed and expanded till it filled the screen, then burst, and reappeared as a brilliant image the size of a man's thumb. His voice cut off, then came through as a crackle.

"Siss kissis sissis," said the image, expanding again, "hisss siss kississ sissikississ." This noise was accompanied by earnest gestures on the part of Rast, and a very determined facial expression. The image grew huge and dim, and burst, then started over again.

Bade spat out a word he had promised himself never to say again under any circumstances whatever. Then he sat helpless while the image, large and clear, leaned forward earnestly and pounded one huge fist into the other.

"Hiss! Siss! Fississ!"

"Listen," said Bade, "I can't make out a word you're saying." He leaned forward. "WE CAN'T GET SUP-PLIES TO YOU!"

The image burst and started over, bright and small.

Bade sucked in a deep breath. He grabbed the Communications microphone. "Listen," he snapped, "I've got General Rast on the screen here and I can't hear anything but a crackle. The image constantly expands and contracts."

"I know, sir," said a gray-smocked technician with a despairing look. "I can see the monitor screen from here. It's the best we can do, sir."

Out of the corner of his eye, Bade could see Rast's image growing huge and dim. "Hiss! Siss!" said Rast earnestly.

"What causes this?" roared Bade.

"Sir, all we can guess is some terrific electrical discharge between here and General Rast's position. What such a discharge might be, I can't imagine."

Bade scowled, and looked at a thumb-sized Rast. Bade opened his mouth to roar out that there was no way to get supplies through. Rast's image suddenly vibrated like a twanged string, then stopped expanding.

Rast's voice came through clearly, "Will you repeat that, sir?"

"WE CAN'T SUPPLY YOU," said Bade. "Halt your advance. Pick a good spot and HALT!"

Rast's image was expanding again. "Siss hiss," he said, and saluted. His image vanished.

Bade immediately snapped on the Communications microphone. "Do you have anyone down there who can read lips?" he demanded.

"Read *lips*? Sir, I—" The technician squinted suddenly, and swung off the screen. He was back in a moment, his face clear and hopeful. "Sir, we've got a man in the section that's a fanatic on communications methods. The other men think he *can* read lips, and I've sent for him."

"Good," said Bade. "Set him to work on the record of that conversation with General Rast. Another thing—is there any way you can get a message though to Rast?"

The technician looked doubtful. "Well, sir . . . I don't know—" His face cleared slightly. "We can try, sir."

"Good," said Bade. "Send 'Supply situation bad. Strongly suggest you halt your advance and consolidate position.' " Bade's glance fell on the latest plot from the map room. Glumly he asked himself how Rast or anyone else could hope to consolidate the balloon-like situation that was coming about.

"Sir," asked the technician, "is that all?"

"Yes," said Bade, "and let me know when you get through to Rast."

"Yes, sir."

***

Bade switched off, and turned to ask Runckel for the exact time Landing Force 3 would be down. Bade hesitated, then squinted hard at Runckel.

Runckel's face had an unusually bright, animated look. He was glancing rapidly through a sheaf of reports, quickly scribbling comments on them, and tossing them to an excited-looking clerk, who rushed off to slap them on the desks of various exhilarated officers and clerks. These men eagerly transmitted them to their various sections. This procedure was normal, but the faces of the men all looked too excited. Their movements were jerky and fast.

Bade became aware of the sensation of watching a scene in a lunatic asylum.

The excited-looking clerk rushed to Runckel's desk to snatch up a sheaf of reports, and Bade snapped, "Bring those here."

The clerk jumped, rushed to Bade's desk, halted with a jerky bounce and saluted snappily. He flopped the papers on the desk, whirled around and raced off toward the desks of the officers who usually got the reports Bade was now holding. The clerk stopped suddenly, looked at his empty hands, spun around, stared at Runckel's desk, then at Bade's. A look of enlightenment passed across his face. "Oh," he said, with a foolish grin. He teetered back and forth on his heels, then rushed over to look at the latest plot from the map room.

Bade set his jaw and glanced at the reports Runckel had marked.

The top two or three reports were simple routine and had merely been initialed. The next report, however, was headed: "Testing Lab. Report on Cause of Vehicle Failure; Recommendations."

Bade quickly glanced over several sheet of technical diagrams and figures, and turned to the summary. He read:

"In short, the breakdown of normal function, and the resultant slow violent pulsing action of the motor, is caused by the abnormally low conductivity of Surface Conduction Layer S-3. The pulser current, which would normally flow across this layer is blocked, and instead builds up on projection L-26. Eventually a sufficient charge accumulates, and arcs across air gap B. This throws a shock current through the exciter such as is normally experienced only during violent acceleration. The result is that the vehicle shoots ahead from a standing start, then rolls to a stop while the current again slowly accumulates. The root cause of this malfunction is the fantastically low moisture content of the atmosphere on this planet. It is this that causes the loss of conductivity across Layer S-3.

"Recommended measures to overcome this malfunction include:

a) Artificial humidification of the air entering the motor, by means of sprayer and fan.

b) Sealing of the motor unit.

c) Coating of surface conduction layer S-3 with a top-sealed permanent conducting film.

"A) or b) probably can be carried out as soon as the requisite devices and materials are obtainable. This, however, may involve a considerable delay. C), on the other hand, will require a good deal of initial testing and experimentation, but may then be carried into effect very quickly, as the requisite tools and materials are already at hand. We will immediately carry out the initial measures for whichever plan you deem preferable."

Bade looked the report over again carefully, then glanced at Runckel's scrawled comment:

"Good work! Carry this out immediately! S.R."

Bade glared. Carry *what* out immediately?

Bade glanced angrily at Runckel, then sat up in alarm. Runckel's hands clenched the side of his desk. Runckel's back was straight as a rod. His chest was inflated to huge dimensions, and he was slowly drawing in yet more air. His face bore a fixated, inward-turned look that might indicate either horror or ecstasy.

Bade shoved his chair back and glanced around for help.

His glance stopped at the map screen, where the huge overblown blot in the center of the continent had sprouted a long narrow pencil reaching out toward the west.

There was a quick low gonging sound, and the semicircular rim atop the Communications microphone lit up in red. Bade snapped the microphone on and a scared-looking technician said, "Sir, we've worked out what General Rast said."

"What?" Bade demanded.

At Bade's side, there was a harsh scraping noise. Bade whipped around.

Runckel lurched to his feet, his face tense, his eyes shut, his mouth half open and his hands clenched.

Runckel twisted. There was a gagging sound, then a harsh roar:

Ka

Ka

Ka

KACHOOOOO!!

Bade sat down in a hurry and grabbed the microphone marked, "Medical Corps."

***

A crowd of young doctors and attendants swarmed around Runckel with pulse-beat snoopers, blood pressure gauges, little lights on long rubber tubes, and bottles and jars which they filled with fluid sucked out of the suffering Runckel with long hollow needles. They whacked Runckel, pinched him, and thumped him, then jumped for cover as he let out another blast.

"Sir," said a young doctor wearing a "Medical-Officer-On-Duty" badge, "I'm afraid I shall have to quarantine this room and all its occupants. That includes you, sir." He said this in a gentle but firm voice.

Bade glanced at the doorway. A continuous stream of clerks, officers, and messengers moved in and out on necessary business. Some of these officers, Bade noticed, were speaking in low angry tones to idiotically smiling members of the staff. As one of the angry officers slapped a sheaf of papers on a desk, the owner of the desk came slowly to his feet. His chest inflated to gigantic proportions, he let out a terrific blast, reeled back against a wall, and let out another.

The young medical officer spun around excitedly. "Epidemic!" he yelled. "Seal that door! Back, all of you!" His face had a faint glow as he turned to Bade. "We'll have this under control in no time, sir." He came up and plastered a red and yellow sticker over the joint where door and wall came together. He faced the room. "Everyone here is quarantined. It's death to break that seal."

From Bade's desk came an insistent ringing, and the small voice of the communications technician pleaded, "Sir . . . please, sir . . . this is important!" On the map across the room the bloated red space now had two sizable dents driven into it, such as might be expected if the enemy were opening a counteroffensive. The thin pencil line reaching toward the west was wobbling uncertainly at its far end.

Bade became aware of a fuzzy quality in his own thinking, and struggled to fix his mind on the scene around him.

The young doctor and his assistants hustled Runckel toward the door. As Bade stared, the doctor and assistants went out the door without breaking the quarantine seal. The sticker was plastered over the joint on the hinge side of the door. The seal bent as the door opened, then straightened out unhurt as the door shut.

"*Phew*," said Bade. He picked up the Communications microphone. "What did General Rast say?"

"Sir, he said, 'I can't reach the coast any faster than a day-and-a-half!' "

"The *coast*!"

"That's what he said, sir."

"Did you get that message to him?"

"Not yet, sir. We're trying."

Bade switched off and tried to think. His army was stretched out like a rubber balloon. His headquarters machinery was falling apart fast. An epidemic was loose among his men and plainly spreading fast. The base was still secure. But without sane men to man it, the enemy could be expected to walk in any time.

Bade's eyes were watering. He blinked, and glanced around for some sane face in the sea of hysterically cheerful people. He spotted an alert-looking officer with his back against the wall and a chair leg in his hand. Bade called to him. The officer looked around.

Bade said, "Do you know when Landing Force 3 is coming down?"

"Sir, they're coming down right now."

∗∗∗

Bade stayed conscious long enough to watch the beginning of the enemy's counteroffensive, and also to see the start of the exploding sickness spread through the landing site. He grimly summarized the situation to the man he chose to take over command.

This man was the leader of Landing Force 3, a general by the name of Kottek. General Kottek was a fanatic, a man with a rough hypnotic voice and a direct unblinking stare. General Kottek's favorite drink was pure water. Food was a matter of indifference to him. His only known amusements were regular physical exercise and the dissection of military problems. To hesitate to obey a command of General Kottek's was unheard of. To bungle in the performance of it was as pleasant as to sit down in the open mouth of a shark. General Kottek's officers were usually recognizable by their lean athletic appearance, and a tendency to jump at unexpected noises. General Kottek's men were nearly always to be seen in a state of good order and high spirits.

As soon as Bade, aching and miserable, summarized the situation and ordered Kottek to take over, Kottek gave a sharp precise salute, turned, and immediately began snapping out orders.

Heavily armed troops swung out to guard the site. Military police forced wandering gangs of sick men back to their ships. The crews of Landing Force 3 divided up to bring the depleted crews of the other ships up to minimum standards. The ships' damper units were turned to full power, and the outside power network and auxiliary damper units were disassembled and carried into the ships. Word came that a large enemy force had made an air-borne landing not far away. Kottek's troops marched in good order back to their ships. The ships of all three landing forces took off. They set down together in the center of the largest mass of Rast's encircled troops. The next day passed embarking these men under the protection of Kottek's fresh troops and the ships' dampers. Then the ships took off and repeated the process.

In this way, some sixty-five percent of the surrounded men were saved in the course of the week. Two more landing forces came down. General Rast and a small body of guards were found unconscious partway up an unbelievably high hill in the west. The situation at this point became hopelessly complicated by the exploding sickness.

This sickness, which none of the doctors were able to cure or even relieve, manifested itself in various forms. The usual form began by exhilarating the victim. In this state, the patient generally considered himself capable of doing anything, however foolhardy, and regardless of difficulties. This lasted until the second phase set in with violent contractions of the chest and a sudden out-rush of air from the lungs, accompanied by a blast like a gun going off. This second stage might or might not have complications such as digestive upset, headache, or shooting pains in the hands and feet. It ended when the third and last phase set in. In this phase the victim suffered from mental depression, considered himself a hopeless failure, and was as likely as not to try to end his life by suicide.

As a result of this suicidal impulse there were nightmarish scenes of soldiers disarming other soldiers, which brought the whole invasion force into a state of quaking uncertainty. At this critical point, and despite all precautions, General Kottek himself began to come down with the sickness. With him, the usual exhilaration took the form of a stream of violent and imperative orders.

Troops who should have retreated were ordered to fight to the death where they stood. Savage counter-attacks for worthless objectives were driven home "to the last drop of blood." Because General Kottek ordered it, people obeyed without thought. The hysterical light in his eye was masked by the fanatical glitter that had been there to begin with. The general himself only realized what was wrong when his chest tightened up, his body tensed, and a racking concatenation of explosions burst from his chest. He immediately brought his body to the position of attention, and crushed out by sheer will a series of incipient tickling sensations way down in his throat. General Kottek handed the command over to General Runckel and reported himself to sick bay.

Runckel, by this time, had recovered enough from the third phase to be untied and allowed to walk around with only two guards. As he had not fully recovered his confidence, however, he immediately went to see Bade.

*   *   *

Bade's illness took the form of nausea, cold hands and feet, and a sensation of severe pressure in the small of the back. Bade was lying on a cot when Runckel came in, followed by his two watchful guards.

Bade looked up and saw the two guards lean warily against the wall, their eyes narrowed as they watched Runckel. Runckel paused at the foot of Bade's bed. "How do you feel?" Runckel asked.

"Except for yesterday and the day before," said Bade, "I never felt worse in my life. How do you feel?"

"All right most of the time." He cleared his throat. "Kottek's down with it now."

"Did he know in time?"

"No, I'm afraid he's left things in a mess."

Bade shook his head. "Do we have a general officer who *isn't* sick?"

"Not in the top brackets."

"Who did Kottek hand over to?"

"Me." Runckel looked a little embarrassed. "I'm not sure I can handle it yet."

"Who's in actual charge right now?"

"I've got the pieces of our own staff and the staff of Landing Force 2 working on it. Kottek's staff is hopeless. Half of them are talking about sweeping the enemy off the planet in two days."

Bade grunted. "What's your idea?"

"Well," said Runckel, "I still get . . . a little excited now and then. If you could possibly provide a sort of general supervision—"

Bade looked away weakly. "How's Rast?"

"Tied to his bunk with half-a-dozen men sitting on him."

"What about Vokk?"

"Tearing his lungs out every two or three minutes."

"Sokkis, then?"

Runckel shook his head grimly. "I'm afraid they didn't hear the gun go off in time. The doctors are still working on him, though."

"Well . . . is Frotch all right?"

"Yes, thank heaven. But then he's Flyer Command. And, worse yet, there's nobody to put in his place."

"All right, how about Sozzle?"

"Well," said Runckel, "Sozzle may be a good propaganda man, but personally I wouldn't trust him to command a platoon."

"Yes," said Bade, rolling over to try to ease the pain in his back, "I see your point." He took a deep breath. "I'll try to supervise the thing." He swung gingerly to a sitting position.

Runckel watched him, then his face twisted. "This whole thing is all my fault," he said. He choked. "I'm just no goo—"

The two guards sprang across the room, grabbed Runckel by the arms and rushed him out the door. Harsh grunts and solid thumping sounds came from the corridor outside. There was a heavy crash. Somebody said, "All right, get the general by the feet, and I'll take him by the shoulders. *Phew!* Let's go."

Bade sat dizzily on the edge of the bed. For a moment, he had a mental image of Runckel before the invasion, leaning forward and saying impressively, "Certain glory and a mighty victory await us."

Bade took several slow deep breaths. Then he got up carefully, found a towel, and cautiously went to wash.

♦♦♦

It took Bade almost a week to disentangle the troops from the web of indefensible positions and hopeless last stands Kottek had committed them to in a day-and-a-half of peremptory orders. The enemy, meanwhile, took advantage of opportunity, using ground and air attacks, rockets, missiles and artillery in such profusion as to stun the mind. It was not until Bade's men and officers had recovered from circulating attacks of the sickness, and another landing force had come down, that it was possible to temporarily resume the offensive. Another two weeks, and another sick landing force recovered, saw the invasion army in control of a substantial part of the central plain of the continent. Bade now had some spare moments to squint at certain reports that were piled up on his desk. Exasperatedly, he called a meeting of high officers.

∗∗∗

Bade was standing with Runckel at a big map of the continent when their generals came in. Bade and Runckel each looked grim and intense. The generals looked uniformly dulled and worn down.

Bade took a last hard look at the map, then he and Runckel turned. Bade glanced at Veth, Landing Site Commander. "What's your impression of the way things are going?"

Veth scowled. "Well, we're still getting eight to ten sizable missile hits a day. Of course, there's no predicting when they'll come in. With the men working outside the ships, any single hit could vaporize large numbers of essential technical personnel. Until we get the underground shelters built, the only way around this is to have the whole site damped out all the time." He shook his head. "This takes a lot of energy."

Bade nodded, and turned to Rast, Ground Forces Commander.

"So far," said Rast frowning, "our situation on paper looks not too bad. Morale is satisfactory. Our weapons are superior. We have strong forces in a reasonably large central area, and in theory we can shift rapidly from one front to the other, and be superior anywhere. But in practice, the enemy has so many missiles, of all types and sizes, that we can't take advantage of the position.

"Suppose, for instance, that I order XX and XXII Tank Armies from the eastern to the western front. They can't go under their own power, because of fuel expenditure, the wear on their tracks, and the resulting delay for repairs. They can't go by forceway network because there isn't any built yet. The only way to send them is by the natives' iron track roads. That would be fine, except that the iron track roads make beautiful targets for missile attacks. Thanks to the enemy, every bridge and junction either is, has been, or will be blown up and not once, either. The result is, we have to use slow filtration of troops from one front to the other, or we have to accept very heavy losses on route. In addition, we now know that the enemy has formidable natural defenses in the east and west, especially in the west. There's a range of hills there that surpasses anything I've ever seen or heard of. Not only is the difficulty of the terrain an obstacle, but as our men go higher, movement finally becomes practically impossible. I know this from personal experience. The result of it is, the enemy need only guard the passes and he has a natural barrier behind which he can mass for attack at any chosen point."

Bade frowned. "Don't the hills have the same harmful effect on the enemy?"

"No sir, they don't."

"Why not?"

"I don't know. But that and their missiles put us in a nasty spot."

Bade absorbed this, then turned to General Frotch, head of Atmospheric Flyer Command.

Frotch said briskly, "Sir, so far as the enemy air forces are concerned, we have the situation under control. And various foreign long-range reconnaissance aircraft that have been filtering in from distant native countries, have also been successfully batted out of the sky. However, as far as . . . ah . . . missiles . . . are concerned, the situation is a little strained."

Bade snapped, "Go on."

"Well, sir," said Frotch, "the enemy has missiles that can be fired at the fastest atmospheric flyers, that can be made to blow up near them, that can be guided to them, and even that can be made to chase and catch them."

"What about our weapons?"

"They're fine, on a percentage basis. But the enemy has a lot more missiles than we have pilots."

"I see," said Bade. "Well—" He turned to speak to the Director of Intelligence, but Frotch went on:

"Moreover, sir, we are having atmospheric troubles."

" 'Atmospheric troubles'? What's that?"

"For one thing, gigantic traveling electrical displays that disrupt plane-to-ground communications, and have to be avoided, or else the pilots either don't come out, or else come out fit for nothing but a rest cure. Then there are mass movements of air traveling from one part of the planet to another. Like land breezes and sea breezes at home. But here the breezes can be pretty forceful. The effect is to put an unpredictable braking force on all our operations."

Bade nodded slowly. "Well, we'll have to make the best of it." He turned to General Sozzle, who was Disseminator of Propaganda.

Sozzle cleared his throat. "I can make my report short and to the point. Our propaganda is getting us nowhere. For one thing, the enemy is apparently used to being ambushed daily by something called 'advertising,' which seems to consist of a series of subtle propaganda traps. By comparison our approach is so crude it throws them into hysterics."

Bade glanced at the Director of Intelligence, who said dully, "Sir, it's too early to say for certain how our work will eventually turn out. We've had some successes; but, so far, we've been handicapped by translation difficulties."

Bade frowned. "For instance?"

"Take the single word, 'snow,'" said the Intelligence Director. "You can't imagine the snarl my translators get into over that word. It apparently means 'white solid which falls in crystals from the sky.' Figure that out."

Bade squinted, then looked relieved. "Oh. It means, 'dust.'"

"That's the way the interpreters translated it. Now consider this sentence from a schoolbook. 'When April comes, the dust all turns to water and flows into the ground to fill the streams.'"

"That doesn't make any sense at all."

"No. But that's what happens if you accept 'dust' as the translation for 'snow.' There are other words such as 'winter,' 'blizzard,' 'tornado.' Ask a native for an explanation, and with a straight face he'll give you a string of incomprehensible nonsense that will stand you on your ear. Not that it's important in itself. But it seems to show something about the native psychology that I can't quite figure out. You can fight your enemy best when you can understand him. Well, from this angle they're completely incomprehensible."

"Keep working on it," said Bade, after a short silence. He turned to Runckel.

Runckel said, "The overall situation looks about the same from my point of view. Namely, the natives are driven back, but by no means defeated. What we have to remember is that we never expected to have them defeated at this stage. True, our time schedule has been set back somewhat, but this was due not to enemy action, but to purely accidental circumstances. That is, first the atmosphere was so deficient in moisture that our ground vehicles were temporarily out of order, and, second, we were disabled by an unexpected disease. But these troubles are over with. My point is that we can now begin the decisive phase of operations."

"Good," said Bade. "But to do that we have to firmly hold the ground we have. I want to know if we can do this. On the surface, perhaps, it looks like it. But there are signs here I don't like. As the old saying goes, 'A shark shows you his fin, not his teeth. Take warning from the fin; when you see the teeth it's too late.' "

"Yes," said Frotch, turning excitedly to Rast, "that's the thought exactly. Now, will *you* mention it, or shall I?"

"Holy fangjaw," growled Rast, "maybe it doesn't really mean anything."

"The Supreme Commander," said Runckel angrily, "was trying to talk."

Bade said, "What is it, Rast? Speak up."

"Well—" Rast hesitated, glanced uneasily at Runckel, then thrust out his jaw, "Sir, it looks like the whole master plan of the invasion may have come unhinged."

Runckel angrily started to speak.

Bade glanced at Runckel, took out a long slender cigar, and sat down on the edge of the table to watch Runckel. He lit the cigar and put down the lighter. As far as Bade was concerned, his face was expressionless. Things seemed to have an unnatural clarity, however, as he looked at Runckel and waited for him to speak.

Runckel looked at Bade, swallowed hard and said nothing.

Bade glanced at Rast.

Rast burst out, "Sir, for the last ten days or so, we've been wondering how long the enemy could keep up his missile attacks. Flyer Command has blasted factories vital to missile manufacture, and destroyed all their known stockpiles. Well, grant we didn't get all their stockpiles. That's logical enough. Grant that they had tremendous stocks stored away. Even grant that before we got here they made missiles all the time for the sheer love of making them. Maybe every man, woman, and child in the country had a missile, like a pet. Still, there's got to be an end *somewhere*."

Bade nodded soberly.

"Well, sir," said Rast, "we get these missiles fired at us all the time, day after day after day, one missile after the other, like an army of men tramping past in an endless circle forever. It's inconceivable that they'd use their missiles like this unless their supply is inexhaustible. Frotch gets hit with them, I get hit with them, Veth gets hit with them. For every job there's a missile. We put our overall weapons superiority in one pan of the balance. They pour an endless heap of missiles in the other pan. *Where do all these missiles come from?*"

For an instant Rast was silent, then he went on. "At first we thought 'Underground factories.' Well, we did our best to find them and it was no use. And whenever we managed to spot moving missiles, they seemed to be coming from the coast.

"About this time, some of my officers were trying to convert a bunch of captives to our way of thinking. One of the officers noticed a peculiar thing. Whenever he clinched his argument by saying, 'Moreover, you are alone in the world; you cannot defeat us alone,' the captives would all look very serious. Most of them would be very still and attentive, but here and there among them, a few would choke, gag, make sputtering noises, and shake all over. The other soldiers would secretively kick these men, and jab them with their elbows until they were still and attentive. Now, however, the question arose, what did all this mean? The actions were described to Intelligence, who said they meant exactly what they seemed to mean, 'suppressed mirth.'

"In other words, whenever we said, 'You can't win, you're alone in the world,' they wanted to burst out laughing. My officers now varied the technique. They would say, for instance, 'The U.S.S.R. is our faithful ally.' Our captives would sputter, gasp, and almost strangle to death. Put this together with their inexhaustible supply of missiles and the thing takes on a sinister look."

"You think," said Bade, "that the U.S.S.R. and other countries are shipping missiles to the U.S. by sea?"

General Frotch cleared his throat apologetically, "Sir, excuse me. I have something new to add to this. I've set submerger planes down along all three of their coasts. Not only are the ports alive with shipping. But some of our men swam into the harbors at night and hid, and either they're the victims of mass-hypnosis or else those ships are unloading missiles like a fish unloads spawn."

Bade looked at Runckel.

Runckel said dully, "In that case, we have the whole planet to fight. That was what we had to avoid at any cost."

This comment produced a visible deterioration of morale. Before this attitude had a chance to set, Bade said forcefully and clearly, "I was never in favor of this attack. And this fortifies my original views. But from a strictly military point of view, I believe we can still win."

He went to the map, and speaking to each of the generals in turn, he explained his plan.

✳✳✳

In the three following days, each of the three remaining landing forces set down. The men of each landing force, as expected, became violently ill with the exploding sickness. With the usual course of the sickness known, it proved possible to care for this new horde of patients with nothing worse than extreme inconvenience for the invasion force as a whole.

The enemy, meanwhile, strengthened his grip around the occupied area, and at the same time cut troop movements within the area to a feeble trickle. Day after day, the enemy missiles fell in an increasingly heavy rain on the road and rail centers. During the height of this bombardment, Bade succeeded in gradually filtering all of Landing Force 3 back to the protection of the ships.

Rast now reported that the enemy attacks were mounting in force and violence, and requested permission to fall back and contract the defense perimeter.

Bade replied that help would soon come, and Rast must make only small local withdrawals.

Landing Forces 7, 8, and 9, cured of the exploding sickness, now took off. Immediately afterward, Landing Force 3 took off.

Landing Forces 3 and 7, under General Kottek, came down near the base of the Upper Peninsula of Michigan, and struck south and west to rip up communications in the rear of the main enemy forces attacking General Rast.

Landing Force 8 split, its southern section seizing the western curve of Cuba to cut the shipping lanes to the Gulf of Mexico. Its northern sections seized Long Island, to block shipping entering the port of New York, and to subject shipping in the ports of Boston, Philadelphia, Baltimore and Washington to heavy attack from the air.

Landing Force 9 remained aloft until the enemy's reaction to General Kottek's thrust from the rear became evident. This reaction proved to be a quickly improvised simultaneous attack from north and south, to pinch off the flow of supplies from Kottek's base to the point of his advance. Landing Force 9 now set down, broke the attack of the southern pincer, then struck southeastward to cut road and rail lines supplying the enemy's northern armies. The overall situation now resembled two large, roughly concentric circles, each very thick in the north, and very thin in the south. A large part of the outer circle, representing the enemy's forces, was now pressed between the inner circle and the inverted Y of Kottek's attack from the north.

A large percentage of the enemy missile-launching sites were now overrun, and Rast for the first time found it possible to switch his troops from place to place without excessive losses. The enemy opened violent attacks in both east and west to relieve the pressure on their trapped armies in the north, and Rast fell back slowly, drawing forces from both these fronts and putting them into the northern battle.

The outcome hung in a treacherous balance until the enemy's supplies gave out in the north. This powerful enemy force then collapsed, and Rast swung his weary troops to the south.

***

Three weeks after the offensive began, it ended with the fighting withdrawal of the enemy to the east and west. The enemy's long eastern and southern coasts were now sealed against all but a comparative trickle of supplies from overseas. General Kottek held the upper peninsula of Michigan in a powerful grip. From it he dominated huge enemy industrial regions, and threatened the flank of potential enemy counter-attacks from north or east.

Within the main occupied region itself, the forceway network and key-tools factories were being set up.

Runckel was only expressing the thought of nearly the whole invasion army when he walked into the operations room, heaved a sigh of relief and said to Bade, "Well, thank heaven *that's* over!"

Bade heard this and gave a noncommittal growl. He had felt this way himself some time before. During Runckel's absence, however, certain reports had come to Bade's desk and left him feeling like a man who goes down a flight of steps in the dark, steps off briskly, and finds there was one more step than he thought.

"Look at this," said Bade. Runckel leaned over his shoulder, and together they looked at a report headed, "Enemy Equipment." Bade passed over several pages of drawings and descriptions devoted to enemy knives, guns, grenades, helmets, canteens, mess equipment and digging tools, then paused at a section marked "Enemy clothing: 1) Normal enemy clothing consists of light two-piece underwear, an inner and an outer foot-covering, and either a light two-piece or light one-piece outer covering for the arms, chest, abdomen and legs. 2) However, capture of the enemy supply trains in the recent northern offensive uncovered the following fantastic variety: a) thick inner and outer hand coverings; b) heavy one-piece undergarment covering legs, arms and body; c) heavy upper outer garment; d) heavy lower outer garment; e) heavy inner foot covering; f) massive outer foot covering; g) additional heavy outer garment; h) extraordinarily heavy outer garment designed to cover entire body with exception of head, hand, and lower legs. In addition, large extra quantities of the heavy cover normally issued to the troops for sleeping purposes were also found. The purpose of all this clothing is difficult to understand. Insofar as the activity of a soldier encased in all these garments would be cut to a minimum, it can only be assumed that all these coverings represent body-shielding against some abnormal condition. The presence of poisonous chemicals in large quantities seems a likely possibility. Yet with the exception of the massive outer foot-covering, these garments are not impermeable."

Bade looked at Runckel. "They do have war chemicals?"

"Of course," said Runckel, frowning. "But we have protective measures, and our own war chemicals, if trouble starts."

Bade nodded thoughtfully, slid the report aside, and picked up one headed, "Medical Report on Enemy Skin Condensation."

Runckel shook his head. "I can never understand those. We've had a flood of reports like that from various sources. At most, I just initial them and send them back."

"Well," said Bade, "read the summary, at least."

"I'll try," growled Runckel, and leaned over Bade's shoulder to read:

"To summarize these astonishing facts, enemy captives have been observed to form, on the outer layer of their skin, a heavy beading of moisture. This effect is similar to that observed with laboratory devices maintained at depressed temperatures—that is, at reduced degrees of heat. The theory was, therefore, formed that the enemy's skin is, similarly, maintained at a temperature lower than that of his surroundings. Complex temperature-determining apparatus were set up to test this theory. As a result, this theory was disproved, but an even more astonishing state of affairs was discovered: The enemy's internal temperature varied very little, regardless of considerable experimental variation of the temperature of his environment.

"The only possible conclusion was that the enemy's body contains some built-in mechanism that actually controls the degree of heat and maintains it at a constant level.

"Now, according to Poff's widely accepted Principle, no complex bodily mechanism can long maintain itself in the absence of need or exercise. And what is the need for a bodily mechanism that has the function of holding body temperature constant despite wide external fluctuation? What is the need for a defense against something unless the something exists?

"We are forced to the conclusion that the degree of heat on this planet is subject to variations sufficiently severe as to endanger life. A new examination of what has hitherto been considered to be the enemy's mythology indicates that, contrary to conditions on our own planet, this planet is subject to remarkable fluctuations of temperature, that alternately rise to a peak, then fall to an incredible low.

"According to this new theory, our invasion force arrived as the temperature was approaching its maximum. Since then, it has reached and passed its peak, and is now falling. All this has passed unnoticed by us, partly because the maximum here approached the ordinary condition on our home planet. The danger, of course, is that the minimum on this planet would prove insupportable to our form of life."

This was followed by a qualifying phrase that further tests would have to be made, and the conclusions could not be considered final.

Bade looked at Runckel. Runckel snapped, "What do you do with a report like that? I'd tear it up, but why waste strength? It's easier to throw them in the wastebasket and go on."

"Wait a minute," said Bade. "If this report just happens to be right, then where are we?"

"Frankly," said Runckel, "I don't know or care. 'Skin condensation.' These scientists should keep their minds on things that have some chance of being useful. It would help if they'd figure out how to cut down flareback on our subtron guns. Instead they talk about 'skin condensation.'"

Bade wrote on the report, "This may turn out to be important. List on no more than two sheets of paper possible defenses against reduced degree of heat. Get it to me as soon as possible. Bade."

Bade signaled to a clerk. "Snap a copy of this, send the original out, and bring me the copy."

"Yes, sir."

"Now," said Bade, "we have one more report."

"Well, I have to admit," said Runckel, "that I can't see that either of these reports were of any value."

"Well, read this one, then."

Runckel shook his head in disgust, and leaned over. His eyes widened. This paper was headed, "For the Supreme Commander only. Special Report of General Kottek."

The report began, "Sir: It is an officer's duty to state, plainly and without delay, any matter that requires the immediate attention of his superior. I, therefore, must report to you the following unpleasant but incontrovertible facts;

"1) Since their arrival in this region, my troops have on three recent occasions displayed a strikingly low level of performance. Two simulated night attacks revealed feeble command and exaggerated sluggishness on the part of the troops. A defense exercise carried out at dawn to repulse a simulated amphibious landing was a complete failure; troops and officers alike displayed insufficient energy and initiative to drive the attack home.

"2) On other occasions, troops and officers have maintained a high, sometimes strikingly high, level of energy and activity.

"3) No explanation of this variability of performance has been forthcoming from the medical and technical personnel attached to my command. Neither have I any assurance that these fluctuations will not take place in the future.

"4) It is, therefore, my duty to inform you that I cannot assure the successful performance of my mission. Should the enemy attack with his usual energy during a period of low activity on the part of my troops, the caliber of my resistance will be that of wax against steel. This is no exaggeration, but plain fact.

"5) This situation requires the immediate attention of the highest military and technical authorities. What is in operation here may be a disease, an enemy nerve gas, or some natural factor unknown to us. Whatever its nature, the effect is highly dangerous.

"6) A mobile, flexible defense in these circumstances is impossible. A rigid linear defense is worthless. A defense by linked fortifications requires depth. I am, therefore, constructing a deep fortified system in the western section of the region under my control. This is no cure, but a means of minimizing disaster.

"7) Enemy missile activity since the defeat of their northern armies has been somewhat less than forty per cent of that expected."

The report ended with Kottek's distinctive jagged signature. Bade glanced around.

Runckel's face was somber. "This is serious," he said. "When Kottek yells for help, we've got trouble. We'll have to put all our attention on this thing and get it out of the way as fast as we can."

Bade nodded, and reached out to take a message from a clerk. He glanced at it and scowled. The message was from Atmospheric Flyer Command. It read:

"Warning! Tornado sighted approaching main base!"

Runckel leaned over to read the message. "What's this?" he said angrily. " 'Tornado' is just a myth. Everybody knows that."

Bade snapped on the microphone to Aerial Reconnaissance. "What's this 'tornado' warning?" he demanded. "What's a 'tornado'?"

"Sir, a tornado is a whirling severe breeze of destructive character, conjoined with a dark cloud in the shape of a funnel, with the smaller end down."

Runckel gave an inarticulate snarl.

Bade squinted. "This thing is dangerous?"

"Yes, sir. The natives dig holes in the ground, and jump in when one comes along. A tornado will smash houses and ground-cars to bits, sir."

"Listen," snarled Runckel, "it's just *air*, isn't it?"

Bade snapped on Landing Site Command. "Get all the men back in the ships," he ordered. "Turn the dampers to full power."

"Holy fangjaw!" Runckel burst out. "Air can't hurt us. What's bad about a breeze, anyway?" He seized the Aerial Reconnaissance microphone and snarled. "Stand up, you! What have you been drinking?"

Bade took Runckel by the arm. "Look there!"

On the nearest wall screen, a wide black cloud warped across the sky, and stretched down a long arc to the ground. The whole thing grew steadily larger as they watched.

Bade seized the Landing Site Command microphone. "Can we lift ships?"

"No, sir. Not without tearing the power and damper networks to pieces."

"I see," said Bade. He looked up.

The cloud overspread the sky. The screen fell dark. There was a heavy clang, a thundering crash, the ship trembled, tilted, heeled, and slowly, painfully, settled back upright as Bade hung onto the desk and Runckel dove for cover. The sky began to lighten. Bade gripped the microphone and asked what had happened. He listened blank-faced as, after a moment, the first estimates of the damage came in.

One of the thousand-foot-long ships had been tipped off its base. In falling, it struck another ship, which also fell, striking a third. The third ship struck a fourth, which fell unhindered and split up the side like a bean pod. The mouth of the tornado's funnel then ran along the split, and the ship's inside looked as if it had been cleaned out with a vacuum hose. A few stunned survivors and scattered bits of equipment were clinging here and there. That was all.

The enemy chose this moment to land his heaviest missile strike in weeks.

It took the rest of the day, all night, and all the following day to get the damage moderately well cleaned up. Then a belated report came in that Forceway Station 1 had been subjected to a bombardment of desks, chairs, communications equipment, and odd bolts and nuts that had riddled the installation from one end to the other and set completion date back four weeks.

An intensive search now located most of the missing equipment and personnel—strewn over forty miles of territory.

"It was," said Runckel weakly, "only air, that's all."

"Yes," said Bade grimly. He looked up from a scientific report on the tornado. "A whirlpool is only water. Whirling water. Apparently this planet has traveling whirlpools of air."

Runckel groaned, then a sudden thought seemed to hit him. He reached into his wastebasket, fished around, and drew out a crumpled ball of paper. He smoothed it out, read for a while, then growled, "Scientific reports. Here's some kind of report that came in right in the middle of a battle. According to this thing, the native name for the place where we've set down is 'Cyclone Alley.' Is there some importance in knowing a thing like that?"

Bade felt severe prickling sensations across his back and neck. " 'Cyclone,' " he said, "Where did I hear that before? Give me that paper."

Runckel shrugged and tossed it over. Bade smoothed it out and read:

"In this prevalent fairy tale, the 'cyclone'— corresponding to our 'sea serpent,' or 'Ogre of the Deep'—makes recurrent visits to communities in certain regions, frightening the inhabitants terribly and committing all sorts of prankish violence. On some occasions, it carries its chosen victims aloft, to set them down again far away. The cyclone is a frightening giant, tall and dark, who approaches in a whirling dance.

"An interesting aspect is the contrast of this legend with the equally prevalent legend of Santa Claus. Cyclone comes from the south, Santa from the north. Cyclone is prankish, frightening. Santa is benign, friendly, and even brings gifts. Cyclone favors 'springtime,' but may come nearly any time except 'winter.' Cyclone is secular. Santa reflects some of the holy aura of the religious festival, 'Christmas.'

" 'Christmas comes but once a year. When it comes, it brings good cheer.' Though Cyclone visits but a few favored towns at a time, Santa visits at once all, everyone, even the lowliest dweller in his humble shack. The natives are immensely earnest about both of these legends. An amusing aspect is that our present main base is almost ideally located for visits by that local Ogre of the Sea, 'Cyclone.' We are, in fact, situated in a location known as 'Cyclone Alley.' Perhaps the Ogre will visit us."

At the bottom of the page was a footnote: " 'Cyclone' is but one name for this popular Ogre. Another common name is 'Tornado.' "

Bade sat paralyzed for a moment staring at this paper. "Tornado Alley," he muttered. He grabbed the Flyer Command microphone to demand how the tornado warning system was coming. Then, groggily, he set the paper aside and turned his attention to the problem of General Kottek's special report. He looked up again as a nagging suspicion began to build up in him. He turned to Runckel. "How many of these 'myths' have we come across, anyway?"

Runckel looked as though a heavy burden were settling on him. He groped through his bulging wastebasket and fished out another crumpled ball of paper, then another. He located the one he wanted, smoothed it out, sucked in a deep breath, and read: "Cyclone, winter, spring, summer, hurricane, Easter bunny, autumn, blizzard, cold wave, Snow White and the Seven Dwarfs, lightning, Santa Claus, typhoon, mental telepathy, earthquake, levitation, volcano—" He looked up. "You want the full report on each of these things? I've got most of them here somewhere."

Bade looked warily at Runckel's overstuffed wastebasket. "No," he said. "But what about that report you're reading from? Isn't that an overall summary? Why didn't I get a copy of that?"

Runckel looked it over and growled, "Try to train them to send their reports to the right place. Yes, it's an overall summary. Here, want it?"

"Yes," said Bade. He took the report, then stopped to wonder, where was that report he had asked for on "reduced degree of heat?" He reached for a microphone, then remembered General Kottek's special report. Bade first sent word to Kottek that he approved what Kottek was doing, and that the problem was getting close attention. Then he read the crumpled overall summary Runckel had given him, and ended up feeling he had been on a trip through fairyland. His memories of the details evaporated even as he tried to mentally review the paper. "Hallowe'en," he growled, "icebergs, typhoons—this planet must be a mass of mythology from one end to the other." He picked up a microphone to call his Intelligence Service.

A messenger hurried across the room to hand him a slip of paper. The paper was from Atmosphere Flyer Command. It read:

"Warning! Tornado sighted approaching main base!"

✷✷✷

This time, the tornado roared past slightly to the west of the base. It hit, instead Forceway Station 1, and scattered sections of it all over the countryside.

For good measure, the enemy fired in an impressive concentration of rockets and missiles. The attack did only slight harm to the base, but it finished off Forceway Station 1.

An incoherent report now came in from the occupied western end of Cuba, to the effect that a "hurricane" had just gone through.

Bade fished through Runckel's wastebasket to find out exactly what a "hurricane" might be. He looked up at the end of this, pale and shaken, and sent out a strong force to put his Cuban garrison back on its feet.

Then he ordered Intelligence, and some of his technical and scientific departments to get together right away and break down the so-called "myths" into two groups: Harmful, and nonharmful. The harmful group was to be arranged in logical order, and each item accompanied by a brief, straightforward description.

As Bade sent out this order, General Kottek reported that, as a supplement to his fortified system, he was making sharp raids whenever conditions were favorable, in order to keep the enemy in his section off-balance. In one on these raids, his troops had captured an enemy document which had since been translated. The document was titled: "Characteristics of Unheatful-Blooded Animals." Kottek enclosed a copy:

"Unheatful-blooded animals have no built-in system for maintaining their bodily rate of molecular activity. If the surrounding temperature falls, so does theirs. This lowers their physical activity. They cannot move or react as fast as normally. Heatful-blooded animals, properly clothed, are not subject to this handicap.

"In practical reality, this means that as unheatful conditions set in, the Invader should always be attacked during the most unheatful period possible. Night attacks have much to recommend them. So do attacks at dusk or dawn. In general, avoid taking the offensive during heatful periods such as early afternoon.

"Forecasts indicate that winter will be late this year, but severe when it comes. Remember, there is no year on record when temperatures have not dropped severely in the depths of winter. In such conditions, it is expected that the Invader will be killed in large numbers by —untranslatable—of the blood.

"Our job is to make sure they are kept worn down until winter comes. Our job then will be to make sure none of them live through the winter."

Bade looked up feeling as if his digestive system were paralyzed. A messenger hurried across the room to hand him a thick report hastily put together by the Intelligence Service. It was titled:

"Harmful Myths and Definitions."

Bade spent the first part of the night reading this spine-tingling document. The second part of the night he spent in nightmares.

Toward morning, Bade had one vivid and comparatively pleasant dream. A native wearing a simple cloth about his waist looked at Bade intently and asked, "Does the shark live in the air? Does a man breathe underwater? Who will eat grass when he can have meat?"

Bade woke up feeling vaguely relieved. This sensation was swept away when he reached the operating room and saw the expression on Runckel's face. Runckel handed Bade a slip of paper:

"Hurricane Hannah approaching Long Island Base."

***

Intercepted enemy radio and television broadcasts spoke of Hurricane Hannah as "the worst in thirty years." As Bade and Runckel stood by helplessly, Hurricane Hannah methodically pounded Long Island Base to bits and pieces, then swept away the pieces. The hurricane moved on up the shoreline, treating every village and city along the way like a personal enemy. When Hurricane Hannah ended her career, and retired to sink ships further north, the Atlantic coast was a shambles from one end to the other.

Out of this shambles moved a powerful enemy force, which seized the bulk of what was left of Long Island Base. The remnant of survivors were trapped in the underground installations, and reported that the enemy was lowering a huge bomb down through the entrance.

In Cuba, the reinforced garrison was barely holding on.

A flood of recommendations now poured in on Bade:

1) Long Island Base needed a whole landing force to escape capture.

2) Cuba Base had to have at least another half landing force for reinforcements.

3) The Construction Corps required the ships of two full landing forces in order to power the forceway network. Otherwise, work on the key-tools factories would be delayed.

4) Landing Site Command would need the ships and dampers of three landing forces to barely protect the base if the power supply of two landing forces were diverted to the Construction Corps.

5) The present main base was now completed and should be put to efficient use at once.

6) The present main base was worthless, because Forceway Station 1 could not be repaired in time to link the base to the forceway network.

7) Every field commander except General Kottek urgently needed heavy reinforcements without delay.

8) Studies by the Staff showed the urgent need of building up the central reserve without delay, at the expense of the field commanders, if necessary.

Bade gave up Long Island Base, ordered Cuba Base to hold on with what it had, told the Landing Site Commander to select a suitable new main base near some southern forceway station free of tornadoes, and threw the rest of the recommendations into the wastebasket.

Runckel now came over with a smoldering stub jutting out of the corner of his mouth. "Listen," he said to Bade, "we're going to have a disciplinary problem on our hands. That Cuban garrison has been living on some kind of native paint-remover called 'rum.' The whole lot of them have a bad case of the staggering lurch from it; not even the hurricane sobered them up. Poff knew what was going on. But he and his staff covered it over. His troops are worthless. Molch and the reinforcements are doing all the fighting."

Bade said, "Poff is still in command?"

"I put Molch in charge."

"Good. We'll have to court-martial Poff and his staff. Can Molch hold the base?"

"He said he could. If we'd get Poff off his neck."

"Fine," said Bade. "Once he gets things in order, ship the regular garrison to a temporary camp somewhere. We don't want Molch's troops infected."

Runckel nodded. A clerk apologized and stepped past Runckel to hand Bade a message. It was from General

Frotch, who reported that all his atmospheric flyers based on Long Island had been lost in Hurricane Hannah. Bade showed the message to Runckel, who shook his head wearily.

As Runckel strode away, another clerk put a scientific report on Bade's desk. Bade read it through, got Frotch on the line, and arranged for a special mission by Flyer Command. Then he located his report on "Harmful Myths and Definitions." Carefully, he read the definition of winter:

"To the best of our knowledge, 'winter' is a severe periodic disease of plants, the actual onset of which is preceded by the vegetation turning various colors. The tall vegetables known as 'trees' lose their foliage entirely, except for some few which are immune and are known as 'evergreens.' As the disease progresses, the juices of the plants are squeezed out and crystallize in white feathery forms known as 'frost.' Sufficient quantities of this squeezed-out dried juice is 'snow.' The mythology refers to 'snow falling from the sky.' A possible explanation of this is that the large trees also 'snow,' producing a fall of dried juice crystals. These crystals are clearly poisonous. 'Frostbite,' 'chilblains,' and even 'freezing to death' are mentioned in the enemy's communication media. Even the atmosphere filled with the resulting vapor, is said to be 'cold.' Totally unexplainable is the common reference to children rolling up balls of this poisonous dried plant juice and hurling them at each other. This can only be presumed to be some sort of toughening exercise. More research on this problem is needed."

Bade set this report down, reread the latest scientific report, then got up and slowly walked over to a big map of the globe. He gazed thoughtfully at various islands in the South Seas.

⁂

Late that day, the ships lifted and moved, to land again near Forceway Station 2. Power cables were run to the station across a sort of long narrow valley at the bottom of which ran a thin trickle of water. By early the morning of the next day, the forceway network was in operation. Men and materials flashed thousands of miles in a moment, and work on the key-tools factories accelerated sharply.

Bade immersed himself in intelligence summaries of the enemy communications media. An item that especially interested him was "Winter Late This Year."

By now there were three viewpoints on "winter." A diehard faction doggedly insisted that it was a myth, a mere quirk of the alien mentality. A large and very authoritative body of opinion held the plant juice theory, and bolstered its stand with reams of data sheets and statistics. A small, vociferous group asserted the heretical water crystal hypotheses, and ate alone at small tables for doing so.

General Frotch called Bade to say that the special Flyer Command mission was coming in to report.

General Kottek sent word that enemy attacks were becoming more daring, that his troops' periods of inefficiency were more frequent, and that the vegetation in his district was turning color. He mentioned, for what it was worth, that troops within the fortifications seemed less affected than those outside. Troops far underground, however, seemed to be slowed down automatically, regardless of conditions on the surface, unless they were engaged in heavy physical labor.

Bade scowled and set off inquiries to his scientific section. Then he heard excited voices and looked up.

Four Flyer Command officers were coming slowly into the room, bright metal poles across their shoulders. Slung from the poles was a big plastic-wrapped bundle. The bundle was dripping steadily, and leaving a trail of droplets that led back out the door into the hall. The plastic was filmed over with a layer of tiny beads of moisture.

Runckel came slowly to his feet.

The officers, breathing heavily, set the big bundle on the floor near Bade's desk.

"Here it is, sir."

Bade's glance was fastened on the object.

"Unwrap it."

The officers bent over the bundle, and with clumsy fingers pulled back the plastic layer. The plastic stood up stiffly, and bent only with a hard pull. Underneath was something covered with several of the enemy's thick dark sleeping covers. The officers rolled the bundle back and forth and unwound the covers. An edge of some milky substance came into view. The officers pulled back the covers and a milky, semitransparent block sat there, white vapor rolling out from it along the floor.

There was a concerted movement away from the block and the officers.

Bade said, "Was the whole place like that?"

"No, sir, but there was an awful lot of this stuff. And there was a compacted powdery kind of substance, too. We didn't bring enough of it back and it all turned to water."

"Did you wear the protective clothes we captured?"

"Yes, sir, but they had to be slit and zippered up the legs, because the enemy's feet are so small. The arms were a poor fit and there had to be more material across the chest."

"How did they work?"

"They were a great help, sir, as long as we kept moving. As soon as we slowed down, we started to stiffen up. The hand and foot gear was improvised and hard to work in, though."

Bade looked thoughtfully at the smoldering block, then got up, stepped forward, and spread his hand close to the block. A numbness gradually dulled his hand and moved up his arm. Then Bade straightened up. He found he could move his hand only slowly and painfully. He motioned to Runckel. "I think this is what 'cold' is. Want to try it?" Runckel got up, held his hand to the block, then straightened, scowling.

Bade felt a tingling sensation and worked his hand cautiously as Runckel, his face intent, slowly spread and closed his fingers.

Bade thoughtfully congratulated the officers, then had the block carried off to the Testing Lab.

The report on defense against "reduced degree of heat" now came in. Bade read this carefully several times over. The most striking point, he noticed, was the heavy energy expenditure involved.

That afternoon, several ships took off, separated, and headed south.

**

The next few days saw the completion of the first keytool factory, the receipt of reports from insect-bitten scouts in various regions far to the south, and a number of terse messages from General Kottek. Bade ordered plans drawn up for the immediate withdrawal of General Kottek's army, and for the possible withdrawal by stages of other forces in the north. He ordered preparations made for the first completed factories to produce anti-reduced-degree-of-heat devices. He read a number of reports on the swiftly changing state of the planet's atmosphere. Large quantities of rain were predicted.

Bade saw no reason to fear rain, and turned to a new problem: The enemy's missiles had produced a super-abundance of atomic debris in the atmosphere. Testing Lab was concerned over this, and suggested various ways to get rid of it. Bade approved the projects and turned to the immediate problem of withdrawing the bulk of General Kottek's troops from their strong position without losing completely the advantages of it.

Bade was considering the idea of putting a forceway station somewhere in Kottek's underground defenses, so that he could be reinforced or withdrawn at will. This would involve complicated production difficulties; but then Kottek had said the slowing-down was minimized under cover, and it might be worthwhile to hold an option on his position. While weighing the various intangibles and unpredictables, Bade received a report from General Rast. Rast was now noticing the same effect Kottek had reported.

Word came in that two more key-tools factories were now completed.

Intelligence reports of enemy atmospheric data showed an enormous "cold air mass moving down through Canada."

General Frotch, personally supervising high-altitude tests, now somehow got involved in a rushing high-level air stream. Having the power of concentrating his attention completely upon whatever he was doing, Frotch got bound up in the work and never realized the speed of the air stream until he came down again—just behind the enemy lines.

When Bade heard of this, he immediately went over the list of officers, and found no one to replace Frotch. Bade studied the latest scientific reports and the disposition of his forces, then ordered an immediate switching of troops and aircraft through the forceway network toward the place where Frotch had vanished. A sharp thrust with local forces cut into the enemy defense system, was followed up by heavy reinforcements flowing through the forceway network, and developed an overpowering local superiority that swamped the enemy defenses.

Runckel studied the resulting dispositions and said grimly, "Heaven help us if they hit us hard in the right place just now."

"Yes," said Bade, "and heaven help us if we don't get Frotch back." He continued his rapid switching of forces, and ordered General Kottek to embark all his troops, and set down near the main base.

Flyer Command meanwhile began to show signs of headless disorientation, the ground commanders peremptorily ordering the air forces around as nothing more than close-support and flying artillery. The enemy behind-the-lines communications network continued to function.

Runckel now reported to Bade that no reply had been received from Kottek's headquarters. Runckel was sending a ship to investigate.

Anguished complaints poured in from the technical divisions that their work was held up by the troops flooding the forceway network.

The map now showed Bade's men driving forward in what looked like a full-scale battle to break the enemy's whole defensive arrangements and thrust clear through to the sea. Reports came in that, with the enemy's outer defense belt smashed, signs of unbelievable weakness were evident. The enemy seemed to have nothing but local reserves and only a few of them. The general commanding on the spot announced that he could end the war if given a free hand.

Bade now wondered, if the enemy's reserves weren't there, where were they? He repeated his original orders.

Runckel now came over with the look of a half-drowned swimmer and motioned Bade to look at the two nearest viewscreens.

One of the viewscreens showed a scene in shades of white. A layer of white covered the ground, towering ships were plastered on one side with white, obstacles were heaped over with white, the air was filled with horizontal streaks of white. Everything on the screen was white or turning white.

"Kottek's base," said Runckel dully.

The other screen gave a view of the long narrow valley just outside. This "valley" was now a rushing torrent of foaming water, sweeping along chunks of floating debris that bobbed a hand's breadth under the power cables from the ships to Forceway Station 2.

***

The only good news that day and the next was the recapture of General Frotch. In the midst of crumbling disorder, Flyer Command returned to normal.

Bade sent off a specially-equipped mission to try and find out what had happened to General Kottek. Then he looked up to see General Rast walking wearily into the room. Rast conferred with Runckel in low dreary tones, then the two of them started over toward Bade.

Bade returned his attention to a chart showing the location of the key-tools factories and the forceway network.

A sort of groan announced the arrival of Rast and Runckel. Bade looked up. Rast saluted. Bade returned the salute. Rast said stiffly, "Sir, I have been defeated. My army no longer exists."

Bade looked Rast over quickly, studying his expression and bearing.

"It's a plain fact," said Rast. "Sir, I should be relieved of command."

"What's happened?" said Bade. "I have no reports of any new enemy attack."

"No," said Rast, "there won't be any formal report. The whole northern front is anaesthetized from one end to the other."

"Snow?" said Bade.

"White death," said Rast.

A messenger stepped past the two generals to hand Bade a report. It was from General Frotch:

"1) Aerial reconnaissance shows heavy enemy forces moving south on a wide front through the snow-covered region. No response or resistance has been noted on the part of our troops.

"2) Aerial reconnaissance shows light enemy forces moving in to ring General Kottek's position. The enemy appears to be moving with extreme caution.

"3) It has so far proved impossible to get in touch with General Kottek.

"4) It must be reported that on several occasions our ground troops have, as individuals, attempted to seize from our flyer pilots and crews, their special protective anti-reduced-degree-of-heat garments. This problem is becoming serious."

Bade looked up at Rast. "You're Ground Forces Commander, not commander of a single front."

"That's so," said Rast. "I should be. But all I command now is a kind of mob. I've tried to keep the troops in order, but they know one thing after another is going wrong. Naturally, they put the blame on their leaders."

The room seemed to Bade to grow unnaturally light and clear. He said, "Have you had an actual case of mutiny, Rast?"

Rast stiffened. "No, sir. But it is possible for troops to be so laggardly and unwilling that the effect is the same. What I mean is that there is the steady growth of a cynical attitude everywhere. Not only in the troops but in the officers."

Bade looked off at the far corner of the room for a moment. He glanced at Runckel. "What's the state of the key-tools factories?"

"Almost all completed. But the northern ones are now in the reduced-degree-of-heat zone. Part of the forceway network is, too. Using the key-tools plants remaining, it might be possible to patch together some kind of a makeshift. But the reduced-degree-of-heat zone is still moving south."

A pale clerk apologized, stepped around the generals and handed Bade two messages. The first was from Intelligence:

"Enemy propaganda broadcasts beamed at our troops announce General Kottek's unconditional surrender with all his forces. We have no independent information on Kottek's actual situation."

The second message was from the commander of Number 1 Shock Infantry Division. This report boiled down to a miserable confession that the commanding officer found himself unable to prevent:

1) Fraternization with the enemy.

2) The use of various liquid narcotics that rendered troops unfit for duty.

3) The unauthorized wearing of red, white, and blue buttons lettered, "Vote Republican."

4) An ugly game called "footbase," in which the troops separated into two long lines armed with bats, to hammer, pound, beat, and kick, a ball called "the officer," from one end of the field to the other.

***

Bade looked up at Rast. "How is it I only find out about this now?"

"Sir," said Rast, "each of the officers was ashamed to report it his superior."

Bade handed the report to Runckel, who read it through and looked up somberly. "If it's hit the shock troops, the rest must have it worse."

"Yet," said Bade, "the troops fought well when we recaptured Frotch."

"Yes," said Rast, "but it's the damned planet that's driving them crazy. The natives are remarkable propagandists. And the men can plainly see that even when they win a victory, some freak like the exploding sickness, or some kind of atmospheric jugglery, is likely to take it right away from them. They're in a bad mood and the only thing that might snap them out of it is decisive action. But if they go the other way we're finished."

"This," said Bade, "is no time for you to resign."

"Sir, it's a mess, and I'm responsible. I have to make the offer to resign."

"Well," said Bade, "I don't accept it. But we'll have to try to straighten out this mess." Bade pulled over several sheets of paper. On the first, he wrote:

"Official News Bureau: 1) Categorically deny the capture of General Kottek and his base. State that General Kottek is in full control of Base North, that the enemy has succeeded in infiltrating troops into the general region under cover of snow, but that he has been repulsed with heavy losses in all attacks on the base itself.

"2) State that the enemy announcement of victory in the area is a desperation measure, timed to coincide with their almost unopposed advance through the evacuated Northern Front.

"3) The larger part of the troops in the Northern Front were withdrawn prior to the attack and switched by forceway network to launch a heavy feinting attack against the enemy. State that the enemy, caught by surprise, appears to be rushing reserves from his northern armies to cover the areas threatened by the feint.

"4) Devoted troops who held the Northern Front to make the deception succeed have now been overrun by the enemy advance under cover of the snow. Their heroic sacrifice will not be forgotten.

"5) The enemy now faces the snow time alone. His usual preventive measures have been drastically slowed down. His intended decisive attack has failed of its object. The snow this year is unusually severe, and is already working heavy punishment on the enemy.

"6) Secret measures are now for the first time being brought into the open that will place our troops far beyond the reach of snow."

On the second sheet of paper, Bade wrote:

"Director of Protocol: Prepare immediately: 1) Supreme Commander's Citation for Extraordinary Bravery and Resourcefulness in Action: To be awarded General Kottek. 2) Supreme Commander's Citation for

Extraordinary Devotion to Duty: To be awarded singly, to each soldier on duty during the enemy attack on the entire Northern Front. 3) These awards are both to be mentioned promptly in the Daily Notices."

Bade handed the papers to Runckel, "Send these out yourself." As Runckel started off, Bade looked at Rast, then was interrupted by a messenger who stepped past Rast, and handed Bade two slips of paper. With an effort of will, Bade extended his hand and took the papers. He read:

"Sir: Exploration Team South 3 has located ideal island base. Full details follow. Frotch."

"Sir: We have finally contacted General Kottek. He and his troops are dug into underground warrens of great complexity beneath his system of fortifications. Most of the ships above-ground are mere shells, all removable equipment having been stripped out and carried below for the comfort of the troops. Most of the ships' engines have also been disassembled one at a time, carried below, and set up to run the dampers—which are likewise below ground—and the 'heating units' devised by Kottek's technical personnel. His troops appear to be in good order and high spirits. Skath, Col., A.F.C., forwarded by Frotch."

***

Bade sucked in a deep breath and gave silent thanks. Then he handed the two reports to Rast. Bade snapped on a microphone and got in touch with Frotch. "Listen, can you get pictures of Kottek and his men?"

Frotch held up a handful of pictures, spread like playing cards. "The men took them for souvenirs and gave me copies. You can have all you want."

Bade immediately called his photoprint division and gave orders for the pictures to be duplicated by the thousands. The photoprint division slaved all night, and the excited troops had the pictures on their bulletin boards by the next morning.

The Official News Service meanwhile was dinning Bade's propaganda into the troops' ears at every opportunity. The appearance of the pictures now plainly caught the enemy propaganda out on a limb. Doubting one thing the enemy propaganda had said, the troops suddenly doubted all. A violent revulsion of feeling took place. Before anything else could happen, Bade ordered the troops embarked.

By this time, the apparently harmless rain had produced a severe flood, which repeatedly threatened the power cables supplying the forceway network. The troops had to use this network to get to the ships in time.

As Bade's military engineers blasted out alternate channels for the rising water, and a fervent headquarters group prayed for a drought, the troops poured through the still-operative forceway stations and marched into the ships with joyful shouts.

The enemy joined the celebration with a mammoth missile attack.

The embarkation, together with the disassembling of vital parts of the accessible key-tools factories, took several days. During this time, the enemy continued his steady methodical advance well behind the front of the cold air mass. The enemy however, made no sudden thrust on the ground to take advantage of the embarkation. Bade pondered this sign of tiredness, then sent up a ship to radio a query home. When the answer came, Bade sent a message to the enemy government. The message began:

"Sirs: This scouting expedition has now completed its mission. We are now withdrawing to winter quarters, which may be: a) an unspecified distant location; b) California; c) Florida. If you are prepared to accept certain temporary armistice conditions, we will choose a). Otherwise, you will understand we must choose b) or c). If you are prepared to consider these armistice conditions, you are strongly urged to send a plenipotentiary without delay. This plenipotentiary should be prepared to consider both the temporary armistice and the matters of mutual benefit to us."

Bade waited tensely for the reply. He had before him two papers, one of which read:

" . . . the enemy-held peninsula of Florida has thus been found to be heavily infested with heartworms—parasites which live inside the heart, slow circulation, and lower vital activity sharply. While the enemy appears to be immune to infestation, our troops plainly are not. The four scouts who returned here have at last, we believe, been cured—but they have not as yet recovered their strength. The state of things in nearby Cuba is not yet known for certain. Possibly, the troops' enormous consumption of native 'rum' has interacted medicinally with our blood chemistry to retard infestation. If so, we have our choice of calamities. In any case, a landing in Florida would be ruinous."

As for California, the other report concluded:

" . . . Statistical studies based on past experience lead us to believe that myth or no myth, immediately upon our landing in California, there will be a terrific earthquake."

Bade had no desire to go to Florida or California. He fervently hoped the enemy would not guess this.

At length the reply came, Bade read through ominous references to the growing might of the United States of the World, then came to the operative sentence:

" . . . Our plenipotentiary will be authorized to treat only with regard to an armistice; he is authorized only to transmit other information to his government. He is not empowered to make any agreement whatever on matters other than an armistice."

The plenipotentiary was a tall thin native, who constantly sponged water off his neck and forehead, and who looked at Bade as if he would like to cram a nuclear missile down his throat. Getting an agreement was hard work. The plenipotentiary finally accepted Bade's first condition—that General Kottek not be attacked for the duration of the armistice—but flatly refused the second condition allowing the continued occupation of western Cuba. After a lengthy verbal wrestling match, the plenipotentiary at last agreed to a temporary continuation of the western Cuban occupation, provided that the Gulf of Mexico blockade be lifted. Bade agreed to this and the plenipotentiary departed mopping his forehead.

Bade immediately lifted ships and headed south. His ships came down to seize sections of Sumatra, Java, and Borneo, with outposts on the Christmas and Cocoa islands and on small islands in the Indonesian archipelago.

Bade's personal headquarters were on a pleasant little island conveniently located in the Sunda Strait between Java and Sumatra. The name of the island was Krakatoa.

***

Bade was under no illusion that the inhabitants of the islands welcomed his arrival. Fortunately, however, the armament of his troops outclassed anything in the vicinity, with the possible exception of a bristly-looking place called Singapore. Bade's scouts, after studying Singapore carefully, concluded it was not mobile, and if they left it alone, it would leave them alone.

The enemy plenipotentiary now arrived in a large battleship, and was greeted in the islands with frenzied enthusiasm. Bade was too absorbed in reports of rapidly-improving morale, and highly-successful mass-swimming exercises to care about this welcome. Although an ominous document titled "War in the Islands: U.S.—Japan," sat among the translated volumes of history at Bade's elbow, and served as a constant reminder that this pleasant situation could not be expected to last forever, Bade intended to enjoy it while it did last.

Bade greeted the plenipotentiary in his pleasant headquarters on the leveled top of the tall picturesque cone-shaped hill that rose high above Krakatoa, then dropped off abruptly by the sea.

The plenipotentiary, on entering the headquarters, mopped his brow constantly, kept glancing furtively around, and was plainly ill at ease. The interpreters took their places, and the conversation opened.

"As you see," said Bade, "we are comfortably settled here for the winter."

The plenipotentiary looked around and gave a hollow laugh.

"We are," added Bade, "perfectly prepared to return next . . . a . . . 'summer' . . . and take up where we left off."

"By next summer," said the plenipotentiary, "the United States will be a solid mass of guns from one coast to the other."

Bade shrugged, and the plenipotentiary added grimly, "And *missiles.*"

Despite himself, Bade winced.

One of Bade's clerks, carrying a message across the far end of the room, became distracted in his effort to be sure he heard everything. The clerk was busy watching Bade when he banged into the back of a tall filing case. The case tilted off-balance, then started to fall forward.

A second clerk sprang up to catch the side of the case. There was a low heavy rumble as all the drawers slid out.

The plenipotentiary sprang to his feet, and looked wildly around.

The filing case twisted out of the hands of the clerk and came down on the floor with a thundering crash.

The plenipotentiary snapped his eyes tightly shut, clenched his teeth, and stood perfectly still.

Bade and Runckel looked blankly at each other.

The plenipotentiary slowly opened his eyes, looked wonderingly around the room, jumped as the two clerks heaved the filing case upright, turned around to stare at the clerks and the case, turned back to look sharply at Bade, then clamped his jaw.

Bade, his own face as calm as he could make it, decided this might be as good a time as any to throw in a hard punch. He remarked, "You have two choices. You can make a mutually profitable agreement with us. Or you can force us to switch heavier forces and weapons to this planet and crush you. Which is it?"

"We," said the plenipotentiary coldly, "have the resources of the whole planet at our disposal. You have to bring everything from a distance. Moreover, we have captured a good deal of your equipment, which we may duplicate—"

"Lesser weapons," said Bade. "As if an enemy captured your rifles, duplicated them at great expense, and was then confronted with your nuclear bomb."

"This is our planet," said the plenipotentiary grimly, "and we will fight for it to the end."

"We don't want your planet."

***

The plenipotentiary's eyes widened. Then he burst into a string of invective that the translators couldn't follow. When he had finished, he took a deep breath and recapitulated the main point, "If you don't want it, what are you doing here?"

Bade said, "Your people are clearly warlike. After observing you for some time, a debate arose on our planet as to whether we should hit you or wait till you hit us. After a fierce debate, the first faction won."

"Wait a minute. How could *we* hit *you*? You come from another planet, don't you?"

"Yes, that's true. But it's also true that a baby shark is no great menace to anyone. Except that he will grow up into a big shark. That is how our first faction looked on earth."

The plenipotentiary scowled. "In other words, you'll kill the suspect before he has a chance to commit the crime. Then you justify it by saying the man would have committed a crime if he'd lived."

"We didn't intend to kill you—only to disarm you."

"How does all this square with your telling us you're just a scout party?"

"Are you under the impression," said Bade, "that this is the main invasion force? Would we attack without a full reconnaissance first? Do you think we would merely make one sizable landing, on *one* continent? How could we hope to conquer in that way?"

The plenipotentiary frowned, sucked in a deep breath, and mopped his forehead. "What's your offer?"

"Disarm yourselves voluntarily. All hostilities will end immediately."

The plenipotentiary gave a harsh laugh.

Bade said, "What's your answer?"

"What's your real offer?"

"As I remarked," said Bade, "there were two factions on our planet. One favored the attack, as self-preservation. The other faction opposed the attack, on moral and political grounds. The second faction at present holds that it is now impossible to remain aloof, as we had hoped to before the attack. One way or the other, we are now bound up with Earth. We either have to be enemies, or friends. As it happens, I am a member of the bloc that opposed the attack. The bloc that favored the attack has lost support owing to the results of our initial operations. Because of this political shift, I have practically a free hand at the moment." Bade paused as the plenipotentiary turned his head slightly and leaned forward with an intent look.

Bade said, "Your country has suffered by far the most from our attack. Obviously, it should profit the most. We have a number of scientific advances to offer as bargaining counters. Our essential condition is that we retain some overt standing—some foothold—some way of knowing by direct observation that this planet—or any nation of it—won't attack us."

The plenipotentiary scowled. "Every nation on Earth is pretty closely allied as a result of your attack. We're a world of united states—all practically one nation. And all the land on the globe belongs to one of us or the other. While there's bound to be considerable regional rivalry even when we have peace, that's all. Otherwise we're united. As a result, there's not going to be any peace as long as you've got your foot on land belonging to any of us. That includes Java, Sumatra, and even this . . . er . . . mountain we're on now." He looked around uneasily, and added, "We might let you have a little base, somewhere . . . maybe in Antarctica but I doubt it. We won't want any foreign planet sticking its nose in our business."

Bade said, "My proposal allows for that."

"I don't see how it could," said the plenipotentiary. "What is it?"

Bade told him.

The plenipotentiary sat as if he had been hit over the head with a rock. Then he let out a mighty burst of laughter, banged his hand on his knee and said, "You're serious?"

"Absolutely."

The plenipotentiary sprang to his feet. "I'll have to get in touch with my government. Who knows? Maybe— Who knows?" He strode out briskly.

* * *

About this time, a number of fast ships arrived from home. These ships were much in use during the next months. Delegations from both planets flew in both directions.

Runckel was highly uneasy. Incessantly he demanded, "Will it work? What if they flood our planet with a whole mob—"

"I have it on good authority," said Bade, "that our planet is every bit as uncomfortable for them as theirs is for us. We almost lost one of their delegates straight down through the mud on the last visit. They have to use dozens of towels for handkerchiefs every day, and that trace of ammonia in the atmosphere doesn't seem to agree with them. Some of them have even gotten fog-sick."

"Why should they go along with the idea, then?"

"It fits in with their nature. Besides, where else are they going to get another one? As one of their senators put it, 'Everything here on Earth is sewed up.' There's even a manifest destiny argument."

"Well, the idea has attractions, but—"

"Listen," said Bade, "I'm told not to prolong the war, because it's too costly and dangerous; not to leave behind a reservoir of fury to discharge on us in the future; not to surrender; not, in the present circumstances, to expect them to surrender. I am told to somehow keep a watch on them and bind their interests to ours; and not to forget the tie must be more than just on paper, it's got to be emotional as well as legal. On top of that, if possible, I'm supposed to open up commercial opportunities. Can you think of any other way?"

"Frankly, no," said Runckel.

There was a grumbling sound underneath them, and the room shivered slightly.

"What was that?" said Runckel.

Bade looked around, frowning. "I don't know."

A clerk came across the room and handed Runckel a message and Bade another message. Runckel looked up, scowling. "The sea water here is beginning to have an irritating effect on our men's skin."

"Never mind," said Bade, "their plenipotentiary is coming. We'll know one way or the other shortly."

Runckel looked worried, and began searching through his wastebasket.

The plenipotentiary came in grinning. "O.K.," he said, "the Russians are a little burned up, and I don't think Texas is any too happy, but nobody can think of a better way out. You're in."

He and Bade shook hands fervently. Photographers rushed in to snap pictures. Outside, Bade's band was playing "The Star-Spangled Banner."

"Another state," said the plenipotentiary, grinning expansively. "How's it feel to be a citizen?"

Runckel erupted from his wastebasket and bolted across the room.

"Krakatoa is a *volcano!*" he shouted. "And here's what a volcano is!"

There was a faint but distinct rumble underfoot.

The room emptied fast.

* * *

On the way home, they were discussing things.

Bade was saying, "I don't claim it's perfect, but then our two planets are so mutually uncomfortable there's bound to be little travel either way till we have a chance to get used to each other. Yet, we *can* go back and forth. Who has a better right than a citizen? And there's a good chance of trade and mutual profit. There's a good emotional tie." He frowned. "There's just one thing—"

"What's that?" said Runckel.

Bade opened a translated book to a page he had turned down. He read silently. He looked up perplexedly.

"Runckel," he said, "there are certain technicalities involved in being a citizen."

Runckel tensed. "What do you mean?"

"Oh— Well, like this." He looked back at the book for a moment.

"What is it?" demanded Runckel.

"Well," said Bade, "what do you suppose 'income tax' is?"

Runckel looked relieved. He shrugged.

"Don't worry about it," he said. "It's too fantastic. Probably it's just a myth."

IF YOU LIKE...
YOU SHOULD TRY...

DAVID DRAKE
David Weber

DAVID WEBER
John Ringo

JOHN RINGO
Michael Z. Williamson
Tom Kratman

ANNE MCCAFFREY
Mercedes Lackey

MERCEDES LACKEY
Wen Spencer, Andre Norton
Andre Norton
James H. Schmitz

LARRY NIVEN
James P. Hogan
Travis S. Taylor

ROBERT A. HEINLEIN
Jerry Pournelle
Lois McMaster Bujold
Michael Z. Williamson

HEINLEIN'S "JUVENILES"
Rats, Bats & Vats series by Eric Flint & Dave Freer

**HORATIO HORNBLOWER OR
PATRICK O'BRIAN**
David Weber's Honor Harrington series
David Drake's RCN series

HARRY POTTER
Mercedes Lackey's Urban Fantasy series

THE LORD OF THE RINGS
Elizabeth Moon's *The Deed of Paksenarrion*

H.P. LOVECRAFT
Princess of Wands by John Ringo

GEORGETTE HEYER
Lois McMaster Bujold
Catherine Asaro

GREEK MYTHOLOGY
Pyramid Scheme by Eric Flint & Dave Freer
Forge of the Titans by Steve White
Blood of the Heroes by Steve White

NORSE MYTHOLOGY
Northworld Trilogy by David Drake
A Mankind Witch by Dave Freer

ARTHURIAN LEGEND
Steve White's "Legacy" series
The Dragon Lord by David Drake

SCA/HISTORICAL REENACTMENT
John Ringo's "After the Fall" series

LITERARY CRITICISM
Breakfast in the Ruins by Barry N. Malzberg

CATS
Larry Niven's Man-Kzin Wars series

PUNS
Rick Cook
Spider Robinson
Wm. Mark Simmons

VAMPIRES
Wm. Mark Simmons